RELENTLESS PURSUIT

PRIVATE PROTECTORS SERIES

ADRIENNE GIORDANO

W0007311

ALG PUBLISHING

1

BILLY TRIPP NUDGED THE NINE-MILLIMETER HOLSTERED UNDER his suit jacket and decided this might be as good a time as any to meet his maker.

All he needed to do was slide that baby out, prop it under his chin and—*bang*—the misery would be over.

After all the death-defying experiences he'd had, killing himself in a hotel ballroom would be sub-par. Supremely sub-par.

Plus, he'd be dead.

"Cheer up, jagweed," Monk said, slapping him on the back.

"Why?" Billy glanced around the massive room at the sea of men and women dressed in sharp tuxedos and sexy, low cut gowns. As ballrooms went, Dante's ranked in the top ten. Funky red walls and icicle chandeliers gave it a more contemporary feel, but it was still a ballroom. And he'd seen plenty of them.

"It could be worse. This job is almost complete."

Billy scanned his immediate surroundings. "Yeah, but,

dude, I'm guarding a *necklace*. There's not even a body attached to it."

Monk grinned. "You shouldn't have let your passport expire."

Dick. Head.

"First of all, I didn't *let* my passport expire. It just happened. An accident."

"You fucked up. Admit it." And then Monk started humming.

Humming? Really? Of course Monk was in a good mood. He'd just returned from overseas where he played with guns and blew crap up. Billy had been scheduled to take the next two-month shift, but got caught up in this expired passport mess.

How had he, an ex-Army ranger working for one of the country's most elite private security firms, forgotten to renew his fu—fudging passport?

And why the hell had he picked this month to promise his mother he would stop swearing? She'd asked him to do it and deserved his attention to the matter, that's why.

Even if it was slowly destroying him.

A woman in her fifties wearing a monster low-cut black gown—*that thing has no business on her body*—wandered to the table and locked in on him. *Cripes.*

"Fabulous, isn't it?" she asked.

He glanced at Monk, who rolled his eyes and stepped away to check his phone. "It is." Billy kept his focus on the room and any potential bad guys. The woman pressed a note into his hand. Great. Another one slipping him her number.

Ceasing conversation, he waited until the woman left and tucked the paper in his pocket with the other two. He'd get rid of them later. This routine, like most things, had lost its novelty long ago. Wasn't *that* a travesty? Early on, he'd enjoyed the steady stream of attention that accompanied women throwing themselves at him. He was a guy. And guys liked to get laid. Pretty simple.

Except it got old. The strange women. The *crazy,* strange women who parked themselves on his doorstep or called him night and day. Hell, he never misled anyone about his intentions. He always told them what it was.

"That was Vic." Monk grinned. "He said to say hi."

Not biting, Billy kept his gaze on the packed room. "Fu— fudge off. I could have had a new passport in a day or two, but Vic wanted to break my balls."

"He's teaching you a lesson. Next time, you won't forget. Besides, we've been in a lot worse places than a fundraiser in South Beach. In December."

Monk might as well take another hit off the crack pipe because he wasn't getting it. "Every time I turn around, Vic is hauling me into his office. And he had to bring up that little infraction when you beat the crap out of me last summer. Christ sakes, you nearly kill me and *I* get in trouble? All because I was ragging on you?"

A couple in their twenties stepped up to the table and Monk nodded. "Evening."

Billy stayed silent but shifted closer to the table. As ticked off as he was about this job, there would be no way he'd let that necklace disappear. Not on his watch. Soon he'd be out of here. Gone.

When the couple moved on, Monk turned back to him. "You're not grasping the point of this assignment. This is punishment for being a grand fucking pain in the ass all the time."

That was his theory? "Then why are you here? What are you being punished for?"

"I asked for it. I'd been gone two months; Izzy is on vacation for a couple of weeks and we're doing a long weekend. I got no problems with this assignment."

Yeah. There's the difference. Billy turned his attention back to the ballroom. "You're on vacation with your Victoria's Secret model of a girlfriend and I'm in purgatory."

A strawberry blonde, her thick hair falling in soft waves around her shoulders, stepped out of the crowd wearing a peach gown with a baggy, draping neckline, but the rest of it —*humina, humina, humina*—clung to her ample hips like snakeskin. "Whoa."

She'd never be called skinny. Not with those hips and a rack that could give a man vertigo. But chunky didn't suit either. Statuesque maybe. Hot, most definitely. Jeepers, he might be hearing angels singing over the orchestra. He elbowed Monk. "Check out this smoker coming our way."

Monk swung his head in the sexy blonde's direction. "That smoker is Kristen Dante. She runs this place. I met her when I got here yesterday."

The boss? She couldn't have been thirty years old. Billy let out a low whistle as Kristen Dante, her sumptuous body balancing on mile high heels, came closer. Damn, the woman had to be six foot in those shoes.

He nudged right up to the table. A woman like her could make a guy like him lose focus and he'd wind up with a missing million-dollar necklace.

"Hello, gentlemen," Madame Hotness said, pushing her hair off her shoulder.

In contrast to the body that made him want to reach out and touch, she had a face sent straight from heaven. Soft and round and sweet with dynamite green eyes. Amazing that she lived in Florida, because her fair skin would get crispy in the sun. Toss in the reddish-blond hair and Billy decided the whole fudging package worked. Big time.

Monk held out his hand. "Hello, Kristen."

The two of them shook hands and Hotness turned back to Billy. "We haven't met, I'm Kristen. Welcome to Dante."

KRISTEN STOOD WITH HER HAND EXTENDED WAITING FOR HIM to say something. This was a big boy and, given her height, she didn't get to look up at a man very often. Not to mention the Calvin Klein model good looks. He wore his collar-length, dark hair fashionably shaggy and his slick Italian suit fit his long body just fine, but he apparently hadn't learned to speak. His sparkling blue eyes communicated their appraisal quite well, however, and she forced herself not to hunch. Her lifetime of weight issues didn't permit comfort when people stared.

This man made an immediate impression though. With those eyes, she imagined he could get into all sorts of mischief. The pinging in her head warned she should run screaming. He had player tattooed all over him.

Peter, the man Vic Andrews called Monk, nudged his partner with his elbow, and the guy wandered back to Earth.

"I'm Billy. Billy Tripp. Sorry. Mindsnap."

O-kay, then. She could only hope this guy had a bigger attention span than what he'd displayed introducing himself. Considering there over ten million dollars worth of jewelry in this room.

She turned back to Peter. "Do you need anything?"

"No, ma'am. We're fine. I'm doing the rounds and checking in with our men. All is quiet."

Familiar slivers of unease curled around Kristen and she turned to see Mr. Mindsnap's gaze plastered to her chest.

Here we go. Yes, they're real. Again, she focused on standing tall, but the effort drained her, forced her to concentrate on anything but her oversized body.

Peter cleared his throat and Billy flicked his attention back to the ballroom.

"We have men by the main doors and by each table," Peter said. "We're rotating every half hour. Were you expecting this big of a crowd?"

"We expected three-fifty, but we're over four hundred. It's a good cause and everyone loves to see millions in jewelry." She pointed to the necklace propped on the stand. "This one will be auctioned tonight."

Billy leaned forward and something in his twinkly eyes had her girly parts on full alert. *Trouble.*

"I'll keep it safe," he said.

But he was staring at her again, taking in her face and her hair, and the pressure of that hungry gaze forced her shoulders down. If only she could ball herself up to hide from the inspection. Did she have food on her face or something? Wouldn't that be perfect? A fat Amazon with food stuck to her cheek.

Her assistant appeared next to her. "Sorry to interrupt. Can I see you a moment?"

If she didn't already cherish Dee, this interruption would have sealed it. Anything to get out from under Billy Tripp's eyes. "Absolutely. Excuse me, guys."

ONCE MADAME HOTNESS—M.H. AS SHE WOULD HERETOFORE be known—left, Billy waggled his eyebrows at Monk, clutched his heart with both hands and gasped. "This could finally be the end. Tell my mother I love her."

Monk cracked up. "What are you doing?"

"Holy shi—sorry, Ma. Holy crud. Do I have drool on my face? Seriously, dude, I'm fudging dumbstruck here."

"I see that. You were staring. She thinks you're an asshole. I tend to agree. If you screw me on this assignment I'll beat you worse than the last time. All I want is a quiet weekend with my girl."

Kristen appeared again; her lips pinched. "Guys, I have..." She motioned to Billy's hands still at his chest "Are you okay?"

"Crap," Monk muttered.

Oops. Billy dropped his hands, stood tall and scanned the room. "I'm fine. Heartburn."

Her gaze bounced between him and Monk before she finally shook her head. She held up the phone with her left hand. No wedding ring. *Perfect.*

"Something has come up in another part of the hotel. If you need me, call my cell."

Oh, sweetheart, Billy thought, *you've got yourself a deal.*

Kristen charged through the lobby doors and was met by two uniformed Miami police officers. "I'm Kristen Dante. I understand we've had a theft."

"Yes, ma'am," the taller officer said.

A young guy in his twenties with slicked back hair stepped up. "My Range Rover was stolen."

She shifted to maintenance mode. "I'm terribly sorry, sir. Was it valet parked?"

"No, it was in the lot."

At least the car hadn't been touched by one of her employees. "Are you staying in the hotel?"

"I checked in yesterday. I should sue your ass."

Sue them? He parked the car himself. How could it be

their fault? But he was a guest. "I apologize for the inconvenience. I'll be sure your hotel bill reflects our gratitude for your business. We will, of course, arrange for any transportation you may need."

The guy pinched his thin, little lips tight and the veins in his neck popped. Kristen folded her hands in front of her and waited. *Don't scream at me, you weasely man.*

"I'll be in the bar," he said and stormed off.

"Nice guy," the officer said.

Welcome to the hospitality business. She turned back to him, checked his nametag. "Officer Jackson, what can I do?"

"If we could get a look at your security footage, maybe there's something there."

She nodded. "I'll take you upstairs."

After ushering the police to the security office, she phoned the victimized guest and offered use of the hotel's fleet of cars for as long as necessary. For tonight, she'd need to track down a driver.

The elevator doors opened just as her phone chirped. Kurt, her assistant hotel manager. She waved the people inside the elevator to continue without her "Hi, Kurt."

"We have a problem."

For the second time, Kristen strode through the lobby doors and, thanks to the popularity of the two nightclubs in the hotel, ran into a crush of people. A gust of wind blew her hair in front of her face and she tucked it behind her ear. She sidestepped, found Kurt waiting for her and guided him from milling guests.

"You're telling me," she said, her voice strained with forced control, "in addition to the stolen guest's car, one of our Bentleys *and* a Mercedes are gone?"

"Yes," Kurt said.

"How did this happen?"

"We don't know. Both sets of keys were locked in the safe."

"Were the cars taken out tonight?"

"Yes, the Bentley was out twice and the Mercedes once."

"And there were no issues?"

Kurt held his hands palm up. "Not a one. Both drivers turned in the keys and went home."

"The police are upstairs in security. Do they know?"

"Yes. They're reviewing footage."

Kristen's phone beeped with a text. The auction of the diamond necklace was about to start. She should get in there.

A second squad car, lights flashing, entered the circular drive already bumper to bumper with cars. Nothing like causing a scene. What a damned night. Kristen and Kurt rushed to greet the officers and waited for them to join her on the sidewalk.

The older officer stood eye to eye with her, while she towered over the shorter one. "Hello, officers. I'm Kristen Dante."

"Ms. Dante, I'm Officer Burns," the bigger one said. "This is my partner, Officer Sams. Busy night here."

Kristen nodded. "We have a large function in the ballroom and the nightclubs, well, they draw a crowd most nights."

"Okay. Any witnesses come forward?"

"Not yet," Kurt said.

Burns's radio crackled and he stepped away.

"The other two officers are upstairs copying the security footage," Kristen said. "What now?"

Sams nodded. "We called for a detective. Someone will come down and follow up. Meantime, we'll do a BOLO—be on the lookout—for the stolen cars. Maybe something will pop. Most stolen cars go to certain locations. We'll concentrate on those areas. Any idea what time this happened?"

"Yes," Kurt said. "Both cars had been taken out this evening between seven and eight. The Bentley was signed back in at 8:45 p.m. and the Mercedes at nine. The keys were put in the safe. One of the valets noticed the cars missing at 10:15 p.m. when he parked a car in the area."

"When was the guest's car stolen?"

Kurt shrugged. "He hadn't moved the car since he checked in yesterday, but went back this evening around 9:45 to retrieve something and the car was gone."

Kristen turned to the officer. "Maybe all the cars were taken at the same time."

If that were the case, something would be on the security footage. And the hotel was busy tonight. Wouldn't someone have seen something?

Burns finished his call and joined them. "A detective is on the way."

"What are the chances we'll recover the cars?" Kristen asked.

"If these guys are any good, they know how to disable the factory antitheft devices. You have LoJack or anything?"

Kristen shook her head, almost embarrassed by it, but between the cost of the cars, the upkeep and the insurance, maintaining a fleet was expensive. With her father's approval, they had avoided the expense of installing additional tracking systems. Now she wondered if that risk had been worth it.

They'd gambled. And lost.

"No tracking. We'd hoped the standard antitheft systems would do the job."

The officer shrugged. "You never know. You could get lucky."

Somehow, he didn't sound as if he believed it.

BILLY CHECKED THE TIME AGAIN. IN A FEW MINUTES, THE necklace would be sold to the highest bidder and he could get the hell out of here. The last bid had been two-and-a-half mil. That, he had to admit, was fudging impressive.

Monk sidled up to him. "Something is happening out front."

A familiar buzz that he'd savored since childhood sparked. Had there ever been a time when he'd been able to resist the call of adventure? *Nope*. "What is it?"

"If I knew, I'd have told you. I heard one of the guests say there's two Miami-Dade squads out front." Monk jerked his head toward the door. "I'll throw you a bone. Go check it out. See if Kristen needs help."

"Have I mentioned I love you?"

"Not recently."

Considering he and Monk were working their way back from what the head shrinkers would call interpersonal conflict, Billy decided not to pursue the conversation. Besides, two squads out front would be a whole lot more fun.

He strolled to the ballroom doors and once out of sight, picked up the pace to the elevator bank. No sense running down thirty flights when he wasn't even sure there was an emergency.

Minutes later, the automatic lobby doors opened for him and he stepped into a mosh pit of people. Yikes. Busy place for a Thursday.

He scanned left, then right, and spotted Madame Hotness conferring with two uniforms. M.H. held her hands folded in front of her, her head dipped so she could hear the shorter cop. Billy laughed. Suddenly, he had a thing for tall women.

M.H. pointed to the door, nodded and turned away from the officers. She headed in his general direction, so Billy put himself in her path. "Can I help with something?"

Lurching to a stop, she wobbled on her sky-high heels and he reached to steady her. She clasped his arm and they stood for a second while Billy's mind went all the places it shouldn't. Now if *this* woman had slipped him her number... Yow.

She stepped out of his grasp. "Is the auction over?"

"Just about. We heard something was up. You need anything?"

"Uh, no. I'm fine. Well, as fine as can be with three cars stolen."

Shazam. "Three? In one night?"

"Two hotel cars and one belonging to a guest. These officers just got here and two others are up in the security office reviewing footage. I think they can handle it. You can head back upstairs. Thank you, though."

Dismissed. Not fun. But three cars boosted in one night? That was enough of a visceral hit to satisfy his jones for excitement. Maybe this hotel gig wasn't so bad after all.

Sirens and then a loud, repetitive beep blared behind him, and he turned to see an ambulance backing onto the sidewalk.

"What is this now?" M.H. hustled to the ambulance and Billy followed.

"I'm the hotel general manager," Kristen said to the paramedics as they hauled a gurney out of the back end of the bus. "What's happening?"

"Possible heart attack, eighteen-oh-two."

M.H. paddled her hands forward. "Go!"

The paramedics tore through the lobby doors, screaming at people to give way, and she turned back to Billy. "I cannot believe this night."

He cocked his head. "It's a humdinger."

And then she did something he'd never forget. In the midst of the raging chaos in her very expensive hotel, she laughed. The sound of it settled inside him and a burst of heat drilled into his chest. He had to have this woman.

"I need to go," she said. "If someone dies in my hotel, I'll kill myself."

Now it was his turn to laugh. South Beach in December. Yep. Not so bad. He pulled his phone from his suit pocket.

"What's up?" Monk said.

"Three cars boosted."

"No shit?"

"I'm gonna get on this. See what I can find out."

"No. Get back up here."

Not so fast, pal. This was the most fun Billy had seen all damned night. He made crackling noises into the phone. "What? Speak up."

"I know you can hear me. Get. Your. Ass. Back. Here."

"I got a bad connection. I'll call you back." He clicked off and wandered toward the parking lot for a sneak and peek.

After snooping around the crime scene and making friends with the cashier in the valet office, his phone rang. Bobby V. Billy stepped into the lobby, suddenly teeming with people, and assumed the fundraiser must be over. The valets would be hopping now.

Billy stuck his finger in his ear to muffle the noise. "Yo."

"Duck and cover. Monk is headed your way."

Pain in the ass. "Are you done upstairs?"

"Yeah. Everyone is gone."

Just then, Monk stepped out of one of the elevators and his gaze zoomed to Billy.

"I'm out." Billy hung up and prepared for this latest battle with his coworker.

Monk halted a foot in front of him, arms folded. "I'm sick of asking what you're doing."

"Stop asking then. Besides, you told me to check it out."

"I told you to see if Kristen needed help. I have since spoken with her and she said she told you she didn't. Where've you been?"

Billy flicked two fingers toward a darkened hallway lined with closed shops. He wasn't about to scream in the middle of that herd of people. He stopped in front of one of the shops and spun to face Monk. "Here's the deal, we got two hotel cars gone. A Bentley and a Mercedes. A guest's Range Rover is also in the wind. After the cops got done, I checked out the parking lot. No broken glass anywhere."

Monk shook his head. "What are you doing?"

Eff's sake, how many times was he going to ask? "Dude, shut up and listen. I made nice with the shorty in the valet office and she said the Bentley and Mercedes were out tonight. Within an hour after the drivers dropped off the keys, those babies were history."

Monk did that puffing up his chest thing—the alpha-dog routine—and stepped closer. "This is not our problem. Kristen wants the cops to handle it. Do *not* piss her off."

Billy waved him away. "She doesn't know I'm poking around."

"And it'll stay that way. Whatever you're thinking, stop. I am not babysitting you. Got it?"

Babysitting? The expired passport was definitely his fault, and maybe he'd screwed up with the almost-being-beaten-to-death-by-a-coworker incident, which he'd severely chastised himself over, but he didn't need someone watching him. What he needed was to figure out this car theft deal and score points with his boss. To get square with Vic and get his life back on track.

"Born to Run" blasted from Monk's phone and he checked the screen. "Now I'm in trouble." He picked up the call. "Hey, Iz...Yeah...I'm finishing with Billy. I'll be right up."

After ending the call with the super-model clone, he shoved his phone into his suit pocket. "I gotta get upstairs or she'll murder me. I promised her a vacation and my work time is over."

"Can we say whipped?"

Monk held up his hands. "It's bullshit like this that got you guarding jewelry. Now, I'm going to my room. Stay the fuck out of trouble."

2

LATE THE NEXT MORNING, BILLY STOOD STREET SIDE IN FRONT of the double towered, thirty-eight story hotel staring at the reflective windows. Such a bizarre color, like aged whiskey. At the very top, stretched *Dante* in giant gold letters. These people knew how to make an effing statement. A Las Vegas style hotel at the southernmost tip of South Beach. This secluded end of Miami was close enough to the activity of the Art Deco district, but without the chaos. Best of both worlds. Brilliant.

He swung his camera up and snapped a few shots.

An ocean breeze blew and Billy tilted his face skyward. As much as he hadn't wanted to come here, he might be in love with the climate. Which was saying something since, at thirty-one years old, he hadn't found the place he wanted to call home. A place that settled his constantly raging mind.

Sure, his family lived in Virginia and he visited a few times a year, but he didn't see himself moving back. And Chicago? Great city, but he'd yet to even rent an apartment. Why bother when he could stay in an executive suite and not mess with buying furniture. All he had to worry about moving were his clothes and his beloved Nikon.

Not a bad life.

"Hi, baby," a sexy blonde said as she and her friend wandered down the sidewalk. Billy gave her bikini-clad ass a gander over the top of his sunglasses. Crazy hot women here.

Just ridiculous. But he'd always been a fan of the ridiculous.

Yeah. South Beach in December.

"Yo."

Billy shifted front and center to see Monk and Izzy walking toward him. Monk wore his typical outfit of cargo shorts, white T-shirt and flip-flops. His head, as usual, was wrapped in one of his many do-rags. Izzy, on the other hand, looked stunning in a white, gauzy cover-up that did a piss poor job of masking the red bikini under it. The wide brim of her hat flopped in the wind and her black sunglasses hid her green eyes.

"What are you doing?" Monk asked for the millionth time.

"I'm standing here. Is that a crime? Hey, Iz."

"Billy, I adore you, but you're horning in on my time with Peter."

"It's not me. Tell your boyfriend to lay off."

"Our room," Monk said, "faces the street. You've been out here half an hour."

Get a life, man. "Seriously, *you* are whacked. In my defense, something is bugging me about those cars getting boosted so soon after they got back. Doesn't that strike you as odd?"

Monk puffed his cheeks, blew the air out and turned to

Izzy. "This is what happens. Relentless. And he wonders why I beat the crap out of him last summer."

"Listen to me a sec—"

But Izzy didn't want to hear it and held up one hand. "I'm going to the beach. Billy, we're having lunch at one o'clock. Join us if you'd like. By the way, I like your haircut. The long hair was cute, but this is better." She poked Monk in the chest. "You've got ten minutes. Then I find a pool boy to entertain me."

With his jealous streak, old Monk wouldn't like that. Billy grinned as she made her way toward the hotel lobby. *Love that girl.*

"One o'clock?" he called, snatching his phone from his pocket to set a reminder. He had no doubt something, somewhere would distract him and he'd lose track of time.

"One o'clock," she hollered back. "Peter, you're down to nine and a half minutes."

Monk held his hands wide. "Happy now?"

"Absolutely. Hey, you'd better follow her." *And get off my ass.* "You don't have to play daddy all the time. Give it a rest. Besides, I'm gonna talk to the valets. See what's what when they park the cars."

"Son of a bitch."

"I already got to a couple front desk people this morning. I thought maybe they'd know what happens with the keys after the valet office closes."

"You're killing me. If you screw this up, Vic will fry your ass. And mine with it."

"You worry too much."

Except Vic had told him to go to South Beach and A) get some rest, B) stop screwing up and C) figure out how to not piss people off. Too bad none of those things came easy.

Truth of it was, he didn't want to be this way. Even when

he knew he was about to cross a line, he struggled to control his active brain. He'd spent most of his life trying to manage his need to be the smart-ass cut-up. Sure he liked when people laughed at his jokes, but at some point, he'd learned to thrive on it and the older he got the more he needed it. When it came to attention, he was a heroin addict with a two hundred dollar a day habit. Lately that habit had beaten him down to being so strung out and confused that he didn't have the energy to stop himself when he screwed up.

And that, he surmised, was how he got here. He had the impression he'd better accomplish all the things Vic had told him to or he'd be waving goodbye to the job he loved.

Still, this car theft thing was juice-a-licious.

He and Monk walked up the covered circular drive where the hotel's front entry consisted of a large sliding door with four sets of manual doors bookending. A bellman stood off to one side. Security cameras swiveled all around and, of course, Monk the obsessive car lover spotted a silvery-blue convertible sitting on the curve of the driveway.

He whistled. "An Aston Martin V8 Vantage. This is a helluva ride right here."

"It's cool," Billy said.

"Cool?"

He shrugged. "I don't even own a car. What do you want me to say?" In Billy's opinion, cars were just another thing to take care of and with his travel schedule, he didn't need the headache. Besides, he was never around enough to drive anywhere. When he needed one, he rented. Or took public transportation.

"This car is worth a hundred and fifty grand."

"It's a great car, so what? We've seen tons of them." He glanced at the license plate. A vanity plate that read Krissy.

Holy crud.

He turned to the valet, Eddie, whom he had spoken to an hour ago. "Is this Kristen Dante's car?"

Eddie eyeballed Monk. "Who are you?"

Gun-shy after the car thefts. "This is my buddy. We work together at Taylor Security." Couldn't hurt to reinforce that they'd been hired to be here. Even if the event they'd been hired for had nothing to do with overall hotel security.

Eddie nodded. "Yeah, that's Ms. Dante's car. She usually parks in the lot, but asked us to keep an eye on it today."

The boss was worried her car would get boosted. The way Monk was hovering, *he* might be the booster.

"I don't blame her," Monk said. "Damn, this is an amazing car."

Again with the car envy. "Let's get focused here."

How funny was that? Billy telling someone else to get focused.

A second valet jogged up and Eddie tossed him a set of keys. "Put those in the box."

"You keep the valet keys in a lockbox? Is it out here?"

Eddie motioned them to a podium to the left of the entrance where his partner was storing keys in a decorative steel box built into the front of the building. The valet closed and locked it, and—pretty slick—the box, painted the exact color of the building, blended into the façade.

"Do you lock the keys in here each time?"

"Unless we get slammed. Then we hang on to them and do a bunch at the same time."

Monk, who had less than five minutes before his girl-friend accosted a pool boy, squatted and studied the lock on the box. "Who has keys to this?"

"There are two of us here full-time. On weekends, we bring in extra guys. There's only two keys so we pass them back and forth. At the end of the shift we turn the keys in."

A young couple walked up the driveway and Eddie greeted them. When Monk stepped away from the box, Billy bent low to examine it. Piece of shit lock could be picked with a paper clip. He straightened, grabbed his trusty pad and pencil from his back pocket and noted it. "Do the keys in the box get turned in every night?"

"Yeah. They store them in the valet office off the lobby. That's where people go when they're ready to pick up. They turn in the ticket, the person working the inside desk gets the keys and calls us on the radio. Doing the back-end stuff inside keeps this area clear. It's nuts here on Friday and Saturday nights because of the clubs."

Billy jotted notes as Eddie yapped. They hadn't seen the clubs yet. "They're on the top floor?"

Eddie nodded. "One in each tower."

The baby-faced bellman who had to be all of twenty years old, leaped from his perch at the side of the door and stood at attention. Billy spotted Kristen, on yet another pair of stilt shoes that he'd dream about for a week, exiting the hotel in a stretchy, light pink dress topped with a loose, short-sleeved cardigan. *Yoi, the rack.* Too bad she had to hide it under the grandma sweater. She carried a briefcase in her left hand and flipped her hair over her shoulder with the other. Billy's knees went soft. Of course, other parts went hard, but he couldn't help that completely male reaction to a woman such as this.

"Hi, guys." She waved to the bellman. "Hi, Bruno."

"Afternoon, Ms. Kristen."

She stopped in front of them. "How's it going?"

"Good," Monk said.

"Yuh." Billy hoped she wouldn't notice the bulge in his jeans. *Jesus.* The second she hit his radar he'd turned into a horny teenager.

After shooting him eyeball missiles—as if he could help staring?—Monk shifted back to Kristen. "Great event last night."

She slid her gaze to Billy who, yes, continued to gawk at her. There couldn't be a single man to disagree with him on this one. And, in his mind, that made it okay. Sort of.

"Despite the police activity, it was a great event. Thank you."

"Here are your keys, ma'am," the valet said.

"Thank you." She motioned Billy and Monk to the car so they'd be out of earshot. "I parked it up here today."

Monk nodded. "Until you figure out what happened last night, it's not a bad idea. It's a great-looking car."

"I love this car."

Monk dropped one of his million-watters on her. "I love this car too."

Billy rolled his eyes. "He's a car freak. Be careful or he'll ask to drive it."

Her eyes flashed and she let out a crack of laughter that left him wanting to hear it at odd hours of the night. Very odd hours. In bed.

"I think you're S.O.L.," he said to Monk.

"Don't take offense. My father is the only other person who has driven it. This car, gentlemen, was my bonus when we opened the hotel."

She ran her free hand over the side of the car, her fingers slowly stroking back and forth, back and forth, back and forth. *Holy crud.* Billy suspected his boner would last a good, long while.

Monk cleared his throat because even he, a guy toasted in love with his girlfriend—who incidentally, was about to find an entertaining pool boy—couldn't remain unaffected by this level of sex appeal.

"Wow," Billy said.

"So," Madame Hotness said, "it would be a very big deal if I let you drive this car."

"I understand," Monk said.

She grinned. "Good. Because if I let you drive then I'll have to let Billy drive too." She turned to him. "Is that what you want?"

"Lady," he said. "that is a seriously loaded question right now."

CLEARLY KRISTEN HAD MADE A MISTAKE. "I'M SORRY?"

"Ah, crap. I knew it wouldn't take long for him to screw me up."

She swung her gaze back to Peter. "I'm sorry?" For some bizarre reason, she had no clue what else to say.

"Kristen!"

The three of them turned toward the door to see her sister, Jess, her perfect legs encased in a tight, sky blue miniskirt, charging toward them.

Kristen gritted her teeth and spun toward Jess. "I'm on my way to a meeting."

"Well, it'll have to wait. Your club manager is an asshole. He treats me like I'm eye candy."

You are eye candy. Normally, Kristen would take her aside and politely correct her in a firm, but hushed voice. With two hotel contractors and staff members witnessing Jess's total disregard of professionalism, Kristen was beyond that. Still, she kept her voice at a reasonable level. "You watch your tongue when guests can hear you. I don't need you causing a scene. And, how dare you, at twenty-four and just now tackling a job, refer to one of my employees that way? You'll do what he tells you."

"Our *father* owns this place."

"And your *sister* runs it. That doesn't give you permission to be nasty to a manager. Go home and chill out. Don't bother calling Dad and complaining. He's letting me deal with your employment here."

Jess fisted her hands at her side. Good. Let her be mad. Time for her to grow up and be responsible for her own actions. "Take the weekend off. Come back to work Monday morning with a better attitude."

"O.M.G."

"That's the best you're getting from me, Jess, and it's more than you deserve right now."

Jess scrunched her sculpted nose. Who knew such facial perfection could so easily transform to a pig face? Then, Jess's man-vibe must have beeped because she glanced over Kristen's shoulder to Billy and Peter.

"Billy Tripp. I heard you were here."

They knew each other?

"Jess," Billy said.

Sticking her arm out, Jess shoved around Kristen, stood smack in front of Billy and studied his extremely appealing body like a prowling panther. An immediate sizzle shot up Kristen's neck and she hated it.

Despised it.

On some physical level, regardless of his staring problem, she was attracted to him. And a guy like Billy Tripp, in all his blue-eyed, dark-haired splendor, would easily fall for her beautiful sister.

And what did *that* say about the three of them?

Nothing good. Billy would be typical, Jess would be her trampy self and Kristen would be sick with envy. Oh, yes, they'd be quite a bunch.

How the hell did Jess always make her feel inferior?

Dammit. She had a master's degree and yet she wasn't smart enough to disregard her sister.

To Kristen's horror, Jess ran a finger down the front of Billy's T-shirt. "Last time I saw you, things got a little rough."

He glanced at Kristen, met her gaze for a second too long and then ever so slowly shifted back to Jess. "That's because you bit me."

"You were manhandling me."

I so don't want to hear this. Not that she hadn't heard her sister's sexual exploits before. No, those were well documented. Particularly on the internet, thanks to her last loser boyfriend.

Peter clapped his hands and the sound pierced the air like a gun blast. "Let's get moving here."

"Excellent suggestion," Kristen said. "Jess, I'll see you on Monday. Do not come here this weekend. Not even for the clubs."

Jess threw her shoulders back and her eyes filled with that cold, menacing brattiness Kristen had seen many times. "You're such a bitch."

The verbal assault left a hot, stinging sensation under her skin. But wasn't this normal? After all she'd done for Jess, this is what she got. In front of virtual strangers no less. Technically they were guests of the hotel, which made the whole scenario more humiliating. With both hands wrapped around the handle of her briefcase, she stepped forward an inch. "Stop. Right now. You're in front of guests. Maybe you don't care, but I do. Keep it up and I won't bail you out of jail next time."

Jess sucked air through her nose, grunted loud enough for Billy and Peter to hear and stormed toward the lobby doors.

"Wow," Billy said.

Apparently he was back to his limited, one-word vocabulary. Kristen turned back to see his gaze focused on her in a way that alerted her insecurities and made her shoulders curl. Why did she let these people all make her feel uncomfortable? She jabbed her finger over her shoulder. "I need to speak to you a minute."

"Here we go," Peter said.

"Just Billy." She strode to the front of her car. Fury whipped at her and she spun around, found Billy right on her heels and smacked her head against his chin. "Ow!"

Pain radiated through her forehead and her vision went white for a second. But then he rubbed the assaulted spot with a gentleness that turned her liquid. Nice hands. Warm hands. *Attentive* hands.

For a leech.

But still, she stayed there, letting him touch her. When was the last time a man had touched her? In any way. Particularly a man one who looked like this. The closeness of his body, all the male heat, burned into her and her stomach squeezed. How desperate was she for attention that she'd take a simple gesture of comfort as affection?

"I'm sorry," he said. "You okay?"

She stepped back. An outrageously good-looking man touching her was the last thing her deprived body needed. A guy like him could make her forget all about being a woman who didn't sleep around. "I'm fine. But I need you to quit staring at me like I have food on my face. And *other* places. If you know what I mean."

Please don't humiliate me into saying you need to stop ogling my boobs.

He raised his hands. "You're right. I apologize. It's...uh... ah, ship."

"Ship?"

"I told my mom I'd stop swearing."

"Oh." Didn't that little fact set her back some? This nutball loved his mother enough to stop swearing. The leech had a heart. "Anyway, please stop staring at me. It makes me uncomfortable."

"Right. No problem."

"Thank you."

"Sure."

She stepped around him and unlocked the car door, but he beat her to it and opened it. Well, that was nice. Even if he most likely slept with her sister.

"Thank you, again." She slid into the car, tossed her briefcase on the seat and turned back to him still holding the door open.

"FYI," he said. "It isn't food on your face. I just like looking at you."

After her meeting, Kristen returned to the hotel only to be told by her assistant that several managers were concerned over Billy questioning them regarding the stolen cars. Suddenly this man was everywhere he shouldn't be. Including her thoughts.

"What kind of questions?"

Dee shrugged. "No idea."

Kristen bit her bottom lip. "I guess I'll find him and ask."

And wouldn't that be fun after their earlier conversation when he announced he liked her looks. Even if she believed a stud like him would be attracted to a fat Amazon, Billy Tripp was clearly a hit-and-run driver and she had no interest in that kind of rejection. She just had to convince her deprived body.

Marching into her office, she called Peter to get the hit-

and-run driver's number. Twenty minutes later, just as she was about to shove a forkful of salad—*so sick of salads*—into her mouth, he strolled into her office in orange swim trunks and a sleeveless T-shirt.

And oh, the arms on this man.

He grinned at her and she realized the fork was still in midair. *Darn it.* She set it in the bowl and shoved everything aside. "Have a seat, Billy."

He slid into one of her guest chairs. "About earlier."

"That's not why you're here."

"Oh."

Leveling her best I'm-in-charge stare on him, she got right to it. "A few of my managers told me you questioned them regarding the thefts last night. What's that about?"

Billy shrugged. "I'm the curious sort. Thought I might be able to help with the investigation."

Keeping a straight face suddenly became a problem. The jewelry guy. Investigating. "How about we leave that to the police?"

"Have they told you anything?"

Not much. She'd never admit that. "They've told me enough."

"Any suspects?"

"Not yet." Why was she even answering him?

"Have they located the cars yet?"

She let out a long breath. Telling him the antitheft systems on the cars had been disabled would only spur his curiosity. Heck, she herself was curious about that one. Clearly these were no amateur thieves if they could dismantle the security system on a three hundred-thousand-dollar car. "I'm asking you to let the police do their jobs."

"I am. In a way. I'm staying clear of them. Doing my own thing."

"Yes, but that's a problem. I run this hotel and you're distracting my employees. I don't want issues with the police."

He propped his elbow on the arm of the chair and tapped his cheek with one finger. A few seconds later he said, "Okay. I'll leave the employees alone. How's that?"

"Perfect."

He sat forward. "See, I'm not unreasonable."

"You also didn't say you'd stop investigating. All you said was you wouldn't bug my employees."

"Ouch."

She folded her hands on her desk. This situation required a certain amount of control. They both wanted it, but she'd be the one to get it. One thing she couldn't stand was a lack control. "Look, Billy Tripp, I didn't come to running this hotel because I'm a pushover for a cute guy. Stay out of the way and we'll get along just fine. Can you do that?"

He stood, placed his hands on the desk and leaned in. "Sweetheart, I can do whatever you need."

3

THE MINUTE BILLY WAS OUT OF HER OFFICE, KRISTEN DIALED her father's number. It would be midnight in Dubai, but she needed his counsel and hoped he'd forgive her.

"Hi, Krissy," he said in the warm baritone that always managed to offer comfort.

She smiled at the childhood nickname. Jess had been the one who had started it. As a toddler, she'd never been able to say Kristen and shortened the name to Krissy. These days, their father seemed to be the only one calling her Krissy. "Did I wake you up?"

"No. I'm reading contracts."

"Dad, it's late. You should be sleeping."

"Then you would have woken me up."

That was true. "But I'm your favorite oldest daughter. I'm allowed."

"How silly of me to forget. You need to come to Dubai and see this property. It might be more beautiful than Dante Miami."

"Dad! How dare you say that to me?" Despite her admonition, a hit of pride bloomed and she did a little chair dance. Dante Miami had been her brainchild and her father had given her the opportunity of a lifetime in designing it. An opportunity she remained grateful for. Dante Dubai would be the newer version and she'd had a hand in that also. All the design elements she'd found lacking in Miami had been corrected for the Dubai hotel. The property would be nothing short of spectacular.

"I know," Dad said, "but you've outdone yourself."

She glanced at the ancient photo sitting on her desk. The two of them stood in front of a half-completed building and Kristen wore a giant hardhat on her nine-year old head. That had been the beginning of her obsession with beautiful buildings. Even then he'd encouraged her ambitions. "Well, thank you. I'm glad you're happy with it."

"Let's talk about the thefts. Are the Taylor Security people still there? We can call them in for recommendations."

Calling them in. That's all she needed. Bad enough Billy was doing his own investigation. "I think the police have it under control, Dad. They took copies of all the security footage and said they would update me today."

"Yes, but honey, how do we keep this from happening again?"

Maybe he had a point. She supposed recommendations on security upgrades in the parking areas were in order. She tapped a pen against her desk. "We do have Ed Freeborn's daughter getting married here."

And when the United States Senate Majority Leader threw a three-day party, all his rich friends came. Particularly when said senator and his friends lived in the Miami area. They'd have high-end cars lining the parking lot.

"Krissy, we want people talking about the beauty of the hotel. Not the thefts. You've been working your tail off to put

Dante on the worldwide map, and people worrying about their safety could destroy us."

"I agree."

"Were we the only hotel hit?"

The pen tapping started to annoy even her. She tossed it on her desk. "I'm not sure. There's been nothing in the papers and I don't want to start asking questions. Do you know anyone at the police department? Maybe they can tell us."

"No, but my lawyer will. After your sister's escapades he's been sucking up to them."

Kristen curled her lip. Leave it to Jess.

"What *is* Jess up to?"

How much should she tell him? Considering her screwball sister had been dumped on her three weeks ago after she'd completed her community service in L.A. *"But it was only a little marijuana."* Everyone knew Jess had more than a few missing brain cells, but that DUI made headlines. "She's okay. We're trying to use her party girl status to draw celebrities. She's good at schmoozing people so we put her to work in the VIP rooms. Last weekend they had her stand on the bar and lead a toast at midnight. I wasn't there, but I heard the crowd loved it."

Her father sighed. She supposed most men didn't want their daughters standing on bars.

"Thank you for taking care of her, Krissy. She needs direction."

And, as usual, I'm the one who gets stuck with her. "I'll do what I can, but you know how she is."

"I know." Dad sounded as if the weight of his youngest daughter had crushed him, pressed every ounce of air from him. Damned Jess. Her antics had already given the man one heart attack.

"Here's an oddity for you. Apparently, Jess knows one of the Taylor Security guys." *And most likely spent an active night in his bed.*

Her father hesitated. "What's his name?"

"Billy Tripp. He's the jewelry guy from last night. Which is what I was calling you about. Not twenty minutes ago, I had him in my office. If you can believe this, he's been doing his own investigating on the car thefts. I mean, Dad, he's the jewelry guy and he's butting into a police investigation."

Silence. Had they lost the connection? "Dad?"

"I'm here."

"What do you think?"

"Honey, Billy was part of the team that got Jess out of Columbia."

In the words of her sister, *O.M.G.* Billy Tripp, Mr. Mindsnap, who couldn't stop staring at her chest, had rescued Jess when she'd been kidnapped by a Columbian drug cartel. Only her sister would march into South America carrying Louis Vuitton luggage. She might as well have been wearing a sign: MY FATHER IS LOADED. KIDNAP ME.

All kinds of surprises these days. "I've underestimated his skills. Shame on me."

"Vic only hires the best. Why he'd have him guarding jewelry is a puzzle, but he must have had a reason. Either way, let him help. As long as he doesn't impede the police, I don't have a problem with it."

But...but...but he kept staring at her chest, making her uncomfortable and she wanted him gone. This could not be happening. "I don't know how I feel about him investigating on his own."

"Krissy, soon you'll have the United States Senate Majority Leader there. We have to put a stop to these thefts."

She sighed. Apparently Billy Tripp would be staying a little while. She didn't have to like it though.

"Go to bed, Dad. I'll call you when we have an update. You'll be home for the senator's party, right?"

"I'll be there. Can't wait to see you."

"Bye, Dad."

Kristen glanced to the doorway and spotted Manny, the only man in her life. Of course, Manny was nine years old with huge, protruding teeth, but he was cute as could be and freakishly intelligent.

"Hello, young man. How was school today?"

Manny held his thumbs up. "Good."

"Excellent. Homework?"

"Nope."

"You hit the jackpot. Did you say hello to your mom?"

He nodded. His mother worked in housekeeping and, as a single mom raising multiple children, couldn't afford post-school care five days a week.

After finding Manny tucked into the employee lounge one afternoon, Kristen had taken a liking to him. The fact that he was reading Thoreau had shocked and amazed her, and she allowed him to hang out in her office a few days a week. After all, she'd spent the majority of her childhood trailing her father around construction sites, which she firmly believed had prepared her for running Dante.

Manny was the classic at-risk child and with his brain, she didn't want him winding up in a gang like his older brother by the time he was fifteen.

Still in the doorway, he shifted from foot to foot. "It's Friday."

Oh, she knew where this was going. "Yes, it is."

The little turd paddled his hands. "Can we go?"

Kristen laughed. "Ice cream it is. You and me, pal. Let's

do it." Not that she'd eat any. Ice cream was one of the forbidden fruits. Along with most other things that were not a vegetable, but it was always fun to watch him and his mother never minded.

The two of them strolled out to the pool area where the crowd grew with new weekend arrivals. Loud, playful voices sang along with the reggae duo entertaining the happy audience. This was why she loved the hotel business. Guests weren't always happy, but when they were, it made the hard work worthwhile.

She and Manny stepped to the snack bar and the sun broke through two palm trees, warming her while the ocean breeze gave a gentle reminder that she should have grabbed a hair clip.

Manny ordered his usual double scoop of chocolate with rainbow sprinkles. Kristen searched for an open table. Nothing.

"Kristen," a man yelled and she turned to see Billy, Peter and a stunning brunette at one of the far tables. Not exactly who she wanted to see at the moment, but after the chat with her father, it would be a good time to confer with the Taylor Security people.

"Manny, I'll be at that table. Come over when you get your ice cream."

"Yes, Miss Kristen."

God, she loved this kid. So polite.

On her way to the table, she stopped one of the waitresses. "Have the people at table six paid their bill yet?"

Tina, the younger sister of a friend, grinned at her. "The hotties?"

Kristen bit her lip. Hotties. Peter, although a little too muscular for her taste, had a killer smile and general confidence about him that drew one in. She didn't quite get the do-rag look, but it somehow worked for him.

Billy? He qualified as a hottie. Times two. And after that line he'd dropped on her about liking the way she looked, he represented something else entirely. Something that meant trouble. Plus, his irreverence reminded her a little too much of her sister.

Kristen patted Tina's arm. "Make sure to put the hotties' check on my tab, okay?"

"Absolutely."

As if he sensed the conversation about him, Billy kept his eyes on her and she fought the urge to hunch. He just never gave up. She'd play this cool. That's what she'd do.

Kristen approached the table and both men stood. "Hi, guys. Having lunch?"

"Just me," Billy said. "Monk and Izzy ate already."

She waved them back to their chairs and turned to the woman sitting with them. Women like this, their perfect cheekbones, full lips and sculpted bodies made her feel like a heifer. She pasted a smile on. "Hello. I'm Kristen Dante."

"This is Isabelle," Peter said. "I'm trying to convince her to marry me."

Isabelle sighed. "Knock it off. I'm living with you. One step at a time."

Peter blew her a kiss and Kristen laughed at their easy banter. The comfort that came with acceptance. A gift really. What an interesting couple.

Billy gestured to the empty chair beside him. "Join us for a few minutes."

"I have a friend with me. If you don't mind."

"Sure."

"Miss Kristen," Manny called.

"Hi, bud. Come on over." She ushered him and his

monster ice cream cone into the chair. "Manny, this is Mr. Billy, Mr. Peter and Miss Isabelle."

"Hello. I have to lick. It's melting so fast."

"Dude," Billy said, "*that* is an awesome cone."

"I know."

Suddenly, Billy was out of his chair, consulting with the couple at the next table and commandeering the lone empty chair for her. Okay, so maybe that was a nice gesture. Maybe. "Manny's mother works at the hotel. He and I have a standing ice cream date on Fridays."

"She never gets any. Just me. And I never pay either."

Kristen burst out laughing. "Sssshhh, Manny. You're telling my secrets."

"Incoming," Billy said, alerting them to the waitress about to serve his food.

His crystal blue eyes devoured the basket in front of him and Kristen knew on sight it contained Dante's famous blue cheese burger.

Salad, Kristen. Salad. Anything more than salads two out of three meals would make her even fatter and who needed that. No, she needed to maintain her self-discipline and not think about the hateful burger.

"Been waiting all day for this," he said.

"That burger got five stars from Gourmet Magazine."

"I know. I saw the write up in the elevator this morning. Had to try it."

"Well, enjoy. I hear they're fabulous."

Billy held both hands out as if she'd committed some grievous crime against humanity. "Oh, come on! You've never tried one? In your own hotel?"

"Billy," Peter said. "Shut it."

Isabelle eyeballed them both. "Don't start, guys."

What was this tension? Before she could think too hard

on it, to her immense horror, Billy shoved the burger at her. "Take a bite. You have to."

She backed away. "No. Thank you."

Still holding the burger, he inched it closer. "Just try it."

Oh, how she wanted to. Just a little nibble. What harm could it do?

A lot.

She held up a hand as the rush of a seven-year-old memory reminded her just how much damage that blue cheese burger could do. She'd been home from grad school on break and heard voices on the lanai. Venturing to the screened doors, she'd spied Jess and her boyfriend talking and was about to say hello to the newest addition to Jess's fan club.

"How long is the fat Amazon home for?" the louse of a boyfriend had asked.

Kristen's body had seized at the insult and she'd hunched back, spinning away from the door to not be seen. Standing there, hiding behind the curtain, she'd waited for Jess to defend her. Surely her baby sister, the one she'd gotten out of messes time and time again, wouldn't let this jerk talk about her that way.

"Two weeks," Jess had said.

At the sound of those two little words Kristen's love for her younger sister had fallen apart. For the first time, she'd allowed herself to see Jess as the spoiled brat everyone else saw. A sharp, knifing pain had torn into her, but she'd remained still, her shoulders slumped with the agony of her sister's betrayal. And then there was nothing. No tears, no anger, just emptiness in her core that told her she'd never be the same.

The next day, the vicious cycle of not eating began. She starved herself, got frustrated with her body's cravings for sugar and then binged until she had to force herself to throw up. On and on it went until she could barely look at herself in the mirror. Until her eyes became shadowed, hollow holes in her skull. And yet, her weight still fluctuated.

A year later, after being hospitalized for dehydration, her secret came out and she was forced into therapy. As a result, she no longer starved herself, binged or jammed her fingers down her throat. But food of any kind was still an evil temptation. Waiting. Calling. Hoping she'd give in.

Fat Amazon.

And now, Billy Tripp sat in front of her, dangling a wicked, juicy, orgasm inducing blue cheese burger in front of her mouth.

Salad, Kristen. Salad. Gently, using just the tips of her fingers, she pushed his arm away. "No. Thank you."

"I haven't bit into it yet. No germs. You have to try it."

"Leave. Her. *Alone*," Peter said, clearly warning Billy he'd stepped over professional boundaries.

But, God, that burger was right there. The sinful smell teased and goaded her into wanting a sample.

Billy waved the burger by her mouth again. "You sure? One little bite?"

If only he knew. "No. Thank you, though."

He shrugged, took a bite of that fantastic looking sandwich, chewed twice, rolled his eyes and melted into his chair. "Unbelievable. So fudging good."

Kristen gave in and laughed at his antics. She couldn't help herself. Or maybe it was just her way of not focusing on the burger and the loss of control it represented. "You know, for someone who couldn't say more than 'wow' yesterday, you've managed to string quite a few sentences together today."

"Oh, Kristen," Peter said. "I like you."

Billy wiped his hands, slapped a hand on her shoulder and squeezed. "I know. Isn't she great?"

After the run in with Jess earlier, Kristen needed every compliment she could get and would gladly take the teasing. "You two make me laugh."

"Kristen," Peter said, "I don't want to get in your business here, but after last night, you may want to review your security."

She swung to Billy who swallowed another huge bite of burger. The man ate like a dinosaur. And yet, he was in phenomenal shape. To be so lucky. "Did you tell him to say that?"

"Not me, babe. But he's right. You may need more cameras in the parking areas. You also need a better lock on the valet box out front. For the record, I saw this before you yelled at me."

Isabelle smiled. "You yelled at him? Good for you."

"Hey!"

She waved him off. "You know I love you, but you get overanxious."

"My grandmother could pick that lockbox," Peter said.

Kristen cleared her throat. Her father had encouraged her to use these guys while they were here. "Can you change the lock for me?"

Billy grinned. "You bet. The valet said they get slammed on the weekends so I'm gonna hang out there tonight and observe. I want to see this system in action."

She sighed. "I see my yelling at you worked splendidly."

With the last bit of sandwich gone, he drummed his hands on his stomach. "I only promised I wouldn't talk to the employees."

Peter eased out a breath and Isabelle patted his arm. To

Kristen, the relationship between these men was a fascinating and clearly complicated thing. "Fine," she said. "I'll give you some latitude as long as you stay out of the police investigation."

"Sounds cool," Manny said. "Can I help?"

Billy glanced at Kristen and she shrugged. "Sure, kid. We'll come up with something for you. Let me think on it."

"Cool!"

This, combined with her newly acquired knowledge of Jess's rescue, made the man's rating soar. A flat-out skyward launch that meant big trouble for a woman whose only love interest in eighteen months had been a hotel. What that said about her, she didn't want to dwell on. Some would call her driven. Ambitious. Others would say lonely. Her? She didn't know. *Focus on work.* "Do you think that's where my problem is? The valets?"

"Don't know yet. I'm guessing not. That's the first place the P.D. would look. I'm thinking about the keys though and how they're handled. Are they vulnerable at any time? Can they be copied and returned before anyone discovers they're missing? That sort of thing."

Kristen's salad from lunch churned in her stomach. Good thing she didn't have the burger. "We could have some kind of conspiracy happening here? Seriously?"

Billy popped the last of his fries into his mouth. "Never hurts to check it out."

4

SUFFERING WITH BOREDOM THAT OCCURRED WHEN NOT playing with guns for several days, Billy opted for an evening run on the beach. Anything to get rid of his stifled energy and the chaos in his brain. When darkness fell, he headed back to Dante and slowed to a cooldown jog when he saw the two jutting towers and the blazing gold letters atop the building. Kristen Dante ran a hell of a ship. Props to her.

His sneaker clad feet dug into the soft sand until he reached the hotel, where he eased his muscles through a series of stretches. He considered a plunge in the ocean, but the night air had dipped into the sixties and he wasn't up for that. He could tough it out with the baddest of the bad, but freezing his nuts off for the fun of it didn't appeal.

Maybe the pool, though. That sucker stayed at eighty-two degrees. He detoured around a few beach chairs that hadn't been collected by the staff and entered the pool area. Towering palm trees lined the sides and, during the day, offered shade to the anti-sun people. A closed bar sat to his left and Billy cruised by it to ensure all the liquor had been cleared.

Affirmative.

Three multi-colored lights illuminated the calm pool water. Not a ripple to be found. Too late for the families, too early for the drunks. The sound of low tide whooshing against the shore filled the air. Yeah, he'd have to do one of the things he excelled at and disturb the serenity. Grabbing a fresh towel from the hut, he threw it on one of the chairs and stripped his stinking, sweat ridden shirt off.

The St. Christopher's medal he wore around his neck—a gift from his mother twelve years earlier—thunked against his chest and he lifted it to his lips before letting it fall. His life had been spared multiple times and he had just enough faith to believe St. Christopher had offered assistance. For that reason, he never took the necklace off.

A clink from one of the distant tables caught his attention. Someone here. In the dark. A primal buzz nipped him. Maybe he'd check it out. He *was* part of hotel security. In a twisted way.

From the same area, a cell phone rang, one of those old-time *bling-bling-bling* ringers, and Billy shifted toward it.

"This is Kristen."

Kristen Dante's no-nonsense voice carried from the hidden area and Billy cocked his head. Kristen. In the dark. *Alone.*

Or maybe not alone.

He stood, frozen in his spot, his mind spinning and spinning and spinning because he had a major boner for this girl and one thing he didn't need was to walk in on her having a private—uh, *chat*—with her boyfriend. *Can we say awkward?* More than that, it would just plain piss him off.

"That's fine," she said. "Increase the credit limit another five-hundred. If he goes over that, I'll speak with him."

The phone rattled against the glass table tucked about ten feet into a recessed section of the patio. A lone lamppost along the palm tree covered walkway offered light, but Kristen remained barely visible. "Never a break," she said.

Screw it. Billy slid his shirt on and took a step forward. Having already been hammered about his overzealous attention, coming at her half naked probably wouldn't suit. Plus he had a few nasty-ass scars from various knife and gunshot wounds and well, 'nuff said there.

He stopped just beyond the opening of the trees. No sense scaring the bejesus out of her. "Kristen? It's Billy."

A yelp sounded and he snorted. That squeak should so not come out of a woman built like Kristen Dante. No, Kristen needed one of those throaty sounds that grabbed a man by the balls and made him want to hear it between the sheets.

"You scared me," she said.

"Can I come back there?"

"Sure."

He stepped into the cover of the trees and found her sitting at a table, alone—*thank you, St. Christopher*. A soft light tucked into the landscaping threw shadows across her. The diffused light shined over her reddish-blond hair and pale skin, giving her an ethereal look that made Billy suck in a breath. Damn, this woman was stunning. She tucked the cardigan she wore a little closer around her and shot him a warning look.

Yes, he was doing it again. *Staring*. She might as well fudging shoot him now because chances were he'd be falling off the wagon a few times.

But, being the quick thinker he was, he retreated one

step to put more space between them. Her shoulders eased back. Mission accomplished.

From the sky, thousands of stars twinkled at him and he tipped his head back. South Beach in December. What a place. And what a brilliant spot for her to be hiding. During the day, this would be a quiet location to eat or read. At night, the trees kept it hidden for total privacy.

Figuring he had stalled long enough to rid whatever discomfort lingered, he brought his attention back to her. On the table sat a salad—*could that thing be any smaller?*—a small bowl and a half-filled martini glass. "Are you having dinner?"

"Yep. This is where I come at night for quiet. Don't tell anyone you've discovered my sanctuary."

He angled back toward the pool. "You want me to go?"

She glanced behind him, tapped her fingers on the table. "Not at all. Sorry, didn't mean to imply you were interrupting. Were you looking for me?"

"No. I just got back from a run. I heard something back here and wanted to check it out."

"Well, thank you for that. It's nice to know you're looking out for us." She gestured to the chair across from her.

Score one for Team Relentless. Or, Team-Trying-*Not*-To-Be-Relentless.

Billy sat, grabbed the hem of his shirt and wiped the last of the sweat from his face. "This is a great spot."

"I come out here when I stay at the hotel. This meal is my dinner special. Soup, salad and a dirty martini."

How much salad could someone eat? "You stay at the hotel?"

She nodded. "On the weekends. It gets crazy in the clubs, so I prefer to be on-site. I have a suite on the thirty-fifth floor."

"And you don't want to get away from work a while? Go home and chill?"

"I have a hotel to run."

"You're not allowed to have a life?"

She sat back in her chair. Getting comfortable. Good deal.

"I have a life. It operates around the hotel as opposed to the hotel operating around me." She sipped her martini. "I would think you know all about that. The job running your life."

"I like the constant change. It satisfies the adrenalin junkie in me."

"You sound like my sister. She always needs excitement."

Ouch. He wasn't sure how he felt about being compared to Jess Dante, a girl who couldn't figure her way out of an elevator, but he'd engage his impulse control and suck it up. For now. While he considered how to prove his intelligence and capabilities and the fact that he was nothing like Jess. "It is interesting that the two of you came from the same parents."

"We didn't. She's my half-sister."

"Your parents are divorced?"

"Yes. When I was five. Dad remarried and he had Jess with his second and now ex-wife. I was six when she was born."

That explained the differences in the sisters' personalities. And man, oh, man, divorce had to suck for a five-year-old. Billy couldn't grasp it. His folks were going strong after forty years, which, apparently, was a rarity these days. Call him a lucky bastard. "Your dad has bum luck with wives, huh?"

She widened her eyes in that you're-not-kidding look. "That's an understatement. He went from my mother, the world-renowned neurosurgeon, to a B-movie actress. He and the actress were a disaster and got divorced when Jess was a baby. She never experienced her parents being married. I remember bits of things from when we were a family. She doesn't have that."

"Is that why you took her on here? No offense, but she's a train wreck."

Kristen sat forward, propped her chin in her hand and, yeah, all he needed to do was inch. A. *Leetle*. Closer. And his arm would brush against hers. So tempting. But he was trying to play by her rules and if he wasn't allowed to stare at her, touching would be deep-sixed.

"You always say what you're thinking don't you?" she asked.

And wasn't that the burden of his life? "Pretty much. It gets me in trouble a lot. Most people can't take it."

"I'm sure."

"It's not that I'm trying to be an asshole. Well, not usually." He grinned. "I have a fairly common birth defect."

The one I made up so I don't have to talk about the real issue.

That got him a full-blown laugh and the sound squeezed his pitter-pattering heart. *Could be love.*

"A birth defect?"

"It's true. I was born without the brain filter most people have that tells them to shut the hell up."

She rolled her eyes. "Please."

Billy held up his hands. "This is a huge problem for me. Personally, I don't understand it. I mean, don't people want honesty?"

"Sure. Honesty is good. My sister is brutally honest."

Oh hell. Again he was being compared to Jess? Was hell considered a swear word? Dang it, he kept slipping. "Is honesty a good thing with her?"

"Sometimes. The problem is her honesty can be toxic. Yesterday she called me a bitch and that hurt."

Ignoring his earlier hesitation about moving closer, Billy shifted forward. He didn't touch her though. Another quarter inch and he might have, but no, he wouldn't do it. He'd stay clear. "I don't think she was being honest in that case. Nasty, but not honest."

Kristen shrugged. "It may not be my truth or yours, but Jess believes it."

This conversation was about to frustrate the hell out of him. *Focus.* "It's not true."

"She thinks it is. We could sit here all night and argue it. Nothing will change, Billy. My point is certain truths, no matter who they belong to, shouldn't be spoken."

"And my point is, you're not a bitch. You're trying to run a business and she was in your way."

Kristen plucked the toothpick with three olives out of the martini glass and bit one off the end. *Oh, jeez.* Did the woman even know how sexy that was? His entirely male reaction knew. And that male reaction was growing. Rapidly. *Hello, slugger.* Billy hummed a tune to himself and hoped he didn't have to stand up for a while.

Kristen swallowed the olive and dropped the other two back in the glass. "But a woman running a business can't be tough or she's considered a bitch."

Unable to stand the pressure of not pouncing on her, Billy sat back. "I agree, but you're not a bitch."

"You're staring at me again."

"Yes, I am." This fudging holding back thing was tough for a guy who liked to play things straight and just go for what he wanted. "I told you I was born without the filter."

"Nice try."

"But this is what I don't understand. I told you yesterday

that I liked looking at you. I don't think it's a bad thing to find a woman attractive. Now I'm staring, and I was honest about why I do that, and yet, it's a bad thing."

Kristen shook her head.

"What?"

"Certain women don't want to be stared at. I'm one of them."

"And why is that?"

KRISTEN STACKED HER SOUP BOWL ON TOP OF THE SALAD PLATE and pushed it aside. *So not going there with Mr. Adonis.* How would he even understand what it felt like to have lived with a self-absorbed actress who never found her skinny enough, pretty enough or just generally *enough.* For years she'd been dealing with her stepmother's foul derision regarding her weight. True, the woman was no longer married to Dad, but given she was Jess's mother, Kristen still saw her and even the briefest visits gouged those old wounds open.

"To answer your earlier question. My sister is indeed a train wreck and yes, that's why I took her on. I've always taken her on. Our parents traveled. My mother would be off saving someone's life and Dad would be making real estate deals. Jess and I stayed with a nanny or her mother, and her mother didn't have much interest in anything that wasn't stunning. Tough woman to please. Not that it's an excuse for Jess's bad behavior, because I'm sick of people blaming their parents for every rotten thing that goes wrong in their lives."

"Once again, I agree."

She really wanted him to stop agreeing with her so she didn't have to like him. Yet, here they were, enjoying a lovely Florida evening with casual conversation. When was the last time that happened? Maybe if she made the time, it would be different. But she hadn't felt enough of attraction's pull to anyone to make that time. Wanting to do so with the man in front of her terrified her.

"What happened to Jess in Columbia?"

She just blurted it out. Talk about a malfunctioning brain filter. But she'd been wondering for two years now what her sister had gone through in that hellish place, and Jess refused to talk about it. Not with Kristen anyway, and she hated the exclusion. She hated that her sister couldn't confide in her. She hated that her sister *wouldn't* confide in her.

Kristen pushed air through her lips, but Billy remained silent, staring at her with those blue eyes that, even in the dark, sparked and made her want to give in to his advances. But she wouldn't. No. She had no need for hit-and-run drivers.

"I'm sorry. I shouldn't have asked. I'm sure there's some kind of professional ethic that doesn't allow you to elaborate."

She curled back into her chair, feeling like a foolish, weak girl for letting a near stranger have a glimpse of her totally dysfunctional relationship with Jess.

"It's not that," Billy said. "The ethics. Although, I don't usually talk about it outside my team. I guess I'm surprised you know I was there."

"My dad told me this afternoon. He wanted me to feel comfortable with you wandering around the hotel asking questions."

Billy cracked his neck. "How much have you heard?"

"Nothing. All I know is she was captured and Taylor Security pulled her out."

"Monk was there too."

"Really." Kristen imagined Peter, do-rag and all,

traipsing through a jungle and decided it fit. He had that warrior look to him.

Billy shook his head. "She was spitting mad when we busted in there. Just kicking and screaming, and I couldn't shut her up. All I had to do was get in there, grab her and haul ass. But she fought me. I kept telling her who I was, that your dad sent us, but she was *pissed*. It had to have been shock, but we needed her to shut the hell up or she'd alert the whole camp. And she wasn't shutting up. I threw her over my shoulder and she bit me."

The last time I saw you things got a little rough. That's what Jess had said to him in front of the hotel. They'd been talking about her rescue. Only Kristen hadn't known it at the time and, given her sister's proclivity to sexual freak shows, assumed Billy had slept with her. "She bit you."

He smacked his hand across his right shoulder. "Right on the back of the shoulder. Drew blood too. I still have the scar."

That didn't surprise Kristen. Jess could be a hellcat.

"By the time I got her out of there, I was dog-assed tired and had to turn her over to Vic. Don't think I didn't hear about that for six months. We finally gave her a shot and sent her to a happy place. Three miles to the helos and we didn't need her screams drawing fire."

Billy stopped talking and the message that he would offer no further details was received. Obviously, there was more, but he wouldn't give it to her.

Kristen folded her hands on the table in front of her. "Did they rape her?"

Thoughts of her little sister being raped by drug lords had plagued Kristen, and the lack of knowing didn't allow her to offer support. No matter how rocky their relationship, she wanted to save her sister.

Billy's gaze ricocheted back and forth, and Kristen's stomach churned. She shook her head, trying to dispel the vision of beautiful Jess enduring such a violation. Billy covered her hand with his and warmth seeped into her, traveled the length of her body and settled in her core. He had a way about him. For sure.

"I don't know," Billy said. "My guess is they tried. If she fought them as hard as she fought me, they probably gave up on her. There were—uh—other women there."

"Oh..." Kristen reached for her martini. Gone. Of course.

"Want another drink? I'll go inside and grab it for you."

"I'm cutting myself off." She tapped the empty glass and reminded herself she couldn't indulge tonight. "I need to stay sharp. I've got a regular in Inferno—one of the clubs—who maxed out the credit on his house account. He's a big shot record label owner in South Beach who brings in a lot of celebrities. Now he's entertaining a group and I have to decide how far I'm going to let him go. But that's my problem to deal with later."

Billy shrugged. "Works for me."

"Thank you for telling me about Jess. I feel better. She won't talk about it."

"Can't say I blame her."

"See, this is one of those times that you being honest worked. I've never known what happened to her and now I have a better idea."

"Y'all are interesting. I'll say that much."

Kristen smiled. "Y'all? Are you from the south? You don't have the accent."

"I'm originally from Virginia. The accent slips sometimes."

"Is Virginia home then?"

"Nah. It's where my family lives. I'm in Chicago most of

the time, but I don't consider anywhere home. When I finally buy a house it'll be because I want it to be my home." He grinned. "South Beach is looking mighty nice. For a number of reasons."

The man was totally flirting with her. And damned if she didn't sort of like it. Billy Tripp had surprised her. He had an aggressiveness to him. A desire to keep digging until he found what he wanted.

Her phone rang and she scooped it up, her eyes still on Billy. "This is Kristen."

"It's Brent. Reed Davis hit his limit."

Of course he has. It wasn't as if good looking guys flirting with her made her happy all that often and on one of the occasions it had happened, her job got in the way. "I'll be right up." She ended the call and dropped the phone.

"I have to go."

"Too bad. Can I help?"

"No, but thank you."

"I'm gonna get cleaned up anyway and check out the valets. I could meet you up there."

She smiled at him. "I'll be fine. It's just a conversation with a guest. He won't give me a problem."

Unlike the man in front of her.

"Regarding problems, you still haven't told me why staring at you is one."

"Caught that, did you?"

He grinned. "Yep."

"Do you have brothers and sisters?"

"Two of each. I'm in the middle."

"And your sisters? Are they pretty?"

"Ew."

She laughed. "I'm just asking if they're attractive. It doesn't mean *you're* attracted to them."

"Yes. They're attractive. Still has an *ew* to it."

"Do they look alike?"

"Not one bit."

Perfect.

"Do people point out their differences?"

"How the hell should I know? I never asked."

"Call your sisters, Billy. Ask them if people ever point out their differences. If they say yes, ask them how it feels. Then I want you to take a long look at my sister. I assure you, it won't be traumatizing. After that, you should be able to figure out why I don't like to be stared at."

5

Billy stood alongside the hotel's main entrance observing the insanity of a Friday night at Dante. Across from him, the valet stand hopped with three guys hauling tail either parking or picking up cars. The boys definitely had a system going, because they were moving cars in and out at blistering speed.

Keys were shifted back and forth between the three valets with ease. If one had a bunch of keys and the other was going to the lockbox, the keys would be passed off. Every thirty minutes the contents of the box were transferred to the valet office inside the lobby. Billy couldn't see any hiccups where keys might go astray.

Unless one of the valets or someone in the office helped.

Guests and partygoers filed by Billy in packs as he jotted notes. Without his pocket notepad, he'd never remember anything.

A black BMW, one of the big ones, parked in the drive. The valet opened the passenger side door, and Billy caught a flash of blond hair. Out stepped Jess Dante wearing a wicked halter style mini dress.

That crazy fudging bi...biddy. Biddy? This no swearing thing was getting out of hand. And what the hell was Jess doing here? *And* who was the country club jagweed with her? Was jagweed a swear word? More slang probably. A guy had to have some leeway on this deal.

"Hey," Billy called, and Jess swung her gorgeous head in his direction.

She let loose one of her sex kitten smiles and marched her bad self over to him.

"Your sister told you to stay away."

Jess eyeballed his Diesel jeans and slick button-down shirt. "And it's your business how?"

"Mainly because I was there when she told you to beat it."

"Who's this?" the jagweed wanted to know.

"Billy Tripp. He's one of the security guys helping my sister figure out how she lost all those cars. Billy meet Alex. He's my—" she turned to him. "Are you my boyfriend?"

"Who cares," Billy said. "Kristen didn't *lose* those cars. In fact, you might try cutting her some slack, since technically she's your boss, by doing what she asks."

The jagweed stepped up. Got right into Billy's space. Jess had landed herself a tough guy here. Billy met his stare. "Dude, you don't wanna go there. Trust me."

"You could speak to her with more respect. You're the hired help and she owns this place."

Hired. Help. Billy went back to Jess. "Tell Mr. Whipped to back off before I embarrass his ass. And you know I'll do it."

"Mr. Whipped?"

Jess smacked his arm. "Shut up, Alex."

He closed his mouth.

"Well trained," Billy said. "Now, get back in that nice Beemer and take off before the valet snatches it."

"We're going up to Inferno," Jess said. "The place rocks on Friday nights."

"No. Leave now and Kristen won't know you were here. She told you not to come back until Monday. Do yourself a favor and bail before she sees you."

"Jess—"

"Shut up," Billy and Jess both said, and Alex stepped back.

"To hell with you. Your bitch of a sister didn't throw me out. I'm going up." Alex brushed his hands together with a smack. "*Khalas.*"

It's finished? Now the preppy dumbass was speaking *Arabic?* What the hell's that about? This guy needed a serious ass kicking, but he was already through the lobby doors and Billy decided it wouldn't be worth getting into trouble with Kristen over. "Nice effing boyfriend, Jess. A real gentleman. Not only does he disrespect your sister, he leaves you standing here. Bravo."

She huffed. "Now someone has to take me somewhere else." She turned her gaze on him.

Billy stuck his hand in his pocket and peeled off a twenty. "Cab fare. Beat it."

BILLY KNOCKED ON THE DOOR TO KRISTEN'S SUITE WONDERING if it was too late to be paying a call. A second later, the door opened. She stood there wearing black yoga pants and a light pink, belted sweater tied loosely at her waist.

He wiggled his fingers at his sides. It would be so easy to just grab the belt and give it a yank.

Focus.

"Is everything okay?" Kristen asked.

"Uh, yeah. Fine. You didn't answer your phone."

"I was on the balcony. What's up?"

"I called my sister."

"I'm sorry?"

"You told me to call my sister."

Her head lopped forward. "And you did it?"

Of course he'd done it. She'd given him an assignment. What did she expect? "You told me to call, so I called."

She held the door open. "Come in. Let's not talk about this in the hall."

Billy stepped into the suite and was greeted by floor to ceiling windows that, in daylight, would offer an ocean view. On his left was a seating area with a red sofa and two cream chairs. The glass coffee table held a small stack of books, one open and face down on top. "Nice room."

"Thank you. Can I get you something?" She pointed to the mini fridge in the corner.

"Nah. I just wanted to tell you my sister said everyone thinks my other sister is prettier."

"I see."

"And that made me a little sick. I love both my sisters. The one I called though? My older sister? She's the effing bomb. So, yeah, maybe my younger sister is prettier on the surface. But my older sister's the one you call when you've got a problem. You remind me of her actually. She's strong and capable and doesn't whine about bullship things. That's what makes her who she is. And you're like that. Plus, you're sexy as hell. Total package. I wanted to tell you that."

Kristen's sea-green eyes darkened. Seriously, he needed to kiss her. Just—*whammo*—lay one on her, but she made no move toward him. Not a bleeping inch.

"Sit," she said.

From somewhere down deep, he managed to find the strength to say, "No. I'm gonna go. I just wanted you to know."

Kristen grabbed his arm, shoved him against the wall and kissed him. Talk about *whammo*.

Holy fudging smokes.

The woman could kiss. And that body? All soft and warm against him. Keeping his hands to himself was impossible, and he didn't bother to fight. He slipped his arms around her and pulled her close to make sure there would be no mistaking his level of arousal. Homeland Security would call this an elevated level.

Extremely elevated.

And unless he backed away from this scorcher of a kiss that made the little voice in his head—the one that he constantly fought to control—scream, *go, go, go,* his elevated level might hit new heights.

Kristen backed away, just an easy slide, and immediately he saw her gaze dart around. He knew exactly what this was. She'd attacked him—*yes, sweet thing, you did*—and the idea of that must have finally absorbed into her most unspontaneous brain.

He grinned at her, kept one arm around her waist and held her still. "So, not bad for a first kiss, right? It didn't have any of that awkward should I do it this way, or maybe that way, or has it been too long, should I stop now thing going on."

And the look of relief, that slack-jawed ease that Billy knew he was brilliant at creating, appeared on her lovely face.

"You are a master at this aren't you?"

Pretty much, yeah. That didn't make him too happy, though. True, seducing women had never been a problem.

For years he'd bragged about it, but hearing Kristen say it sounded a whole lot like a bad thing.

"So, my sister said something else."

Kristen made a move to back away but he continued to hold her there. She glanced down at his arm. "Are you going to let me go?"

"No. Thanks for asking though."

She laughed.

"My sister told me I needed to back off, and I just want to point out that I was not the aggressor in the whole kissing thing. That one's on you, sweet thing, so I get a pass. I'll admit I was staring at you right before *you* kissed *me,* so I probably get a demerit for that."

"What are you doing?"

"My *sister* said when she was single she would never have trusted a guy like me. That's a little hurtful from one's sister, but I'm a big boy."

"She said that?"

"Yeah. We're a family of honest people who occasionally have diarrhea of the mouth."

"Good to know."

"She said if I liked you, I couldn't do my usual routine. That I had to prove to you it's not about getting laid." He made a *pffting* noise. "I mean who doesn't like to get laid? I totally like to get laid. No problem being honest about that. But this is different—"

Kristen grabbed his cheeks. "Relax. You have some kind of ADD brain surge going here."

A flaming ball of humiliation burned in his gut and he smacked his lips together. *Laugh it off.*

He rolled his eyes, made a show of snorting, but that brief silence had burned him. Too late.

"Oh." Kristen's gaze zoomed over his face. "You have it. ADD?"

For once in his life, he stayed silent.

She squeezed his cheeks again. "That's it, isn't it? The impulse control, the non-filtering. You can't help it."

Gettin' a little heavy here. He grasped her hands, guided them from his face. "I'm borderline. I was tested when I was a kid. I deal with it."

And lately, with his life coming apart around him, he was tired of *dealing* with it.

"I'm sorry I made a joke about it," Kristen said. "I didn't realize."

"*Anyway,* I want you to know, I'm gonna take my sister's advice and back off. Not completely. But I'll change my approach with you because it's not about getting laid. I can get laid anytime by anyone. It's not that hard." That sounded bad, but whatever. Besides, this backing off thing would be a good exercise in the Billy-controlling-himself arena. He'd consider it another behavioral strategy. "I like you Kristen. I like talking to you. I won't stare at you—much—but I want you to know I'm interested. Very interested. I'm only dialing it down because I think it's what you want. It's not a rejection. I'm hoping it's the reverse."

Kristen smiled at him and the sweetness nearly destroyed him. Left him wanting to press soft kisses over her cheeks.

"Thank you," she said. "Interested is good. Let's see where it goes. I'm busy around here. I don't have a lot of time and I'm not into hit-and-run-drivers. Are you a hit-and-run-driver, Billy Tripp?"

He winced. "If I'm being honest, yes, I've been known to do that in the past. I'm better now. I promise you I'll never lie. That part of me sucks sometimes. Just saying."

Except that I'm not going tell you Jess showed up and I got rid of her. Kristen didn't need to know that. Could be playing God with the whole honesty thing, but he'd take a chance on a trip to confession. Why remind her that Jess got off on disrespecting her?

Kristen nodded. "I'm okay with that. I have to ask you something. I think I know the answer, but I have to ask."

"Go for it."

"Did you have sex with my sister?"

Shock and maybe even a little hurt drilled him. But he refused to give a voice to that killer combo of emotions. He stared right into Kristen's eyes. "No. Not even close. Not even close in my *thoughts.* Jess makes me nuts. Before coming to South Beach, I only met her that one time and it never occurred to her to say thank you for hauling her out of that prison. That told me all I needed to know about your sister. So, no, I have never been with her. Nor will I ever."

He had standards.

Kristen leaned into him, rested her head on his shoulder. This honesty thing might work out just fine. He rubbed his hand along her back to keep her there.

"I had a feeling you didn't. But there was a familiarity there and I needed to know it was based on what happened in Colombia. Now I know. I'm sorry if I offended you."

"Kris, it takes a lot more than that to offend me. If it was bugging you, I'm glad you asked."

"Me too."

And with that he kissed her. Just one last time before the official backing off started. Besides, Kristen didn't seem to mind the kissing.

He held his hands up and stepped back. "I'm backing off."

She bit her top lip, but gave up and laughed at him. "That's your version of backing off?"

"For tonight anyway. Tomorrow can be the official start. I figured you wouldn't mind."

"I don't mind."

"Well, clearly. What with that whole tongue in my mouth thing."

Maybe that was too much. She walked to the windows facing the ocean. A million swear words zipped through his mind, but for the life of him he couldn't come up with one replacement. To hell with it. *Fuck a damned duck.*

"Kristen, I'm sorry. I pushed it. I'm working on that. I am. It's part of why I'm down here. Vic wants me to control my mouth. Among other things."

Kristen stared out the windows into the blackness of the Atlantic trying to squash the thought that sexy Billy Tripp and that irreverent mouth were the male version of Jess. Only, he couldn't help it. Most of the time. On top of Jess's antics, did she really need more of it from a guy she barely knew? She turned back to him. "What do you mean?"

"I screwed up getting my passport renewed. I forgot. I usually put everything in my calendar so I don't get distracted, but I lost track of this one thing. Instead of letting me rush the passport through and sending me overseas, Vic sent me down here."

That was why he was guarding jewelry. "I was your punishment?"

"Punishment might be overkill. But, yes, Vic knows I like to play with guns and blow shit up and none of that would be happening guarding a necklace."

Oddly enough, Kristen wasn't offended by thinking of

her event as someone's punishment. From a management standpoint, she understood it.

"And then," Billy said, "this juicy car theft thing came up and got me jazzed. I called Vic, by the way, told him you wanted us to take a look at your security. He's good with that. Whatever you need."

"That's the problem—I don't know what I need. Hopefully you can tell me." The Billy-being-bad smile spread across his face and Kristen rolled her eyes. "Don't say it."

"I won't. I'm restraining myself. Barely. Regarding the security, here's my plan. Tomorrow morning I'll check out your parking lot cameras and take a look at the security footage from the theft."

"Fine. I'll clear it with the security team. What else?"

"That's it for now."

"Billy, if you figure out what happened to those cars, I'll love you forever."

"Yes, but will you love me enough to get rid of the SWAT guy who stops to see you once a week?"

She stilled. Not one inch of movement. After a solid thirty seconds of staring at him, and at a complete loss as to whether she should be flattered that he cared, or offended that he'd asked around about her social life, she managed an answer. "Are you nosing around in my personal life?"

"Your entire personal life? No. I did pursue info on your dating status." He grinned and before she could start yelling, forged ahead. "Give this schmo a break. According to my source, he's been humping it across that causeway for five weeks. Either go out with him or cut bait."

"I cannot believe you. And, for the record, it's not SWAT down here. It's SRT—Special Response Team."

"Whatever."

Also for the record, I cannot allow myself to get naked with a man who has a single digit body fat percentage. "He's a nice guy. I don't want to hurt his feelings."

"Ach!" Billy waved his arms. "First of all, no guy I know —and I'm guessing your SRT guy, purely based on what he does for a living will fall into this category—wants to be thought of as nice by a woman he'd like to get busy with. We want you to think of us as your go-to guy. You need something, we want to be the one to give it to you. Whatever it is. So, Mr. Nice would probably rather you drop-kick him than be thought of that way. Personally, I'd like you to cut bait and make room for me."

Crazy man.

Kristen eyed him, let her gaze roam over his long, broad form and wondered just how low his body fat percentage was.

He smacked his hands together. "But hey, I'm backing off. So, you give it some thought and we'll see what's what." He headed for the door. "Sound good?"

"Sounds good."

A little too good.

6

By mid-morning Billy had already been in the security office staring at a computer monitor for two hours. Something was definitely off. He rewound the bit of footage from before the Mercedes got boosted. As sure as he was a pain in the ass, he knew he was missing something.

He froze the screen just as the thief, dressed in a dark jacket, hood up, his head and face hidden from view, reached the car. Billy sat back, folded his arms and glanced at the bank of monitors lining the wall.

From behind him, the hotel security director swiveled from his desk. "Problem?"

"I don't know. I need to run down to the location where the Mercedes was jacked."

His cell phone rang and John Mayer's "Your Body is a Wonderland"—Kristen's newly assigned ringtone—pierced the silence of the room. Oh, how he loved personalized ringtones, but with Kristen's employee sitting here listening... well, just a *tad* awkward. He snatched the phone from the pocket of his shorts.

"Good morning," he answered.

"Hi. What are you doing?"

Why the hell did everyone always ask what he was doing? As if they suspected he was doing something he *shouldn't* be doing.

"I'm reviewing your security footage."

"Find anything?"

"Still working on it. What's up?"

"I have young Manny in my office. He'd like to offer you his services until lunch time." She lowered her voice. "Is there something he might be able to help with?"

Translation: She needed the kid out of her hair. Pronto. Billy to the rescue. And, yes he would remind her of this at a later time. A time when he was attempting to rid her of her clothing.

"You bet. I'm about to head down to the parking lot. He can be my would-be thief."

"I'm sorry?"

"Don't worry about it. I'll take care of him. What time do you want him back?"

"I promised I'd buy him lunch, so around noon would be great."

"Call me when you're ready and I'll send him your way."

"I will. Thank you, Billy. I appreciate it."

"No problem."

He slid his phone in his pocket, braced his hands on the desk and focused on the monitor in front of him.

Something was definitely off.

"Dennis, send this footage to my phone. I'm going to the lot. You're gonna see a kid wandering around there with me."

"Manny?"

It seemed young Manny knew everyone. "Yeah. He'll pretend he's stealing a car. Don't call the cops on him."

Dennis laughed as Billy headed out the door.

He found Manny waiting for him next to a huge planter in the lobby. Billy offered him a fist bump. "What's up, pal?"

"Dude," the kid said by way of greeting.

"Follow me. We're gonna do some reconnaissance. You up for it?"

Manny bobbed his head.

"Let's hit it then."

Within minutes, Billy stood at the exact location where the Mercedes had been lifted. The hotel's fleet of cars—a Bentley, three Town Cars, two Mercedes and a couple of Cadillac stretch limos—were lined up across the aisle. Absent from that uber-expensive showcase were the missing Bentley and Mercedes.

Yes, my darlings, I will find you. They didn't call him Mr. Relentless for nothing.

Phone in hand, he replayed the footage Dennis had sent him, then scanned the area. Camera one. Right there. He swerved his head back to the spot where the Mercedes had been parked, and, using the footage on his phone, traced the path the thief had taken to reach the car.

A quick survey of the immediate area produced another camera. That one should have picked up where the thief had been hiding.

Billy dialed Dennis. "Send me the footage for the camera on the northeast edge of the lot."

"What are we doing?" Manny called from his spot near the theft site.

Billy walked to him. "I want you to stand here for a second. We're trying to figure out where the thief was hiding."

"Cool."

Billy's phone beeped the arrival of an email.

Using the timestamp on the video, he searched for the time of the theft. This camera wouldn't show the car actually being stolen, but it would indicate where the guy had been hiding. *Huh.* No thief.

Billy spun around, looked at camera one for a long moment, shifted to camera two and dropped his gaze to three parking spots on the very edge of the lot. *Maybe.* He waved to Manny to follow him.

"Manny, I want you to start here and walk back to where you were. I think this is where the guy was hiding. I have to compare the footage of you to the thief's approach."

"I'm on it."

Billy smiled. No wonder Kristen liked this kid.

A gray Jaguar driven by an old guy with a smoker of a hot blonde sitting in the passenger's seat entered the lot. Ah, South Beach. He needed to grow old here. But he didn't picture a hot blonde in the car with him. He pictured Kristen. That kind of long-term thinking was something new. Oddly, he didn't fight it.

Billy waved the Jag through and gave Manny a thumbs up.

Manny walked toward the theft site. "I saw one of those cars at a parking building once. They're cool."

"Stop there for a second." Billy watched as camera two swiveled, but camera one stayed stationary. *Jackpot.* "Okay. Go. Yeah, they're sharp cars. Lots of sharp cars around here."

Billy stood in front of a Navigator and waved his arms. One of these cameras had to be grabbing his image. Had to be.

When Manny reached the car, Billy waved him back. "Good deal, kid. Let's go see what we've got."

On their way to the hotel entrance, they passed a large cement storage shed tucked close to the building. One of the steel double doors sat ajar. Billy stared at it a moment. Odd. Those doors should not be unlocked. A light flickering snapped along his forearms.

And him without a weapon.

"Wait here," he told Manny.

"Why?"

"Just wait here. Don't move from this spot. Got it?"

Manny shrugged.

Stepping up to the shed, Billy pressed his back against the closed door and listened for movement. The swishing of palm trees in the breeze didn't constitute a red alert. He nudged the partially open door with his foot. No sounds from inside.

He snuck a look around the door. A shaft of sunlight illuminated the dark space, revealing a couple of wheelbarrows, buckets, hoses and a smattering of gardening supplies. Nothing seemed amiss. One of the maintenance guys must have forgotten to lock the damned door. The thick steel padlock that usually hung on the handle was gone. He stepped inside the shed to hunt for the missing lock.

On the inside wall was a light switch. He flipped it on and glanced around. No lock. Behind him, the door squeaked and, thinking he'd find the at-fault employee, Billy turned.

A big guy, not fat, but wide—*strong*—pushed through the doorway with two men behind him. The space confined Billy. Made him want to bust out.

At once, multiple questions—Who are they? What do they want? How painful will it be?—slammed into Billy's mind. Then there was Manny. The initial flood of brain activity—his fight or flight response—led him to escape options, but the odds of taking out all three of these guys without a weapon? Not good.

The big guy held his meaty fingers up. "Relax."

Billy's gaze bounced between the big guy and his two cohorts. "Uh, no. Thanks."

The second guy drew a nine-millimeter from a waist holster. "Don't be stupid."

"We're gonna talk for a few minutes," the big guy said, a faint, lilting accent peppering his speech. *Arabic?* "Don't be a hothead or a hero and you don't get hurt. Be stupid and it won't go so easy. Your choice."

The skin on Billy's arms vibrated and he counted three breaths as his mind twirled. He could crack the guy in front with an elbow. Who knew if he had a gun handy though? Evading was fruitless with the human wall blocking the door.

And Manny stood in the parking lot.

These jagweeds had him cold.

If anything, Billy could bullshit the best of 'em. Besides, if these dipsticks wanted him dead, he'd already be marching his way to the pearly gates.

He shrugged, keeping his hands loose at his sides. "Let's talk."

With the doors closed and a combined nine hundred pounds of humanity in residence, heat engulfed the shed and sweat dripped down the center of his back.

"Mr. Billy?" Manny called from outside the door.

He slid his gaze left and right, again measuring the two guys behind the number one beefhead. No chance. He took a long breath and prepped himself for whatever would come next. They'd have to cut off his arms and make him bleed out if they expected to use Manny as bait.

"Manny, go back to the hotel and wait for me in the lobby."

One of the beefheads made a move toward the door.

"I wouldn't," Billy said. "Not unless you want me to go fucking crazy on your ass."

Beefhead number one folded his massive arms. "Leave the kid alone. For now."

"Manny?" Billy shouted.

"Yes?"

Jesus. What the hell was the kid waiting for? He'd have to put some mean into it. "Go back to the hotel. Now! I'll be there in ten minutes."

"Snap, you don't have to yell."

Beefhead number one rolled his eyes, waited a minute for Manny to leave and focused on Billy. "This thing with the cars? You're done." He swiped his hands together. *"Khalas."*

Khalas? Interesting.

Beefhead pointed at him. "You have no idea what you're into. Back off and we let you stay breathing. In fact, my boss is impressed with your skills. He'd like to compensate you. Maybe bring you on board."

Damn, if this didn't get Billy all kinds of jacked up. These guys had the granite balls to grab him off the street, let him see their faces and offer him cash to let them steal cars. No fear that he would go to the cops. None. Whatever this operation was, it must be fucking huge. Based on the barely there Arabic accent, Billy's wild guess entailed an international theft ring.

Juicy.

He took a step forward. "Your boss is bribing me?"

Beefhead grunted.

"My boss is offering you either a one-time payout or the possibility of a job. In exchange, you get out of the way when it comes to cars and the Dante hotel."

Billy stood silent, his mind ticking off the possibilities

and reminding him that if they wanted him dead, he'd be there already. They thought he was a wild card. They had checked him out.

From where he stood, wedged into the back of a stagnant smelling concrete shed with the doors blocked, his only chance at getting out would be to let them think he might be interested. "What kind of cash are we talking about?"

The lead guy smiled, a slick, oily *gotcha* kind of smile. "It starts at two-hundred and fifty thousand. Beyond that, we see what opportunities there are and go from there."

On his right, beefhead number two shifted. Billy glanced at him and went back to the talker. "Who's your boss?"

"Not a chance. If you're interested, you work through me. No negotiation."

"I don't know."

The guy nodded. "You think about it. You got until the end of the day today."

Billster, you might just get out of this. "End of day works. How do I contact you?"

"I'll find you." He gave Billy a one-handed shove. "Do what you're told and Kristen Dante's only problem is a few missing cars. Disappoint me and we'll talk again."

Billy remained still, forcing himself not to react, but —*holy crap*—he wanted to pop this douche bag. If Kristen so much as tripped in her office, he'd hunt this crew down and make sure the bodies wouldn't be found.

But he kept quiet while the big guy waved his buddies out of the shed. Manny better have gone up to the hotel.

He followed them into the fresh air. No sign of the kid. Billy shook his head. Relief mixed with a good dose of bewilderment. He breathed in, filling his lungs and clearing his mind. The three men walked toward the street to a black Escalade.

Billy waited until guy number three got into the car and shut the door. The front passenger window lowered, but Billy stayed back.

"I'll find you later," the big guy called.

"Don't bother. Tell your boss to shove it."

HIS BODY STILL BUZZING, BILLY GRABBED MANNY FROM THE lobby and they returned to the security office to find Dennis scanning the parking lot images. Based on the camera locations, all the video would show is the beefheads walking along the path toward the shed. It wouldn't show them entering. Apparently Manny hadn't seen them walk in, because Mr. Chatterbox seemed to believe Billy had been cleaning up a fertilizer spill.

Whatever. As long as the kid was safe.

Billy stood behind Dennis. "Can you get me the footage of my able assistant on these monitors? I need to see both cameras side by side."

Manny grabbed the seat beside Dennis as he poked the keyboard. Images from camera one popped up on the wall-mounted monitor. Camera two footage appeared next to it. "Are you able to synchronize the times?"

"Sure."

More pecking at the keyboard and the footage rolled from camera one showing Manny's approach to the theft site. Camera two showed the Jag driving past. Nothing from the side edge of the lot. No sign of Billy waving his arms.

"Bring up the night of the theft from both cameras and synchronize them."

Images appeared on the next two monitors. "Cue Manny's footage and roll all four."

A minute later, Billy watched as Manny and the thief traveled an identical route in the Dante parking lot.

"Dammit."

"What?" But Dennis's radio chirped that he was needed at the pool. "I have to go."

After showing Billy and Manny how to run the footage on the wall monitors, Dennis hauled ass.

"Your Body is a Wonderland" blasted from Billy's phone. *Crap.* He'd forgotten to turn it to vibrate. "M.H., good timing. Can you come to the security office?"

Where I won't tell you I was bribed by three men. She didn't need to know that right now. Maybe it was a lie by omission, but he couldn't come up with a single good reason to tell her.

Other than it was her hotel.

"M.H.?" she said. "It's Kristen."

"Uh, right." *Almost blew that one.* "Can you come down here? Manny and I want to show you something." Manny grinned up at him. Great kid, this one.

"Sure. Be there in a sec."

Madame Hotness strolled through the office door wearing a midthigh powder blue skirt—*nice*—but she trashed it with one of those buttoned up baggy cardigans. Her hair had been tied into a low ponytail draped over one shoulder, and his fingers twitched with the urge to touch. Even more slaying was the glossy peach lipstick that set her fair skin glowing.

Holy shiznet.

"Hi, Miss Kristen!" Manny practically bowed to his queen.

"Hi, bud. Ready for lunch?"

Manny leaped from his chair and Billy held up a hand. "Sit tight, Boy Wonder." He pointed at the monitors. "Check this out. These two on the left are Manny from this morning. The two on the right are the night of the theft. Manny, roll video from the night of the theft."

Manny did his thing and Kristen grinned at his acumen with the footage. She stepped closer to the monitors, absently flicked her ponytail over her shoulder and there it was, that long, thick hair just in front of Billy. So close. But he'd been told hands off.

Screw that. He'd had a rough morning and deserved to go off leash.

He lightly skimmed her hair, his touch so soft she didn't even notice.

M.H. spun back to him and he dropped his hand. "Okay, I saw it."

Unsure exactly what she meant—*had she busted him?*—Billy waited.

She held her hands to the monitors. "The footage?"

"Right." *Whew.* "Now, watch the footage of my assistant here. Hit it, Manny."

When the segment ended, Kristen nodded. "All right, what does it all mean?"

"See how we replicated the thief's approach to the car?"

"Yes."

"Well, what you're not seeing is me standing in front of a honking big Navigator waving my arms like a dumb as—ashtray." He had to work on a replacement word for ass.

Kristen laughed. "So, no Billy in front of the Navigator. What does that mean?"

"The cameras didn't catch me. I was trying to narrow where the thief was hiding in case we could get a close-up. I couldn't do that."

"Okay..." Her voice carried that doubtful where-are-you-going-with-this tone Billy had heard so often.

"Boy Wonder, roll the night of the theft again. Kris, watch the thief when he gets to the car."

She watched, but shook her head. "All I see is him getting into the car."

"Exactly."

KRISTEN SIGHED. SHE HAD A TON OF WORK TO DO, STILL needed to treat Manny to lunch and Billy wanted to play crime stoppers. "What's your point?"

He folded his arms. "The way I see it, Ms. Dante, you've got two problems."

She glanced at Manny and squeezed Billy's forearm. The feel of his skin against her hand tingled right up her arm.

"Manny, would you please run to my office for a couple of water bottles? They're in the fridge."

He bobbed his head and stood. "Can I get a Coke?"

"You know the answer to that."

He shrugged. "I tried."

"Yes, you did, but your mom doesn't want you to have the caffeine."

"Be right back."

The door closed and she turned back to Billy. "Sometimes I forget his mother is an employee. Little kids have big mouths."

"Gotcha. Good call."

"Tell me about my problems." *Other than I find you very attractive.*

"First, you have a blind spot."

A not-so-nice tingle much different than the one she'd just felt made her hands itch. "You're saying the thief could be one of my employees who knew about the blind spot?"

"No. I'm saying the thief may have had knowledge of the blind spot. How he got that knowledge I don't know. Yet. Of your employees, who knows about it?"

Wasn't that the million-dollar question? "*I* didn't know. How would I be able to tell you who does? And I'm embarrassed by that."

"Don't be. It's an oversight, but either the thief got seriously lucky and picked a good hiding place or someone in this hotel knows about that blind spot."

Kristen absorbed his comments, analyzed the individual parts. Then she'd draw a conclusion based on the whole.

"What's the other thing?"

"The thief walked right up to the car and got in. "Which means he must have had a key."

"How would he have gotten one?"

"I don't know. Had the guest valet parked since he checked in the other night?"

"You think one of my valets copied his key?"

"Kris, I don't know. I'm tossing options. We work through the options and see where we wind up."

She pressed her fingers to her forehead and pinched the skin there. "Every car is logged into the system. If he valet parked, it'll be on his bill." She spun to the computer on the desk behind her and retrieved the guest's folio. Yes, she'd remembered his name after he threatened to sue her. "There's nothing on his folio. He checked in on Wednesday and must have parked it himself."

"Well, that settles that."

"What are our next steps? What do I need?"

"We're going to get rid of that blind spot and not tell

anyone. Only you and I will know. We'll have the cameras adjusted and keep an eye on it."

"You think the thief will come back?"

"They think you're vulnerable, so it's a possibility. Meantime, I'm going to start interviewing your employees and see if I can figure out who knows about the blind spot. You have a problem with that?"

She shook her head. "No. I've alerted the managers you'll be wandering around."

"Good."

"Will you take care of the camera issue for me?"

"Yeah. I'll call Vic. He'll know someone we can trust in this area."

The office door opened and Manny squeezed through carrying two water bottles in each hand and one tucked under his armpit.

Billy pointed to the under arm one. "I'm not drinking that."

Such an infant. Still, he entertained her and nothing about that gave her comfort. Not when he reminded her so much of Jess and her flighty ways. This man, with his quirky humor and relentless curiosity, would pulverize her.

Manny—all big teeth and brown eyes—gagged. "My pits are good and smelly, dude."

"You got nothin', kid. I can show you smelly pits."

Enough. Kristen held up her hands. "Boys, let's not go there, shall we? Besides, I'm ready for lunch." She turned to Billy. "Lunch plans?"

"Uh, yeah. Izzy texted me a while ago." He batted his eyes. "She's afraid I'm lonely. Raincheck?"

"Of course."

"How about we meet tomorrow?" He grabbed his phone from his pocket and tapped the screen. "You name the time.

I can work on what we discussed here and go over everything with you then."

She shouldn't do this. If she had any sense, she would keep it to meeting in her office, where her business mind would stay firmly intact and not be distracted by the fact that Billy Tripp was criminally handsome and made her laugh. "Sure. Check with me in the morning and we'll figure out a time."

THAT EVENING, BILLY DIALED KRISTEN'S CELL. VOICE MAIL. Did the woman ever answer?

Screw it. He went to her office, letting himself into the executive suite with the key card she'd given him, but didn't find her. He checked the time on his phone. Eight-thirty.

Ten to one she's hiding again.

If so, telling her the camera situation was fixed could wait until tomorrow because, workhorse that she was, she deserved her solitude. But, as hard as he was trying to stick to this backing-off thing, he had plans for her. Big plans. Naked, sweaty plans.

Mindsnap.

He took a breath, shook his head to settle his rioting thoughts and headed out to search for Kristen. He stopped at the bar on the first floor and ordered a dirty martini and a beer before heading out to the pool deck. If she wasn't there, he'd have just wasted fourteen bucks on a drink and he'd rather put a bullet through his eye than force down a martini.

Once on the pool deck, he stopped, inhaled the ocean air and closed his eyes. Yeah, South Beach in December. Something about this place settled him. Gave him solitude from his constantly streaming thoughts. Made him feel like he could control his mouth enough to save him from his boss's wrath. Maybe what he needed were casual trips to South Beach between assignments. Time to shut down, stop thinking so damned much and relax. And let's not forget possibly hanging out with one Kristen Dante. He filed it in the to-be-considered drawer in his brain.

Rustling palm trees brought him back to his mission of finding M.H. The clearing for her hiding spot was a few feet in front of him. He took a step, but halted, listening for any signs of life. Aside from kids splashing in the pool, he caught the chink of a fork against a plate from the general direction of Kristen's haven.

He shouldn't sneak up on her. What to do? Call her?

And say what? *"I'm ten feet away with cocktails and want to utilize your hiding space for obscene things done in a variety of positions that will leave us both smiling and extremely satisfied."* Maybe calling her wasn't a class-A plan.

"Psst! Kristen?"

What kind of jackhole stood whispering into a clump of trees? This had to be a man card violation. Vic would have the mother of all cows. Billy couldn't help it if he sucked at this backing off thing. The little voice in his head said, *"Go, go, go."*

Screw it. Martini and beer in hand, he moved closer. "Kristen?"

"Billy?"

"Yeah. Can I come back there?"

"What, are you an idiot? Of course you can."

Oh, honey, how I think I love you.

He stepped into the clearing and there she sat, fork in one hand, an iPad in front of her, tapping the screen with her free hand. Talk about a multitasker.

"Quartz. Take that!" She dropped the fork into her salad

bowl, shoved the iPad away and held her arms up. "I love when I beat the computer."

"Congratulations."

"Thank you. It's the small stuff, you know." She eyeballed the martini glass. "What have you got there?"

"I brought you a fresh drink." He spotted the empty on the table. "Perfect timing."

"Thank you. Tonight I'll indulge in a second. Why not? Have a seat."

"Sorry to interrupt. I called, but you didn't answer."

She dug into the pocket of yet another of her tent sweaters. He needed to have a sweater burning rally. Just round up all those suckers and torch 'em.

"Look at that. It went straight to voice mail."

"Doesn't matter. There's no emergency. Figured you'd want to know your cameras are fixed."

"Already?"

After the three goons in the shed? Fast wasn't fast enough. Holding his hands wide, he made a *pffting* noise. "Babe, please. This is me we're talking about. Besides, my boss wants to keep the Dante clan happy. Vic called one of his contacts at a local company and the guy came out a couple hours ago."

"I love Vic."

Knowing he shouldn't do it, Billy leaned in and ran a finger over the back of her hand. "Do I get any credit? At all?"

Mirroring him, Kristen slowly came toward him, her gaze hot on his. "Sure—" she slapped at his hand and smiled, "—but you're a total failure at backing off."

He laughed, sat back and settled himself more comfortably into his chair. Yep, he had a serious case of smitten. "That's actually not true. If I weren't backing off, I'd have parlayed getting those cameras fixed into something a whole lot more personal."

"Who says I would have given in?"

He shrugged. "I never assume, but it works more times than not."

"And is that enviable? Keeping track of how many times women fall victim to your advances?"

Ouch. "Okay, well, first, I don't keep track. I don't need to analyze my success ratio to know I'm successful more times than not. Second, I've outgrown it. I have no problem admitting I've been a male whore in the past. That's over now."

"Why should I believe you?"

He shrugged. "Some chick went fatal attraction on me, parking herself on my doorstep every day until I begged Vic to send me overseas."

"She wouldn't leave you alone?"

"Not for a second. I never gave her my phone number. Even went to her place rather than taking her to mine."

"How did she find you?"

"I told her where I worked and she followed me from the office. The first time she showed up at my door, I couldn't remember her name. I've never been a morality nut and I like to think I'm loose in terms of how people live their lives, but I went to bed with her and forgot her name. I'd say that falls smack into the fairly disgusting category."

Kristen shrugged. "I'd say disgusting is harsh. This is South Beach. Party central. Money and indiscriminate sex are as common as ocean waves. I personally don't agree with it, but my sister partakes and considers it her right to do so. If two people consent and they're safe about it, I don't think anyone has the right to tell them they can't do it."

A freethinker. *Yeah, I might definitely be in love.* "I bet you'd pass the 'it's me' test."

"I can't wait to hear this one."

"One of my buddies told me about this and—as butt-crack stupid as it is—I have to agree with it. If someone you've taken out once or twice leaves a voice mail and says 'Hi, it's me,' it's an indicator."

"Oh, dear God. An indicator of what?"

"It implies a familiarity, don't you think? A settling in before you even know each other. I hate that. Why does it need to be rushed? If I'm dating someone, I want it to unfold slowly so I can discover things along the way. That's more fun."

"You like the chase?"

"No. No patience for it. But if I want someone, I'll take the time necessary to discover her needs. For instance, I want you and I will sit here all night trying to figure out what makes you who you are. And, my guess is you'd never call me and say 'Hi, it's me.' You'd say, 'Hi, it's Kristen.' And I like that about you. You don't need to push yourself onto people."

Kristen picked up her martini, held it in front of her in a mock toast and sucked down half. For the tenth time since he sat down, Billy laughed. He liked that about her too. Her ability to make him laugh. To not be condescending when he admitted his ADD. To make him never want to leave this table.

Yeah, South Beach in December.

"So, now that I've scared the hell out of you..."

With the martini safely back on the table, she waved him off. "You don't scare me Billy Tripp. Wait, that's a lie. Part of you terrifies me. You distract me. I'm extremely self-disciplined. Right now, my rule of taking an hour to eat in privacy is over. I should be walking the hotel, checking the restaurants and the clubs, schmoozing our VIPs. Yet, I'm sitting here with you having a second martini. And I'm enjoying it."

"That's a problem?"

"I don't have the luxury of time spent distracted."

Billy's phone buzzed. Incoming text. He ignored it. Instead he shot her one of his no-fail smiles. "I don't require a lot of time. I can be thorough in an amazingly short time span."

The phone screamed "Maneater." *Shit—er—ship.* He yanked it from his pocket to shut the thing up. He really needed to change that. These ringtones were causing all kinds of problems. "Hey, Iz."

"What are you doing?"

The age-old question. "I'm talking to Kristen. What's up?"

"Peter is tired. I'd like to hit one of the clubs. You interested?"

Eh, wouldn't be the worst thing that could happen. "I guess. For an hour."

"Good. Meet me in front of Paradiso at ten."

"Got it." He ended the call and immediately set a reminder for 9:55 p.m. "Izzy wants to hit Paradiso tonight. I love the names of the clubs, by the way. The whole Dante's Inferno reference."

Kristen nodded and sat forward. "Here's a little Dante family trivia for you. It's a secret though."

"Ooohhhh, do tell."

"Our childhood nanny used to call Jess Inferno. I was Paradiso. When we designed the hotel I thought it would be fun to have two towers. That's why the decorating is so different. Inferno tower has more drama and dark colors. That's Jess with her fire. Paradiso has a lighter, more subdued palette. That's me."

"Inferno is a nice place to visit, but I wouldn't want to live there."

Billy's phone buzzed again. What now? He was busy here. He grabbed it. A text from Monk. "This should be good."

The message read *Make sure nobody puts hands on my girl.*

"Shut the front door, man, you gotta get a life."

"Everything okay?" Kristen asked.

"Yeah. Monk doesn't want anyone making time with Izzy. The guy is whacked. I'm good, but I'm not that good. I mean, has he met his girlfriend? She can't walk three feet without someone hitting on her." Billy shook his head and, having had enough of Monk and Izzy and their antics, stuck the phone in his pocket.

"If you don't mind me asking, what is it with you two? I'm sensing tension there."

Understatement of the century. "Uh, yeah. That would be the other part of me being down here. Last summer, I mouthed off to Monk and he beat the crap out of me."

"Seriously?"

Billy tapped his fingers on the table. "Yep. Put me in the hospital for three days."

The shock in her wide-eyed look couldn't be denied. *Yeah, sweet thing, I can be that much of a dick.*

"What did you say to him?"

"What didn't I is the question. One of our teammates died a few months back. Killed during an op. Monk was supposed to be working that day, but he was sick so Roy filled in. Our guy Monk, you may have noticed, thinks everyone is his responsibility and the guilt drove him nutso. He didn't sleep for days and I was ragging on him about being crabby. Let's just say, I rode him too hard during a time I shouldn't have and he blew his stack. Sky high."

"And you're still friends?"

"Sure. We just haven't dealt with it yet."

"As in you haven't discussed it? At *all*? You haven't apologized to each other?"

Apologize? Maybe Billy shouldn't have dogged him, but Monk didn't have to beat him to coughing up blood.

Or did he?

Billy had been asking himself that question for months now and still found himself twisted tight over whether he was a crappy person or if the ADD sometimes prohibited him from doing the right thing. Add to that his own mental warfare over losing two well-liked team members in separate incidents within months of each other and he found himself teetering on an emotional ledge. Monk, their defacto leader, the go-to guy when the shit hit the fan, whacking out after Roy's death didn't help, and Billy flat out lost control of his mind. Which led to him forgetting to renew his passport and landed him in trouble with Vic. Right now, all he knew was since the fight with Monk, he constantly felt unsettled and self-destructive. "He put me in a hospital for three days." He held up three fingers. "Three days."

"I realize that. And he needs to apologize, but Peter seems levelheaded. In my limited dealings with him, he doesn't strike me as someone who loses control to that extreme. If you instigated the problem, you should take responsibility for your part in it. Maybe he's waiting for you to do that and he'll apologize."

Apologize.

Kristen reached over and patted his hand. "Be the better man, Billy, and tell him you're sorry."

"I'll think about it."

"You do that. Tell me about the ADD."

"What's to tell? They tested me in grammar school. Found I was borderline."

"Do you take medication?"

"No. Since I was borderline, my parents—my mother specifically—wanted to try behavioral therapy. She busted her ass keeping me on a regimented schedule, controlling my diet, staying consistent with discipline and making sure I got enough physical exercise to burn off the energy. When it comes to parenting a kid like I was, she's a rock star."

Kristen tilted her head. "I don't hear a lot of people say that."

"Hey, not medicating isn't for everyone. Some kids need the medicine and should have it, but for me, for the most part, we managed without it. With the right conditions, I can handle it. Sometimes I go astray."

Like recently.

"So, when your mother asked you to quit swearing, you agreed."

"For what she gave me, the understanding and faith she had, I owe her at least that."

Kristen tapped her hands against the martini glass. "Sometimes you are the most refreshing man, Billy Tripp. You never quite say what I expect."

He smiled. "I've heard that before. And not in a good way."

"I meant it in a good way." She stood and straightened the tent sweater. "I need to get back to work. Thanks for the martini."

He shoved his chair back, stood to walk with her. "Anytime." *As long as you get rid of the muumuu and give a guy some skin.*

Then she not only surprised him, she made him fall a

little bit in love by kissing his cheek. "This was fun. I like talking to you."

"And to think, you didn't like me at first."

"That's because you wouldn't stop staring at the girls. You were being typical, and *you* are anything but."

"I do try to give people something to remember me by."

7

STROBING BLUE AND RED LIGHTS FLASHED AS HOT WOMEN, seriously hot, suntanned women wearing swatches of gauze for dresses, rocked and twisted their bodies in directions that shouldn't be possible for the average human.

The guys didn't seem to mind. Hell, Billy didn't mind, why should the other men?

Cripes, this place was packed. Holding Izzy's arm, he squeezed through the crowd toward the bar where party-goers stood four deep.

Rather than shout at Izzy over Chris Brown via the DJ, he jerked his head to the end of the bar. One of the cocktail waitresses, a college-age blonde in killer heels, micro shorts and an even more deadly black tank top with a sequined neckline, spotted him. He dropped a fifty on her tray. "That's for you," he half shouted. "Can you grab me a couple of drinks while you're at the bar?"

She pocketed the fifty and took his order.

"Good job," Izzy said. "I wish Peter were here."

Yeah, me too. In this meat market, some jackass would be crazy not to hit on her and he didn't want to deal with it.

In front of him, someone pushed through. The back of the guy's head looked familiar.

"Hey," he yelled and—*jackpot*—the guy turned toward him. Jess's boyfriend. The preppy jagweed. She'd better not be, once again, blowing off Kristen's order to stay away or he'd bust her ass out.

"What?" The boyfriend looked Billy up and down.

"Where's Jess?"

"How should I know? Haven't talked to her today."

With that, prepster moved on, leaving Billy dreaming about kicking his ass a time or two. Something about his elitist attitude. He couldn't worry about it now. He would however, keep an eye out for the little sister from hell. Jesus, these Dantes were a lot of work.

Forty-five minutes later, sweating like a distance runner, Billy hauled Izzy off the dance floor. He reached for his phone to check the time because, yes, folks, he was tired and ready for bed. Izzy didn't look so tired. But he'd promised her at least an hour and she'd get it. Dancing. Someone save him.

A couple of texts and a voice mail had come in. One from Kristen. *Go, me.* Some guy dressed in white slacks and a light pink button-down stepped up to Izzy and gave her a perusal. Izzy—bless her heart—did her soft-on–inducing, staring-at-the-package trick and smirked. The guy, clearly not getting the message, nudged closer until his torso connected with the side of her arm.

Guess that staring-at-the-package stunt wasn't so sure-fire in South Beach.

Billy shot him a look before going back to his phone. "She's off limits. Beat it."

The guy moved an inch closer. *Foolish, foolish boy.* Billy straightened. "I'm doing you a large here. I could hurt you, but her boyfriend is certifiable. That guy will take you apart with his bare hands and use chunks of your body as shark bait. Now, beat it." He went back to his phone. "Don't make me say it again."

"Christ," the guy said and stormed off.

Izzy laughed. "Good thing Peter isn't here."

Billy glanced at her and went back to Kristen's message. "He hates when you do that staring thing. You're asking for trouble."

"It usually works."

"Not here it doesn't. From what I'm told, indiscriminate sex in South Beach is not unusual. You probably just gave that buttwipe an invitation. Listen, Kristen is looking for me. I have to step outside and call her. You gonna be okay?"

Izzy waved him off. Being a Krav Maga expert, she'd kick anyone's ass. Even he was a little afraid of her.

The packed-in bodies on the terrace didn't offer much wiggle room, but at least the eardrum shattering music had been contained to the interior. He breathed in ocean air and waited for Kristen to pick up. "Hi, it's me." He laughed at his own stupid joke.

"The second Bentley is gone."

Any humor he'd been feeling plunged like a brick from a third story window. "Be right there."

Dammit.

With more force than necessary, he jammed his phone into his pocket and headed back inside to shuttle Izzy to her room.

When he reached the security office, he knocked once and stepped in. Kristen and two Dante security guards hovered around a monitor. Another guy in a cheap blue suit and tie stood behind them.

Kristen waved Billy forward. "This is Detective Wilson."

He held his hand out and eyeballed Wilson. By the looks of that wrinkled suit, the guy was into the nineteenth hour of an eight-hour shift. "Billy Tripp."

Wilson nodded and a few strands of his dark hair fell onto his forehead.

"Billy is doing a security review for us." She turned to Billy. "The camera you fixed caught the thief's hiding spot."

Yes.

"Keith," Kristen said, "will you replay it so Billy can see?"

Billy inched closer to the monitor as the thief, his head hidden under another hooded sweatshirt and a pair of baggy jeans that sagged at the ass got out of a late-model three series BMW. A good choice of vehicle. It would blend with the other cars, but not necessarily stand out. He strolled to the Bentley, got in and drove off.

Voila. Boosted car.

Wilson's radio chirped and he paused to listen. "Ms. Dante, I have another call. Saturday night in Miami. I'll need a download of this footage."

Ready for him, Keith held up a thumb drive and Wilson took it. "Thank you."

"Unfortunately, we're getting good at this," Kristen said, her voice soaked in fatigue.

And oh, how Billy wanted to help rid her of those worries. In a variety of ways.

Wilson hotfooted it and Billy slid into his spot behind Keith. "Play it back again on the wall monitor. Rewind a little more though. Before he gets out of his car. Then let me see camera one on the monitor beside it."

After watching the video twice, Billy backhanded Keith on the arm. "Let me sit there."

"What is it?" This from M.H.

"Not sure yet."

She crossed her arms and puckered those lush lips that he so wanted to nibble on. "Shall I wait? Or perhaps I'll go back to running my hotel? Maybe try to find my two Bentleys and a Mercedes while you sit here keeping your thoughts to yourself?"

Too damned cute.

He fought the laugh, but couldn't help himself. M.H. shot daggers. The look had him backing out of her reach and holding up his hands. "I shouldn't have laughed. Sorry. I don't know what I'm looking at. There's something here. I'm not sure what it is yet."

"Can you tell me *something*? Anything?"

He backed up another inch. "Not yet."

"Gah!"

She spun on her wicked spiked heel and stormed out.

"Man, she is pissed at you," Keith said.

Yeah, but it fudging destroys me. Not that he'd ever say that to one of her employees, but crimony, the boss lady had it going on. Too bad he had to piss her off though.

The imaginary filter he was born without—the one that should have told him to shut the eff up instead of laughing at her—would have been nice to have. *Shiznet.* He'd beg forgiveness later. After years of practice, he'd gotten good at it. Why that fact suddenly bothered him, he wasn't sure, but it pressed in, made his head ache. He shook it off and focused on the monitor in front of him.

Don't get distracted.

Priority one would be determining how this gangbanger boosted the last standing Bentley.

Keith's radio chirped. Something about a smackdown in Paradiso. Billy wouldn't mind checking out that action, but the footage in front of him beckoned.

Keith grabbed his radio. "I gotta go."

"Right, Skippy. Do I click on these images to drill down?"

"Yeah."

"Call me if you need help."

I could deal with kicking someone's ass.

"It's My Life" came from his phone. Monk. Speaking of kicking someone's ass. Unfortunately, that someone's ass had to be Billy's for abandoning Izzy. But hell, he'd walked her back to the room at least. "What's up?"

"Izzy told me there was another theft." Monk's voice held the raspy sound of sleep.

"The other Bentley is in the wind."

"You need help?"

"Nah. I'm checking security footage. Go back to bed, Gramps."

"Fuck you."

Billy grinned. "That's how you thank me for chasing off some dickweed hitting on your girlfriend?"

"You want a medal? I do it all the time. Comes with the territory."

"Yeah, but she's not my girlfriend and I delivered for you."

"You always deliver. You may fuck it up on the way, but you always deliver."

Point there. "I'll accept that. Go back to sleep and let me get through these videos. I may want you to look at them tomorrow. Something is bugging me. Don't know what. Not yet anyway."

KRISTEN SAT AT HER DESK WEEDING THROUGH EMAILS BEFORE she closed up for the night. Aside from the theft and a drunken brawl, there'd been no further uproars. She checked her clock. 12:30 a.m. Time for bed and to stop thinking about the insurance company freaking out over two lost Bentleys and a Mercedes.

The hotel's already outrageous premiums would skyrocket. And didn't that thought send her stomach into a full spin.

Her cell phone rang. She scooped it up and checked the ID.

Billy.

No, sir. She was still mad at him for laughing at her in her time of crisis. ADD aside, what sane person would do that?

Exactly why getting involved with him would be a mistake. No matter how physically attractive she found him, no matter how much her body tingled every time he touched her, no matter how much he made her laugh, if she had any sense she'd exorcise him from her life. He'd drive her to madness before this was over. And Jess provided enough madness.

Movement in the doorway caught her eye and she whipped toward it to find insano boy on his knees, holding his hands in prayer.

Laughing would be the absolute worst thing she could do. It would only encourage him. Dealing with Jess all these years had taught her that. She rolled her lips in.

"Go away. I'm mad at you."

"But I crawled all the way up here. The crazy-assed looks I got on the elevator? All for you."

She picked up a cork coaster one of the beverage vendors had left her. The thing wasn't all that heavy, but the rubber base gave it some substance. Good enough. She hurled it at him. It connected with his forehead with a smacking sound and bounced off. Perfect shot.

"Ow!"

A second later he slumped to the floor, spread-eagle, and moaned. Such an idiot.

"I think I have a concussion. It's bad. Call 9-1-1."

"Stop it. Get up."

He moaned again and eased his head back and forth on the floor. Buzzing wisps of panic bubbled inside her. Could he not be faking? The thing was cork. How could it do major damage to that hard head?

"Billy?"

"Uhhhhh."

"Billy Tripp, if you're screwing with me, I *will* kill you."

"Uhhhhh."

Maybe she should check. Holding her hair back with one hand, she bent over him. No blood or immediate bruising. "You look fine."

He stared up at her, his eyes shifting left and right. "Where are you?"

"I'm right in front of you."

"I'm blind," he yelled.

"Knock it off. You're scaring me."

Billy closed his eyes and reached his hands up as if trying to grab something he couldn't see. "Don't leave me alone."

She put her hand over her mouth to cover her smile. "I'm right here, dopey."

"Where?"

She reached down, gave him a not so light pat on his cheek. "Here."

His eyes popped open. "I'm healed."

And with that, he hauled her on top of him and kissed her. Soft and warm and gentle in a light sweeping of his lips and—*wow*—he could kiss. A few seconds in, he pulled her closer, slipped his hand around the back of her head as the kiss escalated to something more. Harder. Insistent. Definitely enough for her to know what he wanted.

Reluctantly, Kristen broke away and reminded herself she was mad at him. "You scared the crap out me."

"I'm still blind in one eye. You'll have to kiss me again. Maybe it'll restore my sight."

"Keep it up and I'll really make you blind. If this is backing off, your technique needs work. You mauled me."

"My technique is great. It's just not the technique you're referring to. Besides, gotta admit, that kiss was a smoker. How about we deep-six this backing off thing? I really suck at it." He wiggled his eyebrows. "Not complaining, but a little cooperation from you on the next kiss would be nice."

Kristen levered off the floor and straightened her skirt. "I so hate you."

When his gaze locked with hers, the heat from that kiss lingered, a connection she hadn't felt in such a long time, and her body went loose. What would be so wrong with enjoying him for a little while? Aside from the fact that she'd have to get naked in front of him.

He wrapped his hand around her ankle and squeezed. "I think you're exaggerating."

Fire erupted inside her and she squeezed her fists, her fingernails biting into her palms to distract her. She could handle this. Handle him. "Why are you here?"

Billy rolled to his feet and held up a thumb drive. "Got something that'll make you happy." He batted his eyes. "It's not me."

"Filter!"

He made a pouty face. "Yeesh. Never mind."

"Don't make me kill you. What is it?"

"Pop that baby in."

Kristen loaded the drive into her laptop and Billy

huddled behind her. While waiting for the files to load, something tickled her neck and she scratched at it.

Billy cleared his throat and she looked up at him. "There are water bottles in the fridge."

"I'm good." He pointed to the screen. "Here we go. This is an image of our guy right before he nabs your Bentley."

Kristen tilted her head one way, then the other. All she saw was a guy in a hooded sweatshirt sitting in his car. "What am I supposed to be seeing?"

"His hands."

She moved closer to the screen, scrunched her nose.

"Kristen, you've got great hair."

"Focus. But thank you. I take a lot of pride in my hair." *Fat Amazons tend to do that.* Hair she could control. "What is he holding?"

Billy leaned over her to point at the monitor and his torso brushed her shoulder. *Close.* Gloriously close.

Would it be so bad? Just one night? To let go? If she were capable of one night, no, it wouldn't be so bad. She imagined he'd be an attentive lover.

He'd take his time.

Savor it.

That's what she imagined, but how would she know? And she was too terrified to risk it. Never had she been capable of no-strings sex. Too body conscious, she supposed, to give in to lust's temptation.

And Billy Tripp would be no exception. Not unless he intended to hang around awhile. Which he didn't.

"This, sweet thing, is an antenna. I think."

"Antenna? What the heck for?"

"I've got a call into our tech geek at work, but I think our bad boy here is using that antenna to transmit the encrypted code from the car. Basically, he's grabbing the signal that tells the car it's safe to unlock the doors."

She leaned right and looked up at him. "*Really.*"

"I'm thinking. What I don't know is how the antenna communicates with the car to pick up the signal."

"And how does he start the car?"

"Still working on that."

"Do you still think one of my employees is involved?"

Billy shrugged. "It's possible. In addition to the antenna unlocking the door, I think the thief would still need a cut key that fits the ignition. I'm hoping Gizmo will know something, but this at least tells us how the guy is getting into the cars."

"How do we stop it?"

Billy groaned.

"Oh, I don't like the sound of that."

"Signal jammer. We've used them on ops to block cell phone signals. There's one that would kick ass in your lot and garage."

Perfect. Kristen nodded. "I'll try it. Where do I get one?"

"Hold up, missy. I can get you one, but it's illegal to jam a signal in the U.S. If you get caught, you're looking at a hefty fine from the FCC. And it might extend beyond the parking areas. Could be a problem for cell phones in certain areas of the hotel. You up for the risk?"

She thought about the United States Senator who'd rented half the hotel for his daughter's impending wedding. "Ew."

Billy laughed. "Exactly."

Still, if these thefts continued, Dante's reputation as a world-class hotel would suffer. "Would you do it?"

"I'd be all over that action. Protecting your property is a good enough excuse for me. That's me though."

True. A fine from the FCC would be no fun. "I need to think about it. Maybe talk to my dad. What else can I do?"

"Besides causing traffic pandemonium by assigning guards to check the paperwork of all cars leaving the lot, not much. The only thing suspicious about this guy is that he's dressed like a gangbanger. Otherwise, he opened the door like he owned it. I'd definitely put a guard near that spot so the thief knows his shit is busted."

"I've already done that. Someone is out there now and will be 24-7."

"It's a start, but if I'm right about this antenna thing, cars can be swiped from anywhere on the property. You'd better keep parking your spiffy ride at the entrance."

"Count on that. Should I phone the police tomorrow and let them know about this antenna thing."

Billy shrugged. "I wouldn't until you decide if you're using the jammer or not. Maybe Gizmo will have the 4-1-1 on how the antenna works."

"Good point. I'll talk to my dad first. I hate secrets though."

"Yeah, but you hate your hotel being violated more. Pick your poison."

8

By lunchtime Sunday, with the sun shining and Bob Marley coming through the speakers, Billy dropped into a chair at the poolside café while Monk and Izzy debated whether to split a grouper sandwich.

"I want a salad," Iz said.

"Yeah, blah, blah." Billy turned to Monk. "You have grouper, she has salad and you share. I gotta talk to you about these car thefts."

Monk nodded. "Did Gizmo call you back?"

"Yeah. More on that in a minute. I gotta fill you in." Monk would go apeshit over the shed incident. An ear-shattering lecture would most likely ensue. Exactly why Billy hadn't admitted it to him yet, but it was time to come clean.

"What?"

Here goes. "I had a visitor yesterday. Three in fact."

Monk gave up on the menu and stared at him. "What happened?"

"Billy?" Izzy said. "Are you all right?"

"I'm fine. Three beefheads cornered me in the storage shed near the parking lot."

Monk shook his head. "Goddammit."

"Take it easy. The short of it is they offered me two hundred and fifty grand to conveniently forget about any stolen cars."

"You rattled someone's cage."

"Apparently. And it's got to be a frickin' huge cage. They came at me head-on. No fear."

Izzy gasped.

Billy waved his hand. "It's fine."

"Not really," Monk said.

"Listen, Mr. Negative, this stays between us. Kristen will freak if she finds out. Anyway, one of the guys sounded like he was from the Middle East. And he said '*khalas.*' To make it more interesting, that dickweed Alex, the one Jess Dante is dating? He said '*khalas*' to me the other day. Pretty damned coincidental, right?"

Monk jerked one shoulder.

"Forget it. I'll look into old Alex more. Those boys yesterday were testing me. They know I'm on to something and from what Gizmo told me, this antenna thing might be part of it. He says the antenna has to be within a certain range to the key."

"How big of a range?"

"His guess? Maybe twenty-five feet."

"Where was the key then?"

"I checked on that. A guest needed a lift last night. The driver returned to the hotel just before eleven."

Izzy leaned forward. "The guy was waiting for the driver to return and when he did, the thief used the antenna to steal the signal from the key." She turned to Monk. "I see this kind of genius all the time when I defend people. If only they used it legitimately."

Monk sat forward, drummed his fingers on the table.

"How, with one antenna, is this guy getting into that car?"

"That's what I need to figure out. Gizmo thinks there had to be a second antenna somewhere. Basically, the antennas transmit the signal and trick the car into opening the doors. Then, Giz says, they use the antenna to start the car because the signal enables the ignition. No key needed. Flipping crazy."

"Billy, this sounds fucked up."

"No shiznet there. Maybe the thief assumed the hotel would be transporting guests on a Saturday night and waited."

"Or did someone tip him off?" Izzy asked.

"Check the footage," Monk said. "See how long he was squatting. If he showed up right before the car disappeared, you know he had the driver's schedule. If not, he probably figured a guest would need a ride at some point and waited. I could see that."

"I'll check it."

The waitress swung by and took their lunch order. Once the salad versus grouper dilemma was settled, Monk turned to Billy. "You're getting in deep here. Probably too deep for someone in a jackpot with his boss. When does Vic want you back in Chicago?"

"Don't know."

"Did you think to ask?"

"Yes. I thought about it."

Monk sighed. "This is typical."

"Hey, with Gina about to go into labor, he's not thinking about me. Why put it on his radar? I'll beg forgiveness later."

"That's brilliant," Izzy said. "You're falling back on it being easier to beg forgiveness than ask permission?"

"Why should this time be any different? This is how he

gets jammed up. And then he wonders where he went wrong." Monk turned to Billy. "Not calling Vic was your first mistake."

Here comes the nagging. Fan-fudging-tastic. Billy sat a little straighter. "Do me a solid and don't lecture me. If he was gonna Donald Trump my ass, he'd have done it already."

Izzy wrinkled her nose. "Donald Trump?"

"Fire him," Monk said.

"Where do you come up with this stuff?"

Billy turned to Izzy and grinned.

Monk poked a finger at him. "Don't screw this up. I don't want to hear you whining when you get your ass kicked."

Billy slapped his hand on the table three times. "Tap out. I'd love to sit and chat, but I sense this is going places we've been before. You kids enjoy lunch. I'll be reviewing security footage to find out how long our thief was waiting."

He made his escape, walked around the busy pool and pushed through the patio doors into the hotel. His phone beeped. Voice mail. Missed another call. Damn building had a buttload of dead zones.

Just then, the phone rang. *M.H.* "Hey."

"Where are you?"

He looked up and a boiling hot, green halter dress in the boutique window nearly sent him to his knees. *Hubba bubba.* "I'm in front of the dress shop. I just came in from the pool. Major dead zone for cell reception, babe." He glanced around to make sure he was alone. "You're not using a signal jammer are you?"

"Very funny. I'm heading your way. Wait there."

"Roger that."

He shoved the phone back in his pocket and stepped closer to the window. What a dress. Looked like silk. He immediately imagined Kristen's full figure squeezed into that sucker. *Suh-weet.*

"What are you doing?"

He turned to see M.H. striding toward him. "From now on, nobody is allowed to ask me what I'm doing. Everyone always assumes I'm doing something I shouldn't be. You told me to wait. I'm waiting. *That's* what I'm doing."

M.H. threw her hands in the air. "Whoa, fella. You had your nose pressed to the glass. I was curious."

"Oh."

She waved him off. "Forget that. I just got a call from the Secret Service. They're coming to do a security sweep before the senator's event."

Secret Service. *Shazam.* "Is the president coming? First lady?"

"No."

"That's weird then. Secret Service doesn't usually show up if it's only a senator."

"Yeah, well, half the Senate will be here. Not to mention the House members. They're not taking chances."

"Well damn, Kris. Good for you."

She gawked at him. "I'm not ready for the Secret Service."

Billy stepped out of her reach. "Easy now."

"I need help getting my security up to snuff. You'll know what they're looking for. I'm hiring Taylor Security, mainly you, to storm this hotel and tell me where I'm vulnerable."

Oh, he'd tell her where she was vulnerable. He engaged his version of a filter, squashed a laugh and nodded. Time to be serious. "Not a problem. I'd actually have fun with that."

"Good. I'll call Vic and talk about the fee."

Billy glanced at the halter dress. "It'll be steep."

"How steep?"

"You're not gonna like it."

She folded her arms. "I'm a tough negotiator, Billy."

Eyeing her up and down, imagining those gorgeous curves in that dress, he looked back to the window and pressed his finger to it. "*That* is my fee."

Her gaze shifted to the window, then slowly back to him.

Oh, yeah, you know what I'm thinking.

"It's not really your color."

"Hardy-har. It's exactly *your* color. You wearing that dress during dinner with me will get this deal done. Take it or leave it."

"You're out of your mind—which, frankly, isn't a stretch—if you think I'm putting this body into *that* dress. My boobs will be spilling out."

He shrugged. "I don't see a problem."

"Bastard!"

Normally he didn't like women who yelled at him. This one though, she made it kind of cute. "Those are my terms."

"I'll call your boss and discuss the real fee. If you don't like it, I'll have Vic send someone else."

"You could do that. But I'm already here and I've been prowling this hotel for two days. I know the layout. A new guy would have to start from scratch. If you wanna waste that time, go ahead."

"Bastard!"

Now he laughed. Couldn't help it. Seriously, he might be in love. "So hot, you are."

She pinched her lips tight and held her fist up. "You're such an annoying man."

"I know. It's a curse. What's your answer?"

She grunted and bared her pearly whites at him. "Fine."

"And you won't weasel out?"

Kristen gasped. "Of course not. When I make a deal, I

stick to it. I'm offended you would say that. I'm setting ground rules though."

"Uh-oh,"

"I'm not wearing the dress in public. And especially not in the hotel. I don't need my employees seeing my boobs hanging out. We'll do it at my house."

She held her hand out to seal the deal. Billy took it, held on way too long while their gazes locked. And—*oh, oh, oh* —the feel of her skin against his got his mind working on scenarios that included varied use of those hands.

Finally, Kristen reclaimed her lovely hand.

He reached into his pocket for his phone. "I guess we have a deal then. I'll call Vic and set it up."

"Good. How long will it take you to do the review?"

"Other than cars disappearing, your security is fine. And I'm working on the car issue now. I need to talk to you about that next."

A FEROCIOUS BEATING CLOBBERED THE INSIDE OF KRISTEN'S skull. "Excuse me?"

"Yes?"

"My security is *fine*?" She refused to so much as glance at the dress in the window. Otherwise, she'd kill him. She'd been bamboozled. "You said you'd check my security. That was the deal."

"Yes. And I have checked your security. The terms of our deal have not been violated."

"Bastard!"

"You'd better quit saying that." He stepped closer—too close. Close enough to ignite a yearning for something she knew would be a disaster. He pressed his lips right against her ear and whispered, "It's kinda turning me on."

Heat rushed into her face. Placing one hand on his chest, the rock-hard chest she wanted to take a pick ax to, she shoved him back a step. "If you'd told me up front the security was adequate, I'd have never made that deal."

"Exactly."

"Exactly my butt."

Billy laughed. "And a lovely butt it is."

Now the panic, deep and rooting, had set in. He'd completely manipulated her. "You knew I was feeling desperate and you used it to get what you wanted."

He sighed, as if this conversation was nothing but a bother. "You got what you wanted. *You* wanted to ensure your security would hold up and it will. I'll guarantee that. Isn't that worth one night of wearing an incredible dress? Besides, I've been feeling desperate since the moment I put eyes on you. My desperation comes from a different place though." He grinned. "Much different, but we won't get into that right now."

"I'm...I'm... Gah."

She spun away and stormed off. This man was the biggest colossal pain in the butt to ever enter her hemisphere. He'd bullied her into this deal. She should renege. Tell him to buzz off. She'd entered into the agreement under false pretenses. Had she known the security was fine, she'd never have agreed. Shame on her for trusting him, a total hit-and-run driver of a womanizer, a self-admitted master at seduction.

"Shall I grab the dress for you?" he called after her.

"I hate you, Billy Tripp."

.   .   .

BILLY APPEARED IN HER OFFICE DOORWAY TWO HOURS LATER and propped himself against the doorjamb. "Have you cooled off yet?"

Not. One. Bit. She cocked her head and pasted a smile on her face. "Certainly. Come in."

"Oooh, that's a rather frosty greeting from such a hot woman."

"You'll survive. What can I do for you?"

"You're still pissed at me. Can we put it aside for a couple of minutes? Gotta talk to you about the cars disappearing."

"Whatever you want, Billy."

He put his hands up. "Hey, now. Don't say that. What I want is you naked and horizontal on this desk."

Just how insane could this man possibly be? Kristen closed her eyes and grunted. She wouldn't lose it on him. She wouldn't. He lived for this. The provoking. The battle. The clash of wills. He truly got off on it and the more she screamed at him, the more he goaded.

"Don't forget that filter."

"You're right. I take back the horizontal thing. Naked still goes though."

Kristen finally laughed. As much as she wanted to hurl something at him again, she had to admit he entertained her. In a sick, torturous, demented way, she found this free-spirited, annoying, chaos-inducing man attractive.

That couldn't be good.

She folded her hands in front of her. "At least try a little harder to control yourself. Can you do that for me? Please?"

He remained silent for a moment but nodded. "Sure. For you, I'll do that."

"Wonderful. Now have a seat and tell me why you're here."

"Right." He dropped into one of her guest chairs. "I've

reviewed the footage from the last theft. Our guy simply hung around and waited for one of the Dante cars to go out. And he has a partner."

"Oh, no."

"Yep. I talked to my guy at the office and showed him the footage. It appears they're using two antennas. One needs to be close to the car and the other to the key."

Kristen sat back, replayed what he said. "The key has to be within a certain distance for the signal to be hijacked?"

"Yes."

"If that's the case, any guest parking a car when the thief happens to be in the area would be vulnerable?"

"Yep."

"Get me the signal jammer. My dad told me to decide. I just decided."

As much as she despised the idea of doing something illegal, it appeared the thieves had complete control of her parking lot.

That, she would not allow.

"Good girl. I'll get the jammer."

"Thank you for taking care of this."

He grabbed a sticky sheet from the holder on her desk and made a note. "No problem. Just wear the shoes you had on yesterday when we have dinner. Those were monster."

"First you tell me what to wear and now you're demanding shoes? What am I, a Stepford wife?"

Billy sat back, his blue eyes twinkling a tad too much. "I'd have fun with you as a Stepford wife."

"You make me crazy."

With his gaze steady on her, he leaned in, propped his elbows on her desk, and her chest seized. They sat there a full minute, his eyes on her, her refusing to give in, until he said, "Yeah, but I think part of you likes it. What I need to know is how far I can push, and that only comes with experience."

"And me getting angry."

"Sometimes, yes."

"That's okay with you? That you have to infuriate people to know where the line is? Isn't that the reason your boss sent you here?"

Silence.

"Billy, maybe you need to think of other ways to figure out where the line is."

"Such as?"

"Talking."

"Okay. Let's talk. We'll start by you telling me where your line is."

Damn him.

"Kris?"

"I don't know."

"That's helpful." He held his palms to the sky. "A guy with my issues needs consistent boundaries. I *need* people to clearly communicate their expectations and stick to them. Can you ballpark for me where the line is?"

Go easy here. He'll trip you up. "The problem is, it keeps moving. And that's saying something. Prior to a few nights ago, I would have run screaming from you. I'm not doing that."

"You're running a little bit."

She grinned. "But I'm not screaming. Yet. You infuriate me, but you also entertain me. What scares the hell out of me is you remind me too much of my sister and I don't need that chaos."

"So you've said. What do I do about it?"

"Don't push me over the line."

Billy huffed, stared at the ceiling. "You just told me you don't know where the line is. How am I supposed to—"

"I'll let you know when you're getting close. How's that?"

"I won't take responsibility for you getting pissed at me if I didn't get a warning."

"I'll give you a warning. I promise."

"That's all I ask."

She smiled. "Except for the shoes."

He smiled back. "Those shoes are *monster*."

Her assistant knocked on the door and Kristen glanced up. "What's up?"

"They need you in banquets."

"I'll be right there." She shifted back to Billy. "Are we done here?"

"For now."

"We should probably let the police know about this antenna thing."

"We could, but you just told me to obtain an illegal device."

Apparently, being a criminal wasn't her strong point.

"Kris, I know this scares you. Let me take care of it."

Yes, it did scare her. *He* scared her. But somehow, she trusted her hotel in his hands. "Thank you. As soon as I fix whatever this banquets problem is, I'll check back with you."

"Sounds good. When are we having dinner?"

"As soon as you write me a report telling me what my security detail will be the night of the senator's party."

"I can have that done in an hour."

Kristen laughed. "Good. If the report meets my requirements, I'll set a date."

"Hang on. What are your requirements?"

She inched closer, ran a finger down the front of his shirt

and poked him in the stomach. "I guess you'll know if you don't meet them."

Billy lay stretched on his bed while Monk sat on the edge of the long dresser. The overstuffed red chair by the balcony door looked dang comfy, but apparently the dresser had better appeal.

Either way, his teammate wouldn't leave him the hell alone. Considering he was down here as a punishment, maybe that was Monk's plan. He himself said he'd gotten back onto Vic's not-so-shit list and probably figured if he stayed on Billy, he'd remain in the boss's good graces.

"Does Vic know you're doing the security for this event?"

"Eff's sake. This is not your problem. Go get busy with your super hot girlfriend."

"Fuck off."

"Gladly."

Monk scrubbed—really scrubbed—his hands over his face. "Don't make me kill you. Please. I have no idea where to dump a body here. My point is, Izzy and I are leaving Tuesday. You will be alone and, after your visitors in the shed, that bugs me. Last thing I want is to be babysitting your ass, but if you need me to stay, I'll do it."

Babysitting? Billy engaged the already overused and strained filter and sucked in the salty sea air billowing through the open balcony door. He inhaled long and slow. Long and slow. Yeah, South Beach in December was good for his soul.

I could stay.

Filtering crisis averted, he said, "How generous, but I'll pass. Leave before you piss me off. You're already well on your way."

Speaking of which... He sat up. There was something he'd been curious about for months now, but had never had the opportunity—or the need—to ask. "Back when you beat the crap out of me, did it occur to you to stop pounding on me?"

"No," Monk said.

"Wow."

Harsh. What monumental screw-up in Billy's life made him capable of dogging his friends to the point where they went Norman Bates on him? That he could be that far off-leash, that *stupid,* to push his friend to that kind of rage?

"I was insane," Monk said. "Your problem is you know you're pissing someone off and you keep going. Most of us know when we've gone too far. You don't. You go balls to the wall every time."

Yes, and Billy wanted to control that. Thanks to his mother's patience, he'd spent his life learning how to perform behavioral interventions on himself. After the fight with Monk though, his restlessness had increased, his distractions had become more plentiful and he'd let his control slip when all he wanted was to hang on. And that made his already active mind spin faster, harder, longer.

He needed a break. A break would allow him to lock that control in and not push his friends into such a state of frustration that they physically attacked him. He wanted to relearn how to let go. Wasn't that what responsible people did? They adjusted, learned to bend and see things from the other person's perspective.

He supposed he could start small. "I'm sorry, by the way."

Monk snorted. "*What?*"

Jackhole. "You heard me. I said I was sorry. Be mature and accept my apology. It's the only one I'm giving you."

"I accept your apology. I apologize as well. I lost it on you and you didn't deserve that beating."

An awkward silence filled the space. Billy wiggled one foot so he could think about anything but the freaking weirdness of having a moment with Monk. "I gotta get better about figuring out where the line is. My line must be farther than everyone else's."

"Your line is off the grid."

"I'm trying to figure out where Kristen's is. She's a tough one."

"Did you ask her?"

Billy gave him a what-the-eff face. "She says it's moving."

"Moving?"

"I'm totally fucked. Sorry, Ma! But, really? *Really?* She gives a guy like me a moving line? How am I supposed to hit that target? I already told her I'd back off, which we've determined I suck at."

Monk shrugged. "I don't think staring at her tits the other night was backing off."

"I don't stare at her chest anymore." Billy waggled his eyebrows. "At least not when she's looking."

Monk cracked up. "You're a jackass"

"Yes, but I'm a male jackass."

"You're so goddamned busy trying to figure out where the line is you don't realize you already know."

Billy huffed. "Is any of that crap supposed to make sense to me?"

"You gonna tell me you don't have that voice in your head that tells you to stop? That you're going too far."

"Of course I have a voice. Only mine is dyslexic. It yells 'go, go, go!'"

Monk did the face-scrubbing thing again. "That is fucked up."

Welcome to my world, pal. "Maybe, but it's my fucked up."

"What else have you got to work with?"

Billy lay back down on the bed, rested his hand over his forehead. "I do get pumped when I sense a reaction in people. I'm a junkie when it comes to that."

"What are you? Ten?"

"When I get that feeling, yes. It's euphoric. I love it and I can't stop."

And wasn't that the suckiest of all suckiest things to admit. Some people had alcohol or drugs. He had adrenaline. And lots of it.

"Jesus, you need help."

"Isn't that why you're here?"

Monk angled his head back and forth as if contemplating the destruction of a foreign country. At this point, maybe he was. "This is fairly simple," he said. "When you start to feel adrenaline popping, that's your signal to stop. You gotta fight the addiction."

"Is there a twelve-step program for that?"

"No." Monk moved off the dresser. "Your problem is you like being pain-in-the-ass Billy. You can't decide how bad you want to change. When you want it bad enough, you'll do it. How bad do you want it?"

Billy stared at the ceiling, thought about Kristen and nibbling on that fantastic lower lip of hers. The way she smiled at him and was so easy to talk to. Her patience with his ADD-related issues was enough to make her damned near perfect. "Pretty flippin' bad."

9

KRISTEN NEARLY ROCKETED OUT OF HER CHAIR WHEN JESS threw the office door open and let it bang against the wall. For crying out loud. After a long day, a coronary wasn't on the agenda. Plus, her sister had been told not to come back until Monday.

As usual, she didn't listen.

"Hey, how about knocking? And why are you here?"

"You won't believe it," Jess said, the tone of her voice rising enough for Kristen to recognize distress.

"What happened?"

"He's cheating on me."

"Who?"

"Alex!"

This is why she almost gave me a heart attack? "He's important?"

Disgusted, Jess flapped her arms. "Well, not so much that, but *he* is cheating on *me*. How humiliating."

Looking at Jess in a sky-blue dress that clung to every millimeter of her thin, tanned frame, not to mention her long blond hair flowing over her shoulders, maybe Kristen could understand why it would be humiliating. And, for some childish reason, she found it mildly satisfying. Which on some level, brought on guilt. But finally, *finally,* Jess knew the horror of being on the losing end of a relationship.

"I'm sorry you were humiliated. Who was he cheating with?"

"I saw him at Aria last night. Someone told me she's a front desk clerk somewhere. Can you believe that? A front desk clerk. I've barely been able to leave my bed today."

Cheating wasn't the issue, but the front desk clerk apparently was. *Maybe she's nice? Unlike you.* Kristen shrugged.

"You don't care. You're too busy to worry about me, the troublemaker."

As if Kristen hadn't spent most of her life worrying and cleaning up her little sister's messes. So typical. "I never said that. Jess, I've barely seen you with him. How would I have a clue as to whether he's someone special or not?"

"If you took the time to talk to me instead of throwing me out of the hotel for two days…"

Kristen gripped the arms of her chair, let them absorb her anger. "Don't you lay that on me. You created that situation and I dealt with it. Had you been any other employee, I would have fired you. Plus, when have *you* ever taken the time to ask me how I'm doing?"

No answer. No surprise either. Jess didn't care enough about anyone else to bother and Kristen didn't have the inclination to argue. She stretched a hand across the desk, laid her palm flat. "Look, I have the Secret Service coming here in less than two days. I don't want to fight with you."

Jess scrunched her nose. "Well, that's *just* fine. I guess I'll leave because the queen bitch is too busy to spend time with her sister."

Pressure drummed inside Kristen's chest, building until

it reached her neck and, oh, the ache of it. That helpless suffocation that came from arguing with an unreasonable person. She felt...she felt...*gah!* Being called a bitch, particularly by the bitch in front of her, was getting tiresome. Extremely. "That's the second time you've called me a bitch. It stops now. If it doesn't, you are out of here. For good. And Dad will agree with me. Trust me on that. He's well aware of what goes on around here."

Jess sucked air threw her nose and stuck her chest out.

"Say it," Kristen said. "Please. Give me a reason."

With that, Jess stomped from the office, shoving aside Billy, who stood in the doorway watching the abysmal exchange.

He craned his neck to watch Jess go. "Your sister on a roll. What else is new?"

She clasped her hands together and squeezed. *That's it. Just breathe.* When her fingers cramped, she released them, shook them out and relaxed her shoulders. She focused on Billy. "She called me a bitch again. I work my tail off to help keep her trust fund intact and this is what I get? Being called a bitch because I don't track her revolving love life?"

He reached her desk in three long strides, his face all sharp angles and sculpted bone, and she pushed back in her chair.

"Then tell her to fuck off. She doesn't deserve you. She should be on your side. All the time. And she's not."

"She's never on my side. No matter what it is. If I said the sun was out, she'd say it was cloudy. How did our relationship get to this?"

"I don't know, but it's not your fault. You do a lot for her. At least one of us is on your side. Always. No matter what. I want nothing more than to slay your dragons. Every damn one of 'em. She should feel the same."

That speech turned Kristen mushy and the girl parts got a little warm. She wanted to despise her reaction to him, wanted to lock it away, wanted not to feel this insane attraction.

The girl parts weren't having any of it.

She sat back and crossed her legs, trying to look like a consummate professional rather than the starry-eyed, hormone-crazed teenager she'd reverted to. "Thank you. And, just so you know, that slaying the dragons line? That was a home run, fella."

His smile came lightning fast and he held her gaze long enough to send the simmering girl parts fully ablaze.

"It wasn't a line. It's true."

She looked down. *Danger, Kristen, danger.* But, God, she was starting not to believe that.

"Why did she call you a bitch?"

"She came busting in here complaining her boyfriend dumped her. I didn't even know he *was* her boyfriend. She's had so many men in and out of her life, it's hard to keep them straight."

"That Alex guy?"

"You know him?"

He scratched his chin. "Sort of. We met the other night. Jess showed up here with him Friday night."

Perfect. Not only had her sister called her a bitch—twice —she'd completely ignored Kristen's directive to stay away from the hotel. Also twice. "After I told her not to come back?"

"Yeah, but I busted her ass out." He grinned. "She wasn't happy."

He'd thrown Jess out. A rush of satisfaction consumed her. It took nerve to push a Dante out of her family's hotel.

He did that for me. "It didn't occur to you that her father owned the hotel?"

He shrugged. "You told her to stay away. I knew you didn't want her here and I took care of it. Slaying your dragons, babe. Slaying your dragons."

"The things that go on in my own hotel. Amazing." She slid her hand, palm up, across the desk. "Thank you."

Billy rubbed his fingers over her palm then clasped her hand. "You're welcome. Just wear the shoes with that green dress."

"*Anyway,* Jess was mad because I apparently didn't care that her so-called boyfriend dumped her for a hotel clerk."

Still clasping her hand, Billy squeezed it. "Oh, man, that's priceless. A hotel heiress gets dumped for a desk clerk."

She leaned forward, slid her hand from his and dragged her fingers up and down over his. "I was rather entertained by it."

"Kris?"

"Yes?"

"You need to stop doing that with my fingers. It's causing major problems for me."

She snapped her hand away. "I'm sorry."

"No sweat. Just don't be offended when I stand up and my shorts are tent-poled."

Totally inappropriate. Did he even understand he did this? Kristen slapped her hands over her face. "Billy!"

"Hey, letting you know. That's all. Normal male reaction to a sexy chick."

"You're insane."

"Add horny to the list."

And oh, the girl parts took a hot flash. Between him and

Jess, her brain might bleed. With Jess came disappointment and Kristen had learned to prepare for that. Billy though, she hadn't been ready for him. With him, she suddenly didn't want to prepare herself. Or at least she didn't want to *need* to prepare herself. How twisted. If she didn't prepare, and he disappointed her, she'd be disappointed and not ready for it. But if she bulked up her reserves and self-protected, she'd miss out on the surprises he constantly inflicted.

No way to win.

Billy smacked his hands on the desk. "Back to why I'm here. Your signal jammer will arrive tomorrow morning. I'll get you all set up. Your security recommendations for the senator's party are almost done. Monk is proofreading, and I'll give you those tomorrow as well. That's the bonus for you wearing the hot shoes."

"Again with the shoes?"

"They're smokers."

She rolled her eyes. "Thank you for the update. Now go. I have work to do."

He jumped out of the chair, headed for the door and stopped. "What do you know about this Alex guy?"

"Not a lot. I've seen him around the hotel. His family owns a local bank. They have money, but they're not considered A-list. Why?"

He tapped his fingers against his legs. "Did Jess say what hotel the other chick works at?"

"No. Why?"

"Well, Ms. Dante, I'm curious if they've had any cars stolen from their lot."

. . .

KRISTEN STARED AT HIM, NIBBLED HER BOTTOM LIP AND SENT his mind places she'd slap him for. He'd take that slap. Maybe a few more too.

"You think *Alex* is involved in the car thefts?"

Billy shrugged. "I find it curious he's dating a hotel heiress *and* a clerk from another hotel. Could be he likes banging hotel people. What do I know?"

"I think you know a lot and if you're wondering, maybe I should ask around. I'll check with Jess about what hotel it was. I know most of the owners and managers on South Beach and might be able to find out if they've had any thefts."

"Would they share that with you?"

"Some would. The others will need incentive. I'll do the you-tell-me-your-secrets-I'll-tell-you-mine routine."

"My kind of girl."

She sighed. "If hotels are being targeted and mine is the first to have problems, the other owners will want to be ready."

Had to love a woman who knew how to work a situation. "Any idea where I can find Alex?"

Grabbing her notepad, she scribbled something. "I'll get you his address. Jess asked me to open a house account for him two weeks ago. The business office will have his contact info."

"Excellent response, Ms. Dante. Next question. You got a car around here I can use? Something low key? Boring?"

Still jotting, she shifted her gaze to him. "Why?"

"My camera and I are about to do a little old-fashioned surveillance."

"Billy—"

He held up his hands before she reamed him. This was her place and he had no interest in drawing her fire. Again.

"It's nothing. I'll follow him and see what he's up to. With the right car, he won't know I'm there."

She tapped her fingers on the desk. "Promise me you won't get caught. You're a contractor for my hotel. I don't need you getting into legal trouble. Signal jammer aside, that is."

"Yes, Mommy."

After huffing a breath—and drawing attention to her chest—she shook her head. M.H. really wasn't happy about this. "I have a meeting in ten minutes. It should only take half an hour. Come back then and I'll get you a car."

AFTER KRISTEN'S MEETING, BILLY SQUEEZED HIS SIX-FOOT-three body into her Aston and decided if they were going to be traveling by car together, they'd be making arrangements for something with more leg room. This trip, she drove him to a two-story, pristine duplex on Palm Island just off the causeway.

He surveyed the area where the waning sun washed over the driveway. He knew Kristen's father lived on Palm Island with some of Miami's wealthiest inhabitants and security was *tight*. Yep, if tourists wanted to have a gander, they needed to check in with the guard at the entrance to the island.

Somehow, Billy didn't think this conservative duplex belonged to her father. From what he knew of Tom Dante, the man liked flash. Still, red tiles on the roof gave the concrete block stucco some sass, and a small patch of grass was well-tended and anchored with hardy red and yellow flowers. All in all, a nice, well-kept home.

"Where are we?"

She stepped to the garage door, punched in a code. "My house. You wanted a car and I've got one."

The door slid up in silence. Impressive. An older model dark green sedan sat on the right side of the two-car garage. What was M.H. doing with this piece of shiznet car? He glanced at Kristen still standing at the entrance to the garage, then did a quick walk around the car. A few scratches here and there and paint chips on the driver's side door. Banged up just enough. Not to mention boring as hell. Perfect.

"Whose car is this?"

"It's mine."

Billy spun back to the Aston, its metallic flecks gleaming in the Florida sun. "You went from this P.O.S.—" he pointed to the sedan then to the Aston, "—to that?"

"Hey! Filter."

Screw the filter. "Sorry, but still. Hell of a shock."

"The green one is my old car. It's seven years old."

Why she kept that drab grandma car when she had the Aston, Billy couldn't fathom. "So, the green one is what, the airport car?"

"What's an airport car?"

"It's the car people leave at the airport when they travel because it's such a piece of crap no one would bother to steal it."

"That's a good idea, but no." She waved at the sedan. "It just sits here."

"Why?"

Now she stared at the car. Studying it. "I can't let it go."

Considering he didn't own anything but his clothes and camera, understanding emotional attachments to items would never be his strong point. Which meant he was far from qualified to analyze the fact that she couldn't dump a crappy sedan when she had an Aston Martin. Call him crazy, but that was fudging ridiculous. He nodded though, pretended to understand. "You should sell it. Or, even better, donate it. Someone can make use of it."

But M.H. was still staring at the P.O.S. car.

"Maybe."

Maybe nothing. "Kris, you've got this smoking hot Aston. What the hell do you need this one for?"

"I *don't* need it."

What exactly were they talking about? She didn't need it, but she kept it. Again he hesitated, tried to make sense of it, but being a guy who didn't own a car, it made zero—sub-zero—sense. He blew raspberries. "So get rid of it."

But the look she gave him, her eyes big and wide and searching suggested that was a dumb-ass idea. What she needed from him, nary a clue.

"I can't," she said.

"Why?"

She leaned one hip against the car and patted it. "Because it's me."

Blood roared to his head. *Go, go, go.* With his gaze still on her, he imagined the filter fanning out. *Did my head just explode?* "Huh?"

Looking down at her feet, she shook her head. "Let me get the keys."

He reached for her. "What did you mean by that? It's you?"

A squawking bird flew by the open garage nearly missing the palm tree in front of the house. Her gaze wandered to the tree, then to the ceiling, the wall, her shoe. Billy stayed focused on Kristen now staring out the garage. *That tree won't save you, sweet cheeks.*

"Kris?"

She finally looked at him, their eyes connecting for a second and Billy knew, sure as he was standing there, he wouldn't like what she was thinking. "It's nothing. I'm blathering."

When she stepped toward the house, he shifted to block her. "We're not leaving until you tell me. I'll sit here. You know I'm asshole enough to do it."

"I need to get back. Let me pass and I'll get the keys."

He crossed his arms and sidestepped when she tried to get around him. "Nobody goes anywhere until you tell me what you meant. I will pin you to the ground if I have to." A gasping sound filled the garage and he shrugged. "Don't sound so shocked. This shouldn't surprise you."

"You'd hold me hostage in my own garage? I don't believe it."

"Try me. Please." He wiggled his eyebrows. "I'd get the double bonus of being on top of you." With her hang-ups about her figure, he made sure to keep his eyes glued to her face. But, really, he wanted to look elsewhere. Elsewhere being about eight inches lower. *Filter.* "Just imagine what that would do to me."

Being the cuteness that she was, she pinched her lips together and scrunched her nose. "I hate you sometimes."

"I'll live with it. Now spill."

"We're not having a big discussion about this. It's my problem. Got it?"

"Yes, ma'am."

"My father gave me the Aston last year. I drove this car for six years before that." She walked back to the Aston and, like the day in front of the hotel, eased her hand over the hood and let it settle there. "Look at it. It's gorgeous. Breathtaking even. Sleek and lean and sexy."

Uh-oh.

She turned back to him and stared right smack into his eyes. "*This* car, Billy, is everything I am not. When the top is down, and I'm behind the wheel, I feel it. I feel the vibe— the power—and it makes me forget I'm a fat Amazon."

Did he hear that right? He cocked his head, replayed it in his mind while that frapping bird squawked.

Fat Amazon.

That's what she'd said. For a second, his mind reeled. Not unusual for him, but in this particular instance he found himself speechless. When's the last time that oddity had occurred? Maybe once. In the fourth grade. During recess... *Concentrate here, pal.*

He didn't know what was more offensive, the fat Amazon comment or the car—an object with no life, no vibrancy— being everything she wasn't.

"And what?" He gestured to the butt-ugly sedan. "You think *this* is what you are? This boring piece of crap that wouldn't grab anyone's attention? *That's* what you think?"

On the street, a car went by. The driver gave the horn a shot and waved. Kristen waved back. Probably a neighbor. She turned back to him and the hard stare she gave him might have been a warning. He wasn't sure. "You're out of your mind. Have you *looked* in a mirror lately? Or are you blind as well as crazy? I mean, Christ," he jerked his hands toward her. "You've got the whole ethereal look with the green eyes and dynamite curves. It's sweet and hot at the same time and it destroys me. *Destroys* me. I look at you and I can't decide if I want to do you fast and rough or slow and quiet and—"

Her face contorted into opened-mouth horror and she threw her hands up. "Filter!"

"Fuck the filter." *Sorry, Ma.* "I get a pass this time." He shoved his hands into his hair and gripped the strands. "I cannot believe this piece of crap car is how you see yourself."

Maybe he shouldn't have said that because she stepped closer and got right into his grill. "Don't you dare judge me. Try growing up with Jess, who popped out of her mother flawless, and watch her grow and listen to people tell her how stunning she is. And then have those same people turn to you and ask how school is. Don't come here and think you—who also popped out of your mother gorgeous—can tell me you can't believe it. In my world, Jess is the Aston and I'm the boring sedan."

Refusing to give in, he inched closer backing her against the driver's door of the Aston. "You're boring?"

She angled backward. "Compared to Jess? Yes."

"Bullshit."

With her hand on his chest, she gave him a shove. "Back off."

He stepped closer. "You're not boring. Yeah, you're smart. So what? How many thirty- year-old women run billion-dollar hotels? And it's not because of your father. Your father is a brutal businessman. He wouldn't let his kid run his hotel if she couldn't do it. You don't see Jess running a property do you?" He inched even closer, felt her hot breath on his face. "If I could play back the first time I saw you in that ballroom, I'd show you what I see." He ran his hands over her hips and pulled her close. "That amazing dress glued to your curves. You wouldn't think you were boring if you knew all the things I wanted to do to you that night. And, if you hadn't noticed, I still want to do those things to you."

She breathed in, soft yet harsh, and brought her gaze to his, still refusing to give in. "Filter." Her voice, in contrast to the hard look she gave, ruptured. "Please. Filter."

"No. If ever you *didn't* need me to filter it's right now." He grabbed her around the back of the neck and kissed her. Just slammed his lips against hers, pressing himself into her as she backed into the car. And then her arms came around him and she ignited, returning the kiss with equal force. It sent him spiraling.

He'd stand here all day like this. No question. Well, maybe he wanted more than a kiss from this particular woman, but it was a start. To his happy amazement, he adored her and the more time they spent together, the more time he wanted.

Something new.

Assuming he'd made his point, he backed away. "Was that boring?"

She shoved him. "Don't be an ass."

"It was amazing. *You* made it amazing. *You* made it hot and sexy."

She crossed her arms and leaned against the car. "It's too much for me. *You* are too much for me. You live on the edge all the time, constantly moving and thinking and doing something. I don't have the fortitude for that. I'm a boring sedan. That's where I'm comfortable. What's wrong with that?"

"If what you see is a fat Amazon, I think there's plenty wrong."

"I love how you gorgeous people think you can pay us not-so-stunning people a compliment and think we immediately have to believe it. Guess what, Billy? I've had plenty of men who look like you tell me I'm all that you said. And then the minute my sister shows up and starts flirting, they all forgot about me in order to bag my sister. So, don't you dare come into my life and tell me how I should see myself. You haven't earned that right."

Of course he hadn't. That took time and they hadn't had much of that. One thing he knew was he planned on taking that time. However he could. With his schedule, he couldn't guess how it would happen, but he'd make it work. Suddenly, that's what he wanted. To be spend more time near Kristen. And didn't that revelation rock his totally anti-settled world?

"I may never earn it. But I'll keep trying. If nothing else, I want you to look at yourself and see what I see. Since I got here I've met any number of stunning—and I mean *stunning* —women that I could have banged the hell out of. Five minutes after seeing them, I couldn't tell you what one of them looked like. Nope, when I close my eyes, I see your face, and in my extremely experienced opinion, sweet cheeks, boring women aren't that memorable. Even if I never put my hands on you again, by the time I leave here, I'll make you see what I see."

Kristen backed up a full step. "I don't need to see what you see."

"Yeah, honey, you do. What I see will blow your mind. You'll never again look at that shitty—*dang it*—sedan and think it's you. Is that a problem?"

A few seconds passed and she kept her gaze on his, clearly battling to keep control of her emotions. Eventually, she closed her eyes, shook her head and sighed. "Would it even matter?"

He laughed. "Probably not."

"You're relentless."

"I'm told it's not always a good thing."

"That's for sure."

That stung. A rather unpleasant feeling in this Billy-learning-to-filter class. He probably deserved it. No probably about it. He'd pushed her. Maybe too far. "Lucky for me, your sister has given you experience with it. You're more forgiving than most."

"Not that forgiving."

"But you see beyond the pain-in-the-ass stuff. That, Ms. Dante, is your magic bullet. You take the time to see more than most. I love that about you."

"I like to consider the potential rather than the negatives."

He took her hand, ran his thumb over her knuckles and enjoyed the quiet of standing with her after their argument. "For everyone else. Not when it comes to you. I'm going to change it."

Slowly, with a lopsided smirk, she eased her head side to side. Slightly amused was better than hacked off. He may have just bailed his ass out of this one. "I'm guessing your silence means you don't have any issues with it?"

"I'll give you some latitude. Some."

"Good enough. Now get me the keys for this piece-of-crap, boring-as-hell car that is so not you."

10

At eight o'clock, Billy strolled into Kristen's office wearing his ripped Diesel jeans and a graphic T-shirt that hugged his shoulders in a way that made her girly parts sing. Second soprano.

She set her pen down and sat back to enjoy the view of this sometimes annoying, but mostly entertaining man. Why not? Letting herself savor simple pleasures hadn't been on her to-do list for a long time.

He flopped into one of the guest chairs. "Followed our boy Alex."

"Anything?"

"No. He had an early dinner and made a stop at a bank building. His office?"

"If it was Sixth Street Bank, it's his office. I don't know that he really works though. Rumor is they don't let him touch anything."

"Then he did nothing while he was there. He's been home over an hour and I got bored."

Of course he did. One fact she'd accepted in their short acquaintance was that Billy became bored easily. How that pertained to his current interest in her, she wasn't quite sure. Lucky for her, she knew how to deal with overstimulated, adventure-seeking people. Speaking of which... "I talked to Jess. She welcomed my call like the plague."

Billy laughed.

"I, as per usual, sucked it up and apologized for rushing her out of here earlier."

The worst of that humiliating experience was Jess taking triumph in Kristen needing her help. She hated this competitive streak between them. The constant battle. Years of this nonsense had begun to wear on Kristen. Flat out, she couldn't make herself numb to it anymore. Now it was just plain tiresome.

A mind-freezing thought broke through. Had she helped to create tension by always feeling less physically attractive? As a result, had she sought to become more than Jess professionally and made her sister feel inferior?

Prior to this moment, she'd never given that insidious thought room to grow, but down deep, she knew. She'd silently taken pleasure in her sister's poor grades and inability to attend a top university, much less finish, while Kristen earned a master's in record time.

And it said nothing good about her.

She fiddled with her pen a moment while Billy eyeballed her.

"Oh, whatever you're thinking cannot be good."

So intuitive, this man. Finally, she dropped the pen and shook off thoughts of being the bitch her sister presumed her to be. "The other woman works at the Ocean Blue Hotel."

"That's the place down the road, right? I go by it when I run. Fudging huge hotel."

"Yes. It's our main competitor. I called the GM, who

wasn't exactly forthcoming, but I told him we'd had some thefts we're investigating. According to him, they haven't had problems and I left it at that. I'm not telling him anything until he gives me something."

Billy grinned that slow, wicked grin. The grin was his tell. The indication he was about to say something completely inappropriate.

"I love it when you talk dirty."

"Oh, just shut up."

"So harsh. I'm not surprised the guy wouldn't pony up though. I slapped a tracker on Alex's car so we can figure out where he goes. Maybe we'll find a pattern."

First a signal jammer and now a tracking device. Were they the CIA? "Is that legal?"

"Do you care?"

She thought about it. On some level she cared, but she also wanted to stop the thefts at her hotel. "Yes, but I can't get hung up on it. Not if you think this guy is involved."

Billy shrugged. "I don't know what I think. Besides being curious that he's dating two women who both work at high-end hotels. Like I said, maybe he has a thing for hotel people." He grinned. "I suddenly see how that could happen."

She rolled her eyes.

"Have you had dinner yet? I'll buy." Not bothering to wait for an answer, he stood.

She glanced at his outstretched hand and folded hers on the desk. "You're awfully sure of yourself, Billy Tripp. What if I have plans tonight?"

"Do you?"

"That's not the point."

"Sure it is. If you have plans, that's that, I eat alone. If you don't, I'll buy you dinner. It's not a lifetime commitment.

Besides, you can call it a working dinner. I've tweaked your Secret Service plan and we can go over it."

Smart man. He immediately made it a business issue. No emotional attachments.

That worked for her. It looked like a nice evening and she'd been trapped inside all day. Even workaholics needed fresh air. "I accept. We'll eat on the patio."

"Cool. After that, maybe you'll find me irresistible, let me take you back to my room and do wicked things to you. Any thoughts on that?"

Good God. The girly parts went into the third verse of the I-Haven't-Had-Sex-In-A-While anthem. "Um. No. No thoughts on that. Aside from holy inappropriateness."

He threw his hand over his heart. "Shot down again. And insulted. You're one tough cookie, Ms. Dante."

If only that were true. Particularly when it came to her attraction to him. By now she should be running as far from him as she could. They simply were not compatible. She needed order and routine while he thrived on chaos and adventure. As much as she enjoyed him, he'd be incredibly high-maintenance.

She stood, smoothed her hand down her skirt and wondered just how far she'd let herself go for him.

Probably pretty far.

THE FOLLOWING AFTERNOON, KRISTEN SAT AT HER DESK reviewing the budget for Billy's security plan and let out a low whistle. Big money. Big enough that her stomach clenched and unclenched as she went down the list of expenses.

She closed the file folder. In her opinion, the plan looked thorough and had been signed off by Vic and

Michael Taylor at Taylor Security. All in all, Billy had given her what she'd asked for.

Now she had to live up to her end of the deal.

Her stomach heaved again. She dreaded that dress. All she could imagine were her monster-sized boobs over-flowing the sides. If Jess's mother saw it, she'd be disgusted. Beyond disgusted. But Kristen couldn't think about that. She had to rid her mind of it. Fast.

A knock sounded on her office door and she glanced up to see Billy stroll in.

"Hey, hot stuff," he said.

She took in his short dark hair, the day-old beard and the ever-present Diesel jeans. *Wow.* "Hey, yourself."

"What are you doing?"

"Recovering from the budget crisis your security plan gave me."

"Blah, blah. You know it's worth it."

She nodded. "I do know it."

"Can you take a break? Our boy Alex is on the move and I want to check out all these places he's been. You know the area. Figured we could scope it out together."

Kristen turned to her computer where countless emails waited. She should finish them. But then—well, *Billy*. In jeans that fit his long, muscular body just right.

He leaned in. "Come on, Kris, live a little."

Screw the emails. She shoved the mouse away and stood. "You're on, fella."

"Atta, girl. We'll take the boring-as-hell, so-not-you car. You know where you're going so you drive. I'll give you the addresses."

"Gladly. I love being in charge."

He smacked her on the ass with the back of his hand. "Don't get used to it."

Oh, she'd get used to it. He'd have to adjust. "Hands off, big boy. You work for me."

With that, he wrapped a hand around the back of her head and eased her closer. "And I'll continue to work for you. Anywhere, anytime, sweetheart."

The second sopranos are having a helluva day.

Helluva day.

In the car, Billy tapped at his phone and Kristen took a moment to enjoy the afternoon sun warming her hands on the steering wheel. A light wind blew and salty air wafted through the open driver's side window. Another gorgeous day and she'd spent it inside. Maybe she needed to start taking a few minutes to get outside during the day. Just for the infusion of fresh air.

"First stop is the corner of Beach Drive," Billy said.

"Really?"

"Yeah, why?"

"That's a park. I grew up in that area."

"Let's go see."

Ten minutes later, Kristen turned onto Beach Drive, pulled to the curb and slid the car into park.

"That's a park." Billy snapped a few photos with the camera he'd brought with him.

Nice camera too. Zoom lens and all. It appeared the things Billy purchased were high-quality. He might not want the responsibility of owning a car or a house, but when he spent money, he did it well.

He set the camera on his lap, checked his phone again. "Next stop is Relton Street. It's gotta be close. It only took him five minutes to get there."

Kristen worked into traffic, thinking the steering on the sedan was too tight. And the seat with that seam digging into her? Extremely uncomfortable. It made the fat on her legs spread, and her stomach knotted at the humiliation of Billy seeing all that blubber.

The seat on the Aston never caused this. Or did this car, this *boring* car, bring on the familiar ache of being a fat Amazon?

"Whatever it is," Billy said, "stop it."

"What?"

"The look on your face. You're thinking about something that's making you sad. Stop."

Handsome *and* perceptive. A dangerous combination when it came to the man sitting beside her. "I'm not sad. You're right though, I was thinking about something that's not necessarily good for me."

He dropped his phone and it clattered against the camera on his lap. "It's the car. This car is no good for you. Bad karma. You need to get rid of it."

You might be right.

Squeezing the steering wheel, she focused on the road ahead. "Is that dumb? That a car does this to me?"

"No. What's dumb is keeping a car that does this to you. You could donate it and someone will love it and be grateful. Instead, you're sitting here thinking something that I know —I *know*—will piss me off, and I'm not going there with you."

"Fat Amazon."

He threw his hands in the air. "I said I wasn't going there and, yes, it pissed me off. If driving this car does that to you, I'll drive it off a pier. Do yourself a favor and get rid of this crapper. Drive the smoking hot Aston and embrace the sexy, full-figured bombshell you are. Embrace the hotness."

Kristen made the right onto Relton and parked at the curb. With great and precise effort, she slid the boring-as-hell car into park, leaned over the console and kissed Billy so hard that her body expanded—just inflated—from the rush. The buttons on her blouse might bust with all this excitement.

Billy didn't complain. No, he pulled her closer, returning the kiss with just as much reckless abandon. But that would be typical for him, wouldn't it? To jump right in. No hesitation. No second guessing. No thinking.

Reluctantly, she retreated. "We're here."

"Yes, we are." He grinned and pointed to his crotch where his jeans had gotten snug. Hers wasn't the only body expanding.

Kristen bit her lip. "I mean the address."

He spun his head to look out the windshield, his focus immediately shifting back to the mission. "Coffee shop?"

"Yes."

After retrieving his phone, he stared at the screen. "That explains why he was only here fifteen minutes. Okay. We'll move on, but let's take five and make out more. That was fun."

After days of convincing herself that Billy Tripp was too much like her sister, a troublemaker with a restless spirit, someone who couldn't grow up and settle down, someone who would distract her from her responsibilities, she really couldn't find a whole lot wrong with kissing him for five more minutes.

Five minutes turned into ten, then twenty before she finally backed away and settled her head on his shoulder, breathing in that clean, fresh-air scent of him. She closed her eyes, enjoyed the quiet of the car, the stillness that she'd been lacking for so long.

"You okay?" he asked.

"Perfect."

"Good. Me too."

"I like the quiet time with you. It feels...right. Like this is where I should be at this moment."

"Go, Billy," he cracked. When she tried to lift her head, he brought his hand to her face and rested it on her cheek to hold her in place. "What's your rush? Let's sit a minute."

Yep, he's going to break my heart. "For a few minutes. Then we need to get moving."

Within five minutes, they were on the road again and Billy directed her to a BMW dealership around the block from the coffee shop.

Kristen parked on the street. "You're sure this is the address?"

"That's what it says."

"He drives a Beemer. Maybe it needed service."

"Maybe. He was here a few minutes and gone again. Man, he was busy today."

That didn't bode well for the pile of work waiting for Kristen at the hotel. She sighed. "How many more stops do we need to make?"

Billy checked his phone again. "Three more. Then he stays put for a while. According to this, he's home now."

From the BMW dealership, they tracked Alex to an office building where he'd stayed thirty minutes, a dry cleaners and a residential street in the not-so nice part of town over the Venetian Causeway. She studied the neglected homes with bars on the doors and boarded windows. The whole place felt... wrong. God, people lived like this. People like Manny and his mother. It made Kristen sad and thankful all at the same time.

"Sweet thing, it's good we're in the boring-as-hell car or we'd get carjacked." He shook his head. "Alex was only here a couple of minutes. Does he have a drug problem? Scoring dope maybe?"

Kristen shrugged. "It wouldn't shock me. If he's hanging with Jess, he likes to party."

Her phone rang and, within seconds, Billy's went off. Something told her they'd be heading back to the hotel lickety-split.

"It's my assistant GM."

"I've got Dennis. Ruh-roh." He punched the button. "What's up?"

"Hi, Kurt. What's happening?" Kristen waited for Kurt to break whatever news he had.

Another stolen car.

She swung her head to Billy just as he said, "You are effing kidding me."

"Dammit," Kristen said, talking on her own phone. "I'm on my way back."

She disconnected and shifted the car into gear. Billy was still talking to Dennis.

"Right," he said. "Check the video. I'll be there in twenty minutes." He dropped the phone onto the console and grunted. "Fudging fantastic. So much for the signal jammer."

"A Jag this time," Kristen said.

"Yep. And now I'm pissed."

BILLY STEPPED INTO THE SECURITY OFFICE AND HELD THE DOOR for Kristen to lead the way. Dennis and two security guys stood reviewing footage with Wilson, the detective handling the thefts.

"Gentlemen," Kristen said. "Did the cameras catch it?"

"Yes, ma'am," Dennis said.

Billy nudged his way by Wilson—in yet another crappy

suit—so he could get a look at the monitors on the wall. "Run the video, please."

Within seconds, images flashed on the screens from three different angles and Billy's gaze darted over all three. "These are cameras ten, eleven and twelve?"

"Yes. Southeast end of the lot."

Different area than before. *Shiznet*. There went his blind spot theory. Either that or the beefhead thieves figured out that he'd found that hiccup in the security system. Which meant Kristen had a leak on her staff.

"Does the car belong to an overnight guest?"

"Yes," Dennis said.

Same method as last time. "The owner left the car and within a couple of minutes, a guy wearing a hoodie steps up and—*boom*—car is history." Billy went back to monitoring the video. "Wait. Back it up for me, Dennis."

Kristen moved beside him. "What is it?"

"Not sure yet."

From behind him, Billy heard Wilson sigh.

"Ms. Dante, we have a download of the footage. I need to speak with the owner of the vehicle again and then we'll be all set. I'll keep you updated."

M.H. turned to the good detective, shook his hand and walked him out. A minute later she came back to Billy.

"What is it? I can see your mind working."

He held his finger up. "Stop the video. Nope. Back it up a couple of seconds." He stepped to the monitor right in front of him and pointed. "Right there. Dennis, can you drill down on this? Zoom as far as you can."

Billy's vision blurred as the camera zoomed to the thief's hand. He blinked. *Son of a gun.* "There you go, Ms. Dante."

Kristen inched forward, her nose nearly touching the monitor. "He has a *key?*"

"Yep. My guess is, the signal jammer did its thing and they went to plan B."

"But where would they get a key?"

Billy faced the security guys. "What do we know about this Jag? Was it valet parked?"

"No," Dennis said. "The owner parked it himself."

"And he's an overnight guest?"

"Yes."

"What about his keys? Did he say they were missing?"

"No, he said he keeps them locked in the room safe when he's not using them."

Kristen let out a breath. "Well, that's good. At least we know an employee didn't sneak into his room and copy his keys."

"Where is this guest from?"

Dennis checked his notes. "Georgia. He's here for two weeks. Checked in three days ago."

Kristen twisted her lips. "Could someone have swiped his keys from his jacket? Maybe he was in the restaurant or something?"

"It's a possibility," Billy said. "Someone could have lifted the keys, used a portable key machine to make a copy and then slipped the keys back to him. The cops will get on that though. And, if that's the case, good luck finding that person."

This was just pissing him off. These guys were walking onto the property and simply driving away with cars. Nothing to it. What was really screwing with Billy was dealing with the antenna issue *and* this copied car key thing. Forget about disabling the antitheft systems. These buckwheats were good.

I'm missing something.

"Okay," he said. "Give me a download of these tapes." He

turned to Kristen. "Can I get all the information you have on the guests who have had cars stolen?"

"Sure. We'll go back to my office and I'll print it for you. Why?"

He stared back at the monitor and the thief holding that fudging car key. "I need to figure out what I'm missing. Can I use your conference room?"

"Of course."

"Good. I might be there awhile."

KRISTEN WANDERED TO THE CONFERENCE ROOM TO MAKE SURE Billy was still alive. The man had been locked away for two hours and, with his limited attention span, who knew what he'd gotten into.

The door was slightly ajar and she stuck her head in. He sat in one of the executive chairs, his elbows propped on his knees, staring at the white board spanning the wall. She knocked to get his attention.

"Can I come in?"

He smiled and sat back. "It's your building, sweet cheeks."

"True."

She walked to him, desperately trying to ignore his obvious appraisal. "You're staring."

Still seated, he held one arm out to her and she slid into it. "Sorry. Sometimes I can't help it. I like to look at you. Well, I'd like to do more than look, but you'll yell at me for that too."

Maybe.

She had to be crazy letting herself become enamored with a reckless player.

To avoid his need to stare, she slid from his arm and

moved behind the chair to examine the white board. Across the top he'd written the makes and models of what she assumed where the stolen vehicles. Below that were the owner's names, permanent addresses and the dates the cars were stolen, as well as any that were valet parked. He'd also hung the guest folios she'd printed for him.

"So, what do we have here?"

"Not a clue."

She laughed.

"I've been going over this since I came in here. I've compared all the video footage for each of the thefts. The only thing that's consistent is the thief used the antennas or, in the case of the Jag, a key."

"Is it the same guy?"

"Sometimes. So far, it's been the same guy on the Bentley, the Rover and the Jag. The others were a different guy."

"So only two?"

"Doing the actual stealing. They might be partners. In order to steal the signal with the antenna you need another person to stand close to the car and capture the signal. The times of the thefts have been random. Some are afternoon, some are evening. These guys have serious balls."

"They're confident."

"And I'm going to nail their asses."

"Music to my ears."

He spun his chair to face her and placed his hands on her hips before she could pivot away. A jittery tension shot up her arms as he moved his fingers along her hips in a gentle stroke. *So reckless.* And way too close. Plus, he was practically staring at her crotch. But oh, how she liked those hands on her. Still, she stiffened.

Using one foot, he pushed his chair back and let go of her. At least he was learning her signals.

"Well then," she said. "Secret Service visit tomorrow. Am I ready?"

"You're ready. No problem there. I told Dennis to bring in extra guys for the parking lot while they're here. We'll temporarily shut the signal jammer down too. No sense risking getting caught with that sucker. Don't be surprised if the Service is already checking you out, watching the regular day-to-day goings on."

"And am I ready for *that?*"

He grinned. "Yep. Old Dennis and I had a long talk yesterday. You're golden."

"Good." She leaned back against the table, felt her hips spread and immediately stood tall. "I'll be happy when they're out of here and give my hotel the okay. This is a big event for us."

"You should be fine. Tonight, we have our dinner date and I get to see you in that dress."

Kristen eased out a breath. The last thing she wanted was to wear the dress. A vision of her huge boobs pouring over the neckline made her stomach turn.

"And don't forget the shoes. You promised me the shoes."

"What's with you and the shoes? They're high heels. So what?"

"On you they're more than high heels. On you, they tell the world that you may be tall, but you have no problem towering over a man. Most women your height would stick with low heels. You? You say fudge it and wear them. I love that about you. Crazy hot."

If he only knew. Ordinarily, she'd have been pleased with that assessment. The problem was, he couldn't be further from the truth. She'd read somewhere that high heels made a woman look thinner. The heels, for her, had nothing to do with confidence, but a lack thereof.

"You'll get the heels and the dress, Billy. We're eating at my house though. And I'm not picking you up. You'll have to take a cab. I don't want anyone here seeing me."

He tapped his fingers on his thighs. "You're that uncomfortable about this?"

"You know it, big guy. But I made the deal and I'll stick to it. Plus, I'll give you a good meal. Then we're even. Got it?"

He slapped his hands on his knees and stood. "Got it."

"I'm going home to get ready. See you at eight. Do you need anything?"

He grinned. "I need you naked and in those heels."

"Dream on." Laughing, she shook her head and her ponytail slid over one shoulder. Billy ran his fingers over it and flipped it back.

"Pretty hair, M.H."

"Why do you call me M.H.?"

"That's my nickname for you."

"And it stands for?"

He leaned forward, brushed a kiss over her lips, and her already unstable nerves nearly bawled. Kissing Billy was always an adventure. Sometimes searing, sometimes—like now—with such tenderness it made her forget he'd eviscerate her.

"Madame Hotness," he said.

With that, he stepped around her, backhanded her on the ass and marched out.

Madame Hotness? The man definitely had a vision problem.

11

Kristen stared at herself in her full-length bedroom mirror. She didn't even have the heels on yet and wasn't sure if they would make things better or worse. Then again, wearing this dress couldn't get any worse. She hoped.

Why had she agreed to this stupid deal? Could her boobs look any more like mounds of white whale flesh? "I mean, seriously. A halter dress?"

Tears threatened and she slapped her hands over her eyes. *Get it together.* She took a breath, steadied herself and dragged her hands away to address herself in the mirror. "Now look, this is no big deal. It's a dress. Sure, it's a little tight and your hips are way too wide, but the side slit isn't bad. Your legs are good. It's the rest that's a problem. But you're gonna rock this thing. Think positive."

Glancing back at herself, she tilted her chin up. "Your hair looks awesome. Focus on that. And the legs. The legs are good. And when you put those heels on, forget it. You'll look great." She pointed at herself in the mirror. "Believe it."

I so don't believe it.

But she couldn't take time to worry about it. She slipped

into the stilettos Billy insisted on. "For God's sake, these shoes don't even match the dress." She'd probably die of a stress-induced heart attack before it was over anyway and none of it would matter.

Then the doorbell rang and the panic sliced into her, ripping at her skin. *This is it.* She wrapped her arms around her aching stomach and spun to the mirror again. All she saw were the boobs—the huge, swelling boobs—that so didn't belong in a halter dress. She couldn't move.

Paralyzed.

In front of a mirror.

Her worst nightmare.

The doorbell rang again and she curled her fingers into a tight fist. "You can do this, Kristen. He won't run. He likes you."

As fast as the shoes would let her, she sped to the stairs. "Coming!"

At the door, she stopped, focused on the marking in the grain. *Screw it.*

She threw the door open and Billy—being Billy—shifted his gaze right to her chest. She squeezed her butt cheeks together—*as if that'll make the monster boobs look smaller*—and tilted her head toward the ceiling.

Don't look at him. Don't look at him. Don't look at him.

Sickness pelted her and she bit her lip, willed herself to stand straight. A smacking noise brought her gaze back to Billy, sprawled on the ground, flat on his back and groaning, his head shifting back and forth.

"I'm not falling for that trick again," she said.

"I knew it." Another groan. "I knew that dress would slay me. I can't even stand."

Mr. Hawkins, her sixty-ish neighbor appeared in front of the house walking his dog. Of course, the dog stopped to sniff the tree. Fabulous. Not only did Mr. Hawkins see her, he was staring. At the boobs.

"Kristen. Wow," he said.

She stepped back from the doorway. Damned Billy, making her wear this dress. "Hi, Mr. Hawkins."

Billy rolled to his side and faced Mr. Hawkins. "She looks amazing doesn't she? I'm crippled here. Crippled, man!"

Mr. Hawkins' gaze was still plastered on Kristen. "I'm about to be on the ground with you."

"Oh, for crying out loud," she said. "Mr. Hawkins, thank you, but if you want your regular dose of key lime from my chef, keep walking. Billy, get off the ground before I close this door."

"I think I can crawl." He then got to all fours and did just that, which, all joking aside, was taking it a bit too far. Instinctively, she knew he was trying to make her laugh, but the crawling, the fuss gone amok, made her more conspicuous. She suddenly couldn't get the door closed fast enough. His playfulness was too much. He'd pushed it too far.

Her breath hitched and she gasped into her hand as tears filled her eyes. *Dammit.* What was she doing in this ridiculous dress? Making a fool out of herself. With Billy on her floor. Was she out of her mind?

Now that he'd seen her in the dress, she'd grab one of her slouchy sweaters and button it up to her chin.

She blinked three times to clear her eyes. "Please get up." She spun away. "Please. Just. Get off. The floor."

He shot to his feet. "What?"

Nope. Not gonna freak out in front of him. She rushed to the back of the house toward the kitchen. "Come inside. I'll get you something to drink."

"Kris?"

He came up behind her and grabbed her arm.

"I need a minute." And dammit, her voice hitched again.

"Are you mad at me? I was joking. You look great. That's all."

"No. I'm not mad."

"Then what?"

"My neighbor saw me."

His head lolled forward. "You're crying because your neighbor saw you?"

"Yes! Because women my size do not belong in dresses like this. It's embarrassing to have my sixty-year-old neighbor look at me, with my *tits* hanging out and my hips wanting to bust free. I'm humiliated, Billy. And you rolling on the floor only makes it worse." He stepped forward and she threw her hands up. "No. I don't need to be babied. I need a sweater."

Pushing him aside, she ran to the stairs, her ankles wobbling on the stilt shoes. She just needed a sweater. A sweater would ground her. Bring balance. She charged upstairs, went to her bedroom closet and yanked the closest one off the shelf.

"Hang on," Billy said from behind her.

She whipped around, holding the sweater to her chest. "No."

"I'm sorry. I thought the dress would be fun. I didn't realize it was such a problem. You should have said something."

Great. Now he thinks I'm a freak. "We made a deal. I didn't want to renege."

"I wanted to have a nice evening with you, not throw you into a homicidal rage. Take the dress off."

"We made a deal."

"Fuck the deal," he yelled. "It's only a dress. A dress I

happen to think you look fantastic in. And, from the reaction of your neighbor, I'm not the only one. But if you're not comfortable, if you don't believe it, then I don't want you in it. It doesn't matter that I'm flipping dumbstruck by how amazing you look and will probably dream about you in this dress for the next twenty years. If you're miserable, it's not worth it. So, take off the goddamned dress, meet me downstairs and we'll start over."

He turned to walk away.

"Wait," she said, and he shifted back. "It's a beautiful dress. It's just not me. I feel too exposed."

"And the old lady sweater makes you feel unexposed. I get it, but it's a crime that a woman who looks like you walks around wearing sacks."

"Filter!"

He stepped closer, his heated gaze steady on hers. "The last thing you need is for me to filter. You need a man who is attracted to you telling it straight." He grabbed the sweater and threw it over his shoulder.

"Hey—"

"Get rid of the frumpy sweaters. You've got great tits. *Rocking* tits that make me want to howl. But you insist on dumbing them down with these stupid sweaters."

"Billy!"

Had this man escaped from a mental institution?

Apparently he wasn't done yet because he threw his hands up, palms out. His face flushed red and he gritted his teeth. Then slowly, with a seemingly exhausting effort, he curled his fingers into fists. If she hadn't been ready to kill him, she'd have laughed at his attempts to control himself.

"For some reason, you've got it in your head that, because you're a little bigger than the bean-pole women running around South Beach, you're not sexy. Well, sweet cheeks, I got news for you." With both hands, he pointed to his crotch where his shorts had tented. "Fat Amazons don't give me hard-ons. Fat Amazons don't make me want to strip them naked and lick their entire body. *Fat Amazons* don't keep me up at night thinking about all the things I'd like to do to them."

At that moment Kristen couldn't do anything but stand there slack-jawed.

"Are you done?" she managed.

He cracked his neck side to side, breathed in and out a couple of times. "Uh, sorry. Got carried away. You pissed me off. I want you to see what I see."

"You don't think *I* want that?"

"I don't know what you want."

She waved a hand to her mirror. "I want to stop hating the full-length mirror. And to stop eating salads day after day because I'm afraid carbs will make me fatter. It's a vicious cycle. The less I eat, the hungrier I am and the more I beat myself up because I'm not losing weight."

"That's because your metabolism is shot. You need to feed your body and give it energy. Your body is begging you to feed it, Kristen. If you want to lose weight, start eating more of the right foods every few hours. Working out once in awhile will help, but eating lettuce for the rest of your life is not going to make you thin. Personally, I like you this way."

His gaze locked on her face, he ran a hand up her hip, over her stomach and, yes, across her breasts. Her arms and chest tingled. She closed her eyes and imagined those hands on her bare skin.

How long had it been since she'd allowed a man to really touch her? To explore her naked body?

A long time.

If only she could get out of her own head.

Billy inched closer and the heat of him swarmed her. Even with her Amazonian height and in heels, he stood an inch taller. A big man who made her feel, well, smaller. She stepped closer, slid her arms around his waist and lowered her head to his shoulder. He took his cue and wrapped her in his arms.

"This isn't so bad, huh?" he said.

"Nope. Not so bad."

"I don't understand. All I want is to look at you and all you want is to hide."

She snuggled into him and the perfection of his body snickered at her. *What would he want with me?* She squeezed her eyes closed, forced her insecurities away. Didn't he deserve her at least trying? Maybe she wasn't comfortable in the halter dress, but she could come up with something else he might like. She backed away an inch, stared up at him. "I think I have a compromise. This dress is just not me. I think I have something else you'd like though. Something that I'm comfortable in, but shows off, as you said, my rocking tits."

"Atta, girl." He set her back so he could look at her. "I never meant to make you uncomfortable. I think you're beautiful. That's all."

He might just get laid tonight.

Kristen breathed in and Billy drew his eyebrows together. "What?"

"I was thinking you might get laid tonight."

He pumped a fist. "Yes. Go, Billy. See, sometimes the lack of a filter works."

"But sometimes it doesn't. You need to focus on those times."

"Yes, ma'am."

"Now leave my room so I can change."

He nodded. "No sweaters?"

"No sweaters."

KRISTEN STEPPED INTO THE KITCHEN WEARING A PAIR OF shorts and a V-neck T-shirt that plunged into her cleavage, and Billy's groin area got active. Really active.

He threw himself off the chair onto the tiled floor and rolled to his back, groaning. After what happened upstairs, he figured a little levity couldn't hurt. Most women would have tossed him out on his asterisk for hollering at them that way.

Suddenly, Kristen was straddling him, lowering that beautiful body of hers over him, pressing that luscious rack against him and shoving her tongue into his mouth. But, with her hands against the floor, she was holding herself up. *Nice try, hotness.* He clamped his arms around her and yanked her fully on top of him. She struggled to push herself up and he rolled her over, let his weight sink into her.

"Am I crushing you?"

"No."

"Good." He rolled back over so she was on top again. "You won't crush me either."

If the squinty look was any indication, she was a non-believer.

"Kris, I definitely weigh more than you. If I wasn't hurting you, you won't hurt me. That little experiment proved it."

Slowly, she eased down, testing as she went.

"I'm still breathing." He smacked her on the ass. "Let me have it, M.H. I can take it."

And then things got crazy. She flattened herself against

him and kissed him with a roughness that had him grabbing handfuls of her hair in his grip. An almost angry surge erupted between them and he held her head in place while he nipped at her lips, her jaw, her neck, wherever he could get to.

She pushed away. "We're not doing this on my kitchen floor. Back upstairs you go."

Billy followed her to the bedroom, imagining stripping off her shirt, her shorts, her underwear, her bra. All one by one and very slowly. Finally, his own private peep show.

The minute they hit the bedroom, he grabbed her belt loop, but she slipped away to the windows, where she yanked the heavy drapes closed.

Again he reached for her and began inching her shirt up. She backed away and Billy groaned.

She headed for the adjoining bathroom. "Give me a minute."

Billy stood in the center of the room wondering what the hell he was supposed to do now? Stand there? Sit on the bed? Get naked? What?

Figuring out this woman's thought process was a serious challenge. In some ways, his verbal diarrhea worked. At least no one ever wondered.

If he got naked and slid into her bed, she might freak out. Then again, it was pretty dang obvious what they were doing here, right?

Still. He'd gotten in trouble for a lot less than assuming he was getting laid.

He remained standing. In the middle of the room. Safest place. Better than risking an ass-kicking because he hadn't thought it through. At least when he didn't filter, he wound up somewhere—even if it was the wrong place—rather than stuck in neutral.

The bathroom door opened and, before she shut off the light, he spotted her in a silk robe.

So much for his fantasy of stripping her. He could make the robe work though. Back to business here.

But when he reached for the robe's belt, she slapped his hand away and ran her hands under his shirt, lifting it over his head. At least one of them was stripping. His shorts and briefs went next and then, in the darkness, he saw her shadow hustling to the bed, climbing under the covers. With the robe on.

Hiding again.

And Billy stood there, in the dark, ass naked, wondering what the hell he'd have to do to see Kristen Dante in the raw.

He rubbed his fingers over his forehead. "Uh, sorry, this isn't working for me."

"What is it?"

Yes, Billy's pecker whined, *what is it*? He almost laughed. "You'll sleep with me, let me put my hands all over you, but I'm not allowed to see you nude. What sense does that make?"

"Billy—"

"Are you going to let me see you naked?" Silence hung heavier than the damned drapes. "Well?" He knew what the answer would be and mentally engaged the filter so he didn't blow when she said it.

"No."

"I figured."

"Billy, it's easy for people who look like you to get naked."

"Oh, here we go." He stopped, clamped his teeth together. Screw the filter. "You are not gonna make this about me. This is *your* issue."

"Yes, it is. And I'm trying to tell you how I feel."

"I know how you feel. The tent sweaters tell me how you feel. I get it, Kris. What I don't get is how, after everything we just talked about, you would think I'd see you naked and be —what?—repulsed?"

"I wouldn't think that."

Billy threw his hands in the air. "Then what's the fucking problem?"

"Filter!"

"No filter. It pisses me off that you think I'm that shallow that I'd see you naked and say, 'I'll just throw this one a pity fuck and move on.'"

Kristen sucked in a breath. Yeah, he was being an asshole. Total douche bag. That's what he was. And he refused to blame it on the ADD.

No wonder his friends grew weary of him.

He held up his hands. "Hang on. I'm sorry. Totally out of line."

She slid from under the sheet, flipped the lamp on and sat on the edge of the bed, staring down at the floor. "Yes, you were." She stood, tightened the belt on her rob. "I'm getting dressed."

Blew that one, Billy boy. "Kris—"

She headed for the bathroom. "I need five minutes to get my thoughts together."

That would be the least he could give her. Damn, how could he be so totally inept at controlling himself? For years, he'd been practicing listening skills, focusing on the words and forcing himself to not interrupt. Lately, it had all come apart.

When she shut the bathroom door he sat on the bed, breathed in and out a few times, cracked his neck and forced himself to quiet his mind.

Breathe. He opened his eyes, focused on the closed drapes. "I'll meet you downstairs," he called to her and hoped to hell she wouldn't throw him out.

Five minutes later, she came into the kitchen wearing the same V-neck shirt and shorts. At least she wasn't in one of the tents. Maybe there was hope.

Billy, seated at the table, tapped his fingers. "How pissed are you?"

She leaned against the counter. Arms folded. "Five minutes ago, I was *really* pissed. Now, not as much. Nothing you said was untrue. You're the king of truth and, as long as it's the truth, it should be okay, right?"

"We both know that's crap."

"I have self-image issues. It's true. The problem is, you want me to do something about it and I've never been able to figure out how to do that. It's easy for you to tell me I'm beautiful, and regardless of what you think, I do believe it when I hear you say it. The problem is, when I look in the mirror, I don't *see* it. So, unless you're going to hang out with me all day telling me I'm beautiful, we both have to get used to the fact that I'm uncomfortable being naked."

"Or figure out a way around it."

"If you're up for that, I'm in. If not, walk out of here now. No harm, no foul. I'll understand and we'll continue on as business acquaintances."

"Is that what you want?"

She smiled, but it was that sarcastic you-are-such-a-child smile. "Billy, where are we going with this? Once your work at my hotel is done, you'll leave. You don't live here and you travel a lot. You told me yourself you don't own a home, or even a car because you don't want to be tied down to one place."

"That's not what I said."

She sighed.

"I said I hadn't found the place I wanted to be tied to yet. Don't write me off because of your perception of what I said. The truth is, I'd be ecstatic to find someplace to call home. I'm open to it and very willing."

"Really? You're interested in taking on my hang-ups when all it will probably amount to is a brief affair?"

"You don't know that."

"I know I enjoy your company and you make me laugh, but I have a lot of responsibilities. I like order. I don't need you stomping all over my heart and taking off. I'm not interested in that. If you want a fling, great, fantastic, let's do it. But don't expect me to hand over my insecurities, to allow you into my own personal hell, when you'll probably be moving on sometime soon. It's not fair."

Billy sat back. Blew out a breath. She was right. He'd be going soon. Did he have the right to ask her for anything? Particularly when it came to her vulnerabilities?

Probably not.

"You're quiet," she said.

"It doesn't happen often. I'm processing. I mean, I'm stuck. I want you. I love hanging out with you. You're smart and funny and selfless. I wish you could see yourself the way I see you. Beyond that, it's too early. I don't know what'll happen. I know I don't want to walk out this door. I want more of whatever this is. And that usually doesn't happen. It's gotta be good, right?"

"Sometimes. Sometimes it ends up being painful. I don't think either one of us wants that."

"Hell no. But sometimes it winds up being great. I think we could be great. You get me. You get that I run my mouth and you're not afraid to tell me when I'm pushing too hard. And I love that I listen when you tell me. Usually I don't listen. I press on because I need the attention and I lose sight of the boundaries. I guess, with you, I know I have your attention."

"That, you do."

He held his hand palm up on the table. "What do you think? Can we give this thing, whatever it is, a try? I won't stomp on you."

He'd try damned hard. That he knew. She slid her hand over his and squeezed. "You may not be able to control it. When you leave, I might be heartbroken."

"But when I leave, it might not be for good. We don't know yet."

Come on, Kris. Step to the plate. Would giving him a chance be so wrong? He had a feeling they might be the perfect storm.

"Well, I have a great steak here that my chef prepared. How do you like it?"

He grinned. "Medium well. You?"

She shrugged. "It's been so long since I've eaten steak, I'm not sure."

"So, you were going to cook me a steak and not eat it?"

"Yes."

Twisted. "No. You need to eat some of it." He held his thumb and index finger up and squeezed them together. "Just a little bit. The protein is good for you. Then we'll go for a walk so you don't feel guilty about eating. How's that? A good meal, a little exercise. It's perfect."

A plate covered in foil sat on the counter and she glanced at it for a long moment. *Come on, Kris, eat the steak.*

She turned back to him. "Let's try it. See what happens."

12

A T NINE THE NEXT MORNING, BILLY STOOD ON THE FRINGE OF
the Dante parking lot, scanning his surroundings. Five
guards were stationed throughout each quadrant of the
exterior lot and the parking garage had two more guards
monitoring the exit. He almost *wanted* the beefheads to
attempt a breach of this set-up.

Early sun slipped through cloud cover warming him in
spite of a fifty-five-degree morning. Once the clouds burned
off, it would be another great day in paradise.

I could stay here.

He breathed in the moist ocean air and let the idea of
squatting in South Beach burrow farther into his brain. The
idea was definitely growing on him.

And it wasn't all about the weather.

Kristen Dante had a boatload to do with it, but he didn't
want to spend too much time analyzing it or he'd scare the
crap out of himself. Not doing that. He'd do what he always
did and roll with it. Where he landed, he landed.

Right now, he had to deal with this parking lot. The
Secret Service had arrived at 8:00 a.m. and Kristen got right

to reviewing the security procedures he had suggested. Hopefully, all would go well, she'd pass muster and Billy wouldn't get his ass handed to him because his plan sucked.

He knew it didn't suck though. Vic, Mike Taylor and Monk had declared it solid.

Still, the way Billy's luck was running, he could see a bunch of cars getting boosted the day the Secret Service was on site.

His radio beeped and he slid it from his belt. "What's up?"

"Not sure," Keith said. "A car came in the southeast entrance a few minutes ago. Two young guys. They parked and are sitting there."

Young guys. Didn't sound like the beefheads. Adrenaline poured into Billy's body, that amazing fix for his action deprived psyche, and he sprinted along the outer edge of the lot toward Keith's location. *This might be it*. A chance to nab these fudgers. When he got within range, he slowed to a walk. Just a vacationing guy strolling by. He turned his back to the lot and buzzed Keith on the radio.

"Don't approach me. Act like I'm a guest. Where are they?"

"Blue Volvo parked in row H. Third spot from the left."

"Got it. Go to another area of the lot. Let's see what these guys are up to."

Billy kept walking, but peered at the blue Volvo from the corner of his eye. He reached the far corner of the lot and ducked behind some cars to make his way back to row H.

One of the guys—definitely not one of his buddies—got out of the car, a set of keys in his hand. He wore a blue sweatshirt and yanked the hood up.

Game on. Gotcha, you rat bastard.

Billy's body hummed but he stayed crouched between

two vehicles waiting to see where R.B. went. Finally, he'd nab this guy.

R.B. walked roughly fifty feet to a BMW 7 series sedan. A *bleep-bleep* pierced the air as R.B. unlocked the car and jumped behind the wheel.

That fucking simple. Unbelievable.

Billy radioed Keith to grab the other guy, snatched his nine-millimeter from the holster at his waist and exploded from his spot, hauling ass toward the Beemer.

The young guy hit the gas when he saw Billy jump in front of the car. *Don't you run my ass over.*

Screeching tires fired a brain synapse—the guy in the Volvo bolting—but his eyes remained fixed on the kid in the Beemer.

"Hands up! Now."

R.B. threw his hands up and Billy stepped over, gun still raised, to open the door.

"Hotel security. Out of the car."

The kid, who couldn't have been more than seventeen years old, did as he was told. "You got ID to prove this is your car?"

Silence, but junior's gaze shot left and right.

"Don't try to run," Billy said. "There are guards everywhere."

"Shit."

"You're not kidding."

Thirty minutes later, Detective Wilson strolled into the Dante security office, saw the hoodie-wearing toddler and said, "What have you got?"

Billy had already checked the kid for weapons and parked him in a chair, but the kid wasn't talking. Nor did he have any ID.

"You're looking at what I got," Billy said. "I caught him

trying to nab a car. The car is registered to a guest from Alabama. We located the owner via cell phone. He was walking on the beach when our Boy Scout tried to take the Beemer for a spin. Owner's never seen this kid before. And yet, he had a key to the car. He has no ID. His buddy was in a blue Volvo and scrammed before we could grab him. We got the plate."

Wilson took the note with the plate number. "They're probably stolen anyway. Has he said anything?"

"Other than 'shit'? No. I told the security team to leave him until you got here." Billy grinned. "Didn't want to screw up anything by violating his rights before you Mirandized."

Wilson twisted his mouth. "Thank you."

Billy jerked his head to the hallway and Wilson followed him out. "Can I watch when you question him? I'm trying to figure out how the hell these guys are getting car keys."

Wilson hesitated and Billy jumped in. "I did you a large by calling off the security team when they wanted to question him."

Letting out a breath, Wilson said, "Awright. But you'll watch on a monitor. It'll be my ass if I let you sit in."

"I'm good with that."

"Let's go then."

"Hey, what are the chances these cars could be getting smuggled out of the country?"

Wilson shrugged. "In Miami? Anything is possible."

AFTER A LONG DAY WITH THE SECRET SERVICE, KRISTEN decided the drive home would require more energy than she could summon and opted to stay in her suite at the hotel. Despite a foiled car theft, which the Secret Service never knew about, the security plan had been cleared.

Mission accomplished.

Billy had promised her he'd be by to give her an update on the car theft suspect, and, with that in mind, she'd opted to forego her normal ratty shorts and T-shirt. Instead she chose a nicer pair of ratty shorts with a nicer T-shirt. She'd even made it one of the plunging V-necks he liked. Why not? Give him a thrill.

A knock sounded, she checked the peephole, found Billy on the other side and opened the door. He held out his hand. Hanging from two fingers was a black blindfold.

She couldn't wait to hear this one. Slowly, she took the blindfold from him. "And? What?"

He jerked his head toward her hand. "You're going to have sex with me while I'm wearing that."

Blood surged, but she remained frozen in her spot, rooted like a hundred-year-old tree, her limbs too heavy to move. Was he really standing in the hallway of her hotel proclaiming they'd have blindfolded sex?

Her mouth moved, but the words stayed trapped inside her throat. She tried again and managed a gurgling noise. A hard slap of her hand against her chest knocked the temporary paralysis loose.

She grabbed his arm, hauled him in and checked the corridor. No one in earshot. "You're in the damned hallway."

"Sorry. I got excited."

"I realize that, but a little restraint would be nice." She threw the blindfold at him and made her way to the sofa.

"Come on, Kris. This is a good plan. I wear the blindfold and you don't have to be stressed about me seeing you naked."

She laughed. Typical man. Anything to get a little.

"No, seriously. This is not bullsh—er, dung." He whapped himself on the head. "I figure if we can get you comfortable being naked in front of me, you'll relax and go with it."

"And this has nothing to do with the blindfold being a little kinky?"

He grinned. "Can we say bonus?"

She grinned back. "Can we say *no?*"

He dropped onto the couch. "M.H., you're being too hasty here. This plan has its merits."

"You're insane."

"Pfft, what's your point?" He slid the blindfold over his eyes. "With this on, I can't see anything. Whaddya say?"

Tilting her head, she examined him sitting there, looking beyond ridiculous in that blindfold while he waited for her to respond. Clearly, he was serious. How incredibly funny. And, in an off way, thoughtful.

She puckered her lips, took a tiny step forward and waved her hand in front of his face.

Nothing.

Gave him the finger.

Still nothing.

If he could see anything, he'd be laughing by now. Maybe he had something here. This blindfold might work.

"You still there?" he asked.

"I'm here." Losing her damned mind for even contemplating this idea. Billy Tripp was already creating chaos in her busy life. If she had sex with him, she'd get attached and then she'd be a goner. Total destruction.

But a man who looked like him, all wide shoulders and perfect cheekbones was hard to resist.

He snapped the blindfold off, wiggled his eyebrows. "How about it M.H.? Are we on?"

No. "I don't know." *What?* "It's a little weird."

"It is not. People do this all the time."

"Please. I do *not* want to have *that* conversation with you." Definitely didn't need to know about his past sexual exploits.

"I know you're thinking about it."

She laughed. "I'm totally thinking about it. And I'm not happy."

He sighed and gently rested his forehead against her stomach. Something in that small gesture seized her and she lifted her hands, set them on his head. *Total destruction.*

"What will get you over the finish line?"

Why would she want to cross the finish line when it terrified her? "Tell me about the car thief."

Billy lifted his head, stared up at her like he hadn't quite heard. Yes, she owed him an answer. If she couldn't give him that, she should at least explain. "I need a minute, Billy. Tell me about the thief while I think about you in my bed."

He smacked his hands together. "Now we're talking. His name is Calvin Dobbs. He turns seventeen next week. He lives in Disciples territory."

"A gang member?"

He nodded. "The cops can't prove it. He's never been arrested, but he was questioned about a robbery last year."

Kristen sat on the arm of the sofa and propped her feet on the cushion next to Billy. "Barely seventeen and stealing cars? What a waste."

"Outside of that, the cops didn't get much from him. They turned him over to his parents but fully expect to see him again at some point."

This was her fear about Manny. She hoped that sweet boy never wound up in a gang. She'd make sure of it. Even if Manny's mother had to work long hours, Manny would be tended to.

"Do we know how he got the car key?"

Billy shook his head and ran his finger along her calf, making squiggly lines as he went. The sensation tickled, but the intimacy of his hands on her skin warmed her girl parts.

"He wouldn't say. The kid is probably too terrified to talk. Wilson says he'll probably get probation, which means his gangbanger friends will love him for not being a rat and he'll continue on his path of criminal activity."

Kristen slid to the sofa next to him and commandeered his wayward hand. "So, from what you know, does it help with your investigation at all?"

"Not sure. I need to get into your conference room and add the latest car information to my board. See if there are similarities anywhere. I'm gonna check the GPS on Alex again, see if he's made any interesting stops. Tomorrow I'll retrace his steps again."

"We can head down to the conference room if you'd like."

But if the solid stare he gave her was any indication, Billy had no interest in the conference room.

"In a while. Let's talk about my brilliant blindfold idea. How close am I to the finish line?"

She rolled her eyes. "Getting closer."

"Excellent."

She backed away. "I opened a bottle of wine."

"Good for you."

He made a move for her neck and she nearly jumped off the sofa. "Want a glass?"

"No, but you should feel free to consume all the alcohol you want."

She made her way to the wet bar. "Thanks so much."

"We'll get you good and relaxed."

"How very unselfish of you."

"I do what I can."

After pouring her wine, she sat at the other end of the couch.

"Really?" he said. "You're going to sit all the way over there? After I got you cleared with the Secret Service today?"

Leave it to him to blackmail her with the Secret Service. She inched closer.

"That's so wrong."

She scooted a little closer. "No cars were stolen today, so I'll give you another couple of inches."

He must have had enough and slid next to her. At least he kept his hands to himself. "Your security for the event is in place. Vic has a guy down here who helped us put a team together. I'm meeting with them tomorrow to go over everything."

"Thank you. You've saved my butt on this Secret Service thing."

"I'm sure you'll figure out a way to compensate me." He nudged closer, leaned forward and kissed her neck.

The man had great lips. Those lips traveled down the side of her neck, across her jaw, until he reached her mouth, where he nibbled on her bottom lip.

She slid her arm around his shoulder and held him there.

"She's weakening," he sang.

"Filter."

"Sorry."

He glided his hand up her waist—*please don't press too hard and feel the fat*—to her breasts and hesitated. She didn't stop him and felt him smile through the kiss. And then his palm was flat against her breast, pressing, and her girl parts required oxygen. Copious amounts.

"Happy girl parts," she said.

He snorted, which, had it been anyone else, would have

been a tad awkward. With Billy, it seemed status quo.

She retreated. "Get that blindfold out before I lose my nerve."

He held it up and grinned. "Right here, babe."

Figured. "Here's the plan. You get into the bed, put the thing on and then I'll get naked."

"No. How about, I get into bed and you keep your clothes on. Then we can take them off piece by piece. I have this whole fantasy going about you stripping in front of me."

"Billy, you'll have a blindfold on. What does it matter?"

"Hey, it's my fantasy. Stop ripping it apart."

He made his way to the adjoining bedroom, stripping his shirt off as he walked. Oh, to have that confidence. When he got to the bed, he dropped his jeans and slid off his underwear. Just like that. No hesitation. Then again, if she were built like him, she'd probably have no problem getting naked.

And staying that way.

Well, it could be a goal. Something to work toward.

He snapped the blindfold on and dropped spread-eagle on the bed, his erection poking straight up in the air. "Service me."

Kristen slapped her hands over her face, her cheeks ablaze. "You can't just lay there. It'll make me nervous. You need to participate."

"I'll participate. Just start stripping. How about a little music? Something stripperish."

Not a chance. Still, she sat on the bed, snatched her iPod from the dock and chose a playlist that included Michael Bublé. "It's not stripperish, but it'll do."

She glanced back at him lying there, flat on his back, his gaze—had he not been blindfolded—pointed to the ceiling. She leaned over and kissed him, let her hand travel down the smoothness of his chest and over his perfect pecs. She fiddled with the gold medal hanging around his neck. "You're so beautiful."

I can't believe he wants me.

"Eh, everything landed in the right place."

"I'll say."

"She's weakening," he sang.

Kristen leaned back, waved her hand in front of his face. Nothing. "Can you see anything?"

"Nope. Start stripping."

I must be out of my mind. "Let me close the blinds."

"Hello? We're thirty-five floors up and I'm blindfolded. Leave them."

She bit her bottom lip. Why not? No one could see. She slipped out of her T-shirt and tossed it on the floor. "Shirt is gone."

"We need a stripper pole in here."

"Forget it, sailor. Nice try though."

"Give my horny ass credit for the attempt."

The urge to bury herself under the covers consumed her and she breathed in. "Billy?"

"Right here."

"This feels weird. Like I'm forcing it."

He sat up, blindfold still on. "We don't have to do this. The point is for you to be comfortable."

She nodded, but he couldn't see, so she grabbed his hand and kissed it. "I know. What if we, well, just snuggled for a bit? I'll take my clothes off and we'll just lay here. Would that be okay?"

He flopped onto the bed again. "Come to me, dahling."

Complete lunatic. Talk about innovative though. "Okay. This might work. We'll just cuddle. See what happens."

He smiled. "As long as we cuddle the right parts, I'm all

over it."

For this, she laughed.

Ten minutes later, they were still lying there, Billy naked and Kristen in only her bra and panties, wrapped around each other, skin to skin—with the lights on—and she couldn't stop grinning because his erection was poking her thigh. He wanted her.

And she was almost naked.

With the lights on.

She roamed her hand over his hip. "I love this."

"It's not too shabby."

"Um, how disappointed would you be if we just did this? No sex."

He shrugged. "Pretty darn disappointed. My physical state cannot be a mystery to you. But if you're not ready, we'll wait. The point of this pseudo waterboarding session is for you to be comfortable. Besides, it wouldn't be the first time I took matters into my own hands, so to speak."

She dipped her head into his chest and laughed. "You really need to use that filter."

"Why? It's the truth. I mean, I can't stay in this condition."

Horrifyingly too much information. "But some things I don't need to know. Okay?"

"I'm all about pleasing you so I'll keep my mouth shut."

Not in this lifetime did she imagine him able to stay quiet. "You'll keep your mouth shut? Really?"

"Ease up, girlfriend. I'm trying here. Bad enough I'm not getting laid."

He was grinning though. Teasing her. This man was too sweet to break her heart. From somewhere inside her, she believed it.

Or was at least starting to.

13

BILLY DROVE TOM DANTE'S BORROWED MERCEDES INTO THE BMW dealership and found a spot right in front of the three-stories of windows lining the façade of the building. The sales guys would be tracking them to see what they were driving and what they would see was a hundred-thousand-dollar car that didn't necessarily stand out like Kristen's Aston would.

"Okay, sweet cheeks. Time to car shop."

They'd been trailing old Alex all morning in the P.O.S. sedan and when he went to the same park he'd visited two days ago, Billy decided to cut bait on Alex and trail the guy he had met with. Besides, Kristen wanted the 4-1-1 on why Billy was so bent on Alex and he thought following the other guy would distract her. Right now, he wasn't ready to fess up to the beefhead in the shed and Alex using the same Arabic word. Eventually, he'd have to tell her, but then he'd also have to explain why he'd never shared the shed incident. And he wasn't ready for that.

Alex's buddy led them back to the BMW dealership from their last journey.

"So, we're car shopping?" Kristen asked.

"Pretend car shopping. I'm buying my gorgeous fiancé—that's you, by the way—a BMW for her birthday."

She rolled her eyes.

"M.H., just go with it. It's a cover story. I need to get eyes on this guy."

"I've always liked Beemers."

"Maybe a convertible. Like your Aston." He tweaked her nose. "You'll have to wear a hat with that fair skin."

"Story of my life."

He grinned. "Let's go shopping. Honey."

The minute they walked through the sliding double doors into the slick, black-and-chrome-encased showroom, a salesman approached them. Billy held his arms wide. "My fiancé needs a hot car. I'm sure there's nothing half as gorgeous as her, but do your best."

The sales guy glanced at Kristen then back to Billy. "Certainly. I'm Dave." He stuck his hand out and Billy shook it.

"I'm Jack. This is Elle."

"Nice to meet you Jack and Elle. Did you have a price point in mind?"

"A lot." Billy scanned the showroom and all the desks lining the far wall. No park guy.

Dave took another gander at Kristen's fancy dress and spiked heels and apparently determined she did, indeed, have that I'm-loaded look. "Let's head over here. I have a nice 7 series you might like."

"This blue one is nice." Kristen dragged her hand along the hood of the car like she'd done with her Aston that day in front of the hotel, and Billy breathed deep. Something about the way she did that always turned his thoughts carnal.

He cleared his throat. "Yeah, honey, get in there. See

what you think. Maybe we'll drive it. I'm gonna check out the service department."

"Our service department is the best in Miami," Dave said. "Ranked number one three years running."

"Even better. Take care of my girl while I check it out."

"He has a fetish with service department cleanliness," Kristen said. "So high maintenance."

Billy cracked a smile at her theatrics and headed through yet another set of sliding doors. Another bank of windows separated the white walled room from the garage area. Three men stood at stations helping customers. No park guy. Check that off the list. He wandered around the room, looked out into the service bay where a couple of guys checked incoming cars. No park guy.

"May I help you, sir?" one of the employees at a station asked.

"I'm about to spend a ridiculous, flippin' filthy amount of money on a car for my fiancé. I want to make sure the service department can handle all her hotness."

The service guy stared at him. Totally fudging deadpan. Not even a smile. He did tug on his collar, though, and Billy suppressed a laugh. People never knew what to do with him. Not that he minded. He liked knocking people off their perches and, according to Vic, that was no longer acceptable.

Billy decided to put this poor schmo out of his misery. "You got a service manager around here?"

"Certainly. Tim Dupont. He's in his office. Let me get him."

You do that. Billy wandered a few feet and nosed around a corner where cars were being tended to. Unfortunately, most of the mechanics had their heads inside cars and he couldn't see their faces.

No matter. He didn't think park guy was a mechanic anyway. Not with the gray dress slacks and oxford he'd been wearing that morning.

"Sir?" a man's voice called.

Billy faced Tim Dupont, who wore gray dress slacks and an oxford shirt.

Yeeha. Park Guy.

After getting a tour of the service bays from Captain Tim, Billy decided to wrap his reconnoitering for the day. He grabbed M.H. and told Dave-the-salesman they'd be back after they checked out the Jaguars.

Back to Dante they went and, in the boardroom, Billy stood in front of the white board staring at his notes on the two BMW car thefts. Kristen stood to his right, hands on hips, waiting for him to say something. The quiet, sustained energy she exuded almost sent him into a sexual haze.

Something about this woman, so cool under fire, made him want to rattle her.

He gestured to the board. "There it is."

"What?"

"See any similarities with the Beemers?"

She studied the board. "No."

"Keep looking, M.H."

Her gaze zeroed in on it—*atta, girl*—and then moved to the next section on the board. "The keys."

"Yep."

"The thief had keys to both BMWs. The only other car the thief had a key to was the Jag. The rest were stolen using the antenna."

He turned back to the board. "My guess is Alex is working with Tim Dupont, AKA park guy, AKA service manager, to get duplicate keys made."

"And what? He's paying the service manager for duplicates? How does he get the car information?"

Billy stepped back, leaned against the table and dragged Kristen with him. She propped one hip against the table. Wow, she was close. He kept his gaze on the white board. Her simple presence continued to be a major distraction for his horny ass.

"That's easy," he said. "Someone probably looks at the VIN number through the windshield. Anyone can see it. Maybe our buddy Alex pays the service manager to look up the VIN number in the system and, once he finds the car, he gets the key codes and makes him a dupe."

Kristen scrunched her adorable nose. "It's that easy?"

"With honest people? No. The dealership is supposed to ask for ID before they make duplicate keys. In this case, the guy is on the take and he's not worrying about ID." Billy stepped back to the white board. "And look at this. Both guests were staying at the hotel a while. They may need some time to get keys made, so they want cars that will be around more than one night."

"Billy—"

He held a finger up so he didn't lose his thought. "How do these thieves know which BMWs to pick?"

"Someone in my hotel is sharing guest information."

KRISTEN STOOD STARING AT BILLY, TRYING TO ABSORB THE idea that she needed to locate the one employee who revealed confidential data.

Billy slid a chair out for her then dropped into one himself.

"I guess we need to start questioning employees who have access to guest information? That'll take hours."

"Or we start with Jess."

Kristen groaned. Would her sister do that? Steal guest information for her boyfriend? A guy she barely knew? Impossible. Even with their strained relationship Kristen refused to believe her sister would betray her for a guy who cheated on her. All of this was based on Billy's assumption Alex was indeed involved. And if so...

"Wait. Alex cheated on Jess with a desk clerk from the Ocean Blue. Maybe he's getting guest information for that hotel from her?"

"Makes sense."

"But the GM told me no cars had been stolen."

Billy tapped his fingertips together. "Not yet. He could be grooming her."

"Grooming?"

"Getting her primed. Playing her. If this guy is a decent con he'd have been watching her, figuring out if she were vulnerable enough to fall for his line of crap. If so, by the time he gets done with her, she'll be so love struck she'll give him anything. Including guest information."

"But Jess is far from vulnerable."

Billy leaned forward and rested his hands on her knees. "Yeah, but she's a party girl. Would anyone question her walking up to a computer in this hotel? Even if she was wasted?"

"I don't know."

"Let's find a way to talk to her without accusing. Maybe this richweed figured her for a mark and then backed off when he couldn't get anything out of her."

Kristen's cell phone rang. "This is Kristen...now?...I'll call him. Thanks."

She ended the call and immediately went to work looking for something on her phone. "The GM at the Ocean Blue left a message at the desk. Apparently he left me a voicemail while we were out. He just called again and needs to speak to me ASAP."

"Did he say what he wanted?"

"No, but I'm about to find out." She held the phone to her ear. "Rod? Kristen Dante returning your call...How can I help you?...When?...Do you mind if I put you on speaker? I have my security person with me."

Billy bolted upright. "What?"

"They had two cars stolen today."

Hot da—diggity—dog.

"Rod," M.H. said, "I have Billy Tripp here. Billy, Rod Perkins."

"Rod, what kind of cars were they?"

"One was a Jaguar and one a Mercedes."

Billy motioned like he was turning a key. If the Jag was stolen with a key, the thefts were probably connected.

Kristen nodded. "Rod, I'm wondering if these thefts are related. Would you mind if Billy and I came over and took a look at your footage? If it's the same two men, Billy has been able to implement security upgrades you might be interested in. Going forward, maybe we can somehow work together to protect our properties from these thefts."

"Come on over." Rod hung up.

"Abrupt guy," Billy said.

Kristen dropped her phone on the table. "He's not winning any congeniality contests. That's for sure. Let's see what his footage has. Maybe it'll tell us something."

"M.H., you're extremely hot when you're on a quest for justice."

"Yeah, well, I have the Senate Majority Leader about to

pop in and I don't need any drama. Right now, you and your blindfold are providing enough distractions."

AFTER REVIEWING THE OCEAN BLUE THEFT FOOTAGE AND finding that, yes, indeed, it appeared to be the same men, Kristen left Billy to discuss security upgrades with Rod and came back to the hotel to wait for him.

And here he was, knocking on the door to her suite, and all she wanted was to get her clothes off. Good grief. Normally all she wanted was clothes on. And worse, the man was totally distracting her from the important things. Like running her hotel.

She swung the door open. "Hi."

"M.H., looking splendid tonight."

Nice of him to notice she'd put the low-cut shirt on. She was so bad. Bad, bad, bad.

She grabbed his arm, hauled him through the doorway and said, "Hurry up and tell me what happened so we can blindfold you."

Billy smacked his hands together, shook them in front of him and stared at the ceiling. "Thank you." He dropped to his knees. "Thank you!"

"Enough. I get it. Just tell me."

Moron that he was, he crawled to the sofa and she laughed at him. At least until he settled her on his lap. *No you don't.* She made a move to slide off.

"Nuh-uh," he said, "we've talked about this. You are not going to crush me. Just sit here and quit squirming. Besides, you're getting me excited."

"Filter!"

"What? It's the truth. You're bound to feel the evidence at any second."

"Ooh!" Wow, that was something. Her cheeks burned, a fierce heat storming her system.

"There you go."

"It's rather unnerving."

Billy slid his hand up her legs in slow circular motions, and her want for him simmered slow and steady.

"Enough to get you to strip without me in the blindfold?"

"No."

"Dang it."

Leaning into him, she asked, "How did it go at Ocean Blue?"

"The two cars stolen belong to guests who are both staying more than seven days."

Could be good news. "It ties into your theory about the thieves knowing the guests will be around long enough to get duplicate keys."

"Yep. Old Rod is going to bite the bullet on installing a signal jammer. His moral compass is not nearly as steady as yours."

"I'm not surprised. He runs a tight ship over there."

"And you don't?"

Was that a compliment? She wasn't sure. Running a hotel required constant attention. In her world, days off didn't exist. Her phone always rang. And she always answered. Still, she didn't want to be on the same level as Rod Perkins. "Not like him. He's brutal to work for."

"Eh, he doesn't look so tough."

"Not to you. You play with AK-47s for a living."

Billy tilted his head, thought about it. "True. Oh, guess who I ran into while old Rod was giving me the tour?"

"Who?"

"Alex."

Could Alex being at the Ocean Blue the night of a car theft be a coincidence?

Not a chance.

"What was he doing?"

"He entered the hotel while I was outside checking the front security."

Billy moved his hand up her leg again and, unable to concentrate, she tried to slide from his lap, but he held her in place. She gave up. Not such a hardship. "Probably the nightclub. He's big into the clubs. Kind of early though."

"Or, maybe he was picking up the chick he cheated on Jess with. I tried to follow him, but I lost him in the lobby."

"What do you think?"

The hand moved up to her waist. "I think after you're done torturing me, I'm going to take a cold shower and download the list of addresses Alex visited in the last week."

"Why? We already know he's been to the BMW dealership and is probably involved."

Finally, he shifted her from his lap, levered himself over her and she eased onto her back with him on top of her. He trailed kisses down her neck and all that heat came roaring back. *He's just too good at this.*

He glanced at her between kisses. "I can have Janet from my office run the addresses and scc if she can get me names of the property owners. Then, Madame Hotness, we are going to cross-check the names against your employees and the ones at the Ocean Blue. If we find any matches, it might be a lead to finding the person leaking guest information."

"How long will that take?"

"A day or two."

The kisses continued and she breathed in, tilted her head back and closed her eyes. So good. "I'm going to be devastated if one of my employees is involved in this."

"I know you are. Maybe it won't be the case. Who knows? Besides, it's getting late and I want to play with my blindfold. What do you say, M.H.? How about a no-peep show for Billy before bed? I won't even bug you for sex. Unless you want me to."

Funny man. But all in all, Mr. Good-At-This accomplished his mission. Suddenly the fat Amazon was all about getting undressed and that could only be categorized as a new experience. Such a fool she was. *Live with it, Kristen. Enjoy him while you can.*

"Sorry, big boy. I'm having fun just playing with the blindfold."

And then she made the mistake of looking into his eyes and found his gaze on her, studying her face with such intensity she nearly coiled into herself. She turned away.

"I'm not staring at your chest," he said. "And sometimes I should be allowed to just look at you."

She glanced back at him, his gaze still on her face. And yes, she kissed him. A soft, lingering kiss that made her legs liquefy. Dammit if he wouldn't break her heart when he left. Why couldn't he have stayed a hit and run driver?

At least then she'd have a reason to hate him.

14

Billy stood at the edge of Dante's parking lot, the quiet of the morning relieving his battered mind. Apparently, people on South Beach weren't early risers because pedestrians were nil and only a lone car cruised by. He propped his foot against a light pole and his hamstrings barked at him through the stretch. Good run. He'd drive the piece-o-crap car along the oceanfront to measure, but his body knew distances and his endorphins indicated five miles.

He switched legs, breathed in and bent farther into the stretch. *Yeah, baby*. He could get used to these morning beach runs. Easily.

Billy heard a vehicle approach from behind. He swung his head right and watched a blue cargo van come to a stop. He set his foot on the ground just as the van's door slid open. Three guys jumped out. He didn't recognize them, but had no doubt they worked for the beefhead who'd visited him in the shed.

Heading straight for him, these guys didn't look like they wanted to shoot the shit. One was big and brawny, which was saying something since Billy was no small fry. The shorter ones held their stocky frames in a way he knew sometimes hid strength.

Three of them. Coming right at him. Clearly wanting a piece of whatever he had.

Fierce, juicy adrenaline streamed and Billy whirled around. *Bam!* He jammed an elbow into the closest guy's nose. The vicious crunch made that schnoz toast. The guy reeled back but his buddies pounced before Billy could react. One stuck a cloth bag over his head while the other put him into a bear hug and hauled him backward.

"I'm a little sick of you assholes cornering me."

He snapped his head back and headbutted the guy holding him. Later, that would hurt. Right now, not so much. Not with the adrenaline drowning the pain.

"Son of a bitch," the guy said, still hanging on. "Hold still before I pop you."

"Good luck with that." Billy headbutted him again.

One of the jagweeds grabbed his feet. The other held his torso and they tossed him into the back of the van. Billy kicked out, connected with someone fleshy—one of the shorter, squat looking guys?

"Ow! Fucker."

Something hard and rubbery smacked against his skull. Pain erupted, blurred what vision he had inside the bag.

His stomach pitched and he closed his eyes.

Damn.

Concentrating on the task, he opened his eyes. A spinning sensation forced them closed again.

BILLY CAME AWAKE SLOWLY, HIS SKULL POUNDING LIKE A SON of a biscuit. He kept his eyes closed, felt the warm sun on his face and knew that wherever he was, it was deep shit. A small splash from his left sounded. Water. He caught a barely-there whiff of something foul. Swampy. Finally, he opened his eyes and stared at a bright blue sky. Sunlight scalded him and he slammed his eyes closed.

Something soft, yet prickly tickled his arm. Grass? And his sneakers were wet.

Not wanting to stare up at the sky again, he turned his head sideways and, once more, pried his eyes open.

He sucked in a breath and let it out slowly. Three feet in front of him, a gator sat on the edge of a shallow canal. Huge fucking gator. Seven...eight feet at least. And big around. Gargantuan.

An insane snapping fried his brain. *Focus.* Inching his head sideways, he surveyed the immediate area and with subtle movement, glanced to the right of the gator—*and the shit gets deeper*—baby gators.

Sons of bitches dropped him by a nest. This mama would tear him to shreds. Still, he remained in his spot. No quick movements. "Easy now, girlfriend. I'm not interested in those babies of yours. All I want is to find the fuckers who dropped me here and rip 'em apart. Maybe you can help me with that."

Yeah, that would be good. If he got out of this colossal shit storm, he'd feed those schmucks to this very gator and watch the festivities.

Suddenly, gator girl lunged. Billy whipped his arm in front of his face to block the bite and—*yow*—those prickly teeth sunk into his flesh, tearing through his skin and ripping at him. A howl shredded his throat and he unleashed it while pain nearly split him in half.

For a moment, he stared into the blackness of hungry gator eyes. Attempting to tug his arm free would be futile.

Gator girl chomped harder and Billy grunted against the agonizing pressure of those jaws chowing on him. "Goddammit."

His mind tripped back to a memory of gators swinging into a death roll to tear bone and muscle from its prey. If she went into the death roll, she'd drown him.

No deal, girlfriend.

And then she did it. In one rapid, mind-numbing move that at any other time he'd be mesmerized by, the gator spun on her central axis and yanked him into the water.

Fear surged as water and panic devoured him in one large gulp. Holy hell, he did not want to die in this fucking canal. Short on options, he began kicking his feet, connecting with the underside of the gator over and over and over. The force of his efforts only drained his energy while the weight of this bitch dragged him into the canal.

Gator girl spun and Billy rolled with her. He came out of the water, roaring his agony, the sound puncturing the quiet air. Still clamped onto his arm, the gator, with that unbelievable strength, tried to roll again.

Don't let her roll.

He kicked and punched with his free arm, while primal, animal grunts ravaged him.

Suddenly, his mind went quiet. The battle calm he thrived on. *Relax.*

Stop struggling.

As strong as he was, he'd never win this fight. Not a chance. More likely, he'd die trying. He drew air through his nose, focused on settling his mind and ignoring the agony of this bitch ripping his arm off and swallowing it.

She clamped down again and Billy howled, his body moving into that state of numbness when the pain is too much. *Think.* Find the vulnerable spot.

The eyes.

No matter the species, the eyes were always vulnerable. He drove his fingers into Mama's eye and, suddenly— boom—she let go, hissed and scampered back to her babies.

Just like that.

Pain radiated through his arm, blood spurting like an open faucet and his vision blurred. The bank of the canal shifted. He shook his head, willed himself not to pass out. If he passed out, forget it, game over. With all this fresh blood, he'd be gator bait.

Not wasting time, he leaped up and stumbled as his feet sunk into the soft muck on the edge of the canal. His head spun, but in two giant steps he topped the embankment and started running. Forget the zig-zagging shit he'd heard so many times. He needed to get the hell out of there before mama decided to chase him.

Running from the canal, his head filled with a fierce clanging, he glanced around. Nothing but trees. Where the hell was he? He kept running. He'd find something. Someplace. For a second, he let go of his wounded arm and patted his shorts pocket. Phone still there, but it'd be useless after the swim.

Dammit.

And he was soaked. He grasped his chewed-up arm again. Blood still spewed from between his fingers. He'd be doctoring himself later. Blistered feet from a wet run would be the least of it. Still he needed to cover this bleeding. The only thing he had on him was his shirt, now saturated with who knew what kind of bacteria.

He analyzed his surroundings, his gaze darting over grass, the various trees and exotic vegetation surrounding him.

No palm fronds. Way too sharp. What looked like a bald cypress with Spanish moss growing on it caught his eye.

Perfect.

He ripped his shirt off, flipped it onto his shoulder and grabbed hold of the moss, layering it over the bleeding wound as a temporary dressing. After wrapping the nasty shirt around his arm, he bit one end to tie it off and considered the job done. At least until he could get to safety.

He'd need to have the wound irrigated, cleaned and any dead tissue cut away. All in all, a damned fine day so far. *Not.* To boot, he was pissed. Really pissed.

Might as well start the trek back to Dante. Burn off some of that mad. He ran through the trees, a damned forest, his mind spinning options of where he could be. Couldn't be that far from the hotel. Based on the position of the sun, it was still morning so he hadn't been gone long. He came to a barren, dirt road where the sun shined through the trees on both sides.

He stopped, bent over and sucked in gulps of air. Which direction?

For the millionth time, he bowed to the altar of his army training and grabbed a stick from the brush, jamming it vertically into the ground. Then he marked the shadow with a rock, raised his throbbing arm over his head to ease the pressure and paced while he waited for the sun to shift. When the shadow moved, he marked the new position and drew an imaginary line across the tops of both rock markers.

"There's your east-west mark, Billy boy."

Still squatting, he scanned the access road. North-south. *Pick a direction. North. Go.*

A few minutes later, he hit a large parking area with only three cars. He ran through the dirt parking lot to the paved road where a sign welcomed visitors to Oleta River State

Park. Beyond the entrance sat a main road with a causeway to his right.

Head east. He needed to get to the ocean and back to Dante. And then he'd find the fuckers who made him gator bait.

THROUGH HER OFFICE WINDOW, KRISTEN STARED AT THE glistening ocean and the growing crowd on the beach. She'd called Billy three times in the last hour. Not to mention the two times she'd called him the hour before that.

A clingy person she was not.

No matter what, he always returned her calls. Which meant something was wrong.

Or maybe not. Maybe he'd picked up some gorgeous, skinny girl on the beach and was right now sharing a morning romp.

Naked.

Something Kristen couldn't give him. Still, the idea of him screwing the first willing female sparked her temper.

Bastard.

She almost wanted to believe it. At least then he'd be safe. Relatively speaking. If he'd picked someone up, she'd kill him. And she'd make it bloody. Ugly bloody.

Nagging at her, though, was the idea of him laying hurt somewhere.

Her desk phone rang and, thankful for the distraction, she leaned over and scooped it up. "Kristen Dante."

"I need you to open the service entrance door for me."

Billy. A rush of relief bloomed happy and bright inside her. She eased into her desk chair, ran her palm over her forehead. "Where have you been? I've called ten times."

"My cell is toast. I'm on the loading dock phone. Kris, please, come down and open the door."

And something in his voice, that hitch when he said "please," lacked his normal smart-mouthed confidence. "Why not walk through the lobby?"

He hesitated. "You don't want me walking through your lobby right now."

Something had happened. "I'll be right there."

She kicked off her sky-high heels, grabbed them and sprinted to the far end of the corridor to the service elevator. The ride to the loading dock entrance didn't take long, but it felt like a month. Along the way, she brainstormed where Billy could have been and why he needed to come through the back door, but none of the options were at all settling and she gave up.

When the elevator doors opened, a janitor stood on the other side. Still holding her shoes, Kristen nodded. "Morning, Marcus."

Marcus glanced at the shoes, frowned, but chose to remain silent as he waved her by.

Outside of Marcus, the loading dock lacked other employees and she said a silent thanks. Who knew what she'd find? When she reached the exterior door, she pushed it open and there was Billy, shirtless, his running shorts soaked, his face smeared with mud and something else— blood? Her gaze went to the flash of white where he'd tied his shirt around his forearm. The shirt too was soaked and worse, appeared bloody.

She gasped and the sound echoed in her head. "What happened?"

"Gator."

"*What?*"

He stormed by her into the loading area, stomping

around like a man three days late for his fix. "Those freaking, motherplucking fudgepuppies threw me to a dagnabit gator. Almost tore my freaking arm off! I'm going to castrate those fragging richweeds. Son of a biscuit!" He stopped his frantic pacing and lifted his arm over his head. "This mother hurts."

Kristen remained still, literally unable to move. Had she heard him right?

"Big gator," he said. "Her babies were right there. *Right* there. I had to fight that thing off."

Yes, she'd heard him right. Her stomach swirled into a tight little ball. "How?"

He held two fingers up. "Poked her in the eye. *Boop.* She shit-canned it and ran."

Kristen stepped back, braced herself against the wall, her fingers stretched along the cool expanse of it. Somehow she knew this had happened due to his involvement with her car thefts. It had to be.

He could have died because he was trying to help her. She'd have to live with that, but she wouldn't do it frozen to a wall like a helpless child. Straightening up, she reached for the makeshift bandage on his arm. "How bad is it? You need to get to the hospital. I'll take you."

"Pfft. Not a chance. It's ugly, but I'll live."

"You could get an infection."

He glanced down at his arm. "I'll need IV antibiotics. Got a doctor I can call?"

"Of course. But who did this to you?"

"I was stretching after my run this morning. A van pulled up and three guys tossed me in. One guy whapped me on the head and I passed out. I woke up on the side of the canal next to the gator nest."

His words flew at her, coming too fast to grasp. All she

knew was she'd been worried for good reason. The fact that she'd been so frantic, so utterly paralyzed, by his absence told her their dalliance had become more than she'd anticipated. Or wanted. "That gator could have killed you."

He pressed two fingers over the makeshift bandage and winced. "I think that was the plan. Someone isn't happy with old Billy boy."

"Where was the canal?"

"They dumped me in Oleta State Park. I started running east until I hit the ocean and made my way back here."

"That's more than ten miles!"

In his condition, he'd run all the way back. Unreal.

"Yeah, well, I needed to get back here."

"I would have picked you up."

He slid his phone out of his pocket and waved it around. "Waterlogged. My phone is trashed. All my alarms, gone. This thing is my freaking sanity. At least I back it up every night. Fudging redneck shiznets. I should crack their fudging skulls."

To think, he'd almost been eaten by a gator and he was still trying to keep his promise to his mother. An admirable feat, but unnecessary at the moment. "Billy, your mother would understand if you swore."

He tilted his head. Considering. "I promised."

Kristen could love this man. And not just casually. It would be all consuming, rip-your-guts-out, you'll-never-recover love. *Too late to run now.* "I know you did."

He plucked at the shirt on his arm. "I need to wash up."

"We'll take the service elevator. You can shower and I'll help you patch up this wound. The hotel doctor can get you antibiotics. You can't mess with this. Does it need stitches?"

"I don't think they'll stitch it. Too much chance of infection. The doc will probably have to pack it with a dry dressing. I got some stuff to clean me up in my field kit. Damned arm is stinging pretty good now."

Kristen grabbed his good arm and led him to the elevator. "When we get upstairs, I'll get out first and make sure the hallway is clear."

"I'll try not to bleed anywhere."

With what had happened to him, the man was worried about bleeding in her hotel? In a bizarre way, she found it sweet. "Carpets can be cleaned."

"Still."

They stepped into the elevator and she jabbed at the button for his floor. Hit it again for good measure. Then a third time. "I knew something was wrong when you didn't call me."

Resting against the elevator wall, he leveled his gaze on her and suddenly, flirty, playful Billy returned. "M.H., you were worried about me?"

Admitting it wasn't a problem. The grown-up in her could deal with that. The problem was the idea that yes, she had been worried about him and it meant more than she wanted it to. "I was. You always call me back. Plus, I waited for you on the beach this morning. Thought we could walk together. When you didn't return my calls or texts, I knew something was wrong. You always call me back. I *know* that about you."

He smiled. "I try to anyway."

The elevator dinged, she checked the hallway and hustled toward his room. Once inside, he shut the door behind her and she spun to him, ready to tell him she'd clean the wound, but found him already kicking out of his shorts and underwear. He left them in a pile on the floor and made his way to the bathroom.

"That arm should be looked at."

"I know, but I need to get cleaned up. I feel nasty."

Kristen stood in the entry marveling at his ability to be so completely at ease in his nakedness.

Not to mention the erection he was sporting. Even a mess, the man was stunning.

She averted her eyes. Ignored the heat swirling up her legs into her core.

She scooped his shorts from the floor and turned away from the open bathroom door. Even if he didn't need the privacy, she'd give it to him. "I'll take your shorts home and wash them."

The shower went on. "Thanks," he said, "they stink. The shirt is toast. I'll toss it."

Not knowing what else to do, she shoved the wet shorts and underwear into the laundry bag from the closet and set the bag by the door. She might as well put a call in to the hotel doctor for antibiotics.

Yes, that's it. Distract yourself from the gorgeous man in the shower. The man who quite clearly, assuming her vision was indeed twenty-twenty, needed some form of sexual release. And here she was. Outside the door. A woman who hadn't had sex in eleven point two months.

Call the doctor.

Maybe Billy took fast showers and would be done any minute. Right. Fast showers. She moved to the desk, dialed the operator and asked her for the doctor's number. And still, the shower continued.

"How the hell long does it take to soap up?" she mumbled as she pounded the doctor's number into the phone.

A wallet sat on the desk and she straightened it, aligning the corners with the edge of the desk while she blurted a message to the doctor's service. She hung up and eyeballed that damned open door. Couldn't he have at least closed the door?

"Are you okay?" she yelled. *Because I'm not.*

"Outside of the arm, I'm good."

He's lucky he didn't lose that arm. And still, the shower remained on. Good Lord, what could he be doing in there? Or did she really want to know?

To hell with it. She walked back to the desk, opened his wallet—*forgive me for snooping*—and with her chest about to explode, looked inside. Yep. Condom. Men were so predictable. Still, she was glad for it.

She unbuttoned her blouse, dropped her skirt, ditched the bra and panties and stood naked for a second, praying he wouldn't suddenly pop out of the tub and see her. The bathroom light needed to go.

Now or never. She'd just shut the light, close the door and slide into the shower with him. In a windowless bathroom, it would be dark enough he wouldn't be able to see her.

She hoped.

BILLY STOOD UNDER THE STREAM OF HOT WATER, HIS GOOD arm braced against the wall while he contemplated his erection. Nothing unusual after seeing action. No, the unusual part was having a woman he cared enough about to *not* bang standing a few feet away.

Shiznet.

He glanced at the blood oozing from the wound on his arm as the water washed it away. Butt ugly. The bathroom suddenly went black and he shot to his full height.

"What the—"

"It's me," Kristen said.

The day was looking up because, to his delight, she stepped into the tub behind him. *Please let this be heaven.* He started to turn, but she placed a hand on his shoulder.

"Don't."

"Why?"

"Did you see me?"

He stared at the tile in front of him. "No."

And then she wrapped her arms around his waist and hugged that amazing body to him. *Oh, yeah.*

She kissed his shoulder and held him there. Well, this was a smoking way to end a gator attack. Could gators be kept as pets? Maybe he could fake a daily gator attack?

Mindsnap.

"You could have been killed."

He leaned into the shower spray, bringing her with him and let the hot water soak them. He'd have to turn the water ice cold before they were done. "I think that's what they were counting on."

"I'm so sorry."

She kissed his shoulder again, pressing those gorgeous lips—among other things—into him. Even if it was pitch black, she'd never gotten completely naked with him. And the way she was holding him, running her hands up and down his torso. Total frickin' chaos.

"Kris?"

"Yes?"

"You feel good."

Slowly, he lifted his hands from the wall. "It's dark. I can't see you. I just want to touch. Is that okay?"

She stroked her hand over his chest from behind. "You could have been killed."

"I just want to touch."

No argument. Maybe he was getting somewhere. "Okay?"

"Okay."

Three seconds later his hands were everywhere. Breasts, stomach, legs. Every inch he had touched while wearing that damned blindfold had to be revisited. Not that he could see anything, but the sensation of skin against skin was not lost on him.

She kissed him, glued herself so hard against him his body splintered, slowly, like a wall crumbling from a slow leak, a piece at a time. And, unless she'd gone completely numb, there'd be no missing what *his* body had in mind.

But who the hell could blame him when all her lush skin fried him? He had to have her. Had to.

He backed her into the wall. *Please, let this be okay.*

From somewhere, who knew where, he felt something prick his skin and he backed up an inch to find her holding something. He reached for it. Condom.

He needed this. Needed the release. Needed *her.* "You sure?"

She nodded. Done deal. No talking necessary, thank you very much. He took care of the condom and inched her back against the wall. She wrapped one leg around him.

"Give me the other leg," he said.

"I'm too heavy."

He trailed kisses down her neck. "Kris, I just wrestled a gator. You got nothing on that bitch. Lift up."

His suggestion was ignored and the panic shooting off her, the swinging of her head back and forth while she pushed herself away closed in. Billy touched her cheek to hold her steady and kissed her. "I'll hold you."

"I'll fall."

"I won't let you. I *won't* let you fall."

She quit moving. "You won't fall." He hoped she'd finally believe it.

The answer came when she slid her hands up his arms and around his neck, drawing him closer. *Thank you.* He scooped her up, let her settle her legs around him and held her against the tile as water ran down his back and side. "Okay?"

She nodded.

He slid into her, gasping at the immediate pleasure. Damn, he needed this.

"Thank you." He sank farther into this luscious woman who, from the second he'd seen her, had him completely undone. And knowing what he needed, she put her own hang-ups aside and stepped into this shower.

If this was love, he wanted more of it.

From her. A woman who had enough patience to deal with his hyperactivity and sometimes poor self-control. Kristen Dante might be the poster child girlfriend for ADD sufferers.

"I'm cooked."

"What?" she said.

The sound of her voice, breathy and tight, destroyed him. "You're never leaving this shower. I'll keep you to myself."

His orgasm building, he pushed into her, hoping to hell he wasn't hurting her, but needing the release.

His knees gave for a split second as the orgasm tore through him, and Kristen jerked, reaching out to grab onto something to hold. "You're okay. I've got you."

Still against the tile, she dipped her head forward, rested her cheek against his shoulder. "Thank you."

"No, thank *you*." The slide of her leg over his hip indicated he should set her down. Once on her own power, he pressed her against the wall and kissed her for what would never be enough time. "I owe you one."

"Yes, you do. I plan on collecting."

"Got time now?"

She tapped his injured arm. "Not if you're going to bleed all over the place. Let's see if the doctor called back."

"Spoilsport."

"I'm trying to take care of you."

"Don't yell at me for saying this, but you already have."

"No yelling required. I enjoyed it as much as you did." She linked her fingers with his and squeezed. "I've never done this before. It's crazy fun."

"Hell to the yeah on that one." He smacked kisses over her face. "Any time you want a do-over, just holler."

Except, she was reaching to shut the water off. Do-over aborted.

"I'll holler. Now it's time to fix up that arm. I'll get out first. You stay here."

In the dark, he made a what-the-fudge face. Back in hang-up land? How the eff did it happen that fast? "Kris. Seriously. We just got really, extremely friendly and you're throwing a mental cow over me seeing you naked. I've pretty much got the picture in my head. It's a great picture, so put the damn light on."

She stepped out of the tub and closed the curtain again. "No. Getting into the shower with you took every bit of confidence I had. Before you, I'd never have done it. Baby steps. Please?"

From behind the curtain, he sighed. "Whatever."

"Now you're mad?"

Fucking A he was mad. Not that he'd be stupid enough to admit that because surely, surely, that would be a cataclysmic screw-up that would get him an ass whooping. How many times had *that* happened? Too many to count and he was supposed to be working on this effing filtering thing. But it was so goddamn hard that sometimes he thought his head might explode.

"I'm not mad. I'm disappointed. I don't understand how we could have just pounced each other like we did and you still won't let me see you in the raw. I mean, really, I had my hands all over you. What's the difference if I see?"

"Give me a second."

That was her answer? He squeezed both fists, felt the pain shoot up his injured arm and hissed. *Dammit.* This nightmare of a day was making his brain mushy.

So fucking tired. The relentless pounding in his brain never stopped. Never. Stopped. He smacked his lips together, pressed them tight. How much could a man take? "You still think I'm gonna run in terror if I see you naked?" He snatched a towel from the shelf and wrapped it around him before swinging the bathroom door open. Already, she was in her skirt and buttoning her blouse, pissing him off even more. "Or maybe you think I'm going to compare you to someone else? Your sister maybe? Who, by the way, I've never seen naked. How the hell could I even draw that comparison?"

Kristen's mouth hung open in a look that told him he was dead. Total meat. That filter, or lack thereof, had royally fucked him. He threw his hands up. "Time-out. Totally unfiltered and shitty of me."

But M.H., with her hands on those gorgeous hips and her green eyes shooting body armor piercing bullets didn't look so forgiving. "Not fair to bring Jess into this when you know I have issues with her perfect body. That's evil, Billy."

True. "It's your hot button and I hit it. I get that, but guess what? I'd never consider comparing you to your sister. She doesn't come close to you. Not in her dreams. Get over it."

She shoved her tangled, wet hair away from her face, gripping her head with both hands. "Because you say so? Because if people don't fall in line with what you think, they're obviously wrong? That's crap. The world doesn't work for you, Billy."

"I could spout off at least half a dozen reasons why it would be stupid to compare you to your sister. The first one being your sister is a slut."

"Hey!"

Billy had the distinct impression he just—again—screwed the pooch. "Your sister has banged half the Eastern seaboard. I know that's not a shock to you."

Her face contorted into a tight rage that scared him a wee bit. "She's still my sister. Maybe she's disrespectful to me, but don't talk about her that way."

"I should lie?"

"No, no, no." She jammed her feet into her shoes. "You are not going to make this about you being the king of truth."

"It is what it is."

Kristen shook her fists at him. "This is your problem. You think because it's not a lie that you can just say it. That it doesn't matter because it's the truth according to Billy. Well, dumbass, there's a little something called courtesy and you calling my sister a slut hurts me. And don't give me that garbage about you missing the impulse control filter. I get it about the ADD and how overwhelming it is when your own thoughts and urges feel out of control. But you're a grown man. Stop acting like a toddler."

"Toddler!"

"Yes. Learn to control yourself. You like to pretend you're

not doing anything wrong because these outrageous things you say fall under the safety of being true, but that's baloney. You like the attention and the more outrageous you are, the more attention you get. *You* are a toddler."

She spun and stormed into the bathroom.

"Kris!"

"I can't talk to you now. I need to dry my hair and get back to work."

By the time she came out of the bathroom, Billy was dressed, sitting on the bed contemplating his plight. She'd ripped him a huge one. Monster sized. Probably for good reason, but he wasn't sure. Not of much anyway. All he knew was the burden of his actions was becoming too much. Even for him, who could carry a lot on his back. Between his boss yelling at him, his mother scolding him about the F-bombs, his teammates hounding him and now Kristen calling him a toddler, the lack of filtering kept getting him in trouble.

When did this constant need for attention—positive or negative—converge on him? For years he'd worked to keep his ADD in check, but in the past months his energy for it faded and all he felt was useless and lost. Like traveling on a road that led to nowhere he wanted to be. Obsessing over it only escalated his anxiety and that always led to bad behavior. Maybe it was time for it to stop. For him to work harder at controlling his emotions. And his mouth.

"Kris?"

"Zip it. I need to go."

Before he could grab her, she charged out the door. Right about now would be a good time to swear.

His room phone rang. Could he not get five seconds to think? "What?"

"I've been calling your cell all morning." Monk's voice. "What the hell crawled up your ass?"

Someone was really testing him. "Not what. Who. Kristen is being a pain in the ass because I called her sister a slut."

"Ouch. And you think *she's* the pain in the ass? Get a damned heart, man."

Billy brought the phone away from his ear, held his middle finger to it and put it back to his ear. Juvenile, yes, but this time, worth it. "Now you're gonna start?"

"Just saying."

"She can barely stand her sister."

"You need schmoozing lessons. You *suck* at it."

If this guy were in front of him, Billy would stick his fucking head in the toilet and drown him. Not only would he do it, he'd laugh at his kicking legs. "I *suck*?"

"Yeah. She may not like her sister, but she adores her father and she wants to please him. Part of pleasing him requires her to deal with Jess. She doesn't need you adding to that hot-ass mess."

Such simple observations drove Billy mad—completely insane. This was why he didn't own a car or a house or have a settled life. Who needed all this stress? He flopped back on the bed. "I guess I'm schlepping up to her office to apologize then. Fantastic. By the way, I was thrown to a gator this morning."

Monk laughed. "What?"

"No joke."

"You aren't shitting me?"

"No. Whoever is behind this theft ring isn't happy with me. Three guys, different ones this time, grabbed me and tossed my ass in a canal with a gator. I had to fight that bastard." *Sorry, Ma.* But, hell, slip-ups were to be expected. All around.

"I knew I shouldn't have left you there."

"As *if*. Please. They would have snatched me regardless. Why are you calling?"

"Vic wants to know when you're heading back to Chicago."

Chicago? In December? Maybe never. "Uh, next week?"

"Uh," Monk mimicked. "You don't sound too sure."

"Not before this shindig for the senator. I told Kristen I'd help with security. I talked to Vic about it the other day. He was cool with it. And I got this car theft thing going. After these dog biscuits made me gator bait, I'm hunting their asses."

"For that, I can't blame you, but you gotta give Vic a return date so he can schedule you for something."

Schedule him? Billy flexed and unflexed his hand. Cracked his neck as a burst of hope welled inside. Maybe he wasn't losing his job. "Am I out of the hole?"

"Why are you asking me? *He's* your boss."

"Yeah, but he was fried when he sent me down here. Forget it. I'll call him. I may need help on this car theft thing. A second hotel has been hit. I got some leads but it's too much ground to cover."

"I'll come back."

Like he needed that aggravation? "No. I don't want Izzy mad at me. I'll tell Vic to send one of the guys. Maybe Bobby."

"Oh, jeez," Monk said.

"What?"

"My girl just walked in and flashed me."

Lucky guy. "I guess you'd better fly then. Besides, I need to practice my groveling."

Billy dropped the phone into the cradle, thinking about what it would be like to have Kristen flash him.

It would take a small miracle for Kristen to be that

comfortable with her body. After escaping a gator and the over-the top sex in the shower, he may have used up his quota of small miracles.

He blew out a breath. If he expected to have any sort of a relationship with Kristen, he'd have to get used to her self-image issues. And that would take some work.

15

KRISTEN GLANCED UP FROM HER COMPUTER, BUT KEPT TYPING while she sneered at that pain in the butt Billy Tripp and his bandaged arm. "What is it?"

"I'm sorry."

She stopped typing. Puckered her lips. "You're sorry. *Really*?"

"Yes. I'm sorry."

Did she dare believe it? How many times had she been in this situation with Jess? And how many times had she been disappointed? No thank you, Billy Tripp, she'd learned all she wanted to about meaningless apologies.

"What exactly are you sorry for?"

If he could answer this one, she might believe him. After all, Jess was always sorry, but it was for the wrong reasons. Her apologies stemmed from being forced to make amends rather than owning up to her mistake.

Or hurting someone.

"Plain and simple," Billy said, "I screwed up by busting out the big guns with the Jess comment."

Just like that. No justifying. No excuses. No trying to

convince her he was right. Just a simple admission of his wrongdoing. Blasted luck. All she wanted was to stay mad at him longer. To let him know he couldn't treat her poorly and not pay a price. And now, with him apologizing, he'd taken all the steam out of this engine of anger she had going. How could she have let that happen?

She scrunched her nose. "I hate you, Billy Tripp."

To add to her misery, he leveled one of his playful, devastating grins on her. *Bastard*.

"Oh, M.H., I don't believe that."

She sat back in her chair and crossed her arms in a futile attempt to stay angry. Why did he have to be so good-looking? And when he smiled, his good-lookingness got worse.

He stepped to the desk, held out his hand. "Am I forgiven?"

Too damned handsome for his own good. Or hers, depending on how she looked at it. "Don't ever use my hot spots to satisfy your need for a rush. It's hurtful and tiring and intolerable. Do it again and whatever this is, is over. Got it?"

Still holding his hand to her, he nodded. "Yes, ma'am."

She smacked at his hand. "You're forgiven. But I'm not ready to hold your hand."

Not one word about it had better come out of his mouth either. She'd decide how long it would take to let him touch her again.

"How's the arm?"

"Eh, no big deal."

Manny strode through the door. "Hi, Mr. Billy."

Here, at least, was one male who had never disappointed her.

"Boy Wonder, what's up?"

"Can I help?"

Billy laughed. "You don't know what I'm doing."

"I don't care. It's always cool."

Kristen had to smile. A whopper of hero worship going on there. But after the gator attack, she couldn't have Manny hanging out with Billy. Inside the hotel might be okay, but never outside. Manny could get hurt.

"I got a good project for you," Billy said. "I have a list of hotel guests I need you to look at and tell me which ones are staying longer than say three or four days. Can you do that for me?"

He bobbed his head. "Yeah. I can do it. Cool."

A good compromise. Manny could help him while staying safely inside the hotel and not at Billy's side.

Another smidge of her anger slipped away. *The jerk can't even let me stay mad at him.*

The boys traded fist bumps. "I need to talk to Miss Kristen. Wait for me outside."

After Manny stepped out and closed the office door, Kristen said, "Well played."

He shrugged. "Figured it's not safe for him to be following me around. I'll have him go through your guest list, find out who the long-term ones are and note the ones who drive high-end cars. If nothing else, we can secure them."

"Good idea."

"Are we okay?"

She nodded. "Mostly. You need to control that mouth, Billy. Jess is still my sister. We may not like each other at times, but I love her and want the best for her."

"Message received." The idiot dropped to his knees and threw himself onto his side. "Thank you," he wailed. "Thank you."

And once again, he'd made her laugh when all she wanted was to throttle him.

He popped to his feet again, straightened his T-shirt and held up two fingers. "Scout's honor. I'm on it."

"That's all I ask. And you're buying me dinner later."

"Works for me. Will you eat? And I don't mean salad."

She swallowed. "I'll find something I can eat."

"Let's make it casual. You'll eat and then we'll walk on the beach so you aren't beating yourself up over having a pinhead's worth of red meat. Will that work?"

She'd already walked once today, but the idea of eating meat with dinner—steak perhaps—made her mouth water. Another sunset walk would be a pleasure after this bombing of a day. "Yes. We'll eat at the café overlooking the beach."

"I thought they only served breakfast and lunch?"

"They do. But the general manager can have dinner served anywhere she likes. And tonight she wants to have a quiet dinner with a guy who sometimes makes her crazy."

"Go, Billy," he said.

"Blue cheese burger? Steak? What?"

"The burger. Make it two."

"You eat like a dinosaur. How do you not get fat?"

He shrugged. "I work out. A lot. Tomorrow morning, I'll get my ass out of bed and go for a run. Usually I'll lift, but not with this banged up arm. I'm telling you, M.H., start packing the protein and get some exercise. You'll lose weight."

She thought about it. Never had she even sampled one of the chef's renowned blue cheese burgers. Not even a morsel. The fat in the blue cheese alone could send her into a psychotic break. "Will you split one of your burgers with me? I won't eat the bun. Just the burger. I'm dying to try one."

Billy smacked his hands together. "Perfect. Have half the burger and a boring-ass side salad and you're good to go."

"Then we'll walk after dinner. I won't feel guilty about the fat if we walk."

"Sure, but I'm gonna make you move. No casual strolling. After you start sweating, then we'll stroll."

She nodded. Could she actually be excited about this? Yes. Definitely. She'd get to eat a burger. Not to mention the date with the hot guy.

An evening that sounded like perfection.

AFTER REPLACING HIS TRASHED PHONE WITH A SHINY NEW ONE, Billy sat in the executive conference room studying his notes. Manny had left with his mother, but had provided a neatly handwritten list of current guests who would be staying longer than one week. It was a start.

Each of those guests with high-end cars would be asked to move them to a predetermined spot near the front of the hotel. Billy would then suggest Kristen put a guard on them 24-7 until he figured out who was running the fudging theft ring.

He went back to his laptop and the report detailing the owners of the residences Alex had visited since Billy put the GPS on him. He'd just go through each name and see if anything popped. Then he'd cross-reference it with all the hotel employees to see if there were any matches.

Kristen appeared in the doorway wearing a devastating red wrap dress that made him want to beg for mercy.

"And aren't you making my heart go pitter-patter."

"Ready for dinner?"

Dinnertime already? Damn, he'd forgotten to set an

alarm on the new phone and lost track of time. *Crap.* "Smoking dress, M.H."

She folded her arms. He'd gone too far.

He tore his gaze away. "Sorry."

When he averted his eyes, she dropped her arms.

"Are you ready for dinner?" she asked again.

"Not quite. I'm processing here and I don't want to lose my momentum. Fifteen minutes?"

"Sure. What are you working on?"

"The report of all the places Alex visited. Why don't you look with me? See if anything pops."

M.H. stepped into the room, the devastating red dress clinging to every blazing inch of her as she moved toward him. Jesus, this woman would kill him yet, but he'd never tire of this feeling. That alone was a major change in his way of thinking.

She stood next to him and placed one hand on the back of his chair. The lavender scent of her perfume drifted around him. Nice.

She studied the laptop screen. "These are the names?"

"Yes."

"I don't recognize any of them. For the company names, do you know who the registered agents are?"

"No."

"That's what you need. The company names mean nothing. Registered agents handle receipt of all tax and legal documents for the corporation within its jurisdiction. If the owners of the dealerships lived out of state, they could be clueless about the workings of their own businesses."

Holding up a finger, Billy said, "Good thought."

Three minutes and fifty-nine bucks later, thanks to the wonders of the internet, Billy logged into a handy-dandy database of registered agents in Florida. Piece of cake. He and Kristen made a damned good team.

Now the boring as hell part of this operation started, because he had to search every business old Alex visited.

"Start with the car dealerships," Kristen said.

He grinned up at her. "That's what I was thinking. See? You read my mind. We're perfect for each other."

"Billy, reading your mind could be dangerous. And exhausting."

"Wha, wha."

She laughed as he typed the name of the Jaguar dealership into the database and scanned the corporation details. Kristen leaned forward, her upper body just to the left of his sightline. *Don't look, don't look, don't look.* So what if her dress was hanging down enough for him to get a peek at the rack. *Fight it.*

"Owner," he said, way too loud, and Kristen jumped.

"I'm standing right here; you don't have to yell."

"It's the fudging filter!"

"*What?*"

He paddled his hand toward her chest. "When you leaned over, the top of your dress opened." He held up his hands, but turned his head away. "I didn't look. That's all I'm saying. I fought the urge. It's taxing. On many levels."

Kristen rolled her lips in.

Now she's laughing.

Billy grunted. "You're always telling me to filter. It went against every fiber of my being, but I did it. And it sucked. Really? All I want is to stare at your tits. That's all I'm saying."

He went back to the laptop.

Ignore the woman in the hot red dress.

"Owner," he said again. "RDM Auto Group." He made a note of the name and slapped his pen on the table.

Kristen touched his shoulder and he glanced up. "Thank you for filtering."

And then she placed those beautiful hands of hers against the neckline of the devastating wrap dress, opening it enough to give him a preview of lush cleavage and a black and red lace bra.

Billy whistled low, swiveled in the chair and stared. Yes, stared. And she didn't flinch. He did notice the settling breath she needed to take, but she was handling it. He wasn't the only one trying here.

"Thank you. I want to do amazing things to you. Naked. With the lights on."

Thinking about that wouldn't do him one damned bit of good. She wasn't ready. Not when she had to mentally prepare herself to show him a miniscule bit of cleavage. How flipping ironic. Most women took one look at him and made a dash to get naked. Kristen? She was terrified. His rotten luck.

"Let's focus here." He went back to the laptop. "Leave the dress open though. Please."

"Whatever you say, Billy."

"Oh, *that's* funny. We got the Jaguar dealership here. Registered agent...Bradley J. Murphy. Recognize the name?"

"No."

He wrote down the name. Bradley J. would get his own search.

Next up, the BMW dealership. Owner: MDR Auto.

Hang on. He double-checked the name of the Jaguar dealership. RDM Auto Group.

Ding.

Ding.

Ding.

Those names were awfully similar.

"Tell me Bradley J. is the registered agent," Kristen said.

Billy scanned the file. "Registered agent is Donovan Archer."

Fudgenuts.

He glanced up. "Recognize it?"

"No. Let's do a search on both names. Maybe they're connected somehow."

His fingers flying over the keyboard he typed Bradley J.'s name into the search box.

Lawyer. Employed by Smith, Kline, Abrams and Associates. Billy wrote the firm's name down. "Recognize it?"

"It's a large firm in Miami. Mostly corporate stuff. Check the other name."

He typed in Donovan Archer.

Lawyer.

Employed by—*thank you*—Smith, Kline, Abrams and Associates.

"There's our connection, Billy."

"Okay, boys. What the hell are you up to?"

Billy did a search on Smith, Kline, Abrams and found a website. And an About Us page. With photos. He glanced at the image of Bradley J. on the screen and almost pissed himself.

He'd have to double-check it against the photo he took, but... "I think he's one of the guys Alex met with that first day I followed him." Billy turned back to M.H. "Do you recognize him?"

"No."

Billy sat back and the chair rocked with the movement. He tapped his fingers over his mouth while analyzing the face of Bradley J. Murphy. "Registered agent for the Jag dealership."

"And?"

"Not only is another lawyer at the firm the registered agent for the BMW dealership, but the names of each corporation are similar." He glanced at his notes. "The BMW shop is owned by MDR Auto. The Jag dealership is owned by RDM Auto Group."

"So," she said, sidling up next to him to look at the laptop, "maybe the dealerships are owned by the same person, but he has two different registered agents to make it look like different corporations?"

Hot *and* smart. "Exactly what I'm thinking."

"And you think these registered agents are meeting with Alex and then reporting back to the owner?"

Billy pursed his lips. "Possibly. Or the owner is in the dark while Bradley J. and his coworker are running a car theft ring through his dealership." *An international one.* Voicing that suspicion would require him to tell her about the shed incident and most likely, he'd get in trouble for keeping it from her. Maybe it *was* time to tell her? Just come clean. Would it help matters? Or worry her? He didn't know.

Right or wrong, he'd keep quiet and deal with the consequences later. She might never have to know about the beefheads.

Kristen propped her hip against Billy's chair and it shifted an inch. "Very interesting."

There she stood, the devastating red dress open at the top, the black and red lace bra pretty much flipping him the bird. His punishment for not telling her about the shed. Had to be. *What a life.* He grabbed her arm and guided her down to his lap. She didn't resist. Progress. Finally, he wrapped his hand around her neck and dropped a lip-lock. This, he knew, she enjoyed because she'd always been a willing participant.

"Do you feel dirty?" he asked, nipping her lower lip.

"What?"

"Maybe you need a shower? In the dark?"

She laughed and dropped her head to his shoulder while he trailed his fingers over that teensy bit of cleavage she let him see. She didn't fight him, but he felt her stiffen. As much as it killed him, he stopped. Good enough. For now.

"You make me smile," she said. "You drive me crazy, but you always find a way to make me forget my insecurities. At least temporarily. It's remarkable."

And then she shifted sideways and slid into his lap. The chair wobbled, but he planted his feet to keep them steady.

"See, no problem."

"I'm not too heavy?"

"Can't feel a thing."

She laughed and he nuzzled her neck while moving his hand along her thigh. "To think we've been missing this." She kissed him, long and slow and then grabbed his cheeks. "I don't want to feel this way about you. You'll devastate me. As much as you make me laugh, you distract me."

"I don't see that as a bad thing for a girl who works too much."

"It is when I'm running my father's billion-dollar hotel. I adore you but your free-spiritedness takes a lot of energy. I don't know if I can handle you and the hotel. Then again, in a few days, you'll be gone, back to your adventurous life. So maybe it doesn't matter."

"But South Beach in December is looking pretty good."

She inched back. Set her hands on his shoulders and he

thought he might just die right there. All he could think was that she might be perfect.

"I want you all the time," he said. "It's worse after the shower today. Talk about distracted. The way things are right now, I'll never get enough of you. For the first time, I like that idea. Can we just go with it? Take it one day at a time? Enjoy being together?"

She slid from his lap and stood. "For now. Sure. Eventually though, and probably very soon, you'll leave and my heart will be broken."

Arguing that would be futile. If there was one thing Billy Tripp, Mr. Relentless, was sure of, it was that *her* heart wouldn't be the only one broken.

AFTER DINNER AND A STROLL ON THE BEACH WITH KRISTEN, they snuck into her suite for a quick make-out session before she drove home. Restless from the lack of getting laid, Billy decided it might be a good night for a sneak and peek on Bradley J. Murphy's office. Why not?

His phone rang. Monk. He punched the button. "What?"

"Where are you?"

"I'm in the lobby of the hotel. Where are *you?*"

"I'm standing in front of your room. Stay there. I'm coming down."

Fuck. Sorry, Ma. "You're here?"

"Yeah, just flew in."

"I told you not to. Now Izzy is pissed at me."

"No. Turns out my girl has her eye on a pair of diamond earrings and she's not above bartering for them. We compromised. I would have given her the stupid earrings if she'd asked, which she knows, so I don't get what all the negotiating was about."

Billy laughed. "She's breaking your balls. You know that, right?"

"Pretty much, yeah. I'm getting in the elevator."

Monk stepped out of the elevator wearing his trademark cargo shorts, T-shirt, combat boots and do-rag. The older, dressed-to-impress couple behind him could only stare. They had no idea what to do with him. Fudging priceless. If they only knew how financially loaded the guy was.

"I told you not to come."

"Yeah, you did. Which was a dumb-ass thing to do considering a gator tried to make you her dinner."

Billy's phone rang again. "Vic. I'll call him later."

"Seriously? You gave him '30 Days in the Hole' as a ringtone?"

"I was pissed when he sent me down here."

"You'd better hope he never hears it."

"How's he gonna hear it? It's not like he'll call me on the phone when we're face to face." Billy shook it off. "Besides, I'm about to do a sneak and peek on a law firm."

"Sweet." Monk's phone rang. "Vic. Crap."

"Don't answer—"

"Hello?"

"—it." So much for that.

"Uh," Monk said into the phone. "Billy? No, I haven't seen him...You called my house?" Monk raised his eyebrows and Billy sliced his hand across his throat.

"Izzy told you Billy got eaten by a gator? Uh-huh."

"30 Days in the Hole" blared from Billy's phone. *Shiznet.* The son of a beeswax called from another phone while talking to Monk.

"Here he is now." Monk shoved the phone at Billy.

Dead man. "Hey, boss."

"Straight away, I should kick your ass for giving me that ringtone. Second, you two think I'm an idiot or what?"

Billy said nothing.

"Good fucking answer. And what the hell? A gator?"

"It wasn't that bad. She got hold of my arm. Kristen called the hotel doc and he hooked me up with antibiotics. I'm good to go."

"Get your ass on a plane. Right. Fucking. Now."

This was a teensy problem. After that slamming shower earlier, Billy had no intentions of leaving South Beach for at least a week. Maybe longer. "Can't do that. We committed to helping Kristen with the senator's party in two days. You okayed it. We can't bail on her now. I'm running security."

Monk winced and Billy shot him the bird.

"You motherfucker," Vic hollered. "I sent you down there for a simple assignment that any dickhead could handle. What I wanted was for you to learn a lesson about how your behavior is making everyone around here nuts, and you squeeze me into letting you stay there? And worse, I don't think you've learned anything because you're suddenly into something that gets you served up as gator food. I should fire your ass."

Billy held his breath. He'd been in trouble with Vic plenty of times, more than he wanted to think about, but never did he seriously believe Vic would launch him. "Listen. I didn't go looking for this mess. I totally backed into it. Kristen needed help. She's a client. I was here. What was I supposed to do?"

Monk gagged and Billy gritted his teeth.

"How about not get eaten by a gator?" Vic said.

"Maybe if I'd seen that coming, but who knew?"

"Fuck it. Be back here Sunday night or you're fired."

Sunday? Suddenly Billy had no interest in going back to

Chicago at all. But he earned a ridiculous amount of money doing things that gave him a rush.

Time for him to learn the delicate art of compromise without totally losing his nuts. "How about Monday? I'll need to do a postmortem on the party with Kristen on Sunday. Before you start yelling again, this trip is doing what you wanted. I'm getting better. I'm learning to filter."

"Filter? What the hell are you talking about?"

"The lack of filter is my problem. I don't think, I just act. I'm getting better. Monk'll tell you." Billy looked at Monk. "Right?"

Monk laughed again and Billy shoved him with his free hand. "Monk is busy being a douche but he knows it's true. So, Monday it is then."

"I didn't say it's Monday."

Billy made crackling noises into the phone. "What?"

"I want you back—"

"You're breaking up. Let me get to a better spot and call you."

He hung up. Monk stood in front of him, howling like a man at a comedy show marathon. "Really?" Billy hollered. "You couldn't cover me on that one? You had to tell him you'd found me?"

"Hey, he talked to Izzy while I was on my way down here. He probably figured we'd hooked up by now."

"I wish Gina would have those babies and get him off me. I mean, I'm working on it aren't I?"

"Gotta admit, the gator thing looks bad. From his view, you're being the same Billy who wants in the middle of something and doesn't care how he gets there."

"That's not what happened."

Monk folded his arms. "Careful, buddy. I was here that first night."

Couldn't argue it. In fact, Monk had been the one who'd sent him to the hotel lobby to investigate. "Maybe initially I was bored and pissy and wanted some action, but now, it's more about Kristen and getting her through this. This hotel means everything to her. If I can help her, I'm gonna do it. Gator or no gator."

Monk shrugged. "I hear ya, but it's your ass to lose."

His ass and his job. "Yeah, it is." He checked the time on his phone. "Let's move. I now have four days to figure out who is stealing these fudging cars and if it's an international operation."

16

Billy parked Kristen's boring-as-hell car half a block down from the law office, and he and Monk walked back to the three-story stucco building. A white cargo van was parked in the fire zone in front of the building.

"Cleaning crew," Billy said.

"Maybe. If they're in the building, chances are the alarm hasn't been activated yet. Could get lucky. Let's go around back, get in and out fast."

Traffic along the main road whizzed by, but the back half of the building was sheltered by a crop of large, leafy trees that looked like Arkansas oaks.

Darkness had fully descended, offering nice cover as they strode to the rear of the building. The night air dipped to the low sixties. In Billy's mind, a perfect night for a couple of guys to be out for some illegal snooping. Unfortunately for them, the back entrance of the building was completely visible to the road on the opposing block.

Monk slid his do-rag off, covered his hand with it and unscrewed the light bulb on the fixture beside the door. At least the street wasn't as busy as the one in front. Still, they'd have to be quick about this.

Billy retrieved two sets of latex gloves from his back pocket and they snapped them on.

"Give me your tools," Monk said. "I'm better at locks."

As much as Billy wanted to be an ass and argue, what was the point? Considering Monk, next to Vic, was the best lock buster on the team.

"I don't see any security cameras."

"Me neither. Let's hope it's the same inside."

Within thirty seconds, they were inside a moderately lit corridor.

"They need to upgrade that lock," Billy whispered. "These people have no clue how to keep guys like us out. Maybe they should hire us."

An alarm keypad hung on the wall and Billy checked it. System off.

"Where are we going?" Monk asked.

"No idea. The law firm has the entire building."

"Reception desk?"

"Yep."

They crept along the thick marble floors, padding silently toward the front of the building. Billy stopped at the end of the corridor and shot a look around the two-story lobby with glass entry doors. No security or cleaning people seated at the circular desk.

He spun to Monk and, using hand signals, indicated he'd take the left of the desk and Monk should take the right. They crouched low and quickly moved behind the desk, out of sight from the entrance.

On their knees, they began searching. In the top drawer, Billy found a laminated list of office locations and extensions.

Jackpot. Bradley J. Murphy and Donovan Archer's offices were on the third floor. 305 and 301.

He held up three fingers and motioned to the stairs.

At the top of the stairwell, Billy cracked the door an inch and heard the distant whine of a vacuum cleaner. *Damn.* The sound came from the south end of the building. He turned back to Monk and swirled his finger in front of him. The *go* signal.

Slipping through the door, they slid along the interior wall, avoiding the seascapes that hung in perfect alignment. Nothing like knocking over a painting while on a sneak and peek. After the last painting, Billy came to an office and glanced at the wall plate. 315. To its left was 314. Headed in the right direction.

More hand signals. Forward motion. At the end of the corridor, Billy bent low and checked around the corner. Another long hallway, but the inside wall stopped a few feet down and revealed a large opening. Bullpen?

The vacuum stopped.

A woman stepped into the corridor and Billy reeled backward, jabbing his thumb in the opposite direction. Monk checked the office door they'd just passed, found it unlocked and ducked in. Their hiding space was actually a windowless supply closet.

Great. They'd have to sit here until the cleaning lady went by. Billy checked his phone. Ten-forty. His guess was the third floor was the last one to be serviced and the cleaning crew would be leaving, most likely setting an alarm.

A sliver of light shafted through the bottom of the door. Monk dropped to his belly and peeked under it, looking for feet walking by.

Fifteen seconds later, he jumped up and gave the okay sign. Billy cracked the door, snuck a look. Nothing.

Billy pointed at Monk, indicating that he should check office 305.

The whine of the vacuum sounded again from the north end of the floor. This was, in Billy's opinion, both good and bad news. Good, the cleaning people were still working and the boys had extra time to snoop. Bad, the cleaning people were still working and might spot them.

They'd have to risk it. Monk whooshed his finger in the air and they marched off to their target locations. Billy tried the handle to Bradley J.'s office. Locked. He signaled Monk, who still had the lock picking tools. In seconds, he opened the door and Billy ducked into the pitch- black office.

He retrieved his penlight from his pocket, cupped his hand over the end to dim the glare until his eyes adjusted and he could lower the shades.

A metal three-drawer filing cabinet sat along one wall. To Billy's way of thinking, Bradley J. must not be a big shot because this office sucked. Besides the filing cabinet, the only other furniture was the cheap wood desk, a leather desk chair and two metal guest chairs. Three neat stacks of folders sat on the desk and Billy helped himself to a scan. Next to the folders, a computer monitor cord lay lifeless and unconnected. *Must have taken the laptop home.* Eh, that would have been too much to ask anyhow.

He moved to the filing cabinet, opened the top drawer and winced when a loud creak sounded. *Shiznet.* WD-40 anyone? Not wanting to waste time, he dove in and found client files in alphabetical order. Lucky day.

He found three fat hanging folders labeled RDM Auto Group. He flipped through a few pages of billing records and various meeting notes. Yanking the billing records file, he set it on top of the cabinet.

Dang it, he didn't have his camera. His phone would have to do.

No time to go through the small mountain worth of records. *Get what you can.* He breathed in. Counted twenty to clear his head and closed his eyes. *Focus.* Working with the idea that the car thefts had recently started, he snapped photos of the records from the last three weeks.

Next up, the meeting notes. He flipped through the pages and took more photos. He'd print everything later and read it.

After a few minutes, he checked the time. *Gotta go.* Returning everything to its proper place, he made his way back down the now quiet hall to the rendezvous point inside the stairwell and waited an intolerable forty-nine seconds for Monk to join him.

Who the hell knew where the cleaning people were? Hopefully they were still in the building and hadn't set an alarm.

At the bottom of the stairs, Billy cracked the door open, peeped into the hallway. Nothing. He opened the door a little wider, stuck his head through. Nothing. Good to go.

They hustled twenty feet to the back door, stopped at the alarm keypad and read the display.

What a day. Eaten by a gator, got laid in the shower and the alarm was off. Priceless.

BACK AT DANTE, BILLY AND MONK STRODE THROUGH THE lobby doors and hit the elevator bank with a crush of people heading to the clubs. At midnight this place was a flipping cash cow. M.H. not only knew how to run a hotel, she knew how to make money at it. Another reason to love her. The reasons kept building. Maybe, someone help him, he was ready to take a shot at the dreaded R-word.

A relationship hadn't entered his mind in—hell, had it ever entered his mind? Probably not. He was more the grab and go guy when it came to women. But something about Kristen, her steady reserve, her willingness to put up with his antics, settled his busy mind.

"What's the plan?" Monk asked.

The plan. Yes. He'd think about the mission. Everything else made him want to shit elephants. "We head up to my war room, print out these pictures and see what we've got. You took pictures, right?"

Monk scoffed. "Of course. You think I'm twelve?"

"Just saying."

Monk led the pack onto the elevator and held the door for a wicked-sexy blonde in a tight red dress that left no doubt she was commando tonight. The floor should have melted. That's how hot she was. Billy stared straight ahead. Nope. Not looking again. Not gonna do it.

And, what kind of evil force drops a beautiful woman, going commando, in front of him at the same time he's contemplating a relationship? A couple of weeks ago, he'd have been all over this blonde. Now? Forget it. He didn't know what to do.

Finally, *finally,* the elevator dinged their floor and the doors slid open. Billy jumped off that elevator and didn't turn back.

Monk let out a whistle. "That blonde? Holy hell."

"I didn't notice."

"You noticed."

Billy used the key card Kristen gave him to unlock the

executive suite door. "Hello? Would Izzy *not* be pissed about this conversation?"

They stepped through the doorway and stopped in the inner corridor while Billy located the light.

"Actually, Izzy happens to notice beautiful women. At first, I tried not to respond, but she'd always elbow me and say 'Look, there's one. She's stunning. I wish I had her hair.' I always have a reason why Izzy's better looking." Monk grinned. "It's not hard. Plus, it's not a bad deal. I get to look at beautiful women, purely from a male curiosity stand-point, and not get in trouble."

Billy cupped his hand over his mouth and slid it down his chin. "I don't think Kristen would be comfortable with that."

"Gotta have a level of trust. If there's no trust, it isn't gonna work."

"It's not trust." At least he didn't think so, but it was prob-ably way too early to tell. "It's the body image thing. She thinks she's fat."

"She's not *fat.*"

"*I* know that. She's the one who can't get it through her thick skull. She constantly compares herself to her sister."

"We all have baggage. You think Izzy is easy? Please. She puts up with my shit, I put up with hers. Somehow, you find the compromise."

Reaching the conference room, Billy unlocked the door and flipped the lights on as he stepped in. "How do you find it?"

"There's no shortcut. You get to know each other, figure out which buttons are hot. This game Izzy and I play would never work in the reverse. If she commented on good-looking guys, I'd get nuts. She knows that about me and it's unfair, but it is what it is. Now, I'm sure she probably looks at men all the time and sizes them up. As long as I don't hear about it, I'm good. She, on the other hand, has no issues with me noticing a beautiful woman. If I were to do something more than look, she would kick my ass. Literally."

Nothing about this scenario fit into Billy's abbreviated schedule. He needed that shortcut because he didn't have months, or even weeks, to determine how to help Kristen with her self-image issues. "Well, then, I've got until Monday because Vic ordered me back."

Monk waved that off and dropped into a chair at the conference table. "He was pissed. If you want to stay longer, call him and tell him—no, *ask* him if you can hang out down here while you're waiting for your next assignment. He won't say no. Hell, right now, he wants you out of his hair until Gina has these babies. He needs you not to get killed so he can concentrate on his family. The gator thing rattled him. He thought you were down here blowing off steam. Instead you're getting tossed to a gator by bad guys."

"I wanted to blow off steam. Trust me. I backed into this car theft gig."

"You didn't back into it. You went straight for it. Eyes open. You wanted in on the action."

He got in on it all right. Billy glanced at his war board and shook his head. "Now I want to figure it out before I leave. I owe that to Kristen."

"You think she thinks that? You *owe* her something?"

"No. But I want to finish this for her so she doesn't have to worry about cars disappearing from her lot."

Monk smacked his hands on the table. "Then let's get to work. You, my friend, are short on time."

Billy jerked his thumb toward the white board. "This is what I've got so far."

Monk whistled. "You've been busy."

"A little. You study it while I print these pictures. Give me your phone and I'll do yours."

Once the photos were printed and Monk was brought to speed, they reviewed the new documents.

Using a magnet, Billy secured meeting notes to the white board. "They're careful not to have joint meetings. In none of these notes do Donovan Archer and Bradley J. ever meet."

"And we're sure these two companies are owned by the same person?"

Billy tapped his finger on the registered agents reports he'd bought on the internet. "No, but the names are similar. Let's keep looking and see if we can find a client name."

Monk shuffled through the printouts and sorted them into different piles. "Look for expense reports. Might get lucky with a name."

Together, they categorized all the printouts, stacking them in Bradley J. piles and Donovan Archer piles. Billy picked up an expense report with a copy of a receipt from Dante.

"Hold up, here." The receipt was dated four days ago and time-stamped 10:57 p.m.

"What?"

"This receipt. Bradley J. was in the hotel a few nights ago. He submitted it as an expense."

"Let's see if there are any meeting notes from that night. Maybe we can tie him to something."

Billy went through the stack of meeting notes. Nothing.

Monk's phone rang. "Hey, Iz...Yeah, I know. We're working on something here." He glanced at Billy. "Izzy says hi."

Billy paddled his hands for the phone and Monk tossed it over. He stared at it a minute and decided to face Izzy's wrath like a man. "Are you pissed at me? I told him not to come."

"No. I told him to go. He was worried about you."

"And you got diamond earrings out of it."

"You bet I did. Are you okay?"

Billy glanced at his bandaged arm. "I'm good. No worries."

"Stay safe, Billy. Put Peter on. I'm going to bed and wanted to say goodnight."

And suddenly, Billy's core echoed with the emptiness that came from not having someone to say goodnight to. That gator bite must have infected him with some sort of chemical agent that transformed a man into a wuss. Maybe he needed a stronger antibiotic because this emotional crap was fucked.

He handed the phone back to Monk and checked the time on his cell. Twelve-thirty. Too late to call Kristen. Why was he even thinking this? Particularly when he'd be leaving in a few days. *Wussie-boy*.

Monk ended his call and went back to the printouts. "I'm not seeing any meeting notes from the night at Dante. Did you ask Kristen if she knows this guy?"

"She doesn't. She typically won't hang out in the clubs, though." Billy stopped, held up a hand.

"What?"

"Jess. Between the party girl life and working the VIP lounges, she'd know all the players."

Monk shot two fingers at him. "Good. Let's talk to her in the morning."

"My favorite person."

"Suck it up."

"As if I didn't know that? Really?"

Monk sighed and the voice in Billy's head screamed, *Go, go, go.*

Nuh-uh. Filter engaged. Not going there with Monk again. That irresponsible behavior was what landed him in South Beach in the first place.

He shook it off. Arguing with Monk would take too much effort. "After we talk to Jess, we should check out Bradley J. Maybe tail him awhile. See what he's up to." Billy went to the white board, grabbed a marker. He wrote Alex's name on the board and tapped the marker against it. "We know he's involved with Alex because I saw them in that coffee shop last week." Bradley J.'s name went up next to Alex's. He circled both names and drew a line connecting them. "They have to be working this car theft ring together. It's too much of a coincidence all around. What we need to know is who is doing what."

Monk sat back and planted his hands on top of his head. "Were you able to match any of the hotel employees to the list of homeowners Janet gave you from the GPS?"

"Not the names. I asked Kristen for a list of employees' actual addresses though. There are a lot of rental properties down here. Maybe someone is a renter."

"Good call."

For another hour, the two sat at the table reading and creating a timeline from the various notes, billable hour reports, message slips and phone records they'd acquired on the sneak and peek. Each document sat down the length of the table in chronological order.

They just needed to figure out what it all meant.

Monk stood to stretch. "I need a combat nap. Give me thirty minutes of shut-eye and I'll be good."

"Thirty? Since when?"

Monk rolled his eyes. "This isn't exactly a hot zone. I can take an extra twenty."

A NOISE—PAPER SHUFFLING—FLOATED THROUGH BILLY'S head. He didn't mind so much. After that though, a throbbing in his lower back hammered at him. *Ow.*

Opening his eyes, he stared down at a sheet of paper under his arms, which were cradling his head. He blinked a couple more times, waited for his mind to clear. Right. He'd fallen asleep. Sitting at the conference room table.

More paper shuffling. Must be Monk. Billy lifted his head and focused on an older guy, sixty-ish, full head of black-gray hair, standing on the other side of the table.

He jumped out of his chair, his hands in front of him in case he had to kick someone's ass. After that gator fiasco, he wasn't taking any chances. To his right, Monk, shot off the floor to a standing position, his head swinging left and right in a room survey.

The older guy held his hands wide, the universal *whoa* signal, and stepped back. "Take it easy, boys. I'm Tom Dante."

Billy blew out a huge breath. Should have known by the triple-grand Italian suit. Not to mention the light pink shirt and pocket square. Took a strong man to wear a pink shirt.

Kristen's father. Holy flippin' smokes. He glanced at Monk, who stared at him a sec while the sleepy fog drifted away. *Yeah, buddy, wake up. This is the big cheese and we've got some 'splainin' to do.*

Now that no one's balls had been shot off, Billy let his panicked body settle to his normal, slighty hyper state and held his hand out. "I'm Billy Tripp, sir. Taylor Security? Sorry I startled you."

All three of them shook hands and Billy assumed parade rest while Mr. D. glanced over the stream of paper cluttering the table. "What have you boys got cooking?"

Dicey territory. Somehow Billy didn't think he should admit breaking into a law office. "We're looking into the hotel's car thefts, sir."

Mr. D. eyed him, then transferred his gaze to Billy's bandaged arm. "What happened there?"

Chances were pretty good that he should also *not* tell Tom Dante he'd been attacked by a gator. "Small accident. I'm fine."

"I see."

No, sir, you don't.

"Your Body Is a Wonderland" sprang from Billy's phone. His insides sank. Couldn't get a damned break. He scooped the phone from the table to shut it the hell up. Tom Dante was listening to the ringtone assigned to his daughter. The one about exploring her body.

Billy had to laugh. Had to. These ringtones were getting him into a load of trouble. He punched the button. "Hi."

"Good morning," the daughter in question said. "Where are you?"

"I'm sorry?"

"I'm by the pool. We were going to walk this morning. You forgot me?"

"Uh, no, never." *Except when meeting your father.* "I'm in the conference room." Billy fiddled with the pen on the table. Anything not to look at Tom Dante. "Talking to your dad."

And, yep, Kristen's father shot him a laser look before clearing his throat and smoothing his pristine tie.

"My *dad?*"

"Yep."

"He's not due in until tonight." She hesitated. "I'll be right there. Whatever you do, don't speak."

Talk about having little faith in his ability to filter. Hadn't he been making progress? A little at least?

He tossed the phone on the table, dug his hand into his scalp and gave it a good scratch. Heck of a morning so far. "Kristen is on her way up."

Please don't ask me why your daughter is calling me at six-thirty in the morning. Or about that ringtone.

Mr. Dante looked up at him, his gaze firm, not accusing, but steady in a way that told Billy he'd better watch his six. "I'm anxious to see her. I came home early to help with the senator's party."

Billy nodded. "We took care of the security for you, sir."

"I'm aware. Thank you."

Movement flashed by the door and Kristen swung around the corner wearing biking shorts that clung to her legs nicely and a baggy T-shirt Billy wanted to incinerate. *Friggin' crime.* She took the turn too fast, careened against the door and sent it crashing to the wall. For balance, she grabbed hold of the door handle for support, but momentum swung her forward and she stumbled to one knee.

Jeezus. Now would not be a good time to laugh.

Immediately, she popped to her feet and her ponytail flew over the front of her shoulder. So darn cute. She brushed it back, sucked wind like she'd sprinted upstairs, which given her fear he would say something offensive to her father, she probably had.

Billy grinned at her.

"Hi!" She shot Billy a look then focused on her dad with a big-butt smile on her face that looked as fake as half the Gucci purses in South Beach. "Dad! You're back early."

Her father's face split and the warmth in that smile could have powered the building. Kristen was impossible not to love. *Damn.* The big cheese wrapped her in a hug while Billy and Monk stood around like a couple of bad extras.

"Hi, honey. I got in late last night. Wanted to surprise you this morning."

She backed away from the hug. "Well, you did that. It's so good to see you. You've met Billy. And," she turned to Monk. "Peter. Hi. I didn't know you were back."

Monk aimed a save-me look at Billy.

"He's helping with security for the senator's party."

Mr. D. waved his hands over the table. "Billy was about to tell me what all this is."

Kristen's gaze went to the table, stayed there a minute and then came back to Billy. *Uh-oh.*

"Then I'm just in time."

"These look like meeting notes," Mr. D. said. "Who's Bradley J. Murphy?"

With that, Kristen's head snapped up and the stare she gave Billy should have melted the skin off his bones.

"He's a local attorney, Dad."

"We think he may somehow be involved in the car thefts," Billy added.

"Really?"

"Yes, sir."

With three fingers, Mr. D. tapped the top of the table and a thick gold bracelet slid down his wrist. "How did you get all these documents?"

Monk coughed.

Billy winced. "Sir, it's probably best I don't share that with you."

An awkward silence lingered until Kristen, smart woman that she was, said, "Did you *steal* these?"

Billy pressed his lips together. *Steal.* Harsh word. All they did was snap photos. "No. We did not."

Maybe he was playing word games, but life sucked that way. This whole conversation was like one giant Jedi mindfuck.

"You broke into his office? That's why you said you were tired last night? You lied to me so you could get me out of the way and break into the man's office?"

Billy stayed silent. Admitting they'd broken into the office would make Kristen and her father accomplices.

"What is *wrong* with you?" she hollered. "Dammit, Billy. What if you'd gotten caught? Forget the part about going to jail. Obviously that wasn't a concern, but you are a contractor for this hotel. You put us at stake too."

"Kris—"

She held her hands straight up and waved them back and forth so fast it blurred his vision. *Pissed.* World-class pissed.

So hot.

"No." She pointed at him. "Don't say one thing. You're bound to screw it up. I'm so furious with you, I can't think straight."

The big cheese turned to her. "Kristen—"

"Dad. Please. Don't. They broke into a building. As paid contractors, if they'd gotten caught, it could have been bad for the hotel." She turned back to Billy.

Did she want him to say something? What *could* he say? Couldn't admit it. Not if he intended on keeping them out of any possible legal issues.

"For a man who never shuts up," she said, "you're awfully quiet."

"You told me not to speak."

Not only did she give him the skin-melting look again, she gave it a kick by gritting her teeth. Then she spun on her spanking new sneakers and tore out of the office.

Her father watched her go, staring at the doorway while Billy imagined scooping his balls off the floor. *Not good.* Finally, Mr. D. shifted back. "Well, son, congratulations. Of my two daughters, *that* one is the most unflappable. And you've flapped her."

Monk, of course, being the richweed he was, laughed. "Billy has a tendency for that, Mr. Dante."

Billy eyeballed him. "Really? You're gonna go there?"

"Yes, *really.*" Monk turned back to the big cheese. "Mr. Dante, how about you give me ten minutes to get cleaned up and we'll review the security plan for tomorrow night. Perhaps over breakfast?"

"Good enough. That will give Billy here a chance to experience the wrath of my daughter, whose temper, although rarely seen, can be daunting. Good luck to you, son. You'll need it."

17

KRISTEN JAMMED HER FINGER AGAINST THE ELEVATOR BUTTON and contemplated taking the stairs in case someone—like that damned Billy Tripp—decided to chase after her.

Right now, she needed to be alone and calm the heck down. Maybe she'd take that walk on the beach by herself. If she didn't, she'd find a nice heavy club and use Billy as the test-dummy for a bludgeoning.

The elevator door slid open and she stepped on.

"Kristen!" Billy's voice. *No.* She jabbed at the button.

Last thing she needed was him stepping on this elevator. His voice grew louder just as the door slid closed. "Go away."

Very mature, Kristen.

She tapped the lobby button and waited, her pulse pounding from the blood overfilling her veins.

As soon as she stepped off the elevator, her phone rang and she reached to the waist holder to silence it. She knew who that was and wanted no part of him.

Unless he wanted to die.

In which case, she'd welcome him with open arms. How

did these irresponsible, aggravating, pain-in-the-butt people always land in her path? He broke into a building and didn't even bother to think about the ramifications if they'd gotten caught. Even if he didn't care that, as a paid contractor, going to jail would have reflected badly on the hotel. By now, he should have understood. Yet, knowing how important Dante was to her, he risked it anyway. He didn't care enough to consider her feelings.

Didn't that just break her heart?

She marched to the patio doors and pushed through. One of the maintenance men fiddled with a sprinkler in the shrubs and said a cheery good morning.

Cheery she didn't need right now, but she was still the boss and would be pleasant. She carved a smile onto her face and offered an equally cheery good morning. Oh, if only she could be that happy and not want to murder Billy Tripp.

The man was a royal pain. He came around and insanity followed. Happened every time. Every damned time.

She waved her fists in front of her as she stormed by the empty pool. "Ugh. You are such an idiot, Kristen. This man will destroy you."

"Hey," the destroyer yelled from behind her.

She picked up her pace and rushed through the iron gate separating hotel property from the beach, where a smattering of walkers and runners took advantage of a sixty-degree morning. "Go away, Billy. If you come too close I'll have to kill you. And that's *very* bad for business."

Then she heard him laugh and the miniscule thread of sanity she clung to snapped. Her temples throbbed and she pressed her palms to her head to keep it from flying apart. No, he would not goad her into a fight.

But then he was beside her, grabbing her arm, and she slapped at his grip.

"I'd like to squeeze your neck in my hands and watch your eyes bulge. That's how close I am to killing you."

She spun away and stalked down the beach.

"So flippin' hot," the ass said, and something inside her went apoplectic—just tearing at her like a runaway missile.

She turned and, fists in the air, charged him. Then she lost her balance in the sand, went sailing forward and landed on him with enough force to knock him back a step. He caught her, but the two of them went down with her straddling him.

Before she could smack him, he grabbed onto her wrists and held her as she fought against his strength.

And... he laughed.

"Ohmygod!" She hadn't been this mad in a long time. On her knees, she scooted down, her butt sliding along his stomach as she tried to leverage herself to knee him in the groin.

"Don't you do it," he said, still holding her wrists. "That will seriously hurt me."

At least he wasn't smiling anymore. Finally, he'd gotten the message that she wanted to carve him up.

She continued to wiggle backward until she got to his hips and—*unbelievable*—the moron had an erection. God save her from the entire male species. All they could think about was sex.

Clearly, clearly her tirade was inflicting little fear in him. Trapped in his grasp, and with nothing left to do, she clamped her teeth together and growled at him.

"Oooh." He gripped her wrists tighter. "That scares me."

"Let me up!"

"Will you calm down?"

"No. I'm going to find a hunk of wood and beat you until I crush your skull. Let go."

To his credit, he once again did not laugh. "M.H., you know I'm stronger. I can sit here for a long time. *You'll* get tired of fighting before I do."

Murmuring voices caught Kristen's attention and a couple walked by, their eyes a little wild at the sight before them.

"Hi, folks," Billy said. "Great morning, ay?"

The man nodded and they continued on their way. *Hello?* Maybe someone could give her a hand? Considering she was being held captive. And Billy's stupid hard-on bulged against the back of her leg.

Wait a sec. What was she doing?

He was right. Fighting would be fruitless. But she could torture him in other ways. If nothing else, she knew his weakness and at that moment, had no problem exploiting it. She closed her eyes, drew a breath, relaxed her arms and eased herself into a half sitting, half leaning position on top of him. A few seconds later, the pounding in her head stopped and she opened her eyes.

"Billy," she softened her voice to barely a whisper. "I cannot believe this erection you have."

He grunted. "It's pretty flippin' amazing."

Still holding her wrists, he lightened his grip and stretched his arms over his head, taking hers with him so her upper body shifted closer to him and her breasts were against his chest. "This is much better."

He had no idea. She lowered her head, licked behind his ear and he groaned.

"M.H., I know what you're doing here and it's...uh...not gonna work."

Sure it is. Another lick.

His body, all of it, stiffened under her. "This. Is cheating."

She rocked her hips, pressed herself against him and licked behind his ear again. If any other guests walked by, she'd be mortified.

"Kristen, you will lose this game."

"I don't think so. In fact, at the moment, I seem to be the one in charge." She ran her tongue along his jaw and got another throaty groan out of him. This plan just might work.

"You are seriously going to get it."

Another lick behind the ear. "Promises, promises."

Suddenly, she rolled, the salty sea air whooshing by her, and she landed on her back, the full weight of him pressing into her.

"Ha," he said. "Who's in charge now?"

She closed her eyes. "Billy."

"You think you're so shrewd. What are you gonna do now? I could keep you here all day. All. Day. Long, sweetheart. Won't that be fun?" He glanced around. "This place gets busy around noon."

Clearly, her plan had been hijacked. And he was bastard enough to keep her here while her guests came and went. "Get off."

"Nah. *I* think I might enjoy spending the day like this. Maybe I'll introduce you to the guests? That would be hospitable wouldn't it? Hi, folks, the woman I'm groping is Kristen Dante, general manager of the hotel. You got a need, she can fulfill it. And let me tell you, I've got a need."

Horror aside, she couldn't not laugh. "You wouldn't dare."

"Please. You know I live to go off leash."

"Ms. Dante?"

Her lungs froze. She spotted one of the pool guys hauling lounge chairs to the beach.

How humiliating.

"Hi, Greg. How are you today?" What the heck else could she say when a strange man was lying on top of her?

Greg shot a look at Billy, then back to her. "Are you okay? Need some help?"

Billy grinned down at her. Such a jerk. "I'm good. Thanks. Self-defense lesson."

"Ah." Greg forged on.

Billy snuggled into her neck, sending a jolt of heat down her spine. "I love a woman who's fast on her feet."

"You made your point. Let me up."

He squinted. "Are you going to hit me?"

"No."

"Yell at me?"

"Possibly."

"After you yell at me, will you help me get rid of this hard-on?" He wiggled his eyebrows.

The male mind. So simple.

"I will not. In fact, I hope you walk around all day like a stiff old man. Let me up. I want my walk."

He slid off, rolled to his side. "Okay, sweetness, all set. Let's take your walk and then you can help me with my problem."

She laughed at the protrusion in his shorts. "I'm not doing it."

"I'm gonna make you walk fast. You'll need a shower afterward." He leaned in, kissed her neck. "As I recall, you like showers."

She sure did. Kristen stepped back, smacked his good arm. "I was under extreme stress. You could have gotten killed. It was a spontaneous thing."

"Mmm, imagine if we take our time. You like long showers, M.H.? I typically don't, but if you were in there with me I'd come up with all kinds of reasons to linger."

"Stop."

He locked an arm around her. "It could be amazing."

It could.

And kissed her. Long and slow and gentle. Her girl parts didn't just go crazy, they suffered a major breakdown. Her limbs went soft and loose and she slid her arms around him just wanting to hang on.

This will never work. He's a wildcard.

She backed away from the kiss, focused her gaze on his. "You make me crazy. Sometimes I really want to throttle you."

"I do that to people. I'm sorry."

"Promise me you won't break into any more offices."

He hesitated, but kept his gaze on hers. "I can't do that."

"Billy—"

"I never break a promise and I want that streak to continue. Vic told me I have to be back in Chicago on Monday. I need to fast track this car theft thing."

Monday. The initial blow to her heart penetrated. Let the breaking begin. But really, how long had she thought he'd stay? He should have been gone already.

"Doesn't what I think matter? Or will you just continue to break laws and risk the reputation of my hotel?"

"Of course it matters."

"Then why the hell did you do it? Did you stop to think how this could impact me? That it could possibly hurt me?"

"Kris—"

"We're partners in this and you disregarded my feelings. And that, Billy, I can't stand. Worse, I'm not sure you even feel bad about it."

"No. There you're wrong. I do feel bad. I'm sorry. I need to get this done. Those richweeds tossed me to a gator. That pissed me off, and I made a decision that was unpopular."

She threw her hands in the air. "Unpopular? You just don't get it. I want what I think to matter to you. Clearly it doesn't."

"That's horseshit and you know it. I just didn't see any other way. The information obtained is good. I feel crappy that I hurt you though."

She let out a breath. What were they doing? "They're just cars. It's not worth getting hurt over."

"It's not about the cars anymore."

"What is it then? Your ego?"

"My ego is healthy as can be. This is about helping you figure it out. These fudgers think they can run roughshod over people. It's about shoving it up their asses."

"And is that worth all of this?"

"Sometimes, when it's for the right reasons, yes. Plus, when I only have a few days to figure it out. Time for extreme measures."

"Does Vic have an assignment for you?"

Billy shrugged. "He didn't say. He wants me in Chicago though. I'll make nice and if he's not ready to send me out again, I'll come back here until he does." He inched closer. "South Beach is growing on me."

Somehow, she believed him. "You're trying to get me in that shower."

He nodded. "For sure. But I'm not playing you to do it. If I only wanted to get laid, I'd walk down this beach and find a willing participant. It's not hard."

She rolled her eyes.

"Let me correct that, it's not totally about getting laid."

He lowered his head and kissed her, just a soft touch of his lips against hers. "It's about getting laid with *you*."

Poetry, Billy Tripp style.

She backed away. "I'm still mad at you, but I'm up for a walk. Maybe I'll work off my anger while you continue to tell me how sorry you are. Besides, I'll need to get good and sweaty to justify a long shower."

"Maybe we'll run a little. With your busy schedule, we can carve out extra shower time."

NINETY MINUTES LATER, KRISTEN SLID OUT OF HER SUITE'S pitch-black bathroom wearing a towel that struggled to stay closed over her ginormous boobs. Billy was still in the shower and she hurried to the bedroom, closing the door for privacy.

She should just suck it up and let him see her. He'd been patient and creative by coming up with ways they could be intimate without him seeing her naked. But Billy was a sexual guy and, sooner or later, she'd have to pony up. He liked skin against skin. Not to mention he wanted to put a stripper pole in her suite. Leave it to her, a woman with catastrophic self-image issues to wind up with a man who thought living on a nudist colony would be a dream come true.

He knocked on the bedroom door. "You okay?"

"I'm good."

"I need my clothes. They're on your bed."

She spun and spotted his jeans and a shirt right there on the bed. What now? She could hide behind the door and pass them through to him.

Or she could open the door and let him get them himself.

She opened the door and stood to the side as Billy entered, a towel wrapped around his waist and water drops dotting his shoulders. He glanced down at her covered body, but quickly averted his eyes. Knowing her hang-ups, he obviously didn't want to prolong the look and make her more uncomfortable.

Dangerous, dangerous man with how thoughtful he could be.

"You can look. I won't freak out. Baby steps, right?"

After a few seconds, he sat on the bed, his gaze remaining on her face.

"It's okay, Billy."

"You won't flip out?"

"No. It's like you said the other day, your hands were all over me. I think it's safe to say you know my body."

He grinned. "I do indeed."

"So, we're making progress. A week ago, I would never have stood in front of you in a miniscule towel."

"Progress is good."

Then he looked. A slow drag of his gaze over her towel-clad body. Her pulse quickened and the throb at her temples, the immense pressure of being his sole focus, forced her to close her eyes.

"You okay?" he asked.

She smiled. "I'm good. Getting used to it is all."

"You really are beautiful, Kris. You just don't see it."

She opened her eyes. "Billy—"

"I'm not going to hassle you, but by the time I get done with you, you're gonna believe me. I want you to see what I see."

With that, he stood, dropped his towel and retrieved his underwear from the bed.

To be that confident. That unaffected by stares. It would

be a blessing. She marched to her dresser, dug around for the red lace bra and matching panty and placed them on top.

Behind her, Billy laughed. "That is so wrong letting me see that stuff."

The lingerie. She snatched the bra and panty against her. "I'm sorry."

"I can't believe you wear it for yourself only. That's a crime, M.H."

She turned to him. "I wear it and imagine I'm skinny."

"Once again, a crime." Finally, he stepped to her, slid his hand inside the towel to her stomach and the rough texture of his fingers sent her skin flaming. "Just because I haven't seen you naked doesn't mean I don't have a picture in my head." He grazed his thumb over the underside of her breast and she closed her eyes, breathed in. She loved his hands on her. He always seemed to know just where to touch her. Each little spot that would make her skin pucker.

"Turn around," she said.

"What?"

"I'm going to put this stuff on and let you see. Turn around before I lose my nerve."

In a dramatic flash, he spun backward. "Score!"

Kristen cracked up. "Filter, dopey."

Quickly, she slipped into the underwear and bra, made the necessary adjustments and closed her eyes. *You can do this. He knows your body*. This was just the next baby step. Not completely naked. Heck, most women wore less on the beach.

The lacy underwear was pretty but covered her hips and butt. The bra, too, covered everything. If only she could do something with that bit of flab at her waist.

Stop.

She threw her shoulders back, lifted her head and, with her eyes still closed, breathed deep. "I'm ready."

Liar.

The rustle of clothing distracted her and she opened her eyes. Billy moved toward her, his gaze on her and extremely, mortifyingly predatory. *Stand tall.*

"Wow," he said.

Leaning in, he brushed a kiss over her cheek. "This is not a big deal."

He wrapped his arms around her, dotted kisses along her shoulder and ran his hands down her back. Thankfully, he didn't squeeze or she'd freak over his fingers digging into the fat.

"It feels like a big deal."

"You look amazing. The red is sexy. I love it."

With that, he smacked her on the ass, turned back to the bed and retrieved his shirt. No fuss, no staring at her, no dropping to the floor.

Thank you. Here they were, a couple of lovers preparing for their day. She could do this. No hiding behind a robe or a door.

Billy slid his flip-flops on, stood to finger comb his hair by the mirror. "M.H., unless you want me to strip you out of that underwear, you'd better hop to it. A man can only tolerate so much."

"I can't believe I'm standing here like this."

He cracked a smile. "And I'm damned thankful for it."

"You don't see what I see."

Done messing with his hair, he turned to her, leaned back against the dresser and crossed his arms. "Exactly what I've been telling you. I see a sexy, full-figured woman who knows how to rock some red lingerie. You need to own it.

Embrace the hotness. You're never going to be skinny. You're not built for it. It doesn't mean you're fat."

"Chubby."

He rolled his eyes. "Solid."

This little game was kind of fun. She stepped closer. "Thick."

His gaze moved over her body in a slow, searing path. Not an easy thing for a girl with self-image issues to withstand, but she remained still, stiffening her spine. He was testing her. Wanting to see how far she'd let him go before she imploded. Finally, he looked into her eyes, flashed the crooked bad-boy grin and said, "Rubenesque."

Kristen drew a long breath and blew it through her lips. "You are so getting laid later."

"I have time now."

And yet, his arms remained crossed. He hadn't touched her. Somehow he knew to let her get comfortable playing the game. She went to him, so close, just inches apart and leaned in, cradling her head against his shoulder until he brought his arms around her and let his right hand settle on her ass.

Baby steps.

"I have a meeting with my dad in ten minutes."

"Ho!" Billy shot his hands to the ceiling. "Way to kill a moment, M.H."

She grinned. "I'm sorry. After my tantrum this morning, I don't want to be late. He's still my boss."

"I can wait. Besides, I need to hunt down some info on this Bradley J. Murphy guy. When we were going through his files, I found notes and a bar tab from a meeting he had here last week."

"Really? Where was the receipt from?"

"Club Inferno. Do you mind if I ask the employees if they remember him?"

"No, but be discreet. Your best bet would be to start with Jess. We can look for her after I meet with my dad. She usually gets here at about eleven and spends the afternoon on the VIP pool deck. If Bradley J. was meeting with anyone important, Jess would know. She works the VIPs like nobody's business. If I had faith that she wouldn't bolt at any time, I'd think she'd actually found her niche. With her celebrity contacts, she could do a lot for us."

"Maybe you need to tell her that."

"No. She'll get mad. She'll think I'm pressuring her to do something with her life."

"Aren't you?"

"Sometimes. She's twenty-four years old. No college degree or sustained work history. She's famous, but it's for her bad behavior. That doesn't sit well with me. I also have the name Dante and don't want it being famous because of a sex tape."

Billy raised his eyebrows. "Was it a good sex tape?"

"Billy!"

He threw up his hands. "Joking. I was going for levity. Sorry."

"Totally inappropriate. Filtering isn't just not saying things, it's knowing when jokes are appropriate or not."

He slid his arm around her to keep her from stalking off. "Don't be mad. I'm sorry. Sometimes I suck at this challenge." He trailed kisses down her neck and her breasts tingled. *Oh, boy*.

"I need to go."

"I know."

But he was still trailing kisses up and down her neck, over her shoulders and—where were his hands going? He slid them up her sides and she became an oven. Literally sweating. She loved when he touched her. With him, intimacy didn't send her on a psychotic trip into overthinking land. Knowing she didn't like to be stared at, he always let his hands do the work. The easy touches, the slow slide of calloused fingers against her skin until she shivered.

"I have to go," she said again, but didn't move. "I don't want to leave you though. I love how you touch me."

He trailed the backs of his fingers over the tops of her breasts and stepped back an inch. "My fingers give me a good picture. Whenever you're ready though, you can lose the underwear and we'll have a hell of a good time."

Stretching to tiptoes, she kissed him. "I know. We're almost there. Today was a big step for me. Thank you. You make me feel beautiful and that's never happened before. Makes my girl parts go crazy."

"You should feel beautiful. It's what you are." He held up three fingers. "Three minutes to Daddy, M.H. Get your ass moving."

"What are you doing?"

"I'm going back to my war room to study those notes. Monk went through the security plan for tomorrow with your dad and is now sitting on Bradley J. to see where that bleeper goes. My guess is, if someone wanted to strike your hotel again during the senator's shindig, they'd be gearing up for it today."

"Don't tell me that."

"Sorry, sweet cheeks. Lucky for you, we've got it under control. With the security we have in place, no one will steal a car from here tomorrow night. That, I can promise you."

18

Billy sat in the war room, his flip-flop-clad feet propped on the fancy table and his arms tucked behind his head while he contemplated the puzzling white board. There were so many connections and yet, he couldn't hook any of them.

His interviews of the hotel employees regarding who had access to car keys, the drivers' schedules or anything else transportation related, had turned up nothing. Not even an iota of a suspicion on his part. Good for Kristen that her employees were an honest lot, but bad for his investigation.

Back to Bradley J. Murphy and Donovan Archer. Yes, they were the registered agents for the Jaguar and BMW dealerships. Yes, both those makes of cars had been stolen with the use of keys rather than the antenna. Was it enough to tie these guys to the thefts?

Not yet.

But throw in Jess's cheating wuss of an ex-boyfriend and Billy's mental radar went off the charts. Maybe Alex was responsible for picking up the copied keys and delivering the money to the worker-bee at the dealerships?

Old Alex was the middleman.

Did the dealership owner, or owners—assuming it was two different people, which Billy doubted—even know Bradley J. and Donovan were in on it?

Billy sat forward, gave the war board a stare that should have sawed through it.

"Wow," Manny said from the doorway, and Billy slipped from his trance. "You look mad."

"Manuel, how are you, my friend?"

The kid looked at the board and Billy sucked in a breath. *He shouldn't be looking at it.*

"What are you doing?" Manny asked.

Billy waved his arms to draw Manny's gaze from the board. "Just working on some stuff. You got off school early today?"

"No school today. Teacher conferences."

"Ah." Billy had always hated teacher conferences. In his mind, they'd been the opportunity for educators to tell his parents he needed meds. Back then, school administrators hadn't known how to deal with him and his active brain.

"Can I help you?" Manny asked. "With your stuff? I'll be quiet."

Not a good idea. Billy grinned at the kid. He didn't so much mind him hanging around, but whatever was going on with this war board wasn't for him to see.

"First, you being quiet isn't possible. That I can live with. I'm afflicted with an anti-silence mode myself. Second, I'm doing grown-up stuff, pal, and I don't think it's a good idea for you to be involved."

Immediately, the kid's face collapsed. "Did I do something wrong?"

Billy walked to him and got to eye level. "Not at all. Why would you think that?"

"You don't let me hang out with you anymore. Not since I helped in the parking lot."

Ah, crap. Dead last thing he wanted was for this heck of a nice kid to feel abandoned or left out. "I promise you didn't do anything wrong. It's grown-up stuff, okay?"

In typical Manny style, he swiped a hand across his forehead and smiled the oversized-teeth smile that never failed to entertain. "Whew! I thought I was in trouble because I told my brother."

Uh-oh. Billy's ears thumped, but he kept his lips sealed and his stance neutral until the urge to go full throttle passed. "You're not in trouble. What did you tell your brother?"

The brother Kristen suspects is a gang member.

Manny rocked back and forth. "You know, about helping with the cameras that day. I thought it was cool that I got to help."

The mild thumping in Billy's ears turned to a head rush that spun the room and he fought to remain still. Bleeping son of a biscuit. Manny told his brother the possible gang member about discovering the blind spot. Could this be how the thieves figured out he adjusted the security?

If not, that was one hell of a coincidence.

He stared at Manny, who clearly thought this revelation might end their partnership. At that moment, the one thing Billy knew, without a doubt, was that he didn't want to break this kid's heart.

Not today.

Not ever.

"Listen, Boy Wonder, sometimes things go a little sideways and we have to work around it. It's not a big deal. Don't sweat it."

"Let It Be" sounded from his phone. He snatched it up and punched the talk button. "Hi, Ma. Hang on a sec."

Billy dropped a hand on Manny's shoulder. "You're not in trouble, okay?"

Manny nodded.

"This is my mom. I gotta take it. You know how that is, right?"

Again, he nodded.

"Good deal. I should be done with my work in a couple hours. How about I find you and we grab something to eat or an ice cream? That work for you?"

The kid's cheeks transformed into happy, grinning bunches and Billy felt a stab in his chest. He'd miss this turkey when he left.

Manny bolted and Billy went back to his phone. "Hi, Ma."

"What are you doing?"

He rolled his eyes. Even his mother? Could he get a damned break from people always questioning his actions? "I'm still in Florida working on a security issue at Dante."

Mom clucked her tongue. "Have you met Tom Dante? You know I find him very attractive."

And people wondered where his filtering issues came from? "Uh, no, I didn't realize you find him attractive. If you were here, I'd introduce you. He just got back from Dubai." *Right after I got friendly with his daughter in the shower.* He blew out a breath because—for God's sake—he was talking to his mother and thinking X-rated thoughts about Kristen. "Anyway, nice man."

A knock sounded and Billy glanced up to see the X-rated one in the doorway. He grinned and waved her into the room. "Did I mention I'm crushing on his daughter?"

"Oh, Billy, not her. She's too wild. I read all about her in the tabloids. She's loose."

Tension curled around his neck. His attempt at humor had backfired. What the hell was he supposed to say? *Not the slutty daughter, the other one.* With Kristen standing a foot away? Not a wise move.

"No. *Kristen* is the oldest."

He grinned up at Kristen and she smiled. Very good. Make like his mother asked a question.

"Oh, you mean the *other* sister. The one who runs the hotel?"

"Yes."

Mom sniffed. "I'm so proud. Finally. A decent girl."

"Ma!"

M.H. drew her eyebrows together. This thing was turning into a landslide. He cleared his throat and said to Kristen, "My mother thinks with your brains and our combined good looks, we'll have exceptional children."

"I did not say that," his mother said.

"She did not say that," Kristen said.

Billy went back to his phone. "Ma, don't lie. You know you did."

Too much fun. But one of them was bound to kill him. Still, a vision of Kristen chasing after a brood of kids, his kids, popped to mind. That alone was a shock. Not only the thought of kids, but settling down, staying in one place with one woman had never been on his agenda.

But Kristen, she'd be a terrific mom, just like his own mother, who would support her child, no matter how exhausting that child might be. Kristen's patience with her sister and him, and her love for Manny, they were proof of it.

"I should smack you," Mom said.

Speaking of loving mothers. Billy laughed.

"What are you doing about Christmas?" Mom asked.

Christmas? Billy glanced at Kristen and something in his chest opened up. What that was, he didn't know, nor had it ever happened before, but he liked it. A lot. Suddenly, he knew where he wanted to be for Christmas.

"Not sure yet. I'm due back in Chicago on Monday. I guess I'll get my schedule then. I'll let you know."

"Well, it would be nice to see you. I know you were just here for Thanksgiving, but..."

"I know, Ma. If I don't make it for Christmas, I'll make it there soon. Okay? I gotta go. Can I call you back?"

"How's the swearing going?"

Still staring at Kristen's back, fighting the urge to check out her legs in the midthigh skirt while talking to his *madre,* he winced. "I'm at about seventy percent."

"*Seventy?* That's it?"

He pushed his thumb and index finger into his eyes. All she'd asked was for him to quit swearing and he couldn't give her a one hundred percent? After all she'd done for him? She deserved more. "I'm sorry. It's not easy when I'm around guys who swear all day. It's like being sober around a bunch of drunks. I kinda want to join in."

That made his mother laugh and he grinned at the sound. He could always make her laugh. Which, he supposed, was part of his problem. The sound of someone's laughter always kicked him to high gear and the more people laughed, the more outrageous he got.

"Thank you for trying," his mother said. "I'll talk to you later."

Billy clicked off, tossed his phone on the table.

Kristen spun from the war board. "Everything okay?"

"My mom was checking in. Wanted to know about

Christmas and my swearing. I think I disappointed her on both."

Kristen sat in the chair across from him. "But you're trying. You're definitely getting better. That's worth something, right?"

"She's used to my whacked-out schedule. And the swearing, well..." he shrugged. "What are you doing for Christmas?"

"We go to my dad's on Christmas Eve. It's always fun to see my extended family. Every year Dad hires some fantastic chef. Then I spend a quiet Christmas Day with my mom."

Any room for me? But no, he wouldn't ask. Odd to even be thinking about it. He hadn't spent a Christmas with a woman outside of his family in years.

"I think I would like doing the same thing every year. I never know where I'll be. Can't really make any plans."

Kristen leaned forward and propped her chin in her hand. "I couldn't do that. I like traditions. It's the one time all year we come together and just enjoy being a family. Even Jess shows up. Too bad you're going back to Chicago. You could have come to my dad's with me. We always have guests. It's an open door for wayward friends."

That got his attention. "Really? Your dad just met me."

She laughed. "Yeah, but he was amused. He likes your ambition. Even if you did break ten or twenty laws."

"Don't start, M.H."

She held up her hands. "That's not why I came in here. Jess is on the VIP pool deck. If you want to talk to her, we can go now."

Billy shot from his chair. "I found some bar receipts in Bradley J.'s files that have a weird drink on them. I want to see if she knows whose drink it is. And, by the way, Manny told his brother the gang member about me finding the blind spot."

Slowly, Kristen turned to him with a so-that's-what-happened look.

"Yep," Billy said. "Another piece to the puzzle. I'm not putting it on my board though. I don't want Manny to see it. He thought he was in trouble. That kid breaks my damned heart."

"I know. He's such a good boy. Did you tell him he's not in trouble?"

"Yeah, but it proves your point about talking in front of him. Either way, if he told his brother about the blind spot, maybe the brother shared it with our friend the gang member who got busted. It's a link. I don't know how the hell it ties back to this car dealer thing yet, but we'll figure it out."

The immediate step to that would be talking to Jess about the bar receipts. "Let's go find your sister."

THEY STEPPED ONTO THE POOL DECK, WHERE THE HOSTESS stood by the gated entrance checking names on the guest list. Kristen surveyed the area. Gorgeous, long-legged, bikini-clad women outnumbered the men by three to one. Palm trees swayed in the breeze and offered shade to five cabanas holding tables covered with food. Kristen imagined the profits that would stem from this weekend and hummed to herself.

She turned to one of the gorgeous, long-legged women, this one wearing a haltered mini-dress with a Dante nametag. "Hi, Sherry. Busy day up here."

"Sure is. The senator's guests are arriving. I just called down for extra lounge chairs."

"Good. Whatever we need to do to keep the senator happy, just let me know."

"Yes, ma'am." Sherry turned her attention to Billy and threw her shoulders back so her boobs took center stage. In the halter dress, it wasn't hard, but Kristen supposed the cleavage helped Sherry's tip fund. She couldn't blame a girl for trying to make a living, but the familiar pang of insufficiency nipped her. The beautiful people of the world wouldn't understand.

Billy though, he was scanning the pool deck, ignoring Sherry and her boobs. Excellent. That would earn him extra attention that evening. "Is Jess here?"

"By the bar."

Kristen grabbed Billy's arm, brought him through the gate onto the pool deck and turned to him. "Thank you."

"For what?"

"For pretending to ignore Sherry and her perky boobs."

"What boobs?"

"Exactly. You scored points on that one, Billy Tripp."

"Working for the nudity, M.H. Workin' for the nudity."

"Keep it up and you just might get it."

Tilting his head close to her ear, he said, "You tramp you."

A spark of heat unrelated to the blazing sun, whirled in her core. Oh, to bottle that feeling for his eventual departure. She closed her eyes and willed that nasty seed of a thought away. She'd take what she could get and deal with the carnage later. She opened her eyes and spotted her sister in stiletto heels and a bright pink string bikini that was more string than bikini. "Speaking of tramps, there's Jess."

Immediately, she slapped her hand over her mouth. What a thing to say.

"Filter," Billy mimicked.

"I can't believe I just said that."

"Eh, give yourself a break. It was a moment of weakness." He grinned that silly grin of his. "I have them all the time."

"Don't I know it?"

Kristen stopped to greet guests, thank them for their business and inquire about their needs. Part of her job was keeping these high rollers happy and if sending over champagne would do it, well, she'd suck it up. Within reason.

Each stop brought her closer to Jess, and a wave of insecurity churned in her stomach. As much as Billy didn't like Jess, he was a man and Jess knew how to rattle men.

She glanced at Billy, but he kept busy scanning the pool deck.

"Hi, Jess," Kristen said.

In a well-practiced move, her sister placed her hand on the arm of the older man she spoke with, excused herself and turned to Kristen with a bright, welcoming smile. Jess's mother was an actress after all. "Have you met Brian Dobson? He's an aide to the senator."

After exchanging pleasantries, Kristen borrowed Jess for a private chat.

"What's up?" Jess adjusted the strings on the bottom of her bikini.

Billy, being Billy, watched with a sort of detached fascination. *No.* Kristen straightened her shoulders and thought back to her lacy red underwear and the steamy look he'd given her.

He shoved the photo he'd printed of Bradley J. Murphy toward Jess. "You recognize this guy?"

She glanced at the picture, then back to him, her eyes fusing with his in that same flirtatious manner—the do-me look—she reserved for every other man that came within ten feet of her.

Jess nodded. "He's a lawyer, right? Brad something?"

"Bradley J. Murphy from Smith, Kline, Abrams."

"I saw him last week."

"Who was he here with?" Kristen asked.

"Don't know. I only remember him because he had that snake Alex ask me to deliver a drink to Reed Davis."

"The music guy?" Billy asked.

"Yeah. Reed was in the VIP lounge." Jess shifted to Kristen. "It was that night Reed went over his credit limit and you had to talk to him. I thought the timing was funny that this guy wanted to buy Reed a drink the same night he shot his credit."

"What was the drink?" Billy wanted to know.

"A Cabo Cactus."

A sly quirk of Billy's lips made Kristen think this Cabo Cactus thing was good news.

"What the hell is that anyway?" he asked.

"Cabo Wabo Tequila, triple sec, club soda and a splash of lime. Reed likes the rim of the glass salted with a slice of lime."

For the first time, Kristen found herself in a rare proud moment when it came to her sister. People didn't realize how hard Jess's job could be. She had to keep straight every high roller's personal preferences and make sure those preferences were delivered. Every time.

If only Jess realized her job, the one with access to celebrities and the social circuit she so loved, was tailor-made for her.

"Is that the only time you've seen him?" Billy asked.

Jess shrugged. "I don't remember him from any other time. I meet a bazillion people though. Why?"

To keep him from expounding, Kristen put her hand on Billy's arm. "I'm thinking about hiring him for legal work. Thought you might know him."

"I could ask around."

Kristen shook her head. One thing she didn't need was her already high-strung sister getting in the middle of a car theft ring. "Don't worry about it. You gave me all I needed." She glanced around the pool deck. "You're going to be busy this weekend. Do you need anything?"

Jess puckered her lips. Hesitated. Could her sister actually be afraid to ask?

"What, Jess?"

"Can you raise my budget for the weekend? These big shots are going to be asking for a lot."

The entertainment budget allowed Jess to offer comps to high rollers, but Kristen approved all charges. They would meet privately each week to set the comps limit. But this would be an important weekend for Dante and Jess's schmoozing skills could make the guests happy. Extremely happy.

"I'll look at the budget as soon as I get upstairs. If I raise it, you need to control it. Only the necessary stuff. Got it?"

For once, Jess simply nodded. "I've got it. I know this is a big weekend for you."

"For us," Kristen corrected. "Have you seen Dad yet?"

"I found him when I got here. He left before I woke up this morning."

"He was here early," Billy said.

He sure was. Kristen smothered a smile. Billy bumped her with his elbow and the moment of levity, the naughty shared secret, drifted between them until they finally gave in and laughed.

Jess's gaze darted between them as she waited for

someone to clue her in. Realizing she was not the focus of the situation, she propped her hand on her cocked hip, slathered on her sex-kitten smile and said, "Billy Tripp, you are one fine looking man."

Wasn't this typical? How many times had Kristen watched her sister pounce on a man solely because Kristen had an interest in him? It never mattered if it were a boyfriend, a casual acquaintance, a friend, whatever.

The familiar pinch of jealousy pressed in and Kristen forced her shoulders back, fought the seed of worry that Billy would humiliate her.

"Save it." Billy turned to Kristen. "My attention is elsewhere."

A rush of air filled her. Finally, a man who could resist the temptation of Jess's flirtations. Kristen stood taller when he ran a hand over her lower back. Nothing too intimate in front of her employees and guests, but enough for Jess to know her vicious plan had failed. *Thank you.*

Jess didn't look happy. Not if the miserable scowl was any indication. To make sure they knew just how far reaching her irritation went, she swung her tiny ass around and stalked off. Served her right for spoiling a perfectly civil conversation. And just when Kristen was starting to have hope.

Billy inched his head back and forth. "You're gonna yell at me, but your sister is a witch. She treats you like crap. With what you do for her, you deserve better."

He's right.

"Believe it or not, I won't yell at you. Sometimes, *sometimes,* it's okay when you don't filter."

He opened his mouth and she held her hand up. "Quit while you're ahead."

He snapped his mouth shut. "Good, boy. What's next on Bradley J. Murphy?"

"We head back to my war room to check out Reed Davis. I'm curious if there's a reason Bradley J. was buying him a drink."

Billy unlocked the conference room door with Kristen on his heels. He held the door open for her and she sauntered by, swinging her hips like the blazing hot chick she was. Telling Jess to shove it had scored him big time points. *Big* bleeping points.

Life was good.

"What do you know about Reed Davis?" he asked.

She pulled a chair, sat and crossed her legs, giving him a glimpse of thigh under her short skirt. Unfortunately for him, she wore a blazer over her blouse, but at least the jacket lacked any major frump factor.

"All I know about him is he owns Reed Records. They started as a rap label. Now they do R and B also. I think he's from L.A., but I'm not sure. He's a fixture around South Beach. Extremely visible in community activism."

Billy grabbed his laptop and sat next to M.H. "Let's see what we can dig up on old Reed."

She leaned toward him and the front of her blouse drooped. *Don't look.* He'd just keep his gaze glued to the laptop screen. Well, maybe just a quick gander. He shifted a glance in her direction. Wasn't his fault he could see right down her blouse to the devastating red bra.

"Hey." Kristen smacked him on the head. "Quit looking down my shirt. You need to focus."

He grinned. "I am focused."

She tapped the laptop screen. "This guy donates

millions to gun control and violent crime campaigns in Miami."

Now that the moment was shot to hell, he turned back to the laptop. "But stealing high-end cars isn't a violent crime, M.H. At least not until they threw me to a gator."

"You think Reed has something to do with the stolen cars?"

He shrugged.

"Why not?" Billy scanned the results of his web search. "There's a ton of crap on him. I'll get Janet working on his financials. That's not going to tell us much. If he's in on this car theft ring, he's going to hide the money in an offshore account somewhere. Worth a shot though."

"What can I do?"

He pointed to the pile of papers in front of her. "Go through those meeting notes. See if there's any reference to Reed Davis. Maybe something will kick."

Within twenty minutes, Billy had learned Reed Davis was an expat who grew up in the Middle East—mostly Saudi Arabia—while his father worked as an engineer. Fancy that after Billy's visit from the beefhead with the accent. After returning to the States at age eighteen, Reed attended college and interned at a rap label. Eight years later, he started his own label and Reed Records was born.

This damned Middle East connection coupled with the secret about the beefhead in the shed weighed on him. Time to come clean.

From the corner of his eye, he saw Kristen flip the last page of meeting notes and set it on the stack with the other's she'd read. He spun the chair toward her and tapped his fingers against the table. "I gotta tell you something."

"Oh, Billy. Am I going to hate this?"

"It's not that bad."

"Well then, go ahead and get it over with."

"Sunday morning I was checking the parking lot and three guys approached me. Actually, I was in the maintenance shed trying to find the door lock." He shook his head. "Doesn't matter. These three guys corner me in the shed and they tell me to stay out of the car theft situation. They offered to pay me. They said if I didn't play nice you'd have bigger problems than stolen cars."

She sat back and gripped the arms of her chair, her gaze steady on him, but otherwise he couldn't figure out if she was mad or scared.

He held his hands out. "Let me finish. I told them to shove it."

"Billy!"

"I didn't want to tell you. I was afraid you would freak and I didn't see much good in that. I'm sorry."

"Were these the same guys from the gator incident?"

"No. Different guys. The one guy from the shed had an Arabic accent and he said *'khalas.'* That's Arabic for it's finished or no more. The night I threw Alex and Jess out of here, Alex said *'khalas.'* Which is why I've been so bent on him being connected to these thefts." He waved toward his laptop. "Now I find out that Reed Davis grew up in the Middle East. Kris, I'm thinking we have an international car theft ring in full roar."

Now she placed her hand over her mouth, her eyes a little wide. "And we're in the middle of it."

"I think so."

She turned to the war board, stared at it a minute then walked to it.

"It makes sense. All these little pieces. And again, you kept it from me."

"Hang on. At the time, I didn't see how this information

would change anything and I didn't want to throw more on your plate. I didn't want to scare you. I figured if something came of it, I'd tell you. Which I just did."

She turned back to him, her mouth twisted. "I can live with that. I hate that you kept it from me, but I understand why you did it. And why you've been so diligent about the hotel's security."

"I thought I could control the situation. Plus, I wanted to be sure where my thoughts were going before I told you."

"What do we do now?"

"Did you find anything in those meeting notes?"

"No. Mr. Murphy doesn't specify the client's name. He only refers to him, or her, as 'client.'"

Billy grabbed his phone and dialed Monk, who was still watching Bradley J.

"Yo," Monk said.

"Anything?"

"No. Murphy hasn't left his office all morning. No lunch break yet. I'm guessing any time now."

"You still in contact with that FBI guy from last summer?"

"Sampson?"

"Yeah. The one who wanted to screw Izzy."

Kristen threw her hands in the air and whirled on him. "Maybe we should have you tested for Tourette's."

"Ack! Sorry." Who specifically he was apologizing to, he wasn't sure, but they both deserved it.

Monk, his legendary patience holding up, let out a heavy breath. "Sampson. We coexist. Why?"

"Need to find out what kind of car Reed Davis drives. He owns a record label down here and Jess says he met with our boy Bradley J."

"Call you back."

Monk hung up and Billy said, "He's gonna let me know."

"What are you thinking about Reed Davis?"

"Not sure. But I'm wondering if he could be the R and D in RDM Auto Group and MDR Auto. Nobody probably ever looked close enough to know."

Kristen moved her head side to side. "I'd be stunned. *Stunned*. Particularly with this latest development on Manny's brother. If Reed Davis owns those dealerships, there's no way he's involved with them supplying copied keys to gang members. I'd bet he doesn't know about the thefts. But, I'll leave that to you to figure out." She headed for the door. "I need to check on the senator's guests and the prep work for the wedding tomorrow."

"Do you need me?"

At the door, she turned back to him. "No. I'll call you if something comes up. Will you be around this afternoon?"

"Not sure. I may check out our friend Reed. See if I can find out myself what he drives. Crap."

"What?"

He smacked himself on the head. "Monk has the P.O.S. car. Got no wheels."

"If you promise to be good, I'll let you use one of the hotel cars."

"I could use your Aston."

She smiled at him in that sweet way that fired his engines. "No."

So much for his engines. "Dang."

"I'll tell my assistant to get you a car. Don't get into trouble. Please."

"Not me."

She huffed out a breath, but laughed. "Be careful."

"Always, sweet thing. Always."

19

BILLY HAULED HIS BORED AND TIRED SELF TO HIS ROOM thinking a shower, sex and a good meal—all with Kristen— would make his night. This Reed Davis thing was some hubba-bubba bullshit. He sat on that guy for seven hours and got nothing. Zip. Nada. To top off his mission of nothingness, he'd just followed Reed back to Dante. The man was now upstairs in Club Inferno.

Billy slipped his key card into the lock and shoved the door open to find Monk stretched on the king-sized bed, watching SportsCenter.

Monk muted the sound. "What's up?"

"Nothing."

"Me neither. Murphy went from work to his house. Bobby got here an hour ago and relieved me. I gave him a tracker to slap on Murphy's car. What the hell? You're spying on everyone else."

Some truth to that. Given the bad guys knew how to disable factory installed antitheft systems, paranoia or instinct, Billy wasn't sure which, persuaded him to hide a tracking device on Kristen's Aston. She'd be devastated if that ride disappeared and having his girl upset wouldn't do. Nope. Not gonna happen.

Except, they'd need a damned spreadsheet to keep all the tracking devices straight. "I'm nowhere on this thing."

Monk waved the remote at him. "You're bored. When you're bored you're a pain in the ass." He rolled and got to his feet. "Let's go to the war room and run scenarios. See what pops."

"I've done that a hundred times."

Monk held his arms wide. "Not with me. Let's hit it."

Billy checked his watch, glanced at the bathroom and the shower inside it.

Monk gave him a shove. "You got somewhere to be?"

Yes. He couldn't say that though. In Billy's opinion, this qualified as a real favorfuck. The guy was down here doing him a huge large, but was simultaneously screwing him out of getting laid.

The tick-tock of his investigation clock boomed in his head.

Damn.

He reached for his phone, sent Kristen a text that he needed another hour. He hated putting her off. Maybe they'd stumble onto something and get done quick. Couldn't hurt to be positive. At least that was his mantra on the way to the executive floor.

"Gentlemen," Kristen's dad said from his office just beyond the conference room. "Working late?"

Billy poked his head in the doorway. "Yes, sir."

An exceptional no-info answer. Last thing they needed was Tom Dante in the middle of this.

"Good. I'd like to hear what you have."

Monk leaned back into the hallway and raised his

eyebrows. No shit there. But was Billy supposed to tell the guy he wasn't allowed?

"Uh, sure. Fresh eyes never hurt."

At least until now.

Kristen stood outside the private dining room reading Billy's text while the senator's daughter enjoyed her rehearsal dinner. Billy wasn't done yet. And people said she worked too hard? He was no slouch either.

Well, she'd wait. And be grateful for it. This mission of his started over cars being stolen from her hotel. She knew it was no longer about the cars. It wasn't even about the hotel. Billy was simply mad. Rightly so, she supposed, but his determination, that obsessive intensity she both feared and admired, could cause him to miss the danger.

Could the constant chaos of him throwing himself head-first into peril be indicative of his life? If so, she didn't need it. She needed quiet nights and being settled. Getting attached to him meant never-ending movement and drama. He couldn't help himself. The craziness was part of him.

Some crazy couldn't be fixed.

She shook it off, ducked her head into the senator's party for one last check with the hostess and headed to her office. Might as well clear some paperwork while she waited.

As she unlocked her office door, voices from the conference room disturbed the quiet air. At least she knew where Billy was. She wandered down and halted in the doorway when she saw her father casually leaning back in one of the plush leather chairs while Billy pointed to something on the white board.

What was this now?

Fantastic. Now Dad was involved? And worse, Billy

hadn't even given her the courtesy of a phone call. In that initial moment it appeared her father's arrival meant she was no longer needed.

Would Billy freeze her out?

She sure hoped not.

"Hello," she said.

Billy glanced at her, but kept his features neutral. Stoic. *Oh, yes, you might be in trouble.*

"Hi," he said.

"What are you all doing?"

Dad watched her for a moment, his gaze steady. She tried a smile, but her father knew her well enough. "The boys are going over the results of their investigation. I asked them to fill me in."

Good save, Dad. With her faith somewhat restored, she grabbed the seat next to her father and waved Billy on. "I guess I'm just in time then."

Avoiding eye contact, he shifted to the board again, "We have a whole lot of pieces that aren't fitting." He tapped on Alex's name. "Alex met with the BMW service manager. Turns out they went to high school together. I found that on the internet. My guess is Alex is the middleman and he's getting the copied keys from this guy."

Kristen's father turned to her. "Jess is dating this man?"

"No." Her father tilted his head, knowing full well she was protecting Jess. Old habits die hard. "Not anymore, anyway."

Billy cleared his throat. "We also have the antenna thing. Pretty damned slick. Since we installed the signal jammer, no cars have been stolen using the antenna. I suspect there's someone inside the hotel feeding these guys info."

Please don't let it be Manny.

Billy glanced at her and offered a small nod. He'd

guessed exactly where her mind had gone. How had *he* gotten to know her so well? Too well, she feared. That small nod though, it allowed her to push aside thoughts of Manny being involved.

"There's too much that's convenient," Billy continued. "Based on the info we have, the thieves are targeting guests staying more than a few days. Probably so they can get the keys copied in time. Bottom line, someone in this hotel is giving these people information."

"How do we narrow that down?" Kristen asked. "You've already questioned the employees who have direct access to schedules and guest information."

Billy shrugged. "I don't know. Complicating things is that all this data comes from different departments. The drivers' schedules come from one department, the guest info another and the cameras are dealt with by security. Sure, some of those functions overlap, and one person could have access to it all, but it's not obvious who that person is. The security guys have access to the guest info, but not the drivers' schedules. They'd have to ask for that and I'm not finding anyone who has."

Tom Dante held up his hands. "How is Reed Davis involved?"

"Reed Davis." Billy turned to Monk. "By the way, he drives a Jag. A fascinating coincidence since I think he's the RD in RDM Auto Group. Anyway, we hit on the dealerships after we researched all the residences and businesses Alex had visited."

"And you knew this how?" Kristen's father asked.

"GPS," Billy said.

Dad nodded as if it was no big deal, and Kristen eased out a silent breath when he didn't pursue it.

Billy tapped Bradley J. Murphy's picture on the board.

"That's how we got to Bradley J. and his law firm. Kristen didn't recognize any of the names on the list and suggested we do a search for the registered agents."

Her father sat forward and held one hand toward the board. "You think Reed Davis owns RDM Auto as a front for a car theft ring?"

"Sir, I honestly don't know. He may be the owner, but he might not know anything about the thefts. All I know is I saw Alex meet with the service manager from RDM Auto and accept a large envelope. Then Alex, on behalf of Bradley J., sent Reed Davis his favorite drink last week. Several times. These guys are all associated with each other through the dealerships. Like I said, it's a bunch of individual pieces that don't fit."

"What's next then?" Kristen asked.

"Unless anyone has other ideas, we're stuck."

"But the security for the wedding tomorrow is set, right?"

"That's rock solid. No problems there."

An hour into the senator's daughter's wedding, Billy stood in the hotel's circular drive directing a crush of people toward the open area away from the hotel. "Big frickin' problem," he muttered to himself.

Of all the scenarios he'd conjured for security breaches during the senator's big event, not one of them included a fire alarm going off. To Billy's way of thinking, this had to be a diversion. Someone yanking the alarm would be a hell of a distraction for a car-theft ring bent on breaching security.

"Side of the building, folks. Sorry for the disturbance."

In a few minutes, the side street would be blocked. Freaking mess. Sirens wailed in the distance, alerting him the fire department would be arriving soon. They'd need to get these towers cleared and get everyone back inside.

And he needed to get his ass to that parking lot and make sure no cars disappeared.

To his left, small groups made their way to the lot, most likely to retrieve their cars and leave. The guys covering that area were about to get slammed. The handheld radio he carried chirped. Dennis requesting additional security to help with crowd control. Except, no one could be spared. If anything, they needed to double up on parking lot security.

Billy held the radio to his mouth. "No one from the parking lot moves."

"I need help, Billy. We're moving more than a thousand people here."

"I understand, but the parking lot security stays put. They're about to get slammed with people leaving."

Kristen hustled through the lobby doors and rushed toward him, her strides long and fast and all business. "What's happening?"

"It's a south tower alarm. There's no smoke anywhere. The guys in the security office are checking the footage where the alarm was pulled."

"Is this a distraction so cars can be stolen?"

"That's my guess." Billy waved his arms toward the side street. "This way, folks. Keep moving. We need to clear this area for the fire department." He turned back to Kristen. "Is the senator freaking on you?"

"I beat him to it by offering the open bar for another hour tonight."

"Nice, M.H."

A fire engine pulled into the drive and whooshed to a stop. Kristen swung toward the truck. "I need the fire department to okay everyone reentering or we'll have pristine conditions for an assassination attempt on half the members of the United States Senate."

There's a thought Billy hadn't considered. His stomach did a pitch and roll. This whole thing could be a rouse to get the senator and his powerful friends outside. And that would be bad for business. "Where are the senator's guests?"

"On the beach side. I didn't want them near the street. I had Peter take them down."

"Remind me later to tell you how impressed I am with your crisis management skills."

She half smiled. "I'll do that."

She stepped away to speak with one of the firefighters and a minute later, a team charged to the side entrance of the building where they could enter the hotel unimpeded.

Kristen returned to his side and he said, "Can you handle crowd control for a minute? I need to check the parking lot."

"Sure. I can't go inside. Might as well make myself useful."

Already sweating, whether from the agitation eating away his insides or the suit he wore, even the cool night air offered no relief. He stopped at the automatic gate he'd had installed for the senator's event and glanced at the line of cars attempting to leave. Four security guards stood at the lot exit checking ID and car registrations. Before too long, the place would look like an L.A. expressway during rush hour. People would be pissed.

Too bad. He wasn't about to let one car disappear on his watch.

"You need help?" Billy said to one of the guards.

"Nah. We got it. They'll have to wait is all. If you're good with it, so are we."

"Perfect answer. I'm gonna prowl around some. See if anything looks sideways."

Lights from the fire engine threw flashes of red across the stacked-up cars and Billy moved into the fray. He walked down the first row, angling around guests, all dressed appropriately for clubbing or dinner. No gang bangers. He scanned each car making sure to linger near the high-end ones.

Nothing.

He stopped and checked his immediate surroundings. "Come on, where are you?"

Nothing unusual. He scooted through two cars to the next row, repeating his process while keeping an eye on the first row.

Too much damned ground. He lifted his radio. "Dennis, you got anyone that can help me in the parking lot?"

Not that he counted on that since Den had just been begging *him* for someone. "Give me a couple minutes. The fire department cleared the north tower. Once those guests are in, I'll send you someone."

Good news. The senator and his crew would be heading inside to safety. One problem fixed. Billy continued prowling the parking lot, the crowd thinning as people abandoned their ideas of leaving.

Ten minutes later, after the south tower had been checked and the guests allowed to re-enter the building, Billy approached the parking lot entrance.

"Everything is good here," the guard he'd spoken to earlier said.

"You checked every car?"

"Yes. IDs and registration all match."

Billy smacked him on the back. "Excellent."

He spun back to the cars, scanned the area one last time

and wondered if he was paranoid or if he'd just dodged a big fucking bullet.

AFTER THE CHAOS OF LOCKING DOWN THE HOTEL AND ensuring the fire alarm was indeed the result of a prank, Kristen sat in her suite sipping a martini and hating every second of waiting for Billy to show up. When had she ever been needy?

Worse, in less than forty-eight hours, he'd be gone. History. Out of her life.

And she'd be crushed. So much for self-protection.

She tightened the belt on her silk robe, the red one that matched the lacy underwear he liked. Lucky for him, she stocked multiples of the red.

A knock sounded and she checked the peephole before swinging the door open. Billy stood in the hallway, the top two buttons of his shirt undone, his tie hanging loose while his short dark hair shot up in a rumpled, sexy mess.

"Hi, sailor. How's my hotel security?"

"Hello, Madame Hotness." He looked her up and down. "You are living up to your nickname. And your hotel is safe and sound. Although, I'd hate to be those dumbass teenagers who pulled the fire alarm. The father was *pissed*."

She stepped aside and waved him in. The minute she closed the door, he reached for her belt and tugged. It dropped to the floor and the robe hung open.

An urge to close the robe nagged at her, but she forced herself to stand tall and not curl her shoulders.

"The red again," he said. "My lucky night."

"Are you hungry? I brought some cheese and appetizers up."

Billy dropped onto the sofa and snatched a bit of cheese

from the tray. "How about hot monkey sex first and then we have a snack?"

Her robe remained hanging open and she fought to stand still while Billy made no attempt to control his staring. Unable to withstand the fierce, focused attention, she closed her robe.

"Oh, come on. Please?"

Flattening her hands against her sides, she tapped them against her legs. *You can do this. He likes red.*

"In fact, why not lose the robe?"

Apparently, she wasn't the only one needy tonight. It unsettled her and tingles shot up both arms. She flipped her hand to the bedroom. "How about we go to the other room?"

He vaulted off the couch. "Let's roll."

With him in tow, she stripped off the robe on her way to the bed and tossed it. Billy dragged his hand down the center of her back.

"Very nice, M.H."

And then, from behind, his hands were around her waist, drawing her against him, and then drifting up, over her breasts in a slow torturous route that forced her to draw a breath. *Too much.* She rested her head against his chest, let herself fall into the sensation of him touching her. Had she ever stopped thinking, obsessing, long enough to know she could enjoy sexual attraction? That she could *crave* it?

Never.

Now, all she wanted was his hands on her.

She reached into the side table drawer while he moved his hands up and down her body and trailed kisses over her shoulder and back.

Good God.

"Blindfold," she said.

"Already? Can't I play?"

She spun to him. "You worked to get me to want to be naked with you. You can play later. Please?"

"Deal." He snapped the blindfold on, stripped and eased onto the bed as Kristen made quick work of getting rid of the bra and panties and straddled him.

"Oh, wow," he said. "Not yet. I just want to feel you against me."

With that, she lowered herself on top of him, letting her breasts press against him, skin against skin, savoring the perfection of his body while trying to ignore his single digit body fat.

Yet, somehow, it didn't seem fair to him having to wear the blindfold. Even with his hands traveling over her, why should she be the only one allowed to see? He'd been more than patient and was clearly not repulsed by her body.

He's leaving anyway.

What did it matter? She pushed herself up and smoothed her hands up his chest, twining her fingers in the St. Christopher's medal he never took off.

She glided her fingers up his neck, ran the backs of them against his stubbled chin and cheek and kissed him, long and slow. The gentle touch of their tongues sent fire shooting through her and she groaned. So good. So free.

Here she was, naked, with the lights on, completely at ease sitting on top of him. Never had that happened. Not with her paranoia about crushing the man under her.

Somehow, he'd managed to make her comfortable. No. More than that. He made her feel beautiful and cherished. Not the fat Amazon she'd been living with all these years.

Relief soared. Acceptance. Finally. Anticipation, without warning, urged her upright and—before she thought too much about it—she yanked the blindfold from his eyes.

Billy stared up at the ceiling. "Did you do that on purpose?"

Totally exposed, she dipped her mouth to her upper arm and laughed into it.

Still, his gaze remained straight up. "Seriously? I can look?"

"You can."

She remained motionless, sitting on top of him, her back straight, no hunching, while she absorbed the long, slow swoop of his gaze. Her hair fell over one shoulder and he pushed it back, running his hands over her bare breasts, his palms pressing against her. He grinned and she bit her lip, forced herself not to collapse inside. She didn't want to hide. Not from him.

What she wanted, and what was hard to admit, was for this man to love her. This man who would drive her insane with his constant need for activity and his never-can-be-silent mouth. That's what she wanted.

"You have no idea," he said, "how incredible this feels."

He shot up to a sitting position, wrapped his arms around her and, his face against her chest, held her close. "You're beautiful. You have to know I think that. From the second I saw you, I was dumbstruck. Just flat out stupid with lust. All I ever want is to get my hands on you. I literally cannot wait to touch you. That's how beautiful I think you are."

He shifted her to the bed, sat beside her and ran his hands up and down her body, over her legs and stomach, his lips following the trail of his hands until he'd covered every inch of her. The tingles left in his wake turned to a throbbing sensation that should have broken her apart.

Never had she imagined she could be this free in her own skin.

She reached for the table and the stash of condoms she'd stuck there. "Okay, fella, time to stop teasing me."

"Oh, come on. You can't be giving in this soon. I'm not nearly done."

"How about we have that hot monkey sex you said you wanted and we can play afterward? Compromise? I promise I'll stay naked all night."

"Pinky swear?"

"I'm seriously going to slap you." And yet, she held up her pinky. "I will stay naked, but you have to screw me. Right now."

And then he was inside her and the slow slide into oblivion made her gasp. Perfect. Her thoughts twirled and twirled, the unhurried pace making her insane with wanting.

"You have no idea," he whispered. "No idea. So hot."

"Too slow. Too slow."

He quickened his pace. This was what she wanted. Always. The freedom. This crazy, unabashed ease between them that let her be herself and not worry about the fat Amazon.

Something inside her twisted tighter, a coiling spring about to give and she opened her eyes, placed her hands on his cheeks. She wanted to watch. Wanted to see him looking at her when the euphoria hit. Such joy. Who knew?

She exploded, her body bucking, the contentment drowning her just as Billy lost control, looking right into her eyes.

Perfection.

Finally, he collapsed on top of her, chest to chest, his heart pounding against her. "So bleepin' hot."

She laughed. "I thought that would warrant a swear word."

"I'm filtering. Give me credit."

"Do that to me again and I'll give you all the credit in the world."

"Sweet thing, you're not getting any sleep tonight. And you're staying naked. Just like you promised."

"You're not the only one who can keep a promise."

20

Billy rolled, opened his eyes and met the morning sun cracking through the closed drapes. Harsh. He flipped over and let the softness of Kristen's king-sized bed swallow him.

She lay next to him, her reddish-blond hair a tangled mess against the pillow. Dang, he loved this bed.

He laughed at himself and Kristen stirred. Not wanting to wake her, he remained still. Frozen in his spot. But then her eyes popped open and she stared right at him, blinking a couple of times as if she couldn't quite grasp him being there.

He nudged closer. "Morning, sunshine."

She snuggled into her pillow. "Good morning. What time is it?"

"Nine o'clockish." He inched closer, set one hand on her hip. "You need to be somewhere?"

"Eventually. The senator's brunch is this morning. I'll need to pop over and check on him."

To hell with the senator.

Billy propped himself on one elbow, spotted condoms on the bedside table and decided this would be a terrific time to get laid. "How about I do wicked things to you before you go off to another man?" He ran his finger down the center of her chest, let it wander a little farther and felt her shiver. *Gotcha.* "How would that be, M.H.?"

"I don't see a whole lot wrong with that plan."

Twenty minutes later, just as Billy completed his mission, Kristen's phone rang. Still on top of her, he reached for the phone on the bedside table and tossed it over his shoulder.

"That won't make it stop ringing. The thing is indestructible. In thirty seconds, the voice mail will chirp."

Which it did.

"Told ya."

But then the phone rang again. "Christ sakes," he said. "It's Sunday. Don't you ever get time off?"

"You know the answer to that. Let me up."

No.

Sure he was risking being labeled a toddler again, but he didn't think a few extra minutes in bed was a lot to ask. Not when he'd be leaving in twenty-four hours.

He pressed his weight into her for insurance. "Ignore it."

"I can't ignore it. I have responsibilities. Normally, I would have been downstairs an hour ago making sure everything was set for the senator's guests. Instead, I'm here with you. Where I want to be. Just let me take this call so I can come back to bed."

Kristen scooted from beneath him and retrieved her phone from where it landed. She picked up the still ringing phone and listened as Dennis informed her of what had to be a mistake.

"What?" Billy bolted to a sitting position. "What happened?"

She held up her hand. "How many?"

"Seven," Dennis said. "Including yours. It must have just happened. The valet saw yours not half an hour ago when he parked another car. I'm sorry, Kristen."

Gripping the phone, she closed her eyes. A little peace was too much to ask. She'd known it, but allowed herself to be lazy and stay with Billy when she should have been working.

And now, along with six other cars, her Aston was gone. She could only pray one of the cars didn't belong to the senator. What a nightmare.

"Have you called the police?"

"They're on their way."

"I'll be down in fifteen minutes."

She clicked off and stared at the far wall. Seven cars. They'd been so aggressive with security the evening before, they'd let themselves feel smug. This is what complacency did. *This* is what allowing Billy Tripp to distract her did.

Her gaze remained focused on the wall, her mind reeling off a to-do list while the businesswoman inside scolded her for neglecting her responsibilities.

"Kris?"

She turned to Billy, who had already shoved his legs into his suit pants from last night.

"Seven cars are gone. Including mine."

He stood motionless, his face unreadable. Not a grunt. Not a twitch of his lips. Nothing. For a solid minute, he simply stared at her. In the deepest part of her, she suspected he knew the self-flagellation taking place for letting him divert her attention. For letting him toss away her phone when she was needed.

I can't have this.

Not with him.

"I have to go," she said.

"Kris, don't get crazy. There was nothing you could have done."

"I should have been at work an hour ago."

He folded his arms. "Yeah, and the cars would still be gone. What are you gonna do? Put ten guys on the parking lot at all times?"

She headed to the bathroom. "I have to go."

"This has nothing to do with us being together," he called just as she shut the bathroom door.

THE SECOND HE HEARD THE SHOWER, HE DOVE FOR HIS PHONE. *Got you now, fuckers.*

He punched the screen on his phone and brought up the website. A beautiful red blinking dot appeared and his pulse kicked into a rhythmic warning that an onslaught of adrenaline would soon be unleashed.

After all the false starts and bullshit leads, he might catch these guys.

Kristen's car was on the move.

Immediately, he called Monk and Bobby V. Together, they'd take Kristen's P.O.S. car to recover her Aston.

He hustled into the outer area of the suite and found Kristen's key ring on the desk. This would get him into a boatload of trouble, but he'd beg forgiveness later. He worked the Aston key off the ring and shoved it in his pocket before heading back to the bedroom to finish dressing.

He grabbed his shirt off the floor and buttoned it while jamming his feet into his shoes. *Gotta go.* Except the bathroom door opened and Kristen stepped out, wrapped in a towel, her hair combed, but still wet. *No sneaking out now.* Moving quickly to the closet, she glanced at him. "Where are you going?"

You don't want to know. Decision time. Should he tell her about the GPS? She loved that car. She'd want it back. But she'd also blow a gasket if he went after it. Yeah, he could see her insisting on letting the cops handle it.

No dice.

And then silence, huge and loud and drowning every thought raging inside his head, descended on the room. He looked at Kristen, found her suspicious gaze plastered to him.

"Where are you going?"

Quicker than he imagined she could move, she was on him, snatching his phone and viewing the screen.

Caught.

"What is this?"

"It's your car. Moving down Ocean Drive."

"What?"

"Your car was vulnerable. I hid a tracking device on it."

It was not lost on him how incredibly stalkerish that sounded. He held up both hands. "Before this instance, I have never checked the car's location. Not once. I haven't invaded your privacy. It was a C.Y.A. thing in case the car got boosted."

She waggled the phone. "And what? Now you're going to chase after my stolen car?"

Yes. He remained silent.

"No, Billy. You're not. First, this could be dangerous. Aren't these the people you think threw you to a gator? Second, we can turn the GPS information over to the police." She held up three fingers. "Third, because I have no faith in your ability to stay out of this, I am *ordering* you, as a paid contractor for this hotel, not to get involved."

Ordering him? Really? After all the time they'd spent together, knowing his rebellious streak, *that's* what she was going with? She was out of her mind. He slid the phone out of her hand and shoved it in his pants pocket before heading to the door.

"Billy, did I make myself clear?"

When he reached the door, he gripped the handle, let the cool expanse of it work into his hand. Part of him wanted to give in and tell her he'd stay out of it, but that would never work. He didn't have it in him to stay out of it. He could give in on some things, but not this.

He glanced back at her, still standing in the towel, her hair dripping wet. "Yeah, Kris, you made yourself clear."

Damn him, Kristen thought as she barreled down the hallway to her office. Without a doubt, the man completely ignored her directive and was right now probably chasing down her Aston. So frustrating.

Bad enough the car she adored, a car that, no matter how silly it might be, made her feel vibrant and sexy and forceful, was gone and now she had to worry about Billy getting hurt. Again. She rolled her head side to side to crack the stiffness in her neck.

Damn him.

Her cell phone rang. Dennis. "Hi, Den."

"The detectives are here. We're in the security office."

"I'll be right there. Have we contacted the owners of the vehicles?"

"Two of them. We can't find the others. We're trying to keep it quiet."

A distinct impossibility with seven cars missing. She puckered her lips. "The other cars don't belong to overnight guests?"

"Nothing is coming up in the system."

"Okay. I'll visit the senator's brunch and see if the owners are there."

It would be her luck.

"Where's Billy?" Dennis asked.

Good question. "Out. Try his cell." *Because he won't answer my call.* "Have you seen my father?"

"He's here and looking for you."

I'm sure he is. "Put him on please."

She waited the intolerable amount of time for Dennis to transfer the phone to her father. For the first time, she'd royally screwed up and deserved to be reprimanded. Not that her father would do that in front of staff members. He wasn't that way. He was a tough boss, but not an abusive one. No. He'd save it for when they were alone. God help her—she'd never been the high-maintenance daughter and wasn't about to start now.

"Hi, Krissy," her dad said and a flood of emotion pinched her throat and held until her eyes watered. She'd failed him. He'd handed her his billion-dollar hotel and she'd let him down by getting distracted.

"I'm so sorry, Dad."

"Did you steal those cars?"

Finally, the pinch in her throat eased. "I wasn't available when it happened."

"And if you were, what would you have done? Thrown yourself on top of them? Krissy, I love you, but this isn't about you. Get down here and let's work this problem."

He was right. No time for self-pity. "I'm heading down to

speak to the senator. I'll see if the owners of the other cars are in his brunch."

"I'll do that. I don't need Ed Freeborn using my daughter for posturing in front of his friends. I got that son of a bitch re-elected. He won't give me a hard time."

She couldn't argue that. "Shall I go with you?"

"No. You work with the detectives. Where's Billy? It's time to share what he's found."

A fresh bout of panic seized her and she stilled. "Dad, please, no. Billy is out of the hotel. Plus, his investigation might have legal implications. For him. And maybe for us."

What the hell was she doing?

As conflicted as she was, she didn't want Billy winding up in jail because he tried to help. "Please. Let's wait for him."

Wherever he is.

BILLY STRODE THROUGH THE LOBBY DOORS, STILL WEARING last night's clothes, his nine-millimeter tucked into his waist holster under his suit jacket. Monk and Bobby V. trailed along.

"I'll drive," he said, handing his phone to Monk. "You watch that screen. It has the Aston's location. You tell me where to go and we get the car back."

"Sounds simple enough," Monk said as they made their way to the parking lot and Kristen's P.O.S. sedan.

Once settled, Billy slid the car into gear. "What street are they on?"

Monk punched at the screen, probably to expand the map. "They're going over the causeway."

"Which one?"

"MacArthur."

Easy enough. Of course, they caught every red light on 5th Street and precious time vanished while they waited. He half considered blowing the lights, but with his luck, he'd get jacked up.

Monk blew out a breath. "Crap."

"Crap what?"

"They were on Northwest 20th, turned onto 10th and the signal is gone."

"Hang on a sec. Maybe it'll come back."

"Or," Bobby said, "They're in a garage and the signal is blocked."

The final light before the causeway turned green and Billy pressed the gas. "Which wouldn't be a bad thing, right?"

"Not if you're trying to steal a car back," Monk said.

Within fifteen minutes, they'd turned onto Northwest 20th, a long, garbage littered four-lane street lined with warehouses and broken-down buildings. Any intact windows were covered with bars, the remaining boarded up.

The plus side? For a four-lane thoroughfare, the area was relatively quiet. It being Sunday in a clearly industrial area had something to do with it. Billy slowed the car as he approached the next block and hung a left.

One pass on the narrow street revealed a pallet yard on one side and a single story warehouse on the other. Farther down was a two-story warehouse. Not one other car traveled along this road. Billy waited for Monk to tell him which building might be holding Kristen's Aston.

"It's gotta be this building on the corner. Let's park and take a look."

Billy swung another left and traveled away from their intended target. Half a block down, he found a paved drive that led between two buildings. He'd just tuck the car in there and it would look like someone had come in to work on the weekend.

And, hopefully, someone wouldn't actually come to work on the weekend and wonder who the hell left their car there.

He couldn't worry about it.

The three of them walked back to the suspected building, a squat white cement structure with a loading dock at the back. One side entrance. One in front that he could see. No vehicles outside. If the Aston was inside this warehouse, the driver either left in another car or was still inside.

Billy glanced around the side of the building. No windows, but the ones that ran along the back and the front of the building by the roofline. No help there.

They'd have to risk going in blind.

Noise from the adjacent street, a truck braking hard, caught his attention and he tugged both of them behind the building. The noise slipped away and he nodded to the guys.

Monk dragged his lock-picking tools out of the pocket of his cargo shorts and handed each of them a pair of latex gloves. That Monk. Always the Boy Scout, always prepared.

Monk quietly eased the door open and they listened for voices inside.

Nothing.

They waited another minute. Still quiet. Billy breathed in, held it for a second and exhaled while his heart banged inside his chest. Crazy adrenaline got him every time. For him, it was worse than an illegal substance and highly addictive. He did his best to quiet the chaos in his body.

Finally, he nodded at his cohorts and circled his finger in the air. Time to go.

One by one, they squeezed through the door. The frigid

air-conditioned air blasted Billy. Weapon drawn, he crept down the short entry hall, sticking close to the wall, Monk and Bobby in tow. At the end, he stopped. Listened. When he heard nothing, he peeped around the side of the wall and nearly pissed himself.

"Wow," he mouthed.

Not twenty feet in front of him sat three rows of—Billy did a fast count—*six* cars. Big-time cars. Mercedes, Jaguars, BMWs, a Ferrari. His gaze shot to a Bentley in the middle row and the energy devouring his body exploded. Nearly blew the back of his skull right off. He gripped his weapon tighter and willed himself to stand still while scanning the remainder of the building.

"Let's clear it," Monk whispered, and Billy nodded before stepping into the main area of the warehouse.

Using hand signals, he directed Monk and Bobby to the opposite side and rear of the building. He'd take the front. Given the timing, if the Aston was here, it would most likely be in the front row.

Crouched and moving toward the front, Billy spied an office along the side wall. Lights out. Nobody home. He'd get to that in a minute. They'd hit it lucky that the structure was basically a big open area with no obvious hiding places.

Seemed like whoever owned this building had one thing in mind. Storing cars.

And—*oh, baby*—there sat Kristen's Aston. The plates had been removed, but he knew that car. He'd thought about Kristen and that car in many different ways. *Many* different ways.

He passed a Mercedes and noticed paperwork on the front passenger seat. He tried the front door. Open. Without disturbing the papers sitting on the seat, he studied them. A car title sat on top. Not that he recognized the name, but he made the wild, but most likely accurate assumption that the title was fake. Efficient little bastards. For posterity, and for whatever other reason he'd come up with, Billy snapped a picture of the title with his phone. Couldn't hurt. Then he got a shot of the VIN number. He'd check it out later.

Monk approached from the rear with Bobby trailing behind. "We're clear. What have you got?"

Billy jerked his chin. "Paperwork on the front seat. It's a title. I'm guessing fake. I got a shot of it and the VIN number."

"There's Kristen's car," Monk, the car lover, said.

"We gotta find the button to open the bay door. I'm driving it out of here."

"Does it have a key in it?"

"Doesn't matter. I swiped Kristen's key."

"Billy is a bad boy," Bobby shot.

"Yeah, well..."

And suddenly, they didn't have to worry about finding the button because the bay door made a creaking sound and started to rise.

21

IMMEDIATELY, ALMOST IN UNISON, THE THREE OF THEM pointed their weapons and, with a lack of viable hiding places, hauled ass to the rear of the building and the back door. As he flew through the doorway, his head pounding like a wrecking ball, all Billy could hope was no bad guys would be found on the other side.

Still, they had bad guys inside and he was damned close to getting Kristen's car back. A stack of pallets sat in the open area on the side of the building. Good cover spot for spying.

Billy nodded toward the stack and the guys followed. One way or another, he was driving Kristen's car out of here. Even if it meant disabling someone.

The rumbling of a truck engine drew closer—*no, no, no* —and a not so gentle panic ripped into him.

Son of a bitch.

He nosed around the side of the pallets and spotted a truck backing into the loading bay. Not one of those car-transporting trucks. This one had a shipping container on it.

Monk made a low grunting sound and Billy spun to him.

"Telling you right now, if they load her car on there, I'm jumping into that truck. Somehow, some way. These fuckers are not taking that car."

"Chill. Let's see what they're doing."

And sure enough, the driver, a fifty-something guy wearing jeans and an ancient black T-shirt, jumped out of the cab and pushed the rear door on the container up. He stepped inside and squatted to slide two tire-width portable ramps into place.

Unfortunately for Billy, the quiet roar of the engine on Kristen's Aston filled his head.

His mind went all kinds of crazy working different scenarios on how to take out the guy in the truck and the Aston's driver. Monk could take the truck driver. Billy could handle the Aston while Bobby gave cover.

Billy worked his bullshit scenarios while the Aston was squared away and the young, maybe mid-twenties, guy who'd loaded it jumped off the truck.

"Come inside a second," he told the driver.

To Billy's vast pleasure, the driver left the rear door partially open while he went into the warehouse.

Now.

"I'm jumping in," Billy said. "Follow behind and when the truck stops, slide the door up."

"What?" Monk in his best Daddy voice.

"Don't ask me what I'm doing. I don't have an effing clue. You gotta get that door open though. If they lock it, I'm screwed."

"And what?" Monk huffed. "You're gonna drive the car off a moving truck?"

"Just get the door open."

Billy tore off to the side of the building where he swung his head around the corner. No jag-offs in sight. Nothing.

Three seconds later, he leaped into the back of the container truck and squeezed into the car to hide. He scooted low into the driver's seat, his knees knocking against the steering column. With any luck, the driver wouldn't get back into the container and spot him.

A minute later, Billy heard voices from outside and the sound of the container door ratcheting down.

Success.

When darkness descended, he closed his eyes, reopened them and let them adjust.

He squeezed out of the car, slid along the wall to the front of the car, felt for the bricks behind the tires and removed them.

With nothing else to do, he planted his ass against the driver's side door, one hand on the mirror to steady him, and waited for the truck to come to a stop.

Within minutes, heat saturated the container and reminded Billy just how much he despised dark, enclosed places. Tight, airless spaces that made his lungs ache and sucked the moisture from his body. Drops of sweat trickled down the side of his face and he rubbed his cheeks against each shoulder. The smell of his own sweat in the stagnant air made his throat burn. *Relax.* He breathed through his nose, felt the sting of it and let it out his mouth.

Think about the plan. The truly fucked up plan that had him driving Kristen's hundred-and-fifty-thousand-dollar car off of a moving truck.

He was sure to get killed.

Worse, he'd total the car. Then she'd really be pissed. But he'd be dead. What would it matter?

The distinctive lurch of the truck downshifting jostled him and he grabbed the side mirror to steady himself.

Please stop this thing long enough for my boys to open the door. With the traffic lights on the main drag, they'd have the opportunity.

He had no doubt they'd be back there. One thing about Monk, he might be a pain in the ass, but he'd never leave a teammate. Even if that teammate occasionally pissed him off. Well, more than occasionally.

Billy took more of the hot, stifling air into his straining lungs and suddenly, the truck lurched forward. The driver must have slammed the brakes. Again Billy hung on to the mirror so he didn't fly into the front of the container, alert the driver *and* possibly crack his skull.

And then, like a saving beacon, light shafted into the container and the door slid up. Bobby V. stood there, a big-ass grin on his face, and saluted. Billy had to laugh. Had to.

Before the truck moved—*must be stuck at a light*—Billy glanced out, got his bearings. Still on the four-lane road. *Good*. At least he wouldn't be trying this stunt going eighty. He scanned the opposite two lanes behind the truck. Light to medium traffic in both directions. As long as Monk held back far enough, Billy might pull this off.

From his pocket, for the hundredth time, his phone vibrated. He knew who that was and he wasn't answering. Kristen would have to wait to yell at him. With any luck, he'd get splattered and wouldn't have to worry about it.

Quickly, he grabbed one of the portable ramps. The thing had some heft to it. Good news, bad news. They wouldn't bounce around too much, but they'd be loud as hell scraping against the pavement. Unless the truck driver had the radio up or was afflicted with sudden deafness, he would hear the noise. Too late to ponder a plan B. They had to go for it. Besides there were three of them and only one driver.

Billy jerked his chin. "Grab that end."

Working together, they aligned the ramp with the driver's side tires and hooked it into place off the back of the truck. Done. Within seconds, they had the other side done and Bobby hauled ass back to the P.O.S. car where Monk, of course, shook his head.

The truck started moving, sending sparks of metal flying off the roadway and—*yep*—a loud scraping noise. Hopefully that sudden onset deafness had occurred. Otherwise, Billy was burned. Still, by the time the guy got the truck into park and checked his cargo, Billy would be driving off.

He retrieved Kristen's car key from his pocket, squeezed into the driver's side and fired the engine. Now he had to back this baby out.

Bring in the chaplain. He was about to get grinded.

He shifted the car to reverse, tested the gas pedal to see how touchy it was and squeezed the steering wheel. "Nice and slow, Billy boy. She loves this ride."

A glance at the rearview told him Monk had done the smart thing and given him plenty of room behind the truck for this baby to go ballistic. He eased his foot onto the gas and kept his gaze glued to that rearview. The next group of cars was just far enough back that if he could get safely off this thing, they wouldn't be an issue. They were gaining though.

Brain-searing panic hit him and a thousand little flickers shot up his arms. Sweat pooled under his palms and he hit the brakes, jerking the car to a stop. What if the ramps had lost their alignment when the truck started moving?

Nah. Monk would be signaling.

He checked the rearview again and got his second beacon of the day. This one from Bobby, waving him back.

Thank you.

Billy counted to three, focused on his breathing and

pressed the gas. Suddenly, the sun's rays poured onto the dashboard, the heat filling the car. He swung his head left and right, checking all the mirrors. Behind him, his boys waved him on while his heart nearly detonated.

If he survived this, he might drop dead of a stroke.

The truck began to slow, but with the Aston halfway down the ramps, Billy kept his foot on the gas and checked the rearview. Traffic creeped up and Monk waved his free hand at a furious pace.

"Yeah, buddy, I know, but I'm crapping my pants here."

Another two feet.

One and a half.

One.

He pressed the gas and the car lurched off the ramps. Billy's gaze flew to the mirrors because—*holy shiznet*—he was going backward while everyone else was coming forward. He braked, jammed the car into drive and shot into the left lane as the truck driver eased toward the side of the road.

Billy stared at the open road in front of him while every nerve ending sparked and the little voice screamed *go, go, go.*

"Hot damn." He banged his hand on the steering wheel because, yes, folks, he'd just pulled that sucker off.

Cruising by the truck, he stuck his left arm out the open window and flipped his middle finger up.

"Take *that,* asshole!"

Sorry, Ma.

Behind him, following in the left lane, Monk and Bobby caught up and, to Billy's vast amusement, stuck their arms out and gave the truck driver a double flip-off.

Friends were so important these days.

Billy laughed, but it was time to let Kristen's mega-expensive car show him what it could do.

The buzz of his phone filled the much-appreciated silence within the car. Billy contemplated not answering. It would surely be Kristen and he'd be back to Dante in ten minutes anyway.

But when had he turned into a wuss afraid of a smack-down? He might have the hots for Kristen Dante, but he wasn't afraid of her.

Not much anyway.

"Hi," he said.

"What are you *doing?*"

There's that question again.

"I'm on my way back. With your car."

"What?"

"Yeah and you're welcome."

"Billy! I just reported it stolen."

That might be a problem, since he was driving it. And it didn't have any plates. "Is that detective there? Wilson?"

"Yes, but he's about to leave."

"Well, tell him to cancel the BOLO on the car so I don't get stopped. That would be a *tad* awkward. I'll see you in a few. Tell him to call me. I got some info he's gonna need."

Then he did the only thing a smart guy could.

He hung up.

KRISTEN STOOD UNDER THE LARGE CANOPY COVERING DANTE'S circle drive waiting for Billy.

One foot tap, tap, tapped against the sidewalk as she pondered all the different ways she could kill him.

True, he was a trained operative, but she might be able to drive her four-inch spike of a heel through his brain. That would hurt.

Damn him and his ego. This was retaliation for the gator. And they both knew it.

Which only proved to her that she had lost her mind by getting involved with him. In South Beach, in her own family, for that matter, she was surrounded by egomaniacs. By people who wanted nothing but the next adventure. She was so sick of it. Give her normal, nine-to-five, boring people and she'd be happy.

Ecstatic even.

At the same time, she wanted to wrap the big lug of a man in her arms. The dope cared enough about her to risk his life and go chasing after her car—a stupid piece of machinery—because he knew she cherished it.

And then her beloved Aston, looking every bit of its sexy self, came into view and her throat clogged. Whether that clog had anything to do with the man driving it, she couldn't risk knowing.

Not after she'd spent the last fifty-eight minutes worrying about him.

He parked the car in front of her, got out and her bottled angst broke free. There he was, wrinkled suit, screwy hair, but otherwise in one solid piece.

She turned away, smacked at her cheeks with both hands to focus on anything but crying.

"Kris?"

Time to kill him. She spun and made a beeline. "You shouldn't have done this crazy thing. You could have gotten killed."

He drew his eyebrows together. "You love this car."

"That's not the point!"

He waved her off. "Yell at me later. The plates are gone. Maybe they're in the trunk. Not that I think they are, because you'd have to be a real dumbass to steal a car and then put the original plates in the trunk, but hey, you never know."

"What the hell are you talking about?"

He popped the trunk. "Whoa."

Angling her head, she stared at him. "The plates?"

"No."

"What then?"

"Sweet thing, why do you have titanium alloy sleeves in your trunk?"

Kristen stared into her trunk. *Titanium alloy?* "Those aren't mine. What are they?"

"I'm sure they have multiple uses, but in my experience, they're for Iranian centrifuges used in making enriched uranium."

Despite the seventy-degree temperature, a cold, icy panic settled in her bones. She folded her arms against the chill and dreamed of burrowing into one of her sweaters. Enriched uranium? "Nuclear weapons?"

Billy shut the trunk. "Let's keep our voices down, shall we?"

"That *cannot* be."

He grabbed her arm, inched closer to her ear. "Kris, I don't know. I opened the trunk and there they are. I'll tell ya though, the idea of these guys stealing cars so they can smuggle titanium alloy sleeves to the Middle East? Not effing crazy. That would be huge money. And they'd still get paid on the cars. It's double dipping at its best."

"I don't understand."

Billy guided her to the sidewalk. "Get Dennis to put a guard down here. Nobody touches the Aston. Wilson needs to come and take a look at it. I gave him the warehouse address and he's working on that."

"What warehouse?"

"The cars. We followed your Aston to a warehouse. There are a bunch of high-end cars there. Fake titles on the seats. At least I think they're fake. One of the cars looked like yours, but it was titled to someone else. I got a picture and sent it to Wilson. He needs to get a warrant to search the place."

Whoa, whoa, whoa. "Slow down. You found the cars?"

Billy rolled his eyes, led her away from the brunch crowd entering the hotel. "I think I found the cars. I don't know if Wilson can use the pictures for a warrant though. Technically, they were obtained illegally."

"Because you broke in. After I specifically asked you to stay out of it?"

He held up a finger. "First off, you didn't ask. You ordered. I chose not to follow that order."

Damn him. Her own incessant warnings about not getting involved with him converged and her head nearly shattered.

But Billy didn't get it. No. He was busy dialing his phone. "Who are you calling?"

"Wilson needs to know about these sleeves in your trunk." He turned away from her, waved at Peter and Bobby waiting in her sedan. The one Billy thought was so boring. "And then I'm gonna talk to Bradley J. Murphy."

For the hundredth time today, Kristen thought she might bludgeon him. She held her hands out, her fingers straining into claws. "What is it going to take to get through to you? These people fed you to a gator. God knows what else could happen now that you've stolen a car back. Do you *want* to get killed?"

"Relax."

"And what about Peter and Bobby? If you're stupid enough to get killed, they shouldn't be sacrificed as well."

"They love this crap." Dropping his head back, he sighed then came back to her. "Kristen, I hear what you're saying. I do. But the lid is about to come off this thing. Wilson, I'm guessing, can't do dick because most of the information I have was illegally obtained. The way to put an end to this circus is to get somebody to flip. That somebody is either Alex or Bradley J. My money is on Bradley J. *He's* got the paper trail. Now, get a guard on this car and make sure nobody touches it."

With that, he turned and headed for the boring sedan.

"Billy!"

He kept walking, jumped into the backseat of her sedan and didn't spare her another glance. Unbelievable. How was she supposed to deal with a man who wrestled gators and stole cars? Every day with him would be a missile launch.

She couldn't do it.

Simple as that.

Blowing out a breath, she dialed Dennis and told him to have a security guard watch her Aston until the police could get to it. Upon finishing the call, she turned and saw Reed Davis rushing through the lobby doors. She checked the time on her phone. Reed held a standing ten o'clock brunch reservation. At 10:15 a.m., the chances of him being done with his meal were nil.

Kristen glanced at the valet stepping out of a Jaguar and watched as the keys were handed off to Reed. For his car to be retrieved that fast, he must have alerted the staff he'd be leaving.

Reed Davis was in a hurry.

Where would he be going? If Billy's suspicions about Reed being involved with this car-theft ring where correct, Reed would know the Aston had been stolen back.

He spotted the car sitting on the curve of the drive and

for a brief second, hesitated. Anyone else may have missed it, but not Kristen.

Then Reed's gaze leveled on her and a sharp pinch landed between her shoulder blades. Uncertain of what to do, she smiled at him, held her frozen hand in greeting.

He nodded, slid into the car and cruised down the driveway.

If Reed was involved with this theft ring, he could be trying to flee. Billy was off chasing Murphy; the police hadn't arrived to search the Aston yet and Reed Davis was simply driving away.

Her warnings to Billy about leaving this to the police whispered—*nagged*—at her, but this was the man who may have thrown Billy to a gator.

And he was getting away.

A black Town Car was parked in the drive. Spiked heels notwithstanding, she ran toward the valet and pointed to the car.

"Is that one of ours?"

"Yes. The driver just came in. He's taking it out again and told me to hang onto the keys."

Excellent.

"Give me the keys."

"Ma'am?" Eddie said.

"I need the keys, Eddie. Quickly."

Eddie stared for half a second, clearly confused, but passed off the keys. She darted to the Town Car. With the traffic lights, Reed couldn't have gotten that far ahead. She floored it out of the driveway, the front end scraping along the road when she reached the street. Roaring up Ocean Drive, she spotted Reed's car two ahead of her, stopped at the light on 5th.

Her heartbeat slammed and she squeezed the steering wheel, waited a few seconds and released her grip.

What am I doing?

But she had him. Wherever he was going, she was going with him.

Billy tapped the screen on his phone and found a blinking red light. "He's on the move. Downtown. Over the causeway we go."

"On it," Monk said.

"Okay, he's close. Just got on Biscayne Boulevard. Take the northeast 13th Street exit. We'll hit Biscayne from there."

Bradley J.'s signal led to 4th Avenue. Monk parked at the end of the street while they did a quick recon and waited for Bradley to leave his car, which he'd parked in front of a small two-story building snuggled between a design store and another warehouse.

Finally, Bradley J. exited his car, walked to the door, unlocked it and went in.

"Let's hit it," Billy said. "Park around this corner. We'll walk it. Doesn't look like any windows on the building. We'll have to go in blind."

"Doesn't that sound fun?" Monk said.

"Wha, wha."

Bobby snorted when Monk flipped Billy the bird.

Before they reached the door, Bobby split off to check the back of the building. At the front door, Billy stood to the side while Monk placed his hand on the door. In a soft voice, Billy counted down three, Monk whipped open the door and Billy swung in with Monk on his heels, weapons drawn. They'd done this hundreds of times, like a choreographed dance, sometimes flawless and others, well, those times they were usually met with flying bullets.

No bullets this time.

Sitting at a desk on the far-right side, was Bradley J., who leaped out of his chair, his face stretched in surprise. Most likely, he'd pissed himself. Billy took some satisfaction in that.

Moving forward, gun aimed, Billy slid his gaze around the empty space and found bare cement walls and a catwalk on the second story. That was it. What the hell? The desk was the only item in there.

"Sit," he said

"You're screwing up. You want my wallet? Take it and get out."

The man had a set of stones on him. "No wallet. I'm about to save your ass."

Kristen got stuck at a light in the Design District, but spotted Reed Davis turn onto 4th Avenue.

Tapping her fingers, she counted down the seconds in her head. "Come on light."

When the light turned, she cruised to 4th. *Hello*. There was her sedan parked out of sight from the remainder of the block, where a woman stood on the corner with a stroller. Kristen made the left and saw Reed get out of his Jaguar. He'd parked in front of a vacant lot across from a warehouse. Another car was parked directly across from Reed's. Bradley J. Murphy's? Billy had said he was going after the lawyer.

Billy and his pack of merry men could be in that building. The one Reed Davis was about to walk into.

Dammit. A curling panic squeezed her stomach. Without

a doubt, Billy, Monk and Bobby were armed. But how many other people were in that warehouse and also armed?

She should call 9-1-1.

Shouldn't she?

And tell them what? That she thought a man running a car theft ring, which she had no proof of, was having a meeting.

The police would think she was a mental case.

She needed to do something. Wilson. Tearing her gaze from the building, she grabbed her phone off the seat and checked her contact list for Wilson's number.

Voice mail.

Of course. She left him a message with the location. At the very least, she'd have communicated it to someone. She set the phone in the center console and rested both hands on the steering wheel to get her thoughts together.

A sharp rap hit her window and her heart lurched. She yelped, then stared into the barrel of a gun.

"Out of the car," the large, make that humungous, linebacker of a man said.

His looks alone scared the hell out of her. He had one of those pockmarked faces she used to see in comic books. His age, she guessed, would be around forty, but he'd lost most of the dark hair on his head.

And that gun was pointed right at her. Terror, hot and slick, raced inside her. Her hands began to shake. Whooshing in her head blurred her vision. She blinked, tried to focus.

"Out," he said again.

Just do what he says. Trembling, she flipped open the lock. The man jerked the door open and grabbed her by the arm. His fingers bit into her flesh and, in one jarring motion, snatched her from the car. She stumbled, cursing herself for not wearing flats. Even if she could get free, she couldn't run in these. She'd have to kick them off. Chances were she'd be dead before she got one shoe off.

"You stupid bitch." He dragged her toward the building.

If nothing else, she was about to see if Billy was inside.

BILLY STARED AT BRADLEY J. "HERE'S WHAT I KNOW…"

The front door opened and Billy swung toward it, weapon raised, while Monk stayed on Bradley J. At the door, Reed Davis halted and put his hands up. His gaze went straight to Billy's gun.

"In here. Now," Billy hollered.

Slowly, Reed stepped into the room, arms raised. Billy motioned to Monk, who searched the man for weapons.

"Clean," Monk said shoving Reed over to the desk with Bradley so they could keep an eye on them.

Leaning back on the desk and folding his arms, Reed grinned. "This must be Billy Tripp."

"Bradley," Billy said, "take a look at the guy next to you. He's going to screw you. Hard."

"Shut up," Reed said.

The front door opened again. *Jeez-us.* Billy swung toward it, weapon raised, only to see Kristen being pushed through by one of the beefheads that tossed him to the gator. He held a .45 on her.

Immediately, Billy's brain went to overdrive. He focused on Kristen. The one thing he could have lived without was seeing Kristen with a cannon pointed at her.

His legs, his arms, his chest, everything, buzzed. Images of all the death he'd seen, skulls blown apart, temples with gaping holes, blood-matted hair raced through his mind.

I could lose her.

Sweat pooled in Billy's palm. He tightened his grip on his weapon and fought the surging panic. If Kristen broke a nail, he'd slaughter this fucker. And it would be ugly. And painful. And extremely bloody. He should pop this guy for even putting his hands on her.

What little sense Billy possessed hissed at him.

How the hell did she even get here? Had this guy grabbed her at the hotel? Couldn't be. The place was teeming with people. How could he have snatched her?

Blood raced into his limbs, stealing all that precious oxygen from his internal organs. The lack of focus banged at his skull making him sweat.

Get her out of here.

Monk still had his gun on Reed. Bradley J. sat at the desk looking like he'd witnessed a massacre, clearly crapping his pants. He wasn't going anywhere.

Billy turned his gun and attention to the goon with Kristen. "Drop it!"

No dice. The goon kept the gun jammed against Kristen's head.

Take him out.

From this distance, Billy could nail the shot and Kristen would stay unharmed. She'd be traumatized though.

He took air through his nose, held it a sec and eased it out again. The flood of oxygen relieved his cramping stomach. Thank you.

"Well," Reed swung his head between Billy and the goon, "looks like we have a stalemate here."

"Let her go," Billy said. "She walks out of here and the rest is up to us."

Reed clucked his tongue. "I don't think so."

And where the hell was Bobby?

Billy turned to Bradley J. "You can either be the guppy or

the shark. Old Reed here is gonna try and make you the shark."

"What the hell are you talking about?"

"Think about it. The paper trail on the dealerships leads to you. How the hell do you think I found you? My guess is, you'll get busted for smuggling and Reed can sit back, pretend like he didn't know a damned thing about stolen cars and nuclear weapons while his registered agent takes the heat."

Bradley snapped his head back. "Nuclear weapons?"

This guy could be a terrific bullshit artist, but from the way his gaze bounced around, Billy didn't think so. "Bend over, pal. You're about to get that screwing."

"He's not the only one." Bobby's voice from the catwalk above.

Finally, an appearance from his missing teammate. For effect, Bobby put the laser on his gun to use. Wasn't this sweet? Bobby could hit a target at two thousand yards, and he had his gun trained on Reed Davis's forehead.

Billy's bargaining power for Kristen just increased. Not in his lifetime would he believe they'd let her walk out of here, but he could at least get her away from that monster .45. He glanced at her and their eyes met for a second. His girl was one tough cookie. As spooked as she looked, she wasn't sobbing. Nope. She stood there, staring at him, silently pleading with him to help her. And he would. If he did nothing else, he'd get her out of here. Or die trying.

"Boys, we have a situation." He glanced at Reed. "There are two guns aimed at you. Your boy can't shoot all three of us at once. Do the math. One of us gets shot, your ass is going down."

Billy, still focused on Reed, took a step toward the goon and Kristen. "I'm gonna have Ms. Dante step over here.

Nobody else moves. Got it? And if you think I won't kill you, think again. Not only are you holding a gun to my girl, you threw me to a gator."

For a second, the only sound in the room was the rumble of a truck driving by. "Kristen, come over here."

The goon looked toward his boss. "Let her go," Reed said. "This nut might be crazy enough to shoot me."

"You have no idea."

KRISTEN ABSORBED THE IDEA THAT A GIANT HANDGUN THAT could take apart her head was still pointed at her. Twenty feet in front of her, Billy had his own gun pointed in her direction. He jerked his head to get her moving. And yet, she couldn't. Fear had locked her knees. Simple as that.

"Kristen, move!"

The sharp, dominant tone stung her and suddenly, this was not playful Billy. This Billy, in his wrinkled pants and dress shirt, wore a look of stonelike intensity that rendered her mute. Playful Billy had morphed into warrior Billy and, although comforted by his total lack of fear, Kristen wondered if she knew this man at all.

Either way, warrior Billy prompted her to get moving. With quick steps, silently praying as she went along, she moved toward him. His eyes were on the man behind her, the one with the giant gun, and not knowing what else to do, she stood next to Billy. He slid in front of her, his big body shielding her from both the man with the gun and Reed Davis and Bradley J. Murphy.

She rested her head against the back of his shoulder and a blip of relief loosened her aching limbs. They weren't safe yet, but at least she didn't have a gun pointed at her head. "I'm so sorry," she whispered.

He shushed her. This was bad, and she didn't see how any of them were going to get out of here without someone dying.

"We're making progress," Billy said. "Now, Bradley J., Reed will let you fry on the smuggling charge. That's federal and will put you away for a good, long while. How do you feel about being gang raped in the shower? If that doesn't work for you, you might want to reconsider your loyalties."

Kristen dared to peek at Bradley J. Murphy and saw him staring back, his eyes big and round with the fear Billy had plunged into him. At least she wasn't the only one terrified.

"Tick-tock, Bradley J."

"I only knew about the cars."

"Shut up!" Reed Davis roared, his face contorting into an evil Kristen had never seen on him. Usually this man was charming and slick. Gentle even. Not now.

Bradley turned to him. "You didn't tell me about nuclear weapons. The cars were harmless."

How out of touch were these people that they thought stealing from others was harmless?

Bradley spun to Billy, who still had his gun on Kristen's captor. "All I was supposed to do was be the registered agent. Alex handled dealing with the dealerships. Reed hired people to copy the keys. At the BMW dealership it's the service manager. At Jaguar it's one of the mechanics."

"What about the antennas?" Billy asked.

"I'm not involved in that. That's the gangs. One of Reed's contacts figured out how to start the cars with the antennas. Reed went to one of the gang leaders to get them on board. The gang was paid per car."

"Shut the fuck up." Reed took a lunging step.

"Don't bother," Billy said as Bobby pointed his laser at Reed's chest. "You'll be dead before your next step."

Reed stayed put and Billy nodded toward Murphy. "What about the hotels? Who at the hotels is involved? Who knew about the blind spot?"

Bradley shook his head. "Alex got those people. Someone at the security company that originally installed the cameras told him about the blind spot. At Dante, one of the housekeeper's sons is in the gang. His little brother hangs out at the hotel."

Oh, my God.

"Shit," Billy muttered.

"The gang kid worked the password from his little brother. He helps the mother log which rooms she's completed and has her password. The remote login address wasn't hard to get and they used the maid's password to get into the system. That's how they know how long people are staying."

Manny. A hot slice of betrayal tore into Kristen and her heart broke for the little boy who'd been deceived by his sibling. Kristen knew all about that, which only made the hurt worse.

The entry door flew open and chaos consumed the room as a line of SRT guys in riot gear charged in. A mix of identifying shouts pounded at Kristen and her gaze fixed on the men. Her former captor raised his gun.

No.

A booming sound filled the air, followed by the *rat-a-tat-tat* of an automatic weapon. Kristen's ears nearly bled from the battering sounds and Billy shouted, "Kristen! Down!"

"Drop the gun," someone else yelled.

Shock consumed her. She watched Billy's mouth move, his face twisted in an odd sort of panicked rage, but the words collapsed under the deafening gunfire.

"Get down," he yelled again.

Tired of waiting, he stiff-armed her. She crashed to the floor, knees slamming onto the concrete. The stinging pain drove into her legs. She brought her arms over her head as more shots sounded.

No more. No more.

When her throat began to ache, she realized she was screaming. Forget bravery. Right now, she simply wanted to live through the ordeal. She mashed her hands tighter over her ears, but the barrage of shots kept coming and tears toppled down her face.

Just let me live, just let me live, just let me live.

Suddenly, a huge weight bore down on her.

Don't want to die.

As quickly as the gunfire began, it stopped and the room went still. The officers shouted demands, but Kristen stayed put, afraid to move as her body shivered under the oppressive weight.

"You okay?" Billy's voice broke through the haze.

Her cheek to the cold, harsh floor, she opened her eyes, saw a white shirtsleeve that didn't belong to her. Billy lay on top of her, shielding her from flying bullets.

"I think so." But the tremble in her voice shattered her confidence. "You?"

"I'm good."

When he kissed the side of her head, her body began to quake and she gritted her teeth. She'd lied. When the hell would bullets flying at her make her okay?

"Hands where I can see them," someone yelled and Billy rolled off her.

"Kick that weapon away from you," came from somewhere else, and Kristen prayed Monk and Bobby were unharmed.

"Hands in the air," one of the SRT guys said to Billy.

Kristen pushed her quivering body to all fours and locked her elbows. "I'm Kristen Dante. My family owns the Dante hotel. Billy, Peter and Bobby are part of the hotel's security team. These other men, I believe, are involved in the car theft ring that has targeted my hotel."

Three breaths later, she glanced to her right and spotted an officer handcuffing Billy. Near the desk, Reed Davis and Bradley Murphy were also handcuffed. Behind her, Peter and Bobby stood in the middle of the room enduring a pat down, their weapons nowhere to be seen.

Everyone was safe.

Except her captor. He lay in a heap by the door. Kristen's stomach lurched at the expanding reddish-black puddle under him. How did a random car theft turn into this nightmare?

She turned to Billy. Without stepping from his spot and igniting the officer's wrath, he squatted to eye level with her. "You all right?"

Literally or figuratively? Either way, the answer would probably be a solid, absolute no. This would be life with Billy Tripp. Maybe she wouldn't have guns aimed at her, but she'd always be afraid for him. Always be wondering if he was safe or if he'd thrown himself into danger's path. If she'd learned anything about him it was that, at times, he simply couldn't help himself.

No, what she needed was an office guy. Someone who left in the morning and came home at night. Every night. None of this gun garbage.

What a switch. Just hours ago she'd been thinking Billy Tripp might be a keeper and suddenly all the fear and rage and heartbreak from the last minutes balled into a flaming burst of energy that scorched her body. *Dammit*. With little else to relieve the agony, she let her tears bubble over.

"Ah, Jesus Christ, Billy," an angry, familiar voice said.

Thankful for the distraction, she swiveled to see Detective Wilson storming toward them.

"You couldn't give me a heads up and wait?" he shouted.

Still handcuffed, Billy shrugged. "I didn't know what we had. Could have been nothing."

"This place just got shot up. That's nothing? And you endangered a civilian. We got a 9-1-1 from a lady who saw Kristen get dragged in here or I would have been scrambling to get a warrant."

"First off, I didn't know about Kristen." He looked at her. "Why the hell *were* you here?"

Now it was her fault? "I tried to call you. You didn't pick up and I was afraid Reed would flee. How would I know I'd be dragged from my car?"

Wilson held up his hands. "Both of you stop talking." He turned to Billy. "I'm helping you here. Do not speak without a lawyer. Got it?"

They nodded as Wilson helped Kristen to her feet. "The officers will take you outside while we figure this mess out."

22

By eight o'clock that evening, Billy stood outside Kristen's suite, bone tired and not in the mood for a fight. At least he'd managed to finally take a shower and get clean clothes. Upon his return from the P.D. he'd wanted to come straight to Kristen, but figured ten minutes in a hot shower would settle his already fried brain.

It wasn't like he didn't already have issues with controlling his mouth. Throw in exhaustion and a whole lot of irritation and he was screwed.

Now he stood in front of her door, debating whether he should knock. He hadn't seen or spoken to her since that morning—when she almost got shot—and wondered how welcome his presence would be.

Then again, calling just seemed lame.

He dragged his hand over his face, tugging on his skin as he went along. *Hell of a day, Billy boy.*

Bound to get worse after he knocked on this door. Bad enough that he'd talked to Vic and Mike on the way over and they'd given him a few more bodily holes. Now he'd have to figure out how to make nice with Kristen. Knowing what he did about her, how she hated drama inflicted on her by others, he didn't think any of his weak explanations would suffice.

He had to try though. If only to understand where exactly they stood in this relationship. And when did it become *that*? The big R-word. Next he'd be buying property and life as he knew it would be over.

As much as he tried to conjure distaste for the concept, it wouldn't come. The thought of leaving in the morning with her mad at him, without the chance to mend whatever this *relationship* was, kicked him in the gut. He rubbed at the spot, fully engaged his filter and banged on the door.

A minute later, Jess opened the door, grinning at him with all the smug she could summon.

Here he thought it couldn't get worse.

"She's not interested." Jess took way too much pleasure in that statement.

"I'm shocked to see *you* here."

"Yeah, well, my sister and I don't always play nice, but when someone—namely you—tries to get her killed, I rise to the occasion."

Tries to get her killed. He'd give Jess credit for delivering a solid one-two punch of a line. Fudging great.

He glanced behind her into the suite, but didn't see Kristen. "Is she here?"

"In her room. She just got out of the tub."

"Are you going to let me in?"

Jess puckered her lips. "Nope."

Based on her body language, the folded arms, the steady stare, she wasn't kidding. "I'm not going to upset her—"

"She's already upset."

Billy focused on getting around the guard dog. "I'm not

going to upset her any further. I need to see her before I leave."

"Let him in, Jess."

Kristen stepped from the bedroom dressed in a pair of her yoga pants with the wrap jacket she wore the first time he'd come to see her. And yes, he still wanted to strip her out of that jacket.

"One thing I know," she said, "is he won't go away until he says what's on his mind."

"Uh, *ouch*." No denying the pop of that not-so-disguised insult.

Jess pushed by him. "I'll be back in ten minutes."

"Thank you." Couldn't hurt to be nice to Kristen's family. Even if Jess did irritate the ever-loving-crap out of him. Then again, maybe that's how people felt about him. He blew out a breath. *Yeah, don't go there.*

He stepped into the suite, set his hand on the back of the door and pushed it closed, lingering for a minute before he turned around. *Suck this up.*

Thankfully, Kristen spoke first. "Were you downtown all this time?"

"Yeah. Lots of questions. Mike and Vic did some fast talking and it looks like Monk, Bobby and I are clear. Wilson helped. He's jazzed about my surveillance. He needs to figure out a way to make it all admissible."

"Good. It would be pathetic if, after all you'd done, you were prosecuted."

He gestured to the couch. "Can I sit?"

"Sure."

Not exactly an enthusiastic answer. He shook his head, flicked the fingers of one hand against the other. "If I had known, if I could hit rewind, I'd have never gone after

Murphy today. I would have done what you said and let the cops handle it."

Kristen settled into the cushions, half turning to him. "Is that true? Be honest. For both our sakes. From what Wilson told me earlier, you scared Murphy into flipping on Reed Davis. That's a big deal."

Billy shrugged. "Wilson is keeping it close, but from what I could figure, Davis was smuggling cars to the Middle East, via the Port of Miami. Your Aston was on its way to have a temporary gas tank installed. They drain the gas tank, insert the tubes we found in the trunk and then put enough gas in the temporary tank to transport the vehicle."

"They hide the tubes in the gas tank?"

Billy nodded.

"Who thinks of this?"

"Career criminals."

"So, Reed is making money on the cars and the tubes?"

"Yep. He's an expat with contacts overseas. It's a whole network he's got going. Wilson is hot on checking other major ports to see if he's running the same deal there."

Kristen shook her head and Billy let her absorb the info dump. Finally, he sat forward, propped his elbows on his knees and linked his fingers together. "How pissed are you?"

"It's not about being mad. Not anymore. I'm sad. Heartbroken actually. Your lifestyle isn't good for me. When I saw Reed Davis rushing out of the hotel today, I knew I was at a crossroads. I could either follow the advice I'd given you to let the police handle it and risk him fleeing, or I could follow him. Plus, I was worried about you going after the lawyer. I went against my own edict and followed Reed. I could have gotten us all killed."

"You didn't know."

She pressed his hands between hers and, as sure as he

was sitting here, he knew this might be the last time she ever touched him. He drew a breath and ignored another kick to the gut. This is what it felt like to want a woman he couldn't have.

She didn't want him.

"That's not the point," she said.

"Yeah, I get it. I distract you. I make you do things you wouldn't normally do. Does that have to be a bad thing?"

"It does when it fuels stupidity on my part."

"Ouch," he said for the second time since seeing her and it was starting to piss him off.

She backed away.

"How about credit for getting you out of your own head for a while? Do I get a bonus for that? Anything? Because, hell, Kristen, I think that should be worth something."

"Of course it's worth something. But let's be realistic. What is it that we have? I run a hotel that requires constant attention. I own property here and have roots. My life is here. You own a camera and fly off to do who knows what." She waved her arms. "Your life is out there. In the world."

"Not always."

She shook her head. "I learned one thing today. I cannot sit here while you come and go. My life cannot revolve around you dropping in every once in a while. Worse, I'll never know when you'll be back or for how long. I'll never know if you've been hurt or even if you'll come back. That will destroy me. I can't have it."

His mind raced with bottled frustration and he stood.

Never had he shared such emotional intimacy with a woman, and she was reducing it to a couple of good lays? Unacceptable. He paced the room, waving one hand in the air, hoping something worthwhile would pop into his brain.

"So, that's it? The past eleven days have been a good time

and we part friends never to see or speak to each other again?"

"Billy—"

"Hang on." He stopped pacing, checked himself on what he was about to say and stuck his hands in his front pockets. "That doesn't work for me."

"What?"

"I think you're scared and well, breaking news here, me too. It's been a hell of a few days. Maybe we need to take time and let all this Reed Davis crap unwind. I'm expected in Chicago tomorrow, but I want to come back here after that. I've been thinking about this all week and I want to spend time with you. Take a damned vacation for once. I can do that here. I love this place. I love *you*."

Greetings to the big asshole who, in the course of getting dumped, proclaimed his love. How freaking pathetic.

Screw that.

So what? He'd said it. And meant it. They didn't call him Mr. Relentless for nothing.

Kristen rose from the couch. "You *love* me?"

The dripping sarcasm he'd pass on. "Yes. I do. In case you're wondering, I've never said that to a woman outside of my family. I don't throw those words around."

Not ever. Not even to get laid. Some things were sacred.

Kristen came closer, wrapped her hands around his. "I believe you don't throw them around. And I also believe you think you love me."

"I think?" Had she been sneaking the scotch? "I know what I feel, Kristen. I respect your opinions, but don't tell me what I feel."

"I'm not doing that. I'm being honest and you're the king of truth, so believe me when I say you and I will not work. That's the truth for me. It won't work."

She was tossing him. *Crap.* Normally, he'd happily skip out the door for dodging the I-want-a-relationship bullet. This time though, he was the one shooting. "If you ask me, I'd say we're a great match. You work constantly. When I'm gone, you won't have to feel guilty because I'm distracting you. Then when I'm here, we'll spend as much time together as we can. Why can't we compromise?"

"On what? I just told you it won't work."

"Yeah, I heard, but why do we have to make any decisions right now. Let me go back to Chicago and talk to Vic. If you don't want me here, I'll stay there, but I'll call you in a couple of days. Backing away from a situation brings clarity. Let's get clarity and talk about this again. Can we do that?"

Silence.

Crap.

She held her palm out, opened her mouth and closed it again before dropping her hand.

Maybe he had a shot.

"No."

Tap out.

Game over.

Sure, he could argue with her. Do his Mr. Relentless routine and schmooze her, but why? If she didn't want him, he wasn't going to beg. And didn't that truly suck?

He took a step closer, slipped two fingers under her chin and tilted her head up. "I understand. I'm sorry though. You'll never know how much, but if you want me gone, I'm gone."

She wouldn't look him in the eye, but she nodded. "I don't want you gone. I just think it's best."

And that was that. He'd give her time. Let her think about it. He stepped back. "Call me if you want to talk, okay?"

Then he dropped a quick kiss on her, turned his back and walked out on the woman who had enthralled him on sight. A woman who captured his interest like no other and who would probably take a lifetime to get over.

AFTER A BLEEPING LONG TRAFFIC-SNARLED RIDE IN A CITY where the temperature would cap out at a whopping seventeen degrees, Billy walked into his boss's office. Vic sat behind a battered oak desk that held various stacks of papers, books, sticky notes and general crap that the guy probably hadn't looked at in a year.

"Sit," he said.

After dropping into one of the guest chairs, Billy rested his hands on his thighs and waited. This would be yet another unsavory experience to top off the string of misery hounding him. The minute he'd left South Beach the ache inside him expanded.

Three times he'd told the driver to stop, but then, not wanting to hound Kristen into giving him another shot, he'd told the driver to keep going.

Maybe when the reality of the day before wore off, she'd be more willing to listen. He hoped.

Vic eyed him. "I sent you to South Beach on a multitasked op. You were supposed to control that goddamn mouth of yours and learn some responsibility. Instead, you got mixed up in a car-theft ring that—low and behold—is smuggling titanium alloy sleeves used for Iran's nuclear weapons program. I mean kill me now, Billy."

Billy held up his hands. "I didn't know about the sleeves. All I knew was a client had problems with car thefts. I thought I could help. And besides, I helped bust up that nuclear weapons sh—*ship*. Maybe give me some credit for being a good operator?"

"I'll give you that. But becoming gator bait creates a problem."

"That was an isolated incident."

"That's the fucking problem. They're all isolated incidents."

"Not anymore. I'm better."

Vic shook his head.

"Hey, I'll never be perfect. My mind doesn't work that way, but I'm learning to filter. Plus, well, there's something about South Beach. It relaxes me."

His mind went back to walking along the shore with Kristen. The eccentricity of South Beach made him feel like he belonged there. With her.

Not that it could happen now. She had vamoosed him. Told him to go scratch his ass.

If nothing else, he had learned some filtering skills. Yep, Kristen had taught him some lessons in humility. He was thankful for that, but yearned for a better ending.

"Right," Vic said. "And Kristen Dante doesn't hurt."

He knew.

"Monk?"

"Her father. For some fucked up reason, the man likes you."

The old man inquired about him. Not a bad sign. "What'd you tell him?"

"That you were a royal pain in the ass and I have to check my blood pressure every time I send you on an op."

"Seriously?"

Vic waved him off. "I told him you were square."

"You vouched for me?"

"If I didn't, I'd look like the putz who hired an asshole, wouldn't I?"

"Good point. Thank you, though."

"Don't make me a liar."

"No, sir."

Might be too late.

Vic set his giant hand on a manila folder on his desk. "We got your passport renewed. You ready for an overseas assignment?"

Yes. He still had the job he loved.

"Absolutely."

"It's Afghanistan. Six-week gig. You leave Friday."

"I'm ready. No problems. I'll keep my mouth shut."

Vic raised his eyebrows.

"Well," Billy said. "Let's not expect miracles."

Vic laughed and it was the laugh of acceptance. The laugh of olden days. The laugh that assured Billy he still belonged.

He sat forward. "Listen, if I stay out of trouble, is there a problem with me squatting in South Beach between assignments? Like Monk is doing in Jersey."

"You're using Monk as your precedent?"

"Is it working?"

"No. He's responsible and not messing with a client's daughter. If you fuck her over, Tom Dante will not be happy. You could cost us this account."

Billy shook his head. "Not gonna happen. She's different. Smart and sexy and patient. Turns out, her experience dealing with her crazy sister is good for me. She doesn't freak when I say something inappropriate. She just calls me on my crap and we move on. Right now she's not sure about me, so, yeah, I want to spend time in South Beach and see what happens. I need you to sign off though."

"And you won't piss me off and make me fire you?"

"I'll do my best."

"You won't jerk me around and get lost when I need you on an assignment?"

Now that was offensive. "Have I ever done that?"

"No. But South Beach in the winter and a sexy woman were never involved."

"True. But it's not an issue. She works night and day. She'd go crazy with me around all the time."

Vic shook his head back and forth.

"I can do this," Billy said.

"Here's the deal."

Score.

"We'll try it. The first time you don't return my call in a reasonable amount of time, I'm hauling your ass back here. If I even think you're going half-cocked down there, I will haul your ass back here. If you piss Tom Dante off, I will haul your ass back here. Are we clear?"

Billy nodded.

"Fine. You're going to Afghanistan on Friday. What you do between now and then is your business." Billy stood, but Vic held up a hand. "By the way, good work down there. This guy wasn't even on their radar and you nailed him. *That's* why I hired you. Your instincts are dead on. Maybe this South Beach thing got you focused again. Either way, you made yourself, and this company look good."

Oh, oh, oh, the former big-mouthed-unfiltered Billy would have been all over this action. Ragging on Vic for being a pansy and talking all nicey-nice. Billy grinned. He may have gotten better at filtering, but he was still himself and the idea of walking away from this conversation without commenting on this love fest would kill him. He'd just water it down some. "Boss, are you *proud* of me?"

Vic cracked up. "Billy, I think I am."

That ache inside him? It let up some. Billy stood there, his pansy meter climbing into the red because he didn't actually mind hearing Vic was proud of him. These past weeks had been a brutal assault of self-doubt. A couple of weeks ago he thought he was about to get canned and now his boss was proud of him. Maybe, if he got lucky, he could go back to South Beach and have Kristen feel the same way.

Billy extended his hand. "Let's not tell anyone about this."

Kristen sat on the bed in her suite staring at the lone pair of Billy's Diesel jeans still strewn across the chair. He'd been gone less than twenty-four hours and here she was, in the middle of her workday, hiding in her suite because not only was her heart broken, she didn't have it in her to remove those damned pants from her sight. She'd known from the beginning that getting involved with him, on any level, would be trouble. Disastrous even. Dealing with her sister was enough. She couldn't have Billy coming and going from her life too.

Not if this damned weepiness was the result. Weepiness she hadn't expected. Maybe she should have done what he'd asked and taken a few days to think about it. She had certainly never expected to miss him this much. To feel like the air had vanished from her world. He may have been high-maintenance, but he made her laugh.

And he'd given her a gift...self-acceptance. Of her body, but more than that, self-acceptance of her life and its constant demands.

She glanced at the stupid jeans again and slapped her hands over her eyes. Of course, her cell phone rang. *They can't even leave me alone for a good cry.* She wiped her eyes, drew two breaths and snatched her phone from the bed.

"This is Kristen."

"Ms. Dante, this is Eddie. Can you come down to the valet stand? I have a situation."

"What's the problem?"

"Uh, gotta go, ma'am. Please, come down."

Dammit. It was just as well. She hated pity parties.

Within five minutes, she strode through the lobby doors. The warm air offered comfort and relieved some of her misery. She really needed to make more time to get outside during the day. Particularly now, when she needed to figure out how to heal her ruptured heart.

A car entered the circular drive and the second valet leaped to deal with it. Outside of the few pedestrians entering the hotel, all seemed quiet.

"What's the problem, Eddie?"

He pointed to a giant red pickup. "Someone needs to see you."

"You called me down here because someone needs to see me?"

"Yes, ma'am."

This *was* the hospitality industry. "Any idea what the problem is?

"No, ma'am."

Terrific.

She plastered a smile on and headed down the drive in her stupid stilt heels. On her approach, a man slid out of the truck.

Billy. He's back.

Maybe it didn't mean anything, but the happiness exploding around her couldn't be ignored.

She stopped in front of him, unable to control her smile. "Hi."

He held his hand to the truck. "What do you think?"

Okay. She'd play. She turned and studied the truck. "Um, it's big. And quite red. Whose is it?"

"It's mine."

"Yours?"

"Yep."

She pointed at him. "You bought." She pointed at the truck. "This truck?"

He grinned. "Yes."

This from the man who didn't own anything but his fancy camera. He'd be one of five people in South Beach with a pickup. A red one to boot. "Why?"

"I was hoping you'd keep an eye on it while I was in Afghanistan for six weeks."

What? "Pardon?"

He smacked a hand on the side of the truck. "Yep. My first grown-up purchase. I got to Chicago last night—it's damned cold there by the way—and there I was, freezing my nuts off at the airport while some chick tried to flirt with me and all I could think about was how fast I could get back to you."

"Billy—"

He shot a hand up. "Yeah, no talking. My turn."

Okay.

He raised an eyebrow, clearly as shocked as she was over her silence.

"Leaving here yesterday tore me up. It went against everything I know. All I wanted was to park myself in front of you and badger you into giving me another chance. I controlled myself though. Decided I'd give you a couple days, let things settle down. When I got to Chicago, I talked to Vic. We're square. That meant a lot to me. My job is safe again. Hell, he even told me I did good."

"You did do good."

Billy put his hand up again. "Let me finish. I asked Vic if I could hang out down here between assignments and he agreed. Here is where I want to be. If I'm here, I'm close to you and that's what I want. You understand me, you challenge me and you forgive my screw-ups." He rested his hand on the truck. "I figured I'd need wheels if I was going to spend any substantial time here. I thought a truck would be good. Something I'll be comfortable in."

"Wait. You're staying? In South Beach. Permanently?"

"Not exactly."

Yep, here it comes. Whatever fly-by-night plan her free-spirited lover had. A plan, she would no doubt hate. "What exactly?"

"When I'm on an assignment, I'll be gone. I can't be here all the time."

"Just when you have assignments? What about after that? Are you going to be bouncing around, coming back whenever it suits you while I sit around and wait? I can't do that."

"No. Between assignments, I'm here. All the time. And Vic is good about giving us down time."

Should she even hope? Not without assurances. "Don't mess with me on this, Billy. It's important. I've been a weepy mess all day. I don't want to get my hopes up and be disappointed. I have responsibilities and they don't include sitting on my bed staring at your jeans in the middle of the work day."

"You were staring at my jeans?"

God help her.

"Yes. I can't be doing that."

"What if I'm wearing them?"

"If it's in the middle of my work day, it's still not good."
She took a breath. "I could occasionally make an exception,
though."

"Kristen?"

"Yes?"

"Do I have a shot?"

"I'm standing here, aren't I? Give me something to
believe, Billy. That's all I want."

He leaned against the truck and she noticed the grayish
circles under his eyes. For a man who could function on
very little sleep, he looked tired. Exhausted even.

"Here goes," he said. "I want my voice to be the one you
hear right before you fall asleep at night. And the first one
you hear in the morning. More than that, I want to take care
of you. I can't be here one hundred percent of the time, but
I'll always love you and be faithful. *That* I can do one
hundred percent of the time."

She stood; a bit stunned, totally immobile. At least her
mouth wasn't hanging open. He must have taken it for
hesitation.

"Kris, I'm not asking for a lifetime commitment—yet.
Even I'm not that nuts. We need time to get to know each
other and learn all the day-to-day boring stuff. All I'm
asking is for you to have faith in me. I won't let you down. I
promise. You know I always keep my promises."

"Promise me you won't break my heart."

"No. With my job, that would be a lie, and I won't lie to
you. I can promise you I'll work hard not to break your
heart."

She shook her head. "If you die on me, Billy Tripp, I'll
kill you."

He grinned like the devil he was.

"M.H., when it comes to escaping death, I'm the luckiest bastard there is. In the last ten years I've been shot, I've been stabbed, and now I can add a gator attack to my credentials. I think there's a reason I'm meant to be among the living and I think she's in front of me."

That cracked it. Done deal. As crazy as he drove her, never had she experienced a man like this. One who made her laugh and enjoy life and taught her to be comfortable with her body. She held her hands up and he grabbed hold, entwining his fingers with hers.

"Today," she said, "is one of those days I'd make an exception for you in the middle of my work day."

"I have to leave on Friday. I'm at your disposal until then. And, by the way, you got a room in this shack for me?"

She stuck her bottom lip out. "Unfortunately, we're booked."

"Seriously?"

"Lucky for you, the general manager has a suite in this *shack* with a big bed. I think you'll be comfortable in it."

"A big bed? You naked?"

"Filter, Billy. Filter."

He ran the back of his hand over her cheek and she leaned into it, letting the comfort of his teasing fill her.

"M.H., I keep telling you there are times when you don't want me to filter. Now, show me to my suite."

Want more of the Private Protectors series? Read on to enjoy an excerpt from *Opposing Forces*.

OPPOSING FORCES

BY ADRIENNE GIORDANO

Enjoy an excerpt from *Opposing Forces*, book six in the Private Protectors series:

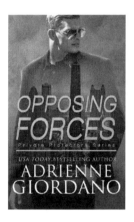

Chapter One

Jillian decided she might be the biggest dingbat in the city of Chicago. Eleven o'clock on a Friday night and she should be doing things that didn't include schlepping to her office in a distribution warehouse on the South Side of Chicago. Just driving down the street on the South Side could get a girl slaughtered.

And yet, here she was, retrieving her beloved two-thousand-dollar camera. The one she'd forgotten in her desk drawer, thereby making her the biggest dingbat in Chicago. One thing she knew for sure, this would never happen again. All she could hope was that someone hadn't made off with it.

This camera was more than just valuable. It represented two years of what she could achieve when she set her mind to it. Pinching pennies, giving up lattes—whatever it took to accomplish her goal of owning a camera every amateur photographer would carve out an eye for. And that was saying something. Considering photographers needed their eyes.

She reached into the drawer and her fingers brushed the soft leather of the camera case. Still there. To be sure, she unzipped the bag and found her precious baby, its lovely lens cover nearly smiling back at her. She snatched it out of the case, set it on her lap and gently ran her hand over the smooth surface. A grown woman shouldn't be so attached to an object.

Eh, why not?

Cameras didn't disappoint her.

Either way, mission accomplished. She sat back in her chair, ran a finger over her forehead. "You got lucky this time." She glanced down at the camera. "Let's get outta here."

She stowed the camera, slung the bag over her shoulder and kicked the bottom drawer closed. A sudden grinding of one of the loading dock doors shattered the eerie quiet outside her office.

A drug delivery at eleven o'clock on a Friday night?

It could happen, but being the assistant distribution manager for Stennar Pharm, she'd have known about it and she didn't remember seeing it on the day's manifest. Unfortunately, in the week since her immediate supervisor had thrown himself off his eighteenth-floor balcony not everything had gone smoothly. Since Greg's death, the VP of distribution, Ned Dillard, had been keeping abreast of the daily goings-on in the department. Even if she didn't know what this delivery was, Ned probably did.

Nothing got by him.

She moved to the doorway. At the loading dock, the growl of the truck engine calmed to an idle. A door slammed.

"Twenty minutes to unload and we're outta here," Cliff Henderson yelled.

Cliff, one of the distribution team members, had obviously been expecting the delivery. The ride down here and the flat-out creepiness of being alone in a huge warehouse must have zapped her senses.

She stepped out of the office, closed the door behind her and made her way to the loading dock.

"Hi, Cliff."

He spun toward her, his face stretched in that holy-crap look people get when surprised.

"Jillian. Wow." He half laughed. "You scared me."

"Sorry. I forgot my camera and had to come back for it."

He glanced at the case. "You don't want to leave that here."

She gestured to the truck. "What's this?"

"Delivery that was supposed to happen this morning. Truck broke down. Pain in the ass on a Friday night."

A delivery that hadn't arrived? She should have been

made aware of that. Jillian glanced at the boxes neatly stacked inside the truck. "You're going to unload this yourself?"

"Not the whole thing. I'll be done fast."

"Can I help you?"

He waved the suggestion away. "Get on with your weekend."

"You're sure?"

"I got this. No problem."

She glanced back at the truck. "If you say so. Just leave the paperwork on my desk and I'll take care of it on Monday."

"Sure thing. Things have been nuts around here since Greg..."

Jillian stared straight ahead. "The poor man. I can't imagine being in such pain that he thought jumping off a building would fix it. I feel horrible for his wife and son."

Her own father would never win any parenting awards, but he'd never allowed his pain to drive him to suicide.

Cliff let out a long, streaming breath. "Let me walk you to your car."

For a week, the employees had been avoiding the subject. Everyone walking around sort of dazed, knowing their coworkers were thinking about Greg, but refusing to talk about it. The unspoken sorrow lay heavy on all of them, but, like the others, Jillian supposed it was better to not think too hard about Greg and his demons. "I'd appreciate that."

Cliff led her to the door and pushed it open. "Good thing the cleaning people don't come in until Saturday. Depending on the crew, you might have lost that camera."

"That's what I was worried about. And I need the camera for a class I'm taking tomorrow."

Another thing she'd pinched her pennies for—a one-day intensive with a world-renowned photographer. The class was only offered once per year and she'd been on the waiting list for four years.

"That sounds fun."

"I'm hoping so." They reached her car and Jillian set the camera bag on the floor behind the driver's seat. She turned to Cliff. "Thanks for walking me out."

"You bet. Be careful heading home."

"I'll lock my doors. Thanks."

Even self-sufficient women couldn't be too careful when it came to being alone at night.

Jackson Lynx added another ten pounds to each end of the weight bar and settled himself on the bench. On Saturday morning, the quiet of the gym in the Taylor Security building could only be considered heaven. No one yapping and wrecking his concentration when he wanted to focus on the day ahead.

Quiet. That's what he needed.

The gym door swung open and Vic Andrews—most likely the nation's loudest loudmouth—entered, wearing a ripped T-shirt that said I'm Just One Big Freaking Ray of Sunshine and a pair of gray basketball shorts. He tossed his gym bag on the floor and smacked his hands together. The clapping noise rocketed off the walls and destroyed the calm.

There goes the serenity.

Vic raised his arms. "Boy Scout, funny seeing you here."

The Boy Scout nickname had been around since their army days when Lynx, two years younger than Vic and fresh out of West Point, had joined Vic's unit as a Second Lieutenant. Vic, being Vic, was the only guy with balls enormous enough to call his superior Boy Scout. Somehow, they'd become friends. War did that to men. Bonded them. Gave them a common purpose and understanding of the insanity surrounding them.

Lynx lay back on the weight bench and gripped the bar. "Since you're here, you might as well spot me."

"Sure. How long you been here?"

"Forty minutes. Don't start."

"I'm not starting. I asked a question."

"Yeah, but I know you're gonna start."

In the five months since Lynx moved to Chicago from D.C., Vic had been nagging him to get out more. Meet some people.

Get laid.

All good things. Just things he wasn't yet ready for. He had someone in mind, though. Jillian Murdoch from his Sunday morning yoga class. She was cute and lush but could derail his plan.

Twelve more days.

"But since we're on the subject," Vic said, "it wouldn't kill you to be spontaneous every once in a while."

"I don't like spontaneous."

"Really? Shocking."

God grant me the serenity to accept the things I cannot change.

Lynx let go of the bar and popped to a standing position. At six foot five Vic had four inches on him, but Lynx knew how to get large with someone without needing bulk. He folded his arms.

"I got an hour before my meeting. Let's make it peaceful. Yes, I should get out and have fun. You know what I'm doing. Don't fuck with my head. I have a plan. That *plan* requires me to stick to a routine. No slip-ups. No emotional upheavals. No pain-in-the-ass friends breaking my balls because I like to keep a schedule. Now, are you gonna shut up and spot me?"

Vic waved both hands at him. "I'm not the one running my mouth and wasting time."

Assuming his point had been made, Lynx dropped to the weight bench again.

Behind the bench, Vic waited for him to start his set. "All I'm saying—"

"I don't care what you're saying. And tell Gina to stop hinting at fix-ups."

"*You'll* have to have that conversation with my wife. She's on a mission to find you a woman and I'm not getting in the middle of it."

Lynx took a breath, held it a second and heaved the bar. His muscles groaned at the added weight, but he exhaled and fully extended his arms. He made it to eight reps before his arms quivered and he set the bar down.

Unaided. Not bad.

"I don't want to insult her."

"Then stop coming to my house for dinner every Friday night. She thinks you're lonely. Why else would a successful single guy be at our house every weekend rather than getting laid?"

True dat. "You don't think I want to get laid? This is no fucking picnic I'm putting myself through."

Without a doubt, there were nights he slept on his sofa to avoid climbing into his cold, barren bed. He was a man who enjoyed the feel of a woman next to him while he slept. In the time since he'd entered a thirty-day rehab for a prescription drug habit that turned borderline scary, he'd been following his program and, as the books advised, staying away from women. For three hundred and fifty-two-

and-a-quarter days he'd been focusing on making himself well, on taking responsibility for his actions and more or less trying not to pummel himself for his mistakes. That meant attending regular support group meetings and concentrating on not relapsing. It had been some of the hardest work he'd ever done. He didn't need his friends testing him.

"Yeah. The big plan. The one-year mark you'll hit in what? Ten days?"

"Twelve. Asshole."

Vic laughed. "*I* get it. My wife isn't convinced. She thinks you need a woman. Can't say I disagree. Except, I don't think you need a woman to marry. You, my friend, need a woman to get busy with. You're like a goddamned monk."

"My life. My choice." Lynx set his hands back on the bar. "Second set."

"I'll talk to her. Tell her to lay off."

"Thank you. Tell her as soon as I'm ready, I'll let her know."

Vic sighed. "Boy Scout, I know you. You'll never *let* yourself be ready. You're so determined to have a plan that you'll make it a habit. Your life will become week after week of rigid schedules. Work every day. The gym every Tuesday, Thursday and Saturday. Recovery meetings every Monday, Wednesday and Friday. Yoga every Sunday. Am I close?"

Close? The fucker was dead-on. Lynx gave the bar a push and ripped off eight reps. Next time he'd shoot for ten at the higher weight. See how he did.

He set the bar back into its cradles and sat up. "I know what I'm doing."

"You need to get a life."

And now the next phase of the lecture would begin. What Vic didn't understand, and probably never would because he wasn't an addict, was that the life Lynx led now was one that kept him in control. To keep his sobriety intact and prove he could be the responsible person he'd been prior to getting hooked on pills. "I have a life," he said. "It's just not the life you think I should have."

ALSO BY ADRIENNE GIORDANO

The Defender

The Marshal

The Detective

The Rebel

JUSTIFIABLE CAUSE SERIES

The Chase

The Evasion

The Capture

CASINO FORTUNA SERIES

Deadly Odds

JUSTICE SERIES w/MISTY EVANS

Stealing Justice

Cheating Justice

Holiday Justice

Exposing Justice

Undercover Justice

Protecting Justice

Missing Justice

Defending Justice

SCHOCK SISTERS MYSTERY SERIES w/MISTY EVANS

1st Shock

2nd Strike

3rd Tango

STEELE RIDGE SERIES w/KELSEY BROWNING

& TRACEY DEVLYN

Steele Ridge: The Beginning

Going Hard (Kelsey Browning)

Living Fast (Adrienne Giordano)

Loving Deep (Tracey Devlyn)

Breaking Free (Adrienne Giordano)

Roaming Wild (Tracey Devlyn)

Stripping Bare (Kelsey Browning)

Enduring Love (Browning, Devlyn, Giordano)

Vowing Love (Adrienne Giordano)

STEELE RIDGE SERIES: The Kingstons w/KELSEY BROWNING

& TRACEY DEVLYN

Craving HEAT (Adrienne Giordano)

Tasting FIRE (Kelsey Browning)

Searing NEED (Tracey Devlyn)

Striking EDGE (Kelsey Browning)

Burning ACHE (Adrienne Giordano)

ACKNOWLEDGMENTS

Writing the acknowledgements page always reminds me how lucky I am to have such patient and dedicated people in my life. As usual, thank you to "my guys" who make me laugh every day. You are the center of my world and inspire me to try harder.

To Kelsey Browning, Tracey Devlyn, Theresa Stevens, Misty Evans and Lucie J. Charles, you ladies always answer my emergency emails and I'm blessed to have you. You're amazing friends.

Milton Grasle, what can I say? Brainstorming action scenes with you is a criminal amount of fun. Thank you for constantly providing the "Milton umph." John and Mara Leach, my dynamic duo, thank you for continuing this journey with me. You'll never know how much it means to me. Carrie Spencer, you deserve a medal for dealing with my website emergencies and for teaching me what a Cabo Cactus is. To Franzeca Drouin and Harold Dzierzynski, thank you for the invaluable research help. I now know how to steal a car. Julie Rowe, Sally Kilpatrick and Jill James, thank you for your ultra-creative suggestions on replacement swear words. Too much fun!

Readers, thank you for taking a chance on letting my stories into your life. To the team at Carina Press, I'm grateful for the support of this series that is so special to me. Thanks for giving my sometimes wacky heroes a home. Finally, thank you to my editor, the fabulous Gina Bernal, who always seems to know how to fix my messes.

A NOTE TO READERS

Dear reader,

Thank you for reading *Relentless Pursuit*. I hope you enjoyed it. If you did, please help others find it by sharing it with friends on social media and writing a review.

Sharing the book with your friends and leaving a review helps other readers decide to take the plunge into the world of the Private Protectors. I would appreciate it if you would consider taking a moment to tell your friends how much you enjoyed the story. Even a few words is a huge help. Thank you!

Happy reading!
Adrienne

ABOUT THE AUTHOR

 Adrienne Giordano is a *USA Today* bestselling author of over forty romantic suspense and mystery novels. She is a Jersey girl at heart, but now lives in the Midwest with her ultimate supporter of a husband, sports-obsessed son and Elliot, a snuggle-happy rescue. Having grown up near the ocean, Adrienne enjoys paddle-boarding, a nice float in a kayak and lounging on the beach with a good book.

For more information on Adrienne's books, please visit www.AdrienneGiordano.com. Adrienne can also be found on Facebook at http://www.facebook.com/AdrienneGiordanoAuthor, Twitter at http://twitter.com/AdriennGiordano and Goodreads at http://www.goodreads.com/AdrienneGiordano.

Don't miss a new release! Sign up for Adrienne's new release newsletter!

Printed in Great Britain
by Amazon

69743052R00210